LOST IN DARA

THE KALEIDOSCOPE CHRONICLES
BOOK ONE

ROBERT BARRETT

THE KALEIDOSCOPE CHRONICLES:
LOST IN DARA

BREWSTER PUBLISHING

First Published in the United States 2024

ISBN 979-8-9899305-2-4

Dedicated to Emma, Jack, and Holly.
Today, you're my favorite.

Listen to your Heart...

Let Go...

Choose Love.

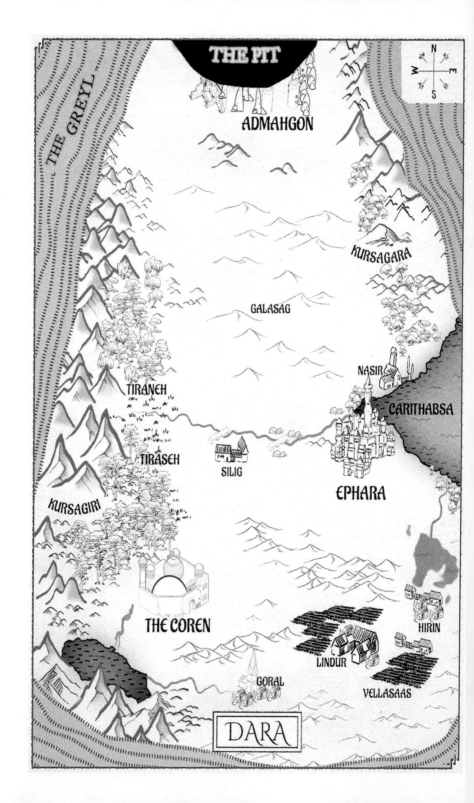

To Eres Ceritha, Esteemed Dubsar for the Historical Society,

In your hands, you hold my latest submission of the first volume of The Kaleidoscope Chronicles.

My first submission to the Society was rejected because it was written from my perspective using material from my diary. Your second rejection noted that I did not include sufficient input from all involved, so the details could not be substantiated. And I am painfully aware of my mother's strong influence as a ranking Society Member in the last rejection.

I hold the Society in the highest regard. Therefore, I have rewritten the Kaleidoscope Chronicles—again—in full accordance with your guidance.

This submission has been rewritten, eliminating any issues with personal bias. At my behest, all of the principals in this truly historic adventure (except for those not present at its conclusion) documented their recollections, which I used for this updated account. I also inserted passages from the Professor's journal and other credible sources when relevant.

Regarding my mother, I assure you that her opinion of this record is sorely tainted by her opinion of me. I implore you, Ceritha, to judge this submission by its merit.

A final point of clarification: I understand the word "butt" is not deemed appropriate for Historical Records. The phrase "get his butt kicked" came from a verbal account by Master Jack. In their colorcasted accounts, Eresi Emma and Holly used this same wording.

By your Marks,

Ber-ha-roi, Loremaster for the Three

JACK'S FIRST LESSON

THREE YEARS AGO.

Tired of waiting for his dad and two sisters, Jack backed out of the shoe store, sprinted down the sidewalk to the White Tiger Dojo, and stepped through the door.

A teenager wearing a black gi looked up from behind a display case filled with training guides and throwing stars. He smiled calmly at Jack.

"We're here..." Remembering he'd run ahead, Jack pushed his tinted glasses up his slightly crooked nose and stared at the floor. "I mean, me and my dad have..."

The young man said nothing and resumed stocking the shelves, his movements precise and methodical.

Jack cleared his throat and stood up straight. "My name's Jack Waite. I'm here to see the Sensei," he said, trying to sound like an adult, not like a ten-year-old. "I have an appointment about starting lessons."

"Welcome to the dojo, Jack. Wait here." The boy turned away and slipped quietly through a curtained doorway behind the display case. To his right, the dojo door swung open, and his dad walked in.

"Remember we agreed, buddy. No more fights. You're taking Martial Arts for defense only, not so you can run around beating up everybody," said Eli, smiling as he stopped next to him and tousled his son's blond mop of hair.

Jack ducked and spun away. He didn't need 'the speech' again. But his dad was right. Even at ten, he fought with much older and bigger boys. Sometimes they started the fight, sometimes he did. Sometimes he won, sometimes he lost. Either way, the bloody noses and colorful bruises kept coming.

Jack explored while his dad waited for the sensei. He'd expected a brightly-lit room covered in mats and packed with grunting students, but instead, this room looked more like a temple than a gym. Smooth wood floors polished to a glossy sheen surrounded the black mat in the center of the room, and a warm glow from paper lanterns illuminated the space. A rising sun logo decorated the far wall.

Jack walked to the end of the room and read the words from a scroll hanging on the wall.

Student Creed and Warrior Ethics:
I avoid violence whenever possible.
I develop significant relationships.
I put the needs of others above my...

"Jack, come meet Sensei Todd."

Walking around the training pit, Jack saw his new teacher for the first time and tried to mask his disappointment. *Well, at least the room is cool.*

Todd looked nothing like a martial arts master, not the kind in the movies. He wore a light blue cardigan sweater, khaki pants...and slippers. Fuzzy brown house slippers.

His father glanced out the window to where Holly and Emma sat waiting on a bench. "I've got more errands with your sisters. The sensei has time to give you a lesson now."

"But, Dad," Jack sputtered, "I mean, I want to." Then he whispered, "But he doesn't look like a Budo trainer."

Sensei Todd walked to the edge of the mat, motioning for Jack to join him. "At first glance, Jack, you do not see a teacher. Always remember, looking at a person is not the same thing as seeing who he truly is." Jack watched his dad leave as the dojo door swung to a close. Nervously rubbing the back of his neck, he stepped forward and stopped in front of the soft-spoken man, instinctively turning his head down and his eyes away.

The man bent down. "Lesson number one. You must learn how to observe your surroundings, your opponent, and most importantly yourself." He reached out and removed Jack's dark glasses. "And these are in your way." He gestured around the room. "Now, tell me what you see."

Jack swallowed hard as he backed up onto the shiny black mat. He felt exposed without the glasses hiding his eyes. Except at home with Emma, Holly, and his dad, he rarely took them off around other people. Strangers always focused immediately on his all-white eyes, then offered up one of a thousand lame 'Ohs' like the apologetic 'Oh, I didn't realize' or the always classic 'Oh, you poor boy'. Not this man. When Jack finally made eye contact, the sensei was not staring at his eyes; he was staring into them.

"A training room?" asked Jack.

The man's grey eyes crinkled as a slight smile crossed his face. "You can do better. Try again. What do you *see*?" Sensei Todd moved forward and knelt.

Jack took a deep breath and studied his surroundings. Lantern light reflected on the ebony walls, highlighting hundreds of overlapping circles patterning the wood. On the mat, a sunburst of dark creases radiated from under his feet, while beneath the grandmaster's knee, another set of lines branched out, intersecting with Jack's lines, forming a new pattern.

"I see a path," he said, staring directly into the man's eyes.

With a slight nod and a bit of surprise in his eyes, the sensei asked, "Anything else?"

Jack hesitated. He was showing a part of himself he rarely shared. But deep down he wanted to commit, and he wanted to walk this new path. "I see a choice."

Sensei Todd slowly exhaled and looked very pleased. "Good. Now for lesson number two."

His hands flew out, he grabbed Jack, and flipped him soundly onto the mat. Groaning, Jack looked up into the eyes of his new teacher.

"Never forget, Jack. Step into the pit only when you are ready to fight."

THE FIGHT

JACK WIPED blood from his mouth. It left a splotch of red on the back of his hand. Every time he changed schools, the second day was always the worst.

As usual, the first day had gone smoothly. The meeting with the vice-principal had been quick and painless. When Jack removed his tinted glasses, she stopped staring at his eyes sooner than most adults, then quickly gave her approval for him to wear his glasses in school. And after the last bell, he found his little sister Holly laughing, surrounded by a gaggle of seventh-grade girls. Walking home, they talked about how this move to a new town might turn out okay.

But that was yesterday. Today was the second day. The worst day.

Now knocked flat on the ground, Jack kept his eyes narrowed. He chose to stay down for a few seconds. The bully standing over him had said "Didn't see you, freak." when he shoved Jack to the pavement. *Freak?* Real original, Jack thought. Like he hadn't heard that a million times over.

Jack took a deep breath, calming himself. *There's no way I'm getting my butt kicked, not on the second day of school, not by this kid.* By fighting he'd risk a suspension or worse, like what happened at his old school. He'd get labeled as the troublemaker, the freak with the white eyes. The other kids would go home and tell their parents who would warn them to stay away, condemning Jack to spend his first year of junior high school alone.

Jack didn't know the bully's name. He hadn't listened during homeroom yesterday when the teacher read roll call. In the hallway between classes, the boy kept staring in his direction which Jack chalked up to curiosity. But this morning before homeroom began, the boy walked straight to Jack's desk and leaned over him.

"They say you've got white eyes." The kid waved his hand a few inches in front of Jack's dark glasses. The other kids stopped talking. "Show me."

Jack ignored him and sat unmoving until the teacher walked in and greeted the class. The bigger boy, his acne-covered face like a squashed orange oozing bad juice, retreated to his desk. Jack stared at the boy. *I'll just call you Wastoid.*

Walking out the south door at the end of the day, he caught Wastoid teasing Holly.

When Jack stepped in to protect her, the bully wheeled around and shoved him to the blacktop. That surprised Jack. The loud-mouthed-ones usually made noise, big barking dogs that quickly backed down. Though not because of his size. At thirteen years old, Jack weighed a whopping ninety-three pounds and was barely tall enough to ride the Starblaster at Brighton Park this summer. But when a person saw his eyes for the first time, they stopped and stared. Except for his former Sensei.

Jack had loved learning Budo from Sensei Todd.

In Japanese, *Bū* meant war and *dō* meant path. Put together.... the Path of the Warrior. Back in Hartford, the dojo had stressed the mental aspect, the Path, more than the fighting. Deep down, Jack was all about the bu. More bū, less do.

Jack had imagined the worst part of getting expelled for fighting was going to be telling his sensei that they were moving to New Hampshire and seeing the disappointment on his teacher's face. But he was wrong. The worst part was after; after Sensei Todd retrieved Jack's training records and handed him the yellow folder, after he shook his hand and encouraged Jack to remember the Path, after Jack walked out.

Two blocks down, he'd sat on the street curb and flipped open the folder. His promotion log was filled with dates and comments by Sensei Todd, handwritten in precise strokes. Underneath his recent test results was a note, written two days before Jack's expulsion for injuring a boy at school.

"I do not recommend Jack Waite for further advancement in the Martial Arts. Though extremely talented physically, Jack has demonstrated an unwillingness to learn self-control. I fear further training would make Jack a danger to himself and others."

Jack rose unsteadily to his feet and tossed the folder into the first trashcan he passed.

∾

NOW JACK TURNED HIS HEAD, ENOUGH TO ASSESS HIS position on the ground, but not enough to trigger a response from Wastoid. To his left, he spied Holly leaning against a green ivy-covered wall, a few of her new friends gathered in a loose semi-circle around her. Jack saw two things immediately.

First, no one else was teasing her. A few kids were staring at his sister's arms and hands, but the rest had turned their attention to him after his glorious fall to the blacktop. Holly was rolling her sleeves down and putting her fingerless gloves back on, covering up the brightly colored marks on her arms. She must have gotten hot by the end of the day and rolled up her sleeves to cool off. *She should know better.* Like his eyes, her arms always drew attention, especially from bullies like Wastoid.

Second, and most importantly, Holly wasn't crying. Her big brown eyes were dry, but sad as she shook her head at him, silently encouraging him to walk away.

Their older sister Emma didn't need his protection because she did a much better job at hiding her marks. But with Holly, Jack took his role as protector very seriously even though she was close to his height and in Seventh Grade with him. A year younger, she'd skipped Second Grade and still teased him about it. He teased her back, too hard at times, and he'd caused most of her tears over the years. But a big brother making fun of his little sister or hiding her favorite blue pen...heck, that was normal. But a bully tormenting her in the school-yard crossed the line. Lucky for this kid, he hadn't made Holly cry. Jack decided to be nice.

He brought his eyes back to center, focusing on Wastoid's dark indigo jeans and white leather sneakers. *Who wears those anymore?* As Jack expected, the kid stood directly in front of him. Jack knew the side or rear position gave more advantage in a fight, but big-mouth bullies always wanted to yell in your face. Still down on all fours, Jack saw his opportunity; Wastoid rocked side to side as he continued to taunt Jack and show off for the other kids.

Jack brought his left foot in and anchored the sole of his sneaker securely on the pavement, then shifted all of his weight onto his left leg. He timed the movement of the boy's feet, slightly rocking to the left, then to the right, back to the left.

Jack grunted to get the kid's attention. At the same time, he threw a short jab with his right fist into the boy's groin. Not a hard shot, since the first strike was the feint. Wastoid flinched and bent over at the waist, reacting like all boys did, and instinctively tried to protect himself. As his head came down, Jack thrust his left arm straight up and drove a heel strike into the boy's temple. Dropping the rest of his weight onto his crouched left leg, Jack swept his right leg into the boy's ankle and knocked him completely off balance. Wastoid slammed to the pavement.

Jack popped up. He whipped off his glasses and glared down at the boy, who was now gasping for air, tears streaming. Jack's eyes, a solid pure white, held the boy's gaze for a moment.

"Do you see me now?"

Holly touched Jack softly on the shoulder. Not speaking, the two of them walked across the school courtyard towards the back gate. A growing murmur trailed behind them as the other kids stepped aside. Holly pushed the gate open, paused, and gave him a reassuring shrug which said, 'It'll be okay' and Jack smiled at her, his half grin saying, 'Yes it will,' and 'No it won't' all at the same time.

Cutting across the violet clover in the field behind the school, Jack pictured his dad, busy settling into his new job at Dartmouth, getting a phone call from the school. Jack knew he hadn't hurt the kid—only knocked the wind out of him and embarrassed him—but his dad wouldn't care. They had changed towns and schools for a fresh start and now he'd screwed it up...on the second day. He already dreaded the inevitable talk, a discussion laced with his dad's disappointment and neatly tied up with a loss of privileges for at least a month. As he walked behind Holly, Jack stared into space and tried not to think about how badly he'd messed up. Methodically cracking his knuckles and enjoying the distraction of the popping sounds, he allowed his mind to wander.

I bet Emma's day has been a heck of a lot better than mine.

SCHOOL PICTURE

EARLIER THAT DAY, Emma stopped walking halfway across the high school parking lot. Something wasn't right.

By the main door, four girls were staring at her, and not in a "Hey, it's the new girl, and we should go say hi" kind of way. Emma recognized the mixture of fear and disgust on their faces. Instinctively, her hand went to her neck as if to cover the colored marks hidden beneath her shirt.

She'd dealt with the staring and whispering before. Their dad had enrolled them into public school for the first time in their lives four years ago in Hartford, Connecticut after the death of their Great Aunt Sarah, who helped raise them. During those difficult years, Emma slowly made a small circle of friends she was comfortable around, but Holly loved going to school and made friends right away. Even though Holly suffered from the same skin condition, she often acted as if the raised colored marks on her arms were works of art still in progress.

But the change to public school wasn't good for Jack. Being stared at by others made him angry, and when a kid teased him about his eyes, Jack always overreacted and started a fight. Emma wasn't sure learning martial arts had been the best solution for Jack; their dad said training at the dojo in Hartford would teach him discipline and self-control. Then Jack hurt a boy and got expelled from school. After paying for the injured boy's medical bills, their dad called a moving company, hauled them out of Hartford, and dragged them here—to Lebanon, New Hampshire.

She was back to ground zero.

Emma tugged on her collar and adjusted her long blonde hair, making sure the marks on her neck were hidden from sight. She forced herself to keep walking toward the entrance as the girls disappeared through the doors. *Maybe I'm overreacting. How would they know about my marks?* After moving into the old house by the lake, she went into town sparingly, limiting herself to drugstore purchases and getting a library card. Besides, yesterday had been uneventful, except for the looks she got for wearing a turtleneck in August.

Head down, she stepped into the noisy lobby. The security guard was yelling at the students in line for the metal detector, reminding them to take their phones and laptops out of their bags. Kids everywhere were joking and calling out to one another. Lebanon was a small town; she guessed these kids had known each other since grade school. Fitting in and making friends was not going to be easy.

Three boys tumbled through the door, goofing off and swinging their backpacks at one another. One of them careened into Emma, knocking her forward into the next girl in line. The girl stumbled and turned around, ignoring Emma. "Geez, Ryan. Walk much?" she said, rolling her eyes at the boys.

Then she looked at Emma.

The girl gasped and stepped backward, bumping into the boy next to her. He started to speak but stopped when he saw Emma. His eyes darted down to the phone in his hand, then he turned away and tapped the shoulder of the boy beside him. Like a virus, a fever of whispers rushed along the line, propelled by a quick elbow, a nudge, and a pointed finger. Everyone's attention turned to Emma, and even the security guard stopped yelling. But then the whispers rose into a chorus of excited voices. No one talked to her yesterday, and they weren't talking to her now. But they were talking *about* her.

Light-headed, Emma shrank back, overwhelmed by the growing

wave of comments. "Did you have any idea she looked like that?" ... "Do you think she's contagious?" She'd heard it all before, but that was back in Hartford where she'd carefully concealed her marks and had a few close friends to shield her. She was alone here.

The girl next to her was wrinkling her nose, staring at Emma like she was one of those slimy pigs they had to dissect in Freshman Biology. *But how could this girl know about her condition?*

The noise in the lobby surged to a crescendo. Her ears burning, she spun around and pushed between the three boys. The one who'd knocked into her raised his hands as if to ward her off like she was a rotting leper. The phone in his right hand had her picture on the screen. Emma gasped, her throat tightening. She wanted to yell at him and every other kid, but she couldn't. She bolted out the front door, but not fast enough.

"Freak," said the boy with the phone.

Emma stumbled across the parking lot, the image burning her brain, tears stinging her eyes. At her car, she yanked open the door and threw her backpack inside, then stopped. She leaned against the side of the car with her eyes closed, trying to catch her breath. She could still see the image on the boy's phone, a picture of her swimming yesterday after the first day of school.

A picture of her standing in the lake. The water came up a few inches below her blue bikini top. Her blonde hair, which she purposefully kept long to hide her neck, was wet and pushed back. The hard sunlight reflected off her wet torso, intensifying every colored mark.

Her marks—and she couldn't remember calling them anything other than marks—started at her ears. Behind her right ear was a thin line made up of four colors—green, yellow, orange, and red, and behind her left ear another set of four colors—also green, but with violet, blue, and indigo. The lines curled like wisps of hair behind each ear before running along both sides of her neck and flowing downward.

Her friends in Hartford had *almost* convinced her that the world wouldn't end if people talked about the marks on her neck. But the colored lines didn't stop there.

From behind her neck, the vine-like bands thickened and passed over her shoulders to reach her collarbones before snaking across her skin and crisscrossing at her breastbone. The orange, yellow, and red lines wove an intricate pattern of thick colors across the top left of her chest as the blue, indigo, and violet lines spread over her right side. In the middle of her chest, the two green lines spun a helix of color going straight down. The marks mercifully thinned and stopped below her ribs, but in this picture with the waterline, no one could know where the marks ended.

She blew out a calming breath. The colored marks on her body were not flat like tattoos. Oh, how she wished they were flat. Nowadays, lots of high schoolers had ink, and she could almost pass them off as a piece of elaborate body art. But all of her marks were raised and bumpy, covered with rough patches that never stopped itching no matter how many creams she used or pills she took. Sometimes, her skin would clear up a little, but she'd learned from painful experience that scratching made everything worse.

Emma hated her skin. Because no matter when or where—in the shower or fully dressed—Emma could always feel the marks, her fingers able to trace every inch. She could never forget how her marks bound her, a rainbow chain pulling her down and crushing her soul.

Another kid must have seen her swimming in the lake, and now every classmate knew about the raised lines scrawled on her skin. In the picture, she looked like a mutant infected with radioactive toxins. She *was* a freak.

"Excuse me." The voice of the security guard startled her. Emma whirled around toward the school. He was walking toward her, but abruptly stopped, his eyes wide with shock as he fumbled to unclip his radio from his belt. He took one more small step but then seemed to reconsider getting any closer. "I'm calling the nurse."

"What? No, I'm leaving." Emma held up her car keys to wave him off. "I don't need a...." Her voice trailed off as she saw the blood on her fingers. Horrified, she looked down. The front of her top was smeared with blood. She ran her hand across her throat and felt the wetness from the scratches she'd stupidly caused while lost in her thoughts.

The guard took another hesitant step in her direction. "Miss, you need to come back inside. You're in no condition to drive."

Behind him at the school entrance, a crowd of kids had gathered, pointing at her with their phones, laughing at her. The sound washed across the parking lot, drowning out the voice of the security guard.

Emma choked back a sob. *This can't be happening.*

"SSHHHUUTTTUUPPP!!" The words exploded out of Emma. The scream still ringing across the parking lot, she climbed into her car and drove away knowing her new life in Lebanon was over.

Wooly-jooly caterpillar
asleep in your cocoon,
Change into a butterfly
And fly me to the moon.
Carry me on silken wings
painted blue and green.
On your back I'll fly away
to worlds I've never seen.

—from "The Wooly-Jooly Caterpillar" by Dorothea Gardner,
1924

3

BUTTERFLY

As she walked with Jack across the back edge of a neglected orchard, Holly twisted the twig in her hand one time, two times. With her left hand still holding the tension in the slender piece of wood, she fished another from her back pocket without looking. Her small fingers felt its bumpy surface. Bending it down, she pushed the ends into her rapidly growing creation, a butterfly.

As she worked, her eyes scanned the ground and the trees like a foraging squirrel. She reached out and snared new pieces of material—a blade of grass gone to seed with its feathery top, a red petal streaked in orange, and a twig from a low hanging branch. A stockpile of grass and flowers stuck out from her pockets and, as she pulled each new item out for use, other pieces cascaded down her legs, tenuously connecting her to the earth and the earth to her.

Building the left wing with blades of field grass, she quickly wrapped and tied off the ends to the top of the wing. Grass tendrils curled around her fingers as she wove them like a basket onto the edge, each blade sliding in and out. She loved the glossy finish of this grass and the sheen in the half-done wing. She could sense a rising tension in the weave. Too much and there'd be wrinkles. Her left hand instinctively twisted the wood on the wing without going past the breaking point.

They squeezed through a gap in the fence and stepped onto King Street. They were halfway home, and Jack hadn't spoken since leaving the schoolyard. He was being quiet on purpose because for her brother, talking ranked second to breathing.

She felt Jack staring at her now, watching her hands and fingers moving. She glanced his way. He'd removed his glasses.

The absence of color in his eyes bothered most people, but Holly loved how they looked and couldn't imagine him any other way. For his birthday last year, she had drawn a picture of his face and used their dad's printer to make copies. She colored his eyes blue on some pages, brown-eyed like hers on others, adding in a few red and purple eyes to make it funnier. She cut and bound the sheets together into a flipbook—first his white eye color, then blue, and so on with the other colors until going back to white at the end. On the last page, underneath the white eyes, she put the word "Brother". When Jack opened the book and riffled his finger through it, the eyes changed colors. Jack loved it. He spent the next two days singing Lucy in the Sky with Diamonds at the top of his lungs with the words changed to a 'boy with kaleidoscope eyes'.

"You know what," Jack said, still looking at the partially complete butterfly in her hands. "You don't have to fix this. You didn't do anything wrong, and you didn't do the fighting. I did." His voice was hard with defiance.

She stopped walking, turned, and looked up at his face. Not far up, though; she'd grown two inches this year. On her tiptoes, she was as tall as he was.

"Yeah, but I feel bad. The boy was a bully and he started it." Holly hesitated. "But, if I'd been more careful he wouldn't have seen my marks. We could have avoided it."

"Avoided?" Jack shot back. "Keep turning away and hiding? I'm tired of wearing sunglasses and keeping my eyes down to avoid freaking out the other kids." He glared at her; rays of sunlight reflected in his eyes. "Emma in turtlenecks? You wearing long sleeves and not raising your hand so you can AVOID getting teased? No, we shouldn't have to hide. Especially you and Emma."

"What do you mean *especially* me and Emma?" she asked, already knowing his answer.

"You know what. All the cool things you can do with your hands. And Emma with music. You're special. Both of you."

"Well so are you," Holly said, knowing she'd lose this argument, like hundreds of times before.

"You're wrong," Jack pushed back. "I don't care what Aunt Sarah said about your skin pigment; it's not just some unfortunate medical condition. You and Emma have something. Me...I have nothing. Nothing but an inhaler for allergies and white eyes which is worse than nothing."

"No, it's not."

"Whatever, Hol. Real convincing with that work of art you're making for Dad." Jack turned his back and stomped off ahead, his hands shoved into the pockets of his jeans, his shoulders slouched.

Holly rubbed at her left forearm, taking care not to irritate any of her swollen colored marks. Last week had been a bad one for her skin. The marks on her arms itched incessantly and she'd scratched them raw in places. She'd stopped using the medicated creams which left her hands too greasy to draw. But she had good days too, where her skin calmed down, revealing the colors that branched into an intricate pattern, sprouting at her shoulders, and stopping at the roots of her fingers. The two green marks, one on each arm, looped around her arms, ending between her thumb and index finger on the backs of her hands. Three more colors—orange, indigo, and yellow—encircled her right arm with each line of color stopping between her fingers. The same pattern—but with blue, red, and violet—covered her left arm. Despite the inflammation, Holly loved her marks, each colored swirl and flowing ribbon. She could never tell Jack that she kept her marks covered more for his sake than her own.

Holly walked after Jack, who was sending up dust clouds in the dirt. His complaining about their talents was nothing new. She wished... Holly found herself stuck, her thoughts stubbornly going nowhere, dragging her heels like Jack up ahead. What did she wish?

That he liked being different? Or that he had marks like her and Emma?"

She knew having marks wouldn't change things for him. After the fight that got him expelled, she suggested giving Jack his own set of marks. He loved the idea. Using markers, she drew thick colored lines up and down his arms, hands, neck, and chest. He asked her to draw colored circles around his eyes as well, to fully unleash the hidden power in his eyes. He wanted x-ray vision but would settle for heat vision. But later that night, when he took a shower, all of his colors washed away.

Holly blinked hard, pushing the memory aside. *No, he wants more than marks, much more.*

Holly looked around, but Jack was nowhere to be seen. Lost in thought, she'd been walking slowly. Picking up her pace, she turned onto Mound Street, lined with old brick houses.

She loved the sidewalks in this part of town with the broken concrete slabs, long surrendered to the force of the spreading roots of the towering cedar trees. She stepped carefully, looking down at the ground, her eyes tracing one of the long deep cracks.

At the alley behind Miller's Print Shop, she turned the corner, and plowed into somebody. Holly frowned at the pair of white sneakers. White leather sneakers.

"Look who we have here." The same bully—the one Jack had called Wastoid—loomed over her, a trash bag in one hand. "You and me never finished talking about your weird arms."

Holly backed up a step. "You and I." Her correction of the boy's taunt came out automatically. Their dad always stressed using good grammar and she had developed a habit of correcting everyone. "It's not correct to say, 'you and me'."

"Say what?" He dropped the bag and grinned at her. "Instead of you trying to learn me a lesson, tell me where your albino brother is hiding."

"Teach me a lesson," Holly interrupted, unable to stop herself. "You can be taught a lesson, but you can't be learned a lesson. And he's not an albino since only his eyes don't have color." Holly got ready to run, but hesitated. *Don't say it.* "Did you get held back a grade or something?"

His grin disappeared. Holly turned to run, but Wastoid grabbed her left arm, squeezed, and twisted her wrist. She winced and squealed in pain.

"Help! Jack!" Holly yelled as her eyes welled with tears. She looked up and down the alley, desperately hoping for any sign of her brother.

"You're the stupid one here. Too stupid to know when to shut it," he said, shoving her at the brick wall and blocking any chance to escape. "Or you got something else to say?"

Holly glanced to her right; a wave of relief washed over her. She stood up as tall as she could and wiped the tears out of her eyes. "Actually, I do," she said, "I'm with Jack."

Jack was sprinting towards them carrying a broken pallet board. He came to a stop and brandished it menacingly at the bigger boy, pulling his attention from Holly. Ducking to the side, she ran to Jack and tugged at his arm, urging him backward, away from Wastoid.

"Hey, freak!" Wastoid stepped forward. "You gonna run away?"

Jack went rigid and his face flushed red with anger. He shook off Holly's grasp and took a step toward him. Holly grabbed his shirt and tried to stop him. She couldn't let him fight again.

CLANG! A metal door on their left slammed open. A grey-haired man wearing overalls and a leather tool belt stepped into the alley. "Jeremy Miller! Get over here!"

Wastoid went pale and threw his hands in the air. "But Dad, I didn't do anything."

"Don't start with me. The principal called. Get inside NOW!" The boy shuffled through the door, glaring back at them.

Mr. Miller turned towards Jack and Holly. He stared at Jack for a long time, a hard expression etched on his face. "Go home. And stay away from my boy." He stepped inside, leaving them alone.

They walked to the end of the alley and broke into a run, racing past parked cars for half a block. At the corner of Water Street, Holly slowed and Jack fell in step next to her. They walked up the steep street side by side.

"I could've taken him," Jack said quietly.

She said nothing. She'd been so relieved when he showed up in the alley, but she didn't want to be the reason for Jack fighting again.

At the top of the hill, Holly paused in front of an abandoned church with an adjacent cemetery, bordered by a wrought-iron fence. The arched gate leading into the graveyard cast a long shadow across her feet.

Jack sat on the curb. "Go on. I need to think about what I'm going to tell Dad."

Beyond the arch rested six rows of untended tombstones, overrun with brown vines. She never understood why their mom and Aunt Sarah were buried here, amongst the forgotten, surrounded by moss-covered headstones with faded inscriptions. Their dad grew up in Lebanon and the town had several cemeteries, all of them much nicer than this one. When they'd moved here in early summer, Holly had wasted no time finding this place. She didn't tell their dad that she was visiting the gravesites or ask him to come with her. Whenever he talked about their mom, which was hardly ever, his voice faltered, like the effort of making the words was too much for him.

Holly's legs automatically propelled her six rows back. She stopped by two gravestones which sat apart and slightly out of line from the others. The white spotless markers rested in front of a pine tree, its trunk a shredded fabric of peeling bark. Holly came here every two weeks to care for the graves, rubbing off stains, brushing away pine needles, and making sure everything was pristine. She bent down and removed the wilted strand of wildflowers she'd left last time.

As she pulled a fresh flower from her pocket, she read her mom's inscription, engraved in a fine cursive script. "Teresa Waite. Devoted Mother. True Love of Eli." Four feet to the left, Aunt Sarah's headstone—adorned with a Star of David—was inscribed with a heavy vertical font which perfectly matched all of Holly's memories of her solidly-built aunt. "Sarah Greenberg. Beloved wife of Samuel."

Holly had no memory of her mom who had died during childbirth. Their dad would only say how smart and creative she was, beautiful, "Beautiful like you and your sister," before drifting off into silence. Holly had only sweet memories of Aunt Sarah who was a nurse and raised them, just like she had helped raise their dad years before.

On the street, Jack hadn't moved from the curb, his chin propped on his hands. Holly carefully placed a blue flower in front of each tombstone and ran back across the cemetery to Jack.

A-C-E-A-B-C-A-F-E-D-C-B-E-G#-B-C-B-A

—The notes from the song – in the Key of A Minor – written by Emma at the age of 5

—Emma's song on the music staff

4

SONGBIRD

EMMA SQUEEZED THE STEERING WHEEL. Going back to school today was out of the question; the idea of walking by other kids made her stomach churn, even though the longer she stayed away would make returning more horrible. The other kids might lose interest, stop showing her picture to their friends, but the moment she walked through the front doors, it would all start again.

Driving through town, she was wrapped in her thoughts, oblivious to the houses and storefronts. When they'd moved to Lebanon at the start of the summer, their dad showed them around his hometown, pointing out his elementary school, remarking how many things had changed. He'd been too upbeat and chatty the whole day, even treating them to sundaes at a small cafe. As if ice cream could make up for Jack ruining her life.

Arriving home, exhausted, she retreated to her room and changed into a clean shirt, before curling up in bed. She closed her eyes, wishing she could fall asleep. But it was no use. She grabbed her portable piano keyboard – the one thing that never let her down – and walked down to the lake behind the house. But after more than an hour of staring at the water, she didn't have the energy to play anything. Each time she closed her eyes, all she could see was her picture on the boy's phone.

Sitting motionless by the edge of the water, Emma listened to the sound of her breath flowing out of her, each exhalation a quiet sigh which floated down the bank, disappearing into the wind across the lake. *That's me...the girl who makes soft sounds. Not the girl who cries and screams in a parking lot, not the center of attention. Not a freak.*

Emma leaned forward and looked at her reflection. Her hair was in shambles. Her blue-green eyes were rimmed red from crying, and there was a streak of dried blood on her cheek where she must have touched her face. She dipped her finger in the water and scrubbed it away. If only she could wash away the marks on her body so easily and wake up normal.

Dad was always telling her to be herself and to give people a chance, that they didn't care about her condition. "Take me, for example," he'd say and then point to his prosthetic eye. "Sure, I get awkward reactions from students when they first meet me, but I don't let it bother me."

Emma would nod and smile and pretend the pep talks helped. But he'd lost his left eye in an accident after college and the blue prosthetic was a close match for his good eye. He didn't grow up dealing with the same pressure and stares from other kids that she, Holly, and Jack got all the time.

A branch snapped and dropped into the lake, and Emma looked across the rippling water. She wished today had never happened. No, what she really wished was that the entire summer had never happened, that they had never moved here at all, and that she was still back in Hartford. She placed her hand on her chest; she could feel the network of raised marks underneath her shirt. *But wishes don't come true, do they?*

She took a deep breath to calm herself. Turning on her keyboard, she closed her eyes, letting her fingers hover in the space above the keys.

As her ears absorbed the sounds of the lake and woods around her, the painful echoes from the school lobby faded into the background. A steady breeze cajoled the surface of the water into ripples that formed overlapping circles of major tones. She listened to the natural rhythm in the flow of the water and played a supporting line on the keyboard in a major key.

She could play something harsh and painful, yet now, here on the lake, repeating the sounds of the morning would be pointless. She relaxed a bit more, expanding her focus to include the underlying sound in the trees—a warm timbre—then starting a rhythmic line with a delicate pace, like a deer stepping its way through the woods.

She had no idea how she did this. Her dad always joked that she was blessed to have this talent and was destined to write a great symphony. Emma didn't think so. She couldn't imagine playing songs in front of other people; even the thought of a piano recital made her want to throw up.

A new set of sounds came from her right. Her fingers moved up the keyboard in response instinctively adding and subtracting notes. Her ears picked up on the E-note coming on the wind, weaving through the branches. She slowed the tempo in synch with the swaying trees and played a three-note arpeggio with her right hand centered on the E chord, then added an F-sharp.

She smiled, pleased with the overall effect, and tapped the record button. Playing the song from the beginning, her fingers effortlessly made small changes in the pattern to match the ambient sounds of the water, the wind, and the trees. She let the fingers of her right hand rest on the keys, holding the final notes, letting them ring out for several measures until no sound remained.

Emma pressed the stop button. She never bothered to write these songs down, because as long as she had the recording, she could recreate it note for note by listening to it. The songs she composed outdoors were momentary creations, beautifully true in one time and place. When she played them inside on the piano, the songs always sounded forlorn like a lost songbird calling for its home.

5

THE WINDOW

"SERIOUSLY? You got into two fights today?" As she and Jack argued, Emma paced up and down the bank of the lake behind their house. Jack and Holly had found her sitting by the water when they arrived home. She squinted her eyes at the mid-afternoon sun reflecting off the water and tried to calm down. "Two fights?"

"You're not listening. The kid's dad came out and stopped us." Jack's mischievous grin quickly turned into a grimace, his left hand gingerly touching the tender cut on his upper lip. "And technically, it was the same kid, so it would have counted as one long fight." He nonchalantly skipped another rock into the lake. Emma frowned; he wouldn't hesitate to start fight number three.

"Not funny. What were you thinking?"

"I don't know. He was teasing Holly and, well, things got out of control."

"Things got out of control, or *you* got out of control?" Emma heard his sharp intake of breath as the short jab of her words hit. Her words came out more like an accusation than she wanted, but they'd had this conversation so many times already.

Jack stopped mid-toss, faced her, and opened his hand. The smooth skipping stone made a small thud on the dirt.

"Fine. You win. I lost control. Again, *Dad*." His eyes narrowed at Emma.

"That's not fair!" Emma shot back. "I'm only saying you have to stop getting into fights." What she wanted to say was that they were stuck here because of him and his stupid fights. "Remember Dad's big speech when we moved here about how every good choice is like opening a door and having more options? And how bad choices lead to dead ends?" Emma looked at Holly for support, but she wasn't looking up, choosing to draw pictures in the dirt with a stick and doing her best to stay out of their argument. Probably just as well. Holly tended to take Jack's side whenever the three of them disagreed.

"What do you want me to do? Walk away and ignore them? Bow down like a lowly servant and say, 'We've had a grand time being called all these names but now we must be on our merry way'?"

"No, of course not. But punching people can't always be your answer..." Emma's voice trailed off. *The boy holding his phone with her picture? Him, she'd punch.*

"So, you're telling me to hide?" Jack said and kept going. "I can't hide my eyes, not like you and Holly can hide your marks. I spend all my time looking down, dark glasses or not. One way or another, I have to face people, and it starts all over."

Holly looked up from her picture as Jack worked himself into a rant, his pent-up frustration now pushing him into motion. They knew each other well, probably a lot better than typical sisters and brothers. They spent most of their time together, each one of them taking turns being the strong one as they dealt with all the problems brought on by their marks and Jack's eyes.

Stomping on the rocks, Jack waved his arms in wide circles. Emma watched and waited. His bursts of anger rushed in like fast-moving thunderstorms. Fortunately, his dark moods blew over just as fast.

Jack pointed at them. "I got it! I'll tell people I'm blind from looking at the solar eclipse last year without using the cardboard viewer we learned how to make in earth science. The solar rays burned my retinas and disintegrated the color in my eyes. But wait! That's not all," he crouched into a fighting stance and Holly giggled as he kept going, "the power of the eclipse altered my brain and gave me super reflexes. Look! Up there! It's Eclipse Man! He's blind, but he's got the power of the dark sun and jungle cat reflexes!" Jack pounced from rock to rock. Humoring him, Emma raised her hands in mock surrender.

"Emma?" Holly spoke up, her head cocking slightly to the left. "Aren't you home early?"

Jack froze, mid-pounce, his imaginary claws ready to swipe. "Yeah. Why are you here?"

Emma sat down on the grassy bank and told them everything about the picture of her swimming in the lake and the reactions of the kids. Holly and Jack listened in horrified silence.

"So, you came home?" Jack gently asked, as Holly picked up a long straight tree branch and began peeling off the bark in skinny strips.

"Well, I considered going back inside..." Emma hesitated. She looked past the two of them. Out on the lake, the wind picked up in intensity, a low hum like an oboe warming up and whipping through the upper tree branches. "But then I screamed."

"You screamed at everyone?" Jack looked surprised. "In front of other people? That's not your usual 'write a song and sulk about it' style."

"Haha...very funny," Emma deadpanned. Inside her head, she could still hear the other kids' voices. "When I got to my car, the security guy confronted me, and I yelled at him. Then I left."

"I'm sorry." Holly walked over, sat down next to her, and slipped her hand into Emma's.

Jack swung his arms in a slow circle then clenched his fists. "Well, if I'd been there—"

Emma sat up straight and blurted, "Seriously? If you'd walked away back in Hartford, if you'd shown an ounce of self-control, we'd still be there, at home, and not stuck here."

Jack's body went rigid. He turned his head to the side, not responding to her outburst which she immediately regretted. He'd been put in a terrible situation today, two terrible situations. She'd

29

been ridiculed and hurt. But while she was moping all day by the lake feeling bad for herself, Jack had been not just ridiculed, but physically attacked while protecting his little sister. And here she was, venting her anger at him about moving.

A gust of wind shook leaves from the trees on the far side of the lake. Jack rolled his shoulders and shifted in place. "I should've backed down. I didn't mean to mess up again."

"I know," Emma said. "And I'm sorry. I didn't mean to yell at you." She paused, hoping he'd forgive her. "It's been a rough day for all of us."

Jack turned to face her and quickly wiped his eyes as a grateful look crossed his face. "It's okay," he said, clearing his throat, "guess I'm not the only Waite with control issues," he teased.

"Haha, that's funny, Eclipse Boy," Emma said. *Funny, but true.*

"It's Eclipse Man," he corrected her. Reverting to his usual state of kinetic energy, he scanned the bank, stepped lightly on several stones, and then hopped onto a turtle-shaped rock half submerged in the lake's shallow water. "And for your information, I showed a lot of control today fighting Wastoid. Ask Holly."

Holly leaned into Emma's side. "The bully. Jack gave him a nickname before kicking his butt."

Jack squatted down on the rock. "Yeah, but I went easy on him. I pulled the first hit, and when I swept his legs, I made sure not to hit his knees." He crouched, lifted his right leg starting the move. "I kicked low and—" His head jerked up to the left, towards the back of the house. "What the heck?"

Off balance on the slippery rock, he toppled backward, his eyes wide in shock, his arms flailing as he hit the water.

Emma doubled over laughing. Holly stood up and walked to the water's edge. Jack burst out of the water sputtering and splashing like a crazed hippo. He climbed back onto the rock and shook his head like a dog, water drops flying in all directions. He ran his hand through his wet hair and froze in place. "There it is again."

"There's what again?" Holly asked. "Jack? Earth to Jack?"

His eyes were locked up the hill towards their house. "There's a stained-glass window on the back of the house." He pointed up the slope. "And it just flashed with a green light. Did you see it?"

Emma craned her head to the left but saw nothing. Odd. She'd spent most of the summer swimming in the lake and never noticed a window. Then again, Jack was the most observant of the three of them. She stood up and stepped close to the water's edge. Her bedroom window on the second floor had blue curtains. To the right, the back corner of the house was swallowed up in a blanket of creeping green ivy. A towering cedar tree, most of its branches dead, blocked her view of whatever Jack was looking at.

"You have to come out here to see it. There's a gap in the tree," said Jack.

Emma shook her head suspiciously. "No way, you're trying to get me out there so you can push me in."

"Let me on your rock," Holly said. She gestured for Jack to move.

Jack jumped in the water and waded to shore as Holly hopped across the stones and took his place on the back of the turtle rock.

Her eyes widened with wonder. "There's a window with all the colors of the rainbow. And it's beautiful."

The cedar tree I planted at the back of the house belongs to the genus *Juniperus virginiana*, a slow-growing evergreen commonly referred to as red cedar. The brownish-red heartwood of the tree is rot resistant.

Related in name is the Lebanon Cedar – genus *Cedrus libani* – which can be found in Lebanon and Turkey in high-altitude forests, mixed with Cilician firs, black pines, and other juniper species.

—Professor Waite's Journal

6

THE LOCKED DOOR

"Did you find anything?" Jack yelled from under the bed in his room on the second floor. He'd spent the last ten minutes rapping and tapping on the walls, tugging on any suspicious-looking baseboards, and inspecting the hardwood floor. So far, he'd found nothing but crinkled candy wrappers and a sock.

Annoyed at not discovering a hidden compartment under his bed, Jack wriggled out and picked the dust bunnies off his black tee shirt. He scanned his room one more time. Unpacked boxes littered the floor, and a rumpled mass of blankets covered his bed. The desk, looking like an armory stocked with airsoft gun parts, was etched with cuts he'd made with one of his penknives. A grin crossed his lips as he remembered his dad's reaction when the desk's front leg, weakened by Jack's incessant carving, had snapped off when packing for the move. His dad made him keep the desk—now held together with a generous helping of duct tape—and confiscated his knife collection as punishment.

He looked up at his poster of Bruce Lee, who stood with his hands at the ready. "*You* got anything? I didn't think so." Jack bent down, retied the laces on his worn sneakers, and walked across the hall into Holly's room. She was sitting at her art desk, her attention

33

focused on the butterfly she had begun making earlier. She'd ignored his plan to search for the secret door.

Holly's room amazed Jack. He used his room like a trashcan, a place to dump stuff. Holly used hers like a giant canvas, and it was decorated as if she'd lived here for years instead of three months. Every surface, including the ceiling, was plastered with paintings of flowers, portraits, and abstracts. Each cubbyhole in the wall cabinet was filled with sculptures, painted boxes, and origami flowers, making her room more art gallery than seventh-grade bedroom. On top of the cabinet sat the lava lamp she'd wanted for her birthday, its unearthly yellow glow and the waxy purple globs of molten wax floating up and down, stretching and pulling their way to the top before morphing into a new shape, burbling back to the bottom. Jack stood still, momentarily enjoying the life and death of each melty blob and forgetting about his search. Sitting at her desk with her back to him, Holly continued to work on the butterfly.

"Hey." He crossed the room and tapped her on the shoulder. "You were supposed to be looking for the window."

Holly ignored him as she added a finishing touch to the butterfly's left wing. She carefully set her latest work down and looked over her shoulder.

"It's not in here," she said flatly.

He groaned loudly at her. His sister had recently discovered the art of sarcasm. Until this year, she had taken everything completely literally. He'd wasted some of his best jokes and funniest lines on her, each time walking away flabbergasted and deflated when she didn't laugh at the punch line. But this year, her humor button had mercifully clicked on.

"What about a trap door?"

"No." Holly crafted the single-word answer into an unmistakable, 'no, don't be a dummy' that made Jack laugh. "Because, (and Jack heard another unsaid 'dummy') I have touched, drawn on, and painted every inch of my room since we moved in. There's no door."

"Okay." Jack shrugged. If there had been a secret door in her room, she would have found it months ago with her habit of touching everything. The multi-hued butterfly rested on her desk, a hinged artist's table with multiple baskets hanging underneath, overflowing with supplies. "You finished? I want to search the attic."

Holly turned to him and placed the butterfly in his hand. It had three-inch wide moveable wings woven from the grass, flowers, and twigs that Holly had picked from the fields while walking home. Each wing radiated color. Green field-grass mixed with blue and purple petals was inserted into the weave. Yellow streaks from dandelion shoots shone like dappled sunlight on the wings. Jack squeezed the legs made from apple tree twigs. The wings of the butterfly flapped in response. She had connected the legs with a cross-hinge made of twigs lashed to the underside of the wings. Jack whistled in awe. "It's beautiful. Your best one yet."

"Thanks." Holly smiled. "I'll put it on Dad's stand and meet you in the attic to keep searching." Holly flitted out of the room with the butterfly.

"More like Dad's Pedestal of Forgiveness," Jack muttered under his breath as he watched her go. Every time she made a mistake, he got in trouble at school, or Emma forgot to call, Holly made a gift for their dad, her way of apologizing. She started with a drawing of a butterfly on a field of flowers, leaving it on the plant stand that had never seen an actual plant. At some point, probably the time Jack broke the kitchen window, her pictures, like a caterpillar in a cocoon, changed into butterfly sculptures of paper and fabric.

Leaving Holly's room, Jack pictured the unavoidable scene later today when their dad came home from his new job at the college. He would bump open the front door with his hip, his hands flipping through the mail. He'd drop his scuffed briefcase onto the corner of his desk, toss the mail down, and then turning, would see Holly's latest butterfly. Immediately knowing that one of them had done something wrong, he'd call them all to the kitchen for the 'talk'. Some things never changed no matter where they lived.

Jack chuckled to himself as he headed upstairs to the third-floor attic. "Might as well enjoy my freedom while I still have it."

He pushed open the door and a rush of hot air and dust hit his face. Stepping inside, he coughed as his fingers fumbled in the dark to find the pull cord. The single bulb popped on with a plink and cast a dim glow around the attic space as Holly walked in behind him.

"Did you ask Emma to come up?" Jack asked, already knowing the answer. "Let me guess. She doesn't want to help."

"She said she's tired."

"Okay, you go right, I'll check left," Jack said, disappointed.

When they'd moved into the house, they had lugged several boxes of their dad's stuff—books and periodicals—up the stairs to the attic, already cluttered with cardboard boxes stacked in pillars like ancient ruins. Jack threaded his way through a maze of stacked books, old furniture, and musty boxes. Most of this once belonged to Aunt Sarah and his dad's parents. The clapboard house, acreage, and lake on the outskirts of Lebanon had been in the Waite family for generations. Their dad grew up here. His parents had both died when he was a teen, so his Aunt Sarah, who had never married, moved in and took care of things. And when their own mom died, Aunt Sarah—a Great Aunt technically though none of them had ever referred to her that way—came to the rescue once again, leaving this old house boarded up.

He bumped into a gold lamp, once beautiful, but now stuck in the dark, not giving any light. Jack rubbed the head of the eagle-shaped finial, both its wings broken off and missing. He pushed aside a stack of boxes labeled Old Testament and started his inspection. Every few feet, reaching around the clutter, he rapped his knuckles on the planked walls and listened for any sound of a hidden door. At the far corner, he turned and worked his way along the back. Twenty feet later and done with his side, he stomped over to Holly.

"Nothing," Jack said as he plopped down onto a cracked leather suitcase. "You find anything suspicious?"

"Nope. Just walls." Holly didn't bother looking up. She was sitting cross-legged in an orange chair, an open shoebox in her lap.

Jack wrinkled his nose; the chair reeked of smoke. "Dad should burn all this junk."

Holly stroked the arm of the chair, covered in a patchwork of orange fabric. "Not this, I like it." With her left hand, she flipped through a stack of old pictures.

Jack reached into the box and pulled out a handful of snapshots. "You're wasting your time. You've been through this box and every other box up here since we moved in. You've never found any more pictures of her."

Her. Their mother. Jack thumbed through the faded pictures in his hand: their dad grilling hamburgers and a four-year-old Holly making a mud castle by the lakeshore when they'd vacationed at this old house, a group shot of all three kids one Christmas morning with Aunt Sarah, and their dad—young and smiling—shaking hands with a large bear-of-a-man. But, like the other boxes they'd searched before, there were no pictures of their mom.

Holly sifted through the box anyway. Their dad told them he and their mom weren't picture-taking people and most of the photos he had were snapped by their Aunt Sarah. Whenever Holly asked, their dad would go quiet, then say it was better to move forward in life, not backward. But then, he'd sit Holly on his lap and pull a small pile of pictures from his left-hand desk drawer. Jack always felt the photos were kind of corny like the photos on greeting cards, but never said that out loud. There was the shot of him in a park with their mom, holding hands, walking away from the camera. Another of Emma on a swingset with their mom in the background. A picture of their mom rocking Jack on her lap. But none with Holly. Jack was one year old when their mom died—Holly a newborn—and neither of them remembered her. He wished he could say something to make Holly feel better.

With the attic as a dead-end, Jack left Holly to herself and trudged down the steps to the second floor. He peeked in Emma's room. She was lying on her bed facing the wall, and Jack kept walking. Emma had a few memories of their mom, but she said they came as vague images, distant sounds. Emma remembered her mom singing. Jack would watch Holly soak up every word like a dry flower desperate for water. She'd rush off, draw yet another rendering of their mom, and present it to their Dad who always said the same thing to Holly, "it's a beautiful drawing, just like you."

Taking the stairs down to the first floor, he jumped the last three steps and landed lightly on the balls of his feet. Hungry, he started off to the kitchen when the grandfather clock in the foyer chimed.

Shoot, I'm running out of time. His dad would be home in an hour and ground him for life, or even worse, make him apologize to Wastoid. Jack stalked outside and walked around the house, his eyes counting off windows. He stared up at the cedar tree and pictured the circular window high above him, hidden by the branches. It was too far up on the house to be in a second-floor room, but the third floor was just the attic.

Minutes ticked by as he rubbed his head and counted the rooms on the second floor, picturing their locations behind the wall of the house. In his mind, he counted the steps from his dad's bed to the dresser, over the easy chair his dad read in every night, on through the bedroom wall, across Emma's bed, and...Jack's eyes popped open. He let out a whoop of triumph and ran to the back door. He burst into the kitchen, the screen door slamming behind him as he yelled.

"Em! Hol! Get down here! I got it!"

"Got what?" Emma replied. She and Holly were sitting at the kitchen table in the corner.

"Oh gosh!" Jack sputtered. "I didn't see you there!"

Emma opened the bag of chips in her hand. "Don't you have superpowers now?"

"Whatever." Jack snatched a handful of chips as Holly playfully tried to block his hand. "Listen, I know where the window is."

"You do?" Holly mumbled, her mouth full.

"You're still looking for the window?" Emma asked. Standing up and moving past Jack to the refrigerator, she opened the door, which banged into the side of the wood bookshelf, filled with cereal boxes, pasta, and snacks. "Shouldn't you be thinking about what you're going to tell Dad when he gets home..." she made a production of looking at her watch, "...in less than an hour?"

"I know, but—"

She reached out and playfully thwacked Jack on the back of the head. "But nothing. Dad's gonna kill you."

"You know, one of these days, I'll see that coming."

"Dream on."

Holly popped another chip into her mouth. "Emma's right. Anyway, it's probably just for decoration."

"But what about the flashing light?" Jack whined.

"Could have been a reflection." Emma set three cold cans of soda on the table, grabbed one, and moved towards the door. "I'm going to my room."

Jack stepped in front of the doorway and spread his arms wide to block her exit. "Hold on! What if there's a hidden room?"

Emma tried to push past him. He braced his arms on the door frame. "Room? You were looking for a window. Holly, help me make him move."

"Where there's a window, there's a wall. And there was a flashing light behind it, which means there's a room. Right?"

Emma stepped back and glanced up, her eyes towards the upper floors. Holly was nodding.

"Now you're curious." He pointed at Emma and then placed the tip of his index finger to his temple. He tried unsuccessfully to arch one eyebrow making Holly laugh. "And having deduced the room's location, I will now prove that it was hidden on purpose!"

Emma sat back down. She frowned at him. "Alright, Sherlock, but make it quick."

"I'll be Dr. Watson." Holly popped up from her chair and stood next to her brother.

"Yes, the game is afoot!" Jack shouted.

Emma groaned loudly.

"Fine. A short game." Jack turned to face Holly. "Dr. Watson, we are standing in the kitchen of a three-story house with only one set of stairs, as far as we know. Using your keen powers of deduction, please tell Detective Emma the location of the hidden door in this room."

Holly slowly turned, pointing. "Maybe behind those cabinets, but..." she walked past Jack and peeked around the doorway into the hall. "...no, that's the living room behind that wall. And there can't be a door on the side or the back wall because that's outside." She smiled, pointing at the refrigerator and bookshelf in the corner. "Your secret door is behind that bookcase."

Jack tipped his imaginary hat to her. "Correct, Watson! That bookshelf is too big for that corner because the refrigerator door bumps it. Plus, this shelf was in Dad's home office in Hartford, and now, all of his books are piled on the floor. Why would he put his bookcase here? It's illogical."

Holly walked to the bookshelf and peered behind it. "There's a door handle."

Jack bowed towards Emma, then strode over to Holly. "Help me move it." They grabbed the back edge of the bookcase and pulled. A box of cereal tumbled to the floor as the bookcase inched away from the wall. Jack kept talking as they slid it several more feet. "What solved the case for me was realizing that the attic space is a lot smaller than yours and Dad's bedrooms combined. There's space above Emma's room."

Emma stood up. She crossed her arms, staring at the exposed door. A metal hasp with a padlock was mounted on the door frame. "Great work, Sherlock. But it's locked."

Holly shook the padlock, then dashed to the kitchen junk drawer, yanked it open, and pulled out a paper clip and a nail file. She went to the door and grabbed the padlock.

"Holly!" Emma yelled at her. Holly froze, her hands on the lock, poised to pick it open. "Hold on. If dad hid the door to a room—"

"*Then* it's a secret room of mystery," Jack pronounced, grabbing a wooden spoon and raising it into the air.

"*Then* we should leave it alone," Emma retorted.

"No. We should vote," Jack argued.

"No, no, and no." Emma shook her head at him. "I know we vote on where to eat and what movie to watch but..."

Jack shook the wooden spoon at her. "But nothing. We always vote, and I vote we open it."

Emma scowled at him. "Fine. I vote no. Besides, you're assuming

Holly can open the lock. Hol, it's your vote. And don't forget how mad you would be if Jack broke into something of yours."

Holly's hands fell away from the lock, seeming to reconsider. Jack saw his chances dwindling. He needed her to take his side.

"Hol," he spoke softly. "There could be pictures of Mom in there."

Emma gasped and punched his arm. Wincing, he kept his eyes on Holly. "Well?"

She took a deep breath. "Sorry, Emma. I'm with Jack."

Holly turned back to the door, putting all her attention on the lock. With the nail file stuck in her mouth like a toothpick, she inserted the paperclip into the keyhole. She moved the paperclip back and forth, her other hand cupping the lock like a fragile egg. She tipped her head down, slid the nail file between her fingers, then inserted its tip into the opening. Up, then right, she pushed the paperclip, turning the nail file clockwise. The lock popped open. Jack let out the breath he'd been holding the entire time.

Eagerly reaching past Holly, Jack removed the lock and grabbed the door handle.

"Jack," Emma said from behind him. "I've got a bad feeling about this."

Jack stared at the door handle. "It'll be fine. We'll investigate and close it up before Dad gets home."

Not waiting for her response, he pulled the door open. A flight of dust-covered wooden stairs rose all the way to the third floor and ended in front of a closed grey door, brightly outlined with thin streams of color slipping through the cracks. A faint rainbow pattern —a wavering mosaic of light—flickered on the stairway wall.

Jack crept up the narrow wooden steps followed by Holly and Emma. At the top of the stairs, he glanced back at his sisters and then slowly turned the doorknob. He felt like an adventurer in one of his video games, exploring the unknown. He didn't know what they would find behind the door, but he desperately hoped it would be something interesting, something more than a cluttered junk-filled attic, or else he'd wasted the entire afternoon. Bracing himself for disappointment, he pushed the door open. A blast of color hit his eyes.

The room was bigger than he'd calculated, at least fifteen feet wide. A wooden table, littered with books and papers dominated the center of the room. The wall to Jack's right was lined with shelves, filled floor to ceiling with an assortment of wooden and metal cylinders, and on the left wall were racks filled with hundreds of colored glass bottles.

In the center of the back wall and directly across from the door was the round window he had seen from outside. Seven segments of glass, each a different color, radiated out from the white glass set in the middle of the window.

Jack stared wide-eyed while, next to him, Emma and Holly gasped. He hadn't seen the window in its entirety from the lake.

The center of the glass was cut in the shape of an eye—a white eye, just like his.

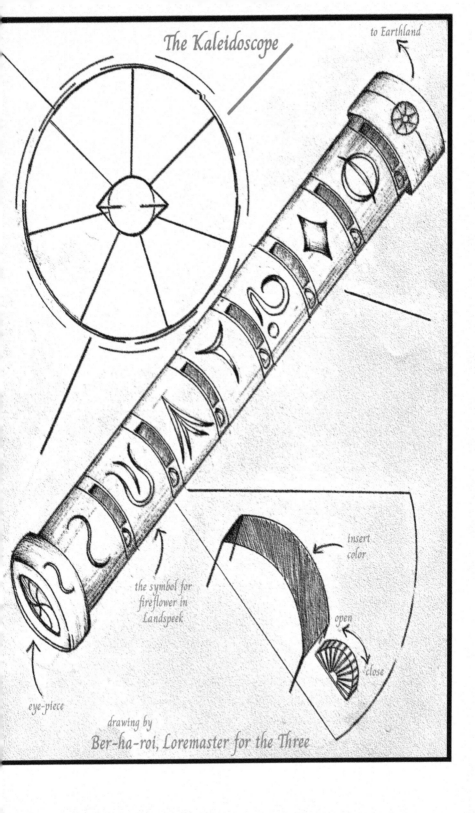

The Kaleidoscope

to Earthland

insert
color

open

close

the symbol for
fireflower in
Landspeek

eye-piece

drawing by
Ber-ha-roi, Loremaster for the Three

THE STUDY

Standing at the wooden table, Emma stopped reading aloud. Piles of notebooks and papers covered nearly every inch of its surface.

"Thanks, sis," Jack smirked, holding up one of the kaleidoscopes he had taken to examine from the series of display shelves behind him. "When I said 'Wow, check out all the kaleidoscopes,' I didn't mean 'Hey, Emma, bore me to death with a history lecture.'"

"You're not as funny as you look," Emma said, her eyes back on the notebooks. The thick notebook she'd been reading to Jack was written in their dad's slanted handwriting. She flipped forward, scanning her dad's writing, her curiosity increasing with each new page. They were dated, and he'd written these more than twenty years ago. She paused at a decorated hand-drawn sketch of an intricate flower-shaped mandala. In the right-hand margin was a list of angles, degrees, and image numbers. Variations of mathematical formulas, which made no sense to her, filled the next dozen pages. She closed the book and flipped through another; these pages listed materials and their RFIs—Refractive Index—whatever that meant.

Hoping to find something she could better understand, Emma pushed that notebook aside and grabbed a black accordion file perched on the table edge. She guessed the collection of kaleidoscopes had value, but as to why their dad had locked them away, she had no idea. She unwound the red cord from the circular closure and pulled out what looked like a bunch of receipts.

"Emma, Emma." Holly insistently tapped the other side of the table to get her attention.

She pulled her eyes away from a bill of sale for an item 'From the Estate of Doctor Aluman, Estate Item Forty-Seven', and glanced up at her sister.

Behind Holly were seven floor-to-ceiling shelves, each overflowing with hundreds of cork-stopped vials. Even empty bottles would have entertained Holly for years, but these were filled. Holly's first round of show-and-tell had been an armful of red bottles. Shoving papers out of the way, she'd dumped the contents of three of them onto the tabletop before Emma told her to stop. Now, she gestured excitedly at a dozen yellow bottles she had laid out like a pirate's gold-toothed grin.

"Amber." Holly picked up and rotated the small glass bottle like a jeweler's loupe in front of one eye. "It has an RF of 1.54. And this one is Yellow Diamond with a 2.417 index." Holly announced the contents of each bottle. "This is a canary feather. This one's Pervana... pervanad..and what's RF mean?"

Emma took the bottle and read the tiny handwritten label. "It says Pervanadyl. According to Dad's notes, RF stands for Refractive Index, but I have no idea what that means."

"These labels are Dad's handwriting." Holly's brown eyes glowed, reflecting the yellow of the bottles. "Did he collect all of these?"

Emma surveyed the shelf-lined wall. "It must have taken him years. There has to be over five hundred bottles."

"Six hundred and ninety-two," Jack chimed in as he slid up to the table and playfully poked Emma in the ribs.

"There's no way you counted them." From years of practice, Emma reached out and lightly smacked the back of Jack's head. Their dad teased him the same way.

"Ouch." Jack grinned, then pointed at the wall of bottles. "I didn't have to. On the shelf with all the purple colors...look at the last bottle."

Holly ran over and grabbed it. "Tanzanite." She squinted at the label. "It's numbered. Six hundred and ninety-two."

"Ta-da!" Jack said, then began mouthing the word 'thankyou' while tipping the brow of an invisible top hat to his imaginary adoring public.

"Don't get cocky," Emma chided. "But this is over the top, even for Dad. I know he gets consumed with work, but he obviously spent years finding all these samples and..." Emma gestured to the other wall. ".... all of those kaleidoscopes. Not to mention the research in these journals."

Jack leaned over the open page of the leather book Emma had been flipping through. "What is this stuff?"

Emma waved her hands over the papers covering the table. "I don't know. The big stack is seven journals filled with handwritten notes and equations way more complex than algebra. The other stack looks like a genealogy project."

"Genealogy?" Holly had now collected bottles from every shelf and piled them on the table. Her hands moving deftly like a weaver's on a loom, she arranged the bottles into the pattern of a rainbow.

"The study of family history...making a family tree." Emma heard the catch in Holly's breath and saw the eager look in Holly's eyes. "Sorry, Hol, I already checked. There's nothing about Mom's family. The notes are about Dad's ancestors."

Jack traced one of the branches with his finger. "Looks like I'm the first and the last Jack."

Emma had already seen that Elishah was the given name for the Waite men, going back hundreds of years. Dad's dad, his dad's dad... all named Eli. "I wonder why you got the first name Jack?"

"Beats me," Jack mused out loud. "But I'm glad. I'm way too cool to be an Elishah."

"Okay, fine, but all these kaleidoscopes hidden away behind a locked door; it feels wrong. No one's been up here for a long time by the looks of the place. And the scattered piles of open books? Why would he have all of this and leave it untouched for years?"

"They could be valuable, and he was keeping them safe," Jack offered up. "I hid my best pocketknives."

"In the hole in the wall you carved behind your bed?" Emma said matter-of-factly.

"What? How do you know that?"

"The night we moved in here, I heard you moving your bed and cutting into the drywall. I guessed you were making a hiding spot."

"But it's such great stuff," Holly said as she rearranged the sample bottles in her impromptu artwork. "Keep it safe for who?" She caught her mistake. "I mean for whom."

"I don't know." Emma hated not knowing the answer. She pictured their dad standing in the scattered, dusty mess: Testing samples of every color she could imagine, recording his findings in these books, using the kaleidoscopes to...to do what? *How do the scopes and the samples connect?* She went back to the leather journal again and started to read, quickly forgetting that Jack and Holly were standing in the same room.

As Holly happily mined the shelves for more colors, Jack returned to the wall of kaleidoscopes and picked up a dark wood barrel carved with a Chinese village. He lifted it and peered through the eyepiece. A brilliant image of repeating lotus flowers (he guessed this was called a mandala based on what Emma had read to him earlier) made of greens, blues, and whites floating in front of his eye. He rotated the barrel slowly clockwise, watching the image shift and change, every variation as breathtaking as the last. Carefully, he placed it back on the shelf. So far, none of the kaleidoscopes he'd picked up had batteries or seemed capable of creating the green flash of light he'd seen outside.

Jack counted the scopes. Eighty-one, no, make that eighty-two. *Who the heck needs eighty-two kaleidoscopes?* Jack picked another one, three-sided and made of colored glass and pewter. On its side the artist...what do you call a person who makes these things...a '*kaleido-scopist*?' A '*kaleidoscoper*?'...had attached a stained-glass butterfly with wings of shimmering pink. On the viewing end, the '*kaleido-guy*' had mounted a glass ball suspended between two delicate prongs of metal. The butterfly, like the carving on the bamboo scope, was decoration, a symbol for the image inside. Jack peered into the scope and spun the glass ball with his fingers. The image rotated, a miniature world—a multi-faceted sphere of iridescent sunshine, rose pink and sky blue. He stared for a long time at the tiny ball of color which, despite its size, made him feel very small.

Jack glanced across the room at his little sister; Holly would love this butterfly scope. The ones laid out on a smaller cloth-covered table in the corner were a different story. Compared to the beautifully carved kaleidoscopes on the shelves, those scopes were rough and plain. He walked over and picked up a particularly ugly scope made out of copper pipe. Like the others on this table, the pipe had seven segments with a small hole drilled between each section. Between the segments, the '*scopologist*' had placed pairs of glass discs. These must be the object chambers Emma read about earlier. A small label—the letters ST4 in his dad's handwriting – was affixed to the bottom of the barrel. *Could his dad have made this?* He raised the scope and looked through it.

"Whoa," He groaned out loud at the icky green and brown splotches inside the scope. Instead of otherworldly creations, this scope projected a blob of pond scum. Green bubbles, bulging as if ready to burst, floated in a brackish slime. It had none of the symmetry of the others, but this image did have more depth and substance. The longer he stared, the more the image appeared biological, like looking at the surface of a liquid in a laboratory.

He picked up a kaleidoscope made of shiny metal—tin, he guessed —also with seven segments. Jack flipped the tube over and read the label, ST22, before peering inside. A swirling yellow field of light filled Jack's eye. He threw out his left hand for balance. Much like the cascading bubbles in the green one, the yellow streaks of color spinning like tiny rays of sunlight seemed almost alive. But these rays of yellow kept changing into new shades as they moved.

Amazing. He followed a glowing ribbon of soft buttercream yellow with his eyes. The color rose into a lighter hue, a cascade of gold. Jack stood motionless, lost in the shifting sands. He tried not to blink, afraid of missing a moment.

"Jack." Holly tapped his shoulder. He jumped and dropped the scope which bounced and rolled under the table. "Sorry."

"S'okay. I was looking through Dad's scope."

She looked at the scopes on the table. "Dad made these? Are you sure?"

"No, but the labels are his writing—ST could be for Scope Test and these are his numbered experiments." Jack bent down, searching for the dropped scope. "You gotta try this one. It's full of a million yellow colors."

He pulled up the edge of the tablecloth, then lifted it to one side. "Hey, Hol, check it out." Holly crouched down beside him.

The green cloth wasn't covering a small table at all, but a polished wooden chest, resting on a shipping crate. Holly stroked the scrolled surface of the chest, her fingers lightly tracing the crevices in the wood.

"It's a treasure chest!" Holly squealed.

"I bet the best stuff's inside." Jack looked crossways at her, a sly smile on his lips.

Not hesitating, they both began grabbing the half dozen scopes still sitting on top.

"What are you doing?" Emma asked. She was frowning at both of them. Jack continued to clear away the scopes, but Holly stopped. "Holly?"

"Ummm," Holly replied slowly. "We found a treasure chest under the scopes Dad made."

"Dad made scopes?" Emma asked. "He made those?"

"Jack thinks they're experiments." She walked over to Emma, looked again through the scope, and offered it to her. "Be careful with it. It's the most beautiful thing I've ever seen."

Emma raised the scope to her eye as Holly continued talking excitedly. "Do you see it? It's like yellow flowers melting into honey."

"Yes, but it's strange, too. The surface is rising and falling, almost like it's alive." Her hands shaking, Emma lowered the scope as an uneasiness she couldn't explain crept over her.

Jack yanked away the dusty cloth that had covered the chest. The dark surface, inlaid with colored stones and an inscription accented with gold filigree, gleamed invitingly. Emma and Holly walked over and stood next to Jack. He reached for the bronze latch.

"Guys." The nervousness in Emma's voice stopped his hand. "Hold on. We gotta talk."

Jack placed his hand squarely on the lid of the chest. He'd discovered this room and now he'd found a treasure chest. There was no way he was going to leave it alone.

"Wait a minute. I'm not sure it's a good idea to play with these. I have a bad feeling." Emma waved the yellow scope at him.

"They're kaleidoscopes. They make pretty pictures." Jack said and rolled his eyes at her, annoyed by his sister's lack of adventure. Next to him, Holly only nodded.

"Nice try," Emma said. "You both know these are more than that. Holly could barely tear herself away from this and you're way too excited." Emma turned the scope over in her hands. "The image in this yellow scope...it scares me."

"Well, I'm not scared."

"And that's the problem. You're never scared, so you rush in. Look at the bruise on your face. Being a little scared might have kept you from getting in a fight today."

Jack slammed his fist on the top of the chest. "I won the fight! And I saved Holly and all you can do is lecture me! When did we vote and make you the mom?"

"Stop it!" Holly stuck her hand between them like a referee separating two boxers. She glared at Jack. "You're being mean." She turned back to Emma. "And so are you."

Emma took a deep breath. "You're right. I wasn't there." She smiled apologetically. "I'm sorry."

Jack offered up half a grin. "Sorry enough to let me open this up?"

He placed his hand on the lid of the still unopened chest just as he had earlier. A bright green light escaped out of the seam under the chest lid, briefly bathing the room in an emerald glow. Jack stepped back in surprise. "You saw that, right? That's gotta be the green light I saw flashing from outside. It's coming from inside the chest."

"But why did it flash now?" Emma asked. "What did you do?"

"It wasn't me," Jack said, then tapped the wooden chest several more times. "See?" He watched Emma's face as she stared intently at the chest. Her brow was furrowed. She was close to saying yes, but he was afraid that if he asked her again, she would reconsider and push back because he was the reckless one. Emma's hand was hovering over the top.

Jack quietly leaned close to Holly and nudged her with his elbow. When she glanced at him, he tipped his head towards Emma and mouthed the words, 'Ask her'.

"So, now can we open it?" Holly asked, looking up at Emma expectantly with her big brown eyes.

EMMA COULDN'T DENY THAT SHE WANTED TO OPEN THE chest. Carvings covered the lid and sides, long sweeping lines with repeating accent marks, like musical notes. And she needed to know the source of the mysterious green light which seemed harmless. They'd been next to the chest when the light flashed and nothing bad had happened. She leaned down and listened; whatever was inside was not making ticking sounds. *Ticking sounds? Seriously? As if their dad had hidden away a bomb!* She made her decision. "We need to be quick. Dad will be home any minute."

She flipped the bronze latch and raised the lid which creaked at the hinges. Laid inside, cushioned by reams of black silk, was another kaleidoscope, its body made of nine sections. Emma sighed with relief. *It's just another kaleidoscope.*

Slim and cylindrical, the metal barrel of the kaleidoscope was black like iron. After the eyepiece, the next seven sections of the barrel shimmered with flame-shaped streaks of color—the first section with deep ruby reds, the second with fiery oranges, the third with golden yellows, and so forth, to the last section with streaks of violet—mirroring the seven colors in a rainbow. Gold bands with inset screws separated each of the sections. Emma guessed immediately from the craftsmanship their dad had not made this one; he wasn't this good with tools. Her earlier fears forgotten, she picked up the scope.

"Cool!" Jack reached over and snatched the scope out of her hands.

"Hey!" Emma tried to take the scope back, but he danced backward. "Be careful. That one is probably worth a fortune. You're going to be in serious trouble if you break it."

"I'm pretty sure the fight and imminent school suspension already count as serious trouble. And remember, if Dad didn't want us to find this, he would have put a lock on the chest."

"A lock on the chest? He hid the room behind a locked door!"

"Just saying." Jack shrugged his shoulders like casting off a cloak. He turned the rod in his hands, his fingers lightly twisting at one of the gold bands. He held up the scope to his eye and looked through it. "Hmmm...besides, it's already broken. There's no image inside. No colors or anything. All I see is black."

"Wait, I know what's wrong." Emma reached her hand out. Jack stared at her for a long moment before handing it over.

"See these engraved symbols on each part? Dad made drawings of them." She led them over to the center table and handed the scope to Holly who smirked at Jack. Emma flipped through the leather journal. "I'm pretty sure there was...yeah, here it is!" She pointed to a detailed drawing. "The eyepiece controls the opening. Rotate right to close and left to open."

Holly turned the eyepiece. The circle of overlapping metal plates began to open.

"It's working," she said. "It's like the pieces of a camera shutter." The kaleidoscope clicked, and Holly looked inside. "Nope, it's still broken."

Emma, her excitement building at finding more answers, flipped to another page. "Dad wrote all this like he was trying to decipher a code. The engravings are copied here, but I can't find the meanings."

Holly traced her fingers across the symbols drawn on the page. "Each section is marked with a different symbol. You know, if I were making this, I'd make everything match. Maybe the symbols are for the colors?"

Jack took the scope from her and rotated one of the small, knurled wheels set next to each band. "Every band has a slot that opens when you turn the wheel. What if the symbols are for what goes in each slot? You know, take the stuff from all those sample bottles over there, stick the material in the holes and..." Jack put the kaleidoscope up to his right eye and froze.

"And what?" Holly asked. Jack didn't respond. "Hello? Earth to Jack."

He stood silent, the scope still pressed to his eye. He raised his left hand slowly and reached forward.

"What the heck are you doing?" Emma asked.

"Are you seeing this?" His voice trailed off as he lowered the scope. "It's working like the yellow scope." He put the scope back to his eye as he talked. "The red is super vivid. But the color in this one is beyond the scope."

"You mean on the wall?" Emma asked.

"No, there's a slice of red color in front of me. And there's something through the color, something real.... something I can almost touch." Jack mumbled as his left hand grasped at the air.

"Let me try it." Holly left the table and nudged him in the side, so he gave her the scope. "Nope. I don't see anything."

"Weird. Could be a reflection from where I'm standing." Jack pulled her over a few feet, put his hands on her shoulders, and aimed her body like a rotating turret. "Straight ahead at the wall... it's red with swooshy lines."

Emma resumed her study of the drawings, hoping to make sense of the crazy words with too many vowels that ran together. "Balgagaar...daan...Sii." Maybe it's one of those old languages Dad teaches."

"Nope," Holly said. "Still nothing." She squinted suspiciously at Jack. " Are you messing with me?"

Emma gave up on the words and traced her finger along their dad's drawings. He had captured every detail on the kaleidoscope's barrel including the seven slots, each next to an engraved symbol. But his drawing of a colored window didn't match the window in this room.

The colors in *this* window were in the order of the rainbow. Emma smiled. She still remembered the memory trick ROYGBIV from science class. Instead of showing their window exactly, the sketch placed the red segment at the top.

She flipped to the next page. He had redrawn the color wheel but with the seven pie-shaped slices of color spaced apart. From the red slice, a wavy arrow shot out, passed through a triangle, and then connected to a red sphere. He'd written 'pure red light' next to the arrow.

"I give up." Holly gave the scope back. "You did get hit on the head today. Maybe that's why you're seeing things."

Jack shrugged and looked through the scope again. "There. It's projecting the glowing circle of red light right in front of me. I can almost reach it."

Come on," Emma said out loud to herself, trying to block out the others. The answer was frustratingly close. She stared at her dad's color wheel drawing. "Wait a minute, what if the wheel represents the scope Jack is holding?" Emma said, working the problem out loud. "Then it would mean the scope is connected to this red color ball, connected by..." she slowly reread her dad's note. "...by the pure red light." The answer flashed across her mind and Emma excitedly jabbed the notebook with her index finger. "I got it! The red section of the scope creates the pure red light that connects to this other place."

Emma gasped. *Jack is looking at a red circle. He's looking at the other place!* She spun around towards her brother, now looking through the scope with his other arm thrown across Holly's shoulders.

"Jack! No, no, no! Jack, put it down!" Emma yelled as she lunged forward.

"It's a door," Jack said. "It's a red door."

"Jack! Put it down!" She grabbed his hand and the kaleidoscope too late.

Without a second thought, Jack stepped through the door.

"Colors are the deeds and sufferings of light."

—A quote found in Professor Waite's Journal attributed to Goethe

8

SEEING RED

JACK SAW RED. To the right and the left. Above and below him. Red as far as his eyes could see.

He tried waving his hand in front of his eyes, desperate for something to focus on. His mind reeled. His hand, his arms, and his body were gone. He ordered his limbs to move in search of any sensations. Nothing. Lost in the endless red sea, the fear rushed in on invisible waves.

"Holly!" He tried to yell.

No sound. He was shouting only in his head. He didn't understand what happened. He'd been looking in the kaleidoscope, stepped forward and now he was someplace else, wrapped in crimson silence.

But something was changing far out in the boundless wash of red color. Coming toward him was a tiny point of reddish-orange light, vibrating up and down. The dot came closer and closer, yet he couldn't tell if it was getting bigger. He couldn't make out its size. The endless red light surrounding him gave no sense of scale.

I must be somewhere beyond the red door, but how? And where is Holly?

Suddenly his vision was filled with not one dot, but a storm of dots, flying toward him too fast to count. Fear squeezed his mind. When the first red light reached him, nothing happened, and Jack relaxed. But slowly he began to feel a sensation in his eyes. He wished he could blink it away, but his eyes wouldn't close. They began to itch as a tiny thread of light wriggled across his eyeballs. He desperately wanted to rub his eyes and make it go away, but he was powerless. He had no arms. He had no hands. He had only eyes.

As more dots approached him, he began to panic. One of the drops darkened and hardened into a sharp point. Then the scarlet spear shifted its angle and dove directly into his eyes.

He wanted to scream. Blinding pain clouded his mind as he tried futilely to look away. A thin needle of red light forced its way through the fabric of his vision, deeper and deeper. Jack yelled in his head, attempting to fight off the relentless pressure. He prayed for blackness, wishing he could pass out to escape the suffering when suddenly the light fractured in a burst of radiance. The unbearable agony released.

Jack sank into the absence of pain and lost himself in the pool of burgundy now bathing his vision. Relaxed, he marveled at the stars twinkling in the expanse. No...wait...those weren't stars. Those were other points of light. Another wave coming his way.

Terrified, Jack wanted to shut his unclosing eyes as an assault of color, scarlet and ruby like the heat of a campfire, flared and flamed.

9

ORIGAMI

Searing pain. Bent bones.

Holly jerked back to consciousness in the sea of red. *I must be dreaming. People can't fold.*

She remembered being latched onto Jack's arm in the study and rushing forward when he lifted the kaleidoscope to his eye. She had found herself floating in an endless red space that seemed to cradle her, suspending her in a vial of warm liquid. Then her right leg had tingled and folded in half.

Bending. Snapping. Cracking.

Holly stared at her folded leg. The terrible pain was gone, but that made no sense. *I should still be in pain.* She blinked uncomprehendingly at the sole of her right foot which now pointed straight up her leg and rested above her kneecap. Her leg had bent backward in the middle of her shin. The bottom of her leg was folded in half.

Holly studied the bend. There ought to be broken bones and blood. Instead, the surface of her leg tapered inwards, flattening out into a hard fold with a paper-sharp crease.

Images from her room, shelves dotted with small origami birds and flowers, flashed into her head as she traced the fold in her leg with her eyes. Holly had always loved the idea of turning a two-dimensional square, flat and lifeless, into a three-dimensional object filled with purpose. She spent hours on their construction, picking them up, and running her fingers along their sharp, deliberate folds.

Her pain, the awfulness in her leg before she passed out, could be described as simply as that; her leg was folded.

Tingling.

A pressure in the red mist began to squeeze her arms, the same pushing sensation as before. The pressure built, now concentrated on spots above her elbows, with another dull ache bearing down on her left shinbone. Holly tried going elsewhere in her mind, far away to the shelf in her room which held a crisp stack of washi paper. She imagined making one of her paper boxes: the countless steps, the book folds and the cupboard folds, undone and redone. She envisioned the dull hand-tool used to create the creases. It was called a bone folder.

Holly's arms snapped backward and folded up behind her back. Red-hot shafts of pain ripped through her body. Her shinbone bent sideways, and as Holly cried and began to pass out again, she felt a tingling in her neck.

I am the paper.

SAND AND SHADOW

JACK LAY ON HIS BACK, his body exhausted from the red nightmare, and tried not to panic. He couldn't see.

He closed his eyes. *It's okay. I just need some time for my eyes to rest and recover.*

Counting to ten, he waited before tentatively touching his fingers to his eyes. He inhaled and opened them again. Nothing. He strained to focus, hoping for any glimpse of light or color, but all he saw was black.

The kaleidoscope was gripped in his right hand, and he could feel hot sun beating down on his face. A warm bead of sweat inched down the side of his nose. He wiped it away with the back of his hand, a smile on his lips despite his circumstances. *At least I have arms again.* He gave his legs a fond pat. *And legs.* But any relief of having his body back was overshadowed by the darkness in his eyes.

"Holly!" Jack yelled, the sound of his voice sucked away by hot swirling winds. His voice cracked; his throat was still raw from his soundless screaming inside the scope. Holly must have been dragged along with him. He could have sworn he felt her next to him for a fraction of a second after he stepped into the red door. "Holly, are you there?"

Jack gritted his teeth. *Think, Jack. You can't see, and your position is unknown.* He'd gone somewhere, most likely triggered by looking inside the kaleidoscope. *Your sister may be hurt or in danger.* His sensei's calm voice spoke to him, and he unconsciously responded as if back in formation at the dojo, steadying himself.

Flexing his hands, he tensed and relaxed the muscles in his shoulders, arms, and legs. Satisfied that he wasn't injured, he placed his hands on the ground—it was hot and sandy. Bewildered, he pushed himself into a kneeling position. *Hot sand?* Jack grabbed a handful of the warm grittiness and looked down. *You can't see, stupid. Try something else.* He raised his hand to his nose and sniffed. *Earthy and dry, and definitely not a beach smell.* Jack ground the soles of his sneakers back and forth and got the expected crunch. *Definitely sand.*

Jack rose into a defensive stance, both hands at the ready. He fought against the urge to search his surroundings with his eyes. Instead, he swiveled his head back and forth, listening. The dry wind pushed and pulled at his t-shirt, but he heard nothing else. He wished Emma were here; she was so much better at listening. *Did she watch us disappear?* A horrible idea hit him. *She must think we're dead.* Then a voice, weak and scared, called out.

"Jack! Jack, where are you?" It was Holly's voice, and she was close. Relief washed over him.

"Holly! I'm over here!" He took small shuffling steps in the direction of her voice, keeping his feet close to the ground, and hoping not to trip on some unseen object. "Are you all right?"

"No." Her voice quivered. "I can't move."

"What? Are you stuck in the sand? Are you hurt?" *Please, please don't be hurt.* She didn't answer him. "Hol, you have to keep talking." Unsure of which way to go, he stopped. "Count out loud, okay?" No response. "Okay?"

Jack waited as the seconds stretched on in silence.

"One, two, three..." Holly began to count, her voice shaky, and Jack quickened his pace, afraid she might go quiet again. "...Four, five..." The sand crackled under his feet as he stumbled across the unseen ground. "...Seven, eight, ow!"

Holly squealed as he stepped on her and toppled to the ground.

He scrambled up, kneeling beside her, feeling with his hands. She seemed to be lying on her back, flat on the sand. He reached out and accidentally poked her in the face.

"Stop! What are you doing?" demanded Holly.

"I can't see you."

"What do you mean?"

"Okay, don't panic. When I woke up here, I couldn't see."

"You're blind? Holly asked, her voice shaking. "Where are we? What happened?"

He sat back on the sand, caught off guard by her question. Blind sounded a lot worse than not seeing. "I think we just traveled through the kaleidoscope. I don't know how, but all I saw was red light, and it burned my eyes, and now I can't see."

"I saw the red too. But my body folded, and I felt like my bones were breaking," Holly explained. "Somehow it doesn't hurt anymore, but my arms and legs are still numb." Jack cringed at the idea of her suffering.

My little sister was folded. And I had my eyes burned out. He didn't want to think about the agony of the scope. He reached out with his right hand and found Holly's unmoving arm. He kept his hand still as a wordless apology, unable to say anything, knowing he should try and comfort her. But he couldn't see how.

MINUTES PASSED, AND HOLLY SAID NOTHING AS JACK SAT in silence next to her. Finally, after what felt like an eternity of waiting, the numbness in her body faded.

"I can get up now," Holly said, trying to sound upbeat, as she rolled away from Jack and climbed to her feet. Dusting herself off, she watched her brother, hoping he'd say that his sight was coming back. But he said nothing.

"How are your eyes? Look at me," Holly said. Jack's head hung down; his blond hair pushed up in an unruly mass.

"They don't hurt, but nothing's changed." Jack rubbed his palms in his eyes.

Above them, the sun was already low in the sky. "I think it's late afternoon here. Will the kaleidoscope take us home when your eyes feel better?" She was scared, but at least her body was working. She didn't understand why his sight hadn't returned as quickly as the feeling in her arms and legs.

He frowned. "I don't know. I don't even know where we are."

"It's a red desert." She knelt and picked up a handful of sand. Up close, the sand had swirls of reddish-brown, speckled with gold...she'd never imagined sand this beautiful. "There are dunes in every direction, but I don't see any trees or buildings." The crimson sand stretched out in front of her, covered in sculpted ripples. There were some boulders in the distance, huddled low to the ground as if afraid to stand up to the winds, but nothing else.

"Maybe we're in Egypt, like the Sahara desert."

Jack shrugged while running his fingers on the barrel of the kaleidoscope. "Maybe. These markings could be hieroglyphics, but..."

"But you think we're somewhere else."

"I don't know. What happened to you and me seemed so...bizarre." He hesitated before looking up in her direction, afraid to put his fear into words. "I think you should explore."

"Uh-uh. I'm not leaving you," Holly argued. Sitting in the middle of the desert made no sense but separating herself from Jack—even a short distance—scared her.

"Listen, you said it's getting late. We need to find help before it gets dark."

"Yeah, but we should look together," Holly insisted.

"How about you do the looking." Jack tapped his cheek below his right eye. "I know you're scared, and so am I, but we don't have time for you to lead me around by the hand."

He was right. Her throat was parched and they needed to find help. They needed to find water. "Fine, but I'm keeping you in sight the entire time." Jack sighed loudly at her choice of words. "Oops. Sorry."

Holly rose and turned away, not knowing what else to say. He was as confused as she was about why he hadn't recovered.

Dragging her feet across the sand, Holly walked away from Jack. After forty steps with the sand pulling at her sneakers, she stopped, afraid to lose sight of him across the dunes. She turned left and walked a little farther in that direction, her eyes searching the rolling seas of red and brown for signs of other people, all the while checking over her shoulder.

Jack sat in the same spot, his face streaked in sandy sweat and his eyes downcast, looking like a holy man praying for rain. Holly stopped. A black mist seemed to swirl in a circle around his body. She scanned the sky, and the sun was a red ball hovering low on the horizon but there were no clouds. She looked again at Jack; the darkness around him was gone.

11

NO WAY HOME

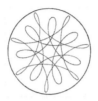

EVENING WAS COMING FAST. *What if we're still here at night?* With her eyes on the dune rising in front of her, Holly pushed herself into motion, smacking her legs with her hands to knock off the grit and beat down the fear gripping her insides.

In front of her, the ground rose steadily towards a low ridgeline, the rising dune blocking her view of the other side. The sky above the crest twinkled, and she picked out three faint points of early starlight, tiny drops of yellow embedded in a swirl of red velvet. Losing daylight would make things worse. If she hurried, she would be able to see beyond the ridge before going back. She glanced back at Jack, then pushed herself into a run, her feet slipping on the loose sand as she climbed to the top.

Cresting the peak, the sand suddenly collapsed under her feet. She tumbled down the far side, toppling headfirst into a towering fence stretched like a fabric wall at the bottom of the unfamiliar sands.

"Help! Jack!" She'd landed face-first into the cloth barrier with her feet trapped ankle-deep in the soft sand. The stretchy beige wall was already collapsing under her weight. With a ripping sound, the material tore apart, and she fell through the fabric and struck the ground elbows first.

"Ow!" She was stuck with her top half through the wall and her bottom half still behind. Holly wriggled back and forth on the ground like a snake shedding its skin. As she tried to pull her legs through the hole, her feet got hopelessly tangled up in the ripped cloth that seemed to tighten with her every move. She grunted, rolled onto her back, and gasped; a small girl with light brown eyes was smiling down at her.

"Are you lost?" asked the little girl. Holly smiled, relieved. The girl —barefoot and dressed in a light brown tunic—had spoken in English, though with a strange, lilting rhythm.

Holly stopped struggling. She'd found help! The girl, who looked about six years old, pulled a short, curved knife from the sash tied around her waist. She pointed it at Holly, the serrated edge glinting in the twilight. Holly kicked her feet afraid she had misunderstood. *Oh no, she's going to—*

"Don't be scared. You're stuck in the wind fence. I'll help you get out."

The girl crouched down at the point where Holly's legs disappeared through the stretchy material now sealed around her ankles. She poked her knife through the fabric, then made a swift cut around Holly's ensnared legs. Holly pulled her feet free and sat up in the dirt, fascinated by the knife's tip which began glowing a bright orange color as if heated in a forge. With the tip of the blade, the girl traced the incision she'd made, stood up, and slid the knife into her sash. No trace of the cut in the repaired cloth wall remained.

"Your knife glows?"

"I needed to mend it. Cloth woven from vella fixes itself, but not as strong. Father says a good farmer always mends his fences."

Holly shook her head, confused by the girl's words. *At least the girl spoke English.* "Can you tell me where I am?"

"You're on father's vella farm by the south wall of Lindur." She pointed behind her to the well-tended fields full of tall brown stalks laden with yellow pods. Holly had never been so happy to see a farmer's field. She and Jack could get help. "What village are you from?" asked the girl.

"Umm...Lebanon. In New Hampshire?" The small girl smiled

blankly while tugging at the hem of her brown woven tunic. The words clearly meant nothing to her.

"Have you heard of America?" Holly held her breath. The girl frowned and picked up a broken stalk from the path bordering the field. Holly's hopes dropped. "How about Earth?" she suggested, feeling silly for asking.

The girl's eyes popped in surprise, and Holly relaxed. *Of course she knows Earth. It's not like we could be on a different planet.*

The girl took a step backward, whipped her knife out and screamed.

"Shard! Shard!" She grabbed Holly's hand and yanked her forward. Holly spun around, following the girl's frightened gaze. The sun had deepened into a dusky red, and as the light vanished beyond the dunes, a black figure pushed against the cloth fence Holly had fallen through. The point of a blade pierced the fabric, then slashed downwards, ripping through the cloth. A black leg thrust through the ragged opening.

The girl screamed again, dropped Holly's hand, and fled down the path.

"Wait! Come back!" Holly cried, but the frightened girl had already darted between the crop rows and vanished from sight. Holly wheeled around.

"Darn it, Jack!" Holly grabbed his hands and pulled him through the rapidly closing hole in the fence. "You scared her away."

"WHAT THE HECK, HOLLY!" Jack exploded, staring wild-eyed as he slid the pocketknife into the back of his jeans. "You were supposed to stay close, and then you screamed for help and now you're on the other side of this...this..." Jack waved the kaleidoscope at the wall. "...whatever this is. And you're all right?"

"Hey, your eyes work!" She pictured him running across the sand to her rescue.

A smile flashed across his face. "Yeah, right before I heard you yelling. What happened?"

"I fell into the vella," she said, then saw his confusion. "The wind fence, I mean. The girl said that it's made from vella. She spoke

English but never heard of America! And Jack, she helped me get free, and she had a knife with an orange blade. It glowed!"

"Slow down, Hol." Jack raised his hands. "What girl?"

"The girl that was here. She said she lives here with her father. She got scared and ran away before I could tell her it was you. I forgot to ask her name."

"Ran away where?"

"Down the path and into the field." Holly gasped. "But it doesn't matter now! You can see. You can use the scope and take us home!"

"You're right!" Jack exclaimed. He quickly wiped each end of the kaleidoscope's barrel with the edge of his shirt. "Grab onto me, like in the study."

Holly linked her right arm with his left, then to leave nothing to chance, grabbed his left hand with both of hers and squeezed tight. As Jack raised the kaleidoscope to his right eye, Holly stiffened; she didn't want to be folded again. She waited, but nothing happened.

"We're not..." She hesitated as she turned her head towards Jack. He switched the scope to his left eye, then shook his head as he lowered the scope and pulled away from her.

"Going home? No, not yet. I'm not seeing anything but dark red," he said, waving his hand back and forth in front of his face. "Maybe it's too dark out here for it to work right." Jack studied the scope while muttering to himself. After a few moments, he blew out a long breath.

Holly blinked in disbelief. When she got the use of her arms and legs back, she was sure Jack would get his sight back and then poof... take them back home.

Jack looked around. "You said she went that way?"

"What?" Holly said, struggling with her disappointment. She couldn't understand how Jack could be so calm. "Yeah, I guess to her house. We're on her father's farm. But—"

"But nothing. You did great," Jack smiled at her reassuringly, then started down the path. "Come on, we can get help, find out where we are, and try Dad's scope again."

Holly couldn't move, her eyes fixated on the barrier behind them.

Jack walked back to her and put his arm around her shoulder. Holly leaned into him grateful for the gesture, surprised by his sweetness. She didn't know if he could feel her trembling. She didn't care.

"I'm scared." She whispered the words.

"Me, too," Jack admitted, but she felt his eagerness to move. "But we could be close to that girl's house, so we just follow this path until we see some lights."

"No, not because of the dark." She needed him to understand her right now. She pulled on his arm, keeping him next to her. "Don't you understand? She never heard of America, maybe not even Earth. We're really lost." She found the white glint of his eyes in the waning light. "I'm afraid if we go down that path"—she started to cry—"we'll never get home. We'll never see Emma again. Or Dad." She wiped her cheeks as she broke down into sobs.

"We'll get back home." He awkwardly tried hugging her, something he would never do back home. Holly started to pull away, but he wouldn't let go. She took several deep breaths.

"I'll get us home." Stepping back, he paused as if weighing invisible odds, his face surprisingly serious. "I promise."

She knew he meant it. She wished she could believe him or could find any small fragment of hope. She wanted to tell him his promise meant something, but she couldn't. He always talked big...big plans and big promises.

Holding hands, they walked fast. The night sky deepened, with faint illumination coming from a few stars and the slivered moon. As they neared the end of the path, an imposing wall of vella, barely visible in the dark, blocked their view as the path turned hard to the right. Holly slowed and squeezed Jack's hand.

"You got a plan?"

"We'll find the farm and go home," Jack reassured her but sounded less confident than before. He stopped and fumbled in his pocket.

"Hey, what was that word the girl screamed over and over? Shard? What's a shard?" He flicked open the blade of his pocket knife.

"I don't know. But whatever it is, she was afraid of it."

They turned the corner. A few hundred yards away was a group of buildings, surrounded by a fence with bright yellow lights.

Jack whooped with excitement and let go of her hand. "See, Hol? I told you it'd be okay."

A horn blasted somewhere close to their right. Holly jumped. Jack reached out and pushed her behind him. The sound faded fast into the dunes, replaced by muffled voices as indistinct words wove their way through the stalks in the field.

"Should we hide?"

"No, let's stay put. It's probably just the farmers," Jack said, but slid the kaleidoscope down the back of his pants. "Stay behind me when they get here, okay?"

"NOW!" a shout rang out behind them. A flash of red light burst at their feet as a heavy net landed on their heads and knocked them to the ground. Jack landed on top of her. Low voices surrounded them as three figures emerged from the vella. Holly tried to move, but the net was too heavy.

"Ouch! Move your elbow!" She complained, struggling to free her left arm. Wriggling under Jack, she peered through the webbing.

Eying her was a fat man with a hard, round belly and a strange beard, split into two halves by the large scar on his chin. He wore a tooled leather vest over a long-sleeved shirt and maroon pants tucked into a pair of desert boots. A curved knife with a jeweled hilt hung from his belt. He held up the glowing lantern in his hand, frowned, and then set it on the ground.

"By Daria's bosom!" the man exclaimed. "Amir, you need to teach your daughter the difference between people and shards. Mina's roast will be tough as my boot soles by now because you've got me out here protecting you from children."

"Better to be safe," the voice came from off to the left. "Besides, Shorta, everyone knows you'll have no trouble eating that roast."

Their captor looked annoyed as he pulled on both ends of his beard and stared at her. She felt Jack shifting his weight.

"Umm, Mister Shorta, sir," Jack cleared his throat. "My name is Jack. Can you let us out now?"

"Silence, boy," Shorta said, still frowning at Holly. "Show me your arms, girl."

Holly squirmed, but she was still pinned under Jack. The man squatted down beside her. "Show me your arms."

"I would but I can't move," Holly snapped. "You dropped a net on us."

The big-bellied man stood up and placed his hands on his hips. "Looks like we have our hands full with this girl as well! What's your name?" The man was smiling at her, but there was no humor or kindness in his eyes. "Girl, your name!"

"Holly. My name is Holly," she answered flatly.

"Very well, Holly. Both of you are under arrest. Kuzrul, get them up."

A wiry red-haired man stepped close to the net and grabbed its edge. Holly gasped. He had a thin red mark on each arm. The smooth lines curled along his forearms and down to his hands, ending between his thumb and forefinger.

This man had marks—just like her.

12

DARK TIMES

"WHY ARE YOU ARRESTING US? What did we do?"

Freed from the net, Jack helped Holly to her feet and tried to make sense of their situation. Holly had a stunned look on her face and was staring at the ground deep in thought.

Based on the desert and these men's strange clothes, Jack knew they weren't close to home. They could be somewhere in the Middle East, or Africa, but the inhabitants of a faraway desert country wouldn't answer in perfect English. He tried to push his worries about being far from home to the back of his mind. He needed to focus on the immediate problem.

"Search them," said the man called Shorta.

"Search? What?" Jack sputtered as the men, the one called Kuzrul and another man with his red hair pulled back in a knot, stepped forward.

Shorta stood several feet away, his arms crossed as he stared at Jack. He felt like an item in an auction with this man estimating his worth. Instinctively, Jack narrowed his eyes to slits and avoided eye contact. In the best of situations, his white eyes never got good reactions from people, and this was not a good situation. He took a deep breath.

Shorta scowled at him but said nothing. The man called Kuzrul walked behind Jack and grabbed him by the shoulders. Resisting would be a waste of time; Jack slowly spread his arms out from his sides.

Kuzrul began patting down his pockets. He'd hid the kaleidoscope inside his jeans but had no doubt they would find it and everything else in his pockets. Amir searched Holly. She'd tugged her long sleeves down over her hands, doing her best to hide her marks from the men.

Both men wore short-sleeved woven tunics, but much plainer than Shorta's. Now Jack understood Holly's reaction—both men had red marks like his sisters.

Kuzrul slid the scope out of Jack's pants. The man held the scope up in the air, along with Jack's small pocketknife. He sighed as the man dropped his pocketknife into a cloth bag before handing the kaleidoscope to Shorta. The rotund man turned it slowly in his hands.

"Where did you get this?"

"It's mine. It belonged to my father," Jack said, unable to contain his anger any longer. He made full eye contact for the first time. He wanted to get a reaction.

Shorta flinched and stepped backward. Jack barely hid his smug smile. The man's eyes narrowed at Jack. *Well, score one point for me. Looks like my eyes get the same reaction no matter where I end up.* He waited for the inevitable remark about his eyes. But the fat man said nothing. He held Jack's gaze with a hard stare, then turned to Holly. "Amir. Bring her here."

Amir grabbed Holly by the wrist and dragged her roughly in front of Shorta. Jack stepped forward but Kuzrul, the man next to him, grabbed him by the shoulders and forced him to stand still. The large man leaned down, looming over Holly, and waved the kaleidoscope in front of her face. "Where did you get this, little one?"

"Like he said. From our dad," Holly answered flatly.

Chuckling softly, Shorta tucked the scope into his belt. "Even my own children would not have the nerve to offer up such lies to my face." He gripped the collar of her shirt and pushed her hair from her neck as Holly squirmed. Jack pulled against Kuzrul but couldn't break free. "Not there." He pulled up the sleeve on her right arm, and then her left, before quickly stepping back, snorting with disgust.

"A thief and a Farker," Shorta said, sneering at Holly. "Seven Marks? Come now, it's bad enough that you rebels desecrate yourselves to pass as Twos and Threes, but to give yourselves more Marks than even possible? And not even good fakes. Pitiful."

"Like you've said before, Shorta, these are truly dark times in the Seven when even the young have no respect for our way of life," Kuzrul said, releasing his grip on Jack.

"Dark times indeed," said Amir as he picked up the lantern.

"We're not thieves! The kaleidoscope belongs to us," Jack blurted out. He had no idea what a 'Farker' was, but they had to get the scope back.

Shorta strode over, his mouth twisted in anger. "As for you, boy," his voice dropped threateningly," I have no idea why you chose to mutilate your eyes. You Farkers, running all over Dara with your fake marks and angry faces. Well, if removing color is the latest Farker protest, I'll make a statement of my own."

Shorta grabbed Jack by the hair and yanked his head back. From the corner of his left eye, Jack caught a flash of steel. The knife blade pressed into Jack's cheek, an inch below his eye. Shorta's head hovered inches from his face.

"If you don't like living in Dara, go. Perhaps if you grovel at the Coren's gate, the Red Guardian will let you leave. Though I doubt you'd be worth my spit in any of the Seven." The man's breath reeked, and Jack gagged. "So, tell your despicable friends not to waste money on colorcasting their eyes. He flicked the tip of the knife; Jack winced as the blade nicked his cheek. "I'll cut them out. For free."

The natural tendency of humanity is to desire privilege and pleasure. We understand human freedom is based on the choices made by humans themselves, but these choices carry an inescapable burden of responsibility. When fully wrestled with and understood, this responsibility can cause humankind to rise above its base urges and reach upwards to become united, centered, and free.

The freedom to live with purpose, think critically, and act thoughtfully is central when considering the most vital of questions: How is it we should carry on our lives as individuals, and how will this action translate into a society?

—Professor Waite's Journal

13

THE COURTHOUSE

ARMS WRAPPED around Holly's waist, his wrists tied to the pommel of the saddle of the beast they were riding, Jack bounced along in furious silence. The small cut on his cheek didn't hurt; Jack had been hurt a lot worse in fights back home. But he was mad. He'd concluded that Shorta must be a sheriff, and apparently the mean and nasty kind of sheriff that enjoys picking on little kids.

They were riding in a group at a slow trot. Shorta's men had placed them on top of one of their horse-sized mounts with lizard-like scales and the large feet of a camel which started riding in a slow trot. The village protector's mount had the same dust-colored lizard skin as the other animals but stood a foot taller and had a huge rear-end. *Like his master.*

Jack stared sullenly at Shorta's broad back up ahead of him on his lizard-horse. These animals moved with an uneven, swaying gait, and Jack's frustration with their predicament grew with every step.

He forced himself to pay attention to the unfamiliar surroundings. They'd ridden by a farm, taking a dirt road past countless rows of vella plants. Ten minutes later, they arrived at the edge of a town. As they rode, the village sprang up around them, a collection of twisted structures with pitched rooflines. Each building had a glowing orb mounted on its roof, and the beams of light crisscrossed their path.

Curious faces rapidly appeared and disappeared in the diamond-shaped windows at the sound of their passing. Jack assumed these were their houses, though unlike any type of house he had ever seen. As far as Jack could tell, in this land called Dara, all the houses were made out of sand.

Not much bigger than cottages, the houses sat on simple square foundations, but then swirled upward with curved walls that had no interest in being a simple shape. Carved windows, latticework openings, and geometric etchings punctuated the sand walls. They looked like delicate pieces of lace that could be blown away by the slightest wind. He traced the steep roof of one building with his eyes, the textured sand carved into ripples like water falling. The roof sharply peaked at least twenty feet in the air.

Up ahead, Shorta came to a stop and dismounted in front of a poorly lit three-story building. Stone steps led up to an arched entrance, and a set of broken wooden doors sat propped to the side.

Kuzrul hopped off his mount, then untied their hands before lowering Holly from the saddle. Jack slid to the ground and landed next to her. The man pointed up the steps to the doorway, his meaning clear. Tattered panels of embroidered drapes hung from metal rings in the doorway and billowed in the warm night wind.

"Amir, tell the mayor we're back. Kuzrul, head on home," said Shorta.

As a young boy in a dirt-splotched tunic ran down the steps and took the reins, Holly nudged Jack with her elbow and pointed. He also had one red mark on his arms, like Shorta's men. As he walked away, the boy snuck a suspicious peek at Jack. He wondered if every newcomer to this town got the same unfriendly reception.

Holly, still looking exhausted, stumbled as her foot caught on the edge of the high step. Jack caught her by the elbow and helped her sit as Shorta sighed loudly in annoyance from behind them. Jack spun around to face him. Knife or no knife, he was tired of being bullied today.

"We're tired." Jack, two steps higher, met the village protector at eye level. He felt his temper flaring. Seeing Holly collapse had magnified his weariness. Now, faced with the scornful way this man looked at them, the same treatment they had been getting all their lives on the playgrounds and classrooms, he'd had enough. "We're thirsty and we're hungry. I don't care if you hate me. Trust me, I'm used to it. But..." he forced the edge out of his voice, trying to sound a lot calmer than he felt. "She's my little sister, and I'm responsible for her."

Shorta stared back, his eyes unblinking, unreadable. Jack had expected a reaction, possibly good, more than likely bad, but now he was stuck with no reaction. Jack stared back. Still nothing. He held the man's gaze. More seconds passed. *You gotta be kidding me. I'm in a staring contest.* He kept staring into Shorta's unwavering eyes. *Yup. I'm standing on the steps of a giant sandcastle caught in a staring contest with a knife-wielding sheriff.* Jack blinked, amazed at the absurdity of the day.

"You are wasting my time, Farker," Shorta said through clenched teeth. "Lucky for you, the mayor is waiting, or else I would gladly cut you again right here. Move."

Jack frowned. The man kept calling them Farkers; Jack didn't know what the word meant, but judging by the way Shorta spat the word, it was not good. The reality that they were a long, long way from home sank in further. He took Holly's arm and helped her up the stairs towards the entrance. *Hopefully the mayor will be more reasonable.*

When they stepped onto the landing, the heavy curtains parted. Shorta directed them forward with a dismissive flick of his finger. As they walked under the arch, Jack noticed there was no motor or anyone pulling cords to move the panels. The dark metal rings were now glowing with an inky blue light and sliding across the rod by themselves.

They entered a wide hallway framed by four-foot-high hardened sand walls leading to a set of tall black doors. On the other side of the walls, rows of carved benches rubbed smooth from wear sat empty. This was a room for waiting. Jack sighed at the strange familiarity of the place. He'd spent way too much time in halls like this waiting for principals, much to the disappointment of his dad. He imagined people sitting on these benches, signing in and waiting for their turn to be helped or judged. He glanced back at Shorta's sour face. *Definitely judged.*

As they approached the doors, he expected them to magically open like the curtains, but they remained shut. Each door had a red disk embedded into the wood where the handle should have been. Jack pushed against the red circles, but the doors didn't budge.

Shorta shoved Jack aside and stared at him with a shocked expression. He tugged on his beard as if evaluating Jack all over again, exposing the tip of a thin red mark on the side of the man's neck, visible above his shirt collar. *He's got a mark like Emma.*

The sheriff reached out and placed his palm on the disk. The door swung open without a sound. He pointed at a set of metal circles embedded in the floor. "Each of you, step inside a circle and wait."

Jack took Holly's hand. He assumed this large circular room was the Mayor's court. Thirty feet ahead of them sat a raised judge's bench carved with a sun hovering over the dunes. Spiraled columns supported the ceiling, decorated with a faded mural. The floor was cracked and peppered with divots. They stopped at the line of four multi-colored rings embedded into the floor, spaced a few feet apart. Holly lifted one foot, but then took a step back, squeezing his hand tight.

Jack took a deep breath and stepped inside his circle. Nothing happened. Relieved, he dropped Holly's hand as she safely walked into her own ring. Striding past them, Shorta crossed the room and stopped at the left side of the judge's bench. He reached around the side and tapped something out of sight. Nothing happened.

Shorta glanced in their direction and scowled. Muttering to himself, he bent down and pounded the side of the bench with his fist.

The metal circles in the floor switched on like a hot wire. A shimmering ring of iridescent light rose and surrounded each of them. Jack dropped into a defensive stance, carefully avoiding any contact with the surrounding energy field. Next to him, trapped in her ring, Holly was pointing at her feet, as if sending him an urgent message through the blurry walls.

Jack pulled his eyes away from the wall of wavering colors and looked down. Segments of color—like the window they'd found in their dad's secret study—had appeared on the floor, radiating from the center point of the ring. Spinning in a slow circle, he tried to make sense of what he was seeing. His eyes swimming with colors and feeling off balance, he stumbled forward into the force field. Reacting instinctively, he reached out to stop his fall, cringing and expecting to be burned as his hands hit the glowing wall, but instead, the light was no hotter than a windowpane on a sunny day. He rapped his knuckles on the surface. It was solid.

Jack shifted into a side stance, brought one knee up, and launched a kick solidly into the shimmering light. The impact jolted his leg as he contacted the unyielding surface. He dropped to one knee in pain and massaged his ankle. Next to the judge's bench, Shorta was watching him, seemingly puzzled by Jack's attempt to escape.

"Shorta!" An angry-faced wiry man in a pale blue robe burst through a doorway to the left of the bench. The man's bare feet slapped the floor as he cinched the sash of the robe around his waist. "Exactly which part of 'do not disturb' don't you understand? I made myself perfectly clear the last time. Barring a full-on attack, throw the upstarts in a cell."

"Yes, Mayor." Shorta bowed his head slightly as the skinny man walked behind the judge's bench to his chair. Still standing, the man leaned forward menacingly, his sleeves riding up his bony wrists. This man had two colors—red marks on both hands, but a second mark of blue on his right, intertwined with the red.

He outranks Shorta. Jack made a mental note. Shorta and his men had one color mark; the extra mark must equate to rank.

"By your Marks, Mayor, but..." Shorta sounded apologetic. "...I wouldn't dare disturb you again without a very good reason."

Jack rolled his eyes and turned to Holly. "Geez, what a brown-noser," Jack mumbled.

"SILENCE!" the mayor screeched at him. "You DO NOT speak in my chambers unless I tell you to!"

Shorta jabbed his finger at Jack. "I told you! He's rebellious and he's clearly mutilated himself. Look at him."

The mayor threw up his hands in exasperation. "So now we have girls pretending to be Sevens and a boy who has removed his Marks? Young man, were you Marked?"

Jack ignored him. His mind stuck to one word. *Girls.* The man had said girls pretending to be Sevens.

"Trust me, Mayor. This boy is a problem." Shorta waved to a doorway on the far side of the chamber as the Mayor stepped down from his bench and walked around to the front. "And I'm convinced they are all working together and clearly up to no good."

Jack whirled to his right. A guard walked into the room with Emma firmly in his grasp.

Inside the cocoon, released enzymes dissolve the caterpillar and turn its body into soup. Floating in this sticky liquid are specialized cells called imaginal discs. These discs – which have been present, yet asleep, inside the caterpillar – develop into the eyes and the wings and the other needed parts of the mature butterfly.

In essence, the caterpillar has been walking around with tiny unformed wings inside its body the whole time.

—from "The Wonderful World of Insects" by Sessina, Master of Bugs

14

SQUISH

"Emma!" Holly forgot everything around her. Her eyes latched onto Emma as the guard placed her in the circle next to Holly. Immediately, the ring activated and surrounded her with a glowing barrier.

"Are you all right?" Emma asked, her voice barely above a whisper. "I was afraid I'd lost you."

"Yeah, we're okay." Holly felt her eyes welling up and knew she wouldn't be able to stop crying once she started. "I mean, we're not hurt. But it's all so much...we thought we left you at home." The idea of home and their dad pushed Holly over the edge, and the tears fell down her round cheeks. "What about Dad? He won't know what happened to us."

"You two. Quiet." The stoop-shouldered guard stepped up between them, blocking Holly's view of Emma. The new separation hit her like a cruel blow to her gut. She backed up inside her circle until her heel tapped the barrier. Their guard, a gray-haired man with a beak nose, slouched and shifted his weight back and forth. Holly raised her right hand to the light wall and tapped it lightly, hoping to get Emma's attention. The guard glanced back at her and shook his head. She stopped tapping, pasted an innocent grin on her face, and leaned casually into the barrier. The guard turned back towards

Shorta and the Mayor who were locked in conversation at the other end of the room.

Squish. Holly jerked her hand off the light wall, surprised by the unexpected sensation. She looked at the spot where her palm had rested. A faint hand-shaped indentation, still visible in the surface of the light barrier, was slowly filling itself back in as Holly examined her hand. It felt normal. Maybe it was the reflection of the light wall, but her red and yellow marks now looked brighter than her other marks. Fascinated, she placed her palm back onto the light wall and closed her eyes. She concentrated on the warm smooth texture.

Squish. Holly opened her eyes. Her hand was sinking into the enclosure. Waves of light spilled around her thumb and rippled up between her fingers like water. Holding her hand as still as possible, she forced herself to relax. She scanned the room to check if anyone had noticed. They hadn't.

"So what? All Farkers are belligerent, and he's an Unmarked boy," the mayor was saying loudly as he stepped behind the judge's bench.

"No, it's more than that. He tried to push the door like he'd never seen a colorlock."

"Who cares?" The mayor stopped next to Shorta and cinched the sash on his blue robe. "Unless you have a good reason, I'm going back to bed."

Shorta pulled the kaleidoscope out of his bag and waved it under the mayor's nose like a fancy cigar. "Here's my reason." The guard next to Holly stepped forward to get a better view.

The mayor's eyes grew wide. He took the scope and traced the engravings on the barrel with his bony fingers. He began to raise it to one eye, and Emma flinched in her lightcell.

"Excuse me, Mister Mayor." Jack's voice, deeper than usual, bounced loudly around the chamber. He was trying to sound older, hiding the awkward cracks and squeaks of his thirteen-year-old voice. He hated sounding like a mouse. "I wouldn't do that."

Shorta turned crimson, ready to explode, but the mayor held up his other hand for silence.

"No? And why not?"

"Because looking through that scope will either kill you or send you to another world. Based on the day we've had, I'm not sure which one is worse."

"Kill me? Another world?" he scoffed but lowered the scope carefully to his waist. "Listen to me, young man. Lying, stealing, and rebellious self-mutilation may be tolerated in the capital, but not here in Lindur, and most certainly not by me. Tell me the truth. You stole this."

"No, it's ours, and we want it back."

The older man laughed harshly, a sneer pulling his thin lips tight. Turning the scope over in his hands, his eyes went wide. "By my Marks, Shorta, you fat bastard, I take back everything I've ever said about you. Do you know what this could be?" He was grinning wildly. "No, of course you don't. If this is the Prophet's Eye, we are going to be rich!"

Holly saw Jack move into a striking stance, his fists clenched. To her right, Emma was pushing frantically against the light barrier with both hands. Holly looked at the mayor who kept toying with the scope and she suddenly understood. *Oh my gosh, if the scope works for him, we'll never get home.*

"Heed me, boy." The mayor brandished the scope like a trophy. "This is now mine. What I do with it is none of your or your tattooed friends' concern." He waved his other hand at the girls dismissively.

He thinks our marks are tattoos. He won't believe anything we say unless... Holly's hand was still sunk partway into the wall of light. She focused on the sensation dancing on her skin: warm but even deeper, the pulling of an underwater current. Concentrating, she pushed, and the barrier split apart, filling her nose with an acrid, metallic smell.

"Shorta. Take them away," the mayor said, already polishing the barrel of the kaleidoscope with the sleeve of his robe.

But Shorta stood staring wide-eyed at Holly, his mouth open. He poked the mayor in the shoulder and pointed. The mayor looked up. His arms fell slack, the scope held loosely in his hand.

Holly, her right arm already extended beyond the light wall, leaned forward, and stepped through it with her left leg. The guard backed away, muttering to himself. The light tugged on her skin, sticking to her like quicksand. She fought the heaviness and pulled her right leg and—with one last tug—her right foot out. She felt electric.

Standing as straight and tall as possible, she rolled up her sleeves and marched across the chamber towards the mayor. Her marks seemed to be shimmering from the contact with the light wall. She stopped directly in front of him, looked up, and cleared her throat. She knew what she wanted to say. She hoped she could say it right.

"These are my marks and they're real." She held them up, brandishing them like a shield. The mayor cowered away from her. A surge of excitement filled her from her toes to her fingertips.

"We are not Farkers," Holly stressed every word, trying to sound more in control than she felt. "Believe me. I am telling you the truth. You don't want to look in our scope."

15

THE RED GUARDIAN

EMMA YAWNED AND STRETCHED. She was too wound up to sleep.
On the other side of the wooden door of her cell, she could hear their
guard talking to himself, complaining about being on duty so late,
muttering angrily as he cleaned their wooden dinner bowls and plates.
The offerings they got once locked in their cells had been sketchy at
best: a small loaf of spiced bread; a jelly spread; and a bowl of cream
soup with tasteless chunks of meat.

They'd been placed in separate wooden cells; Holly was next to
hers, and Jack was across the hall. While eating, the girls shared what
happened to each of them when they showed up in the desert. As best
as they could figure, they'd arrived at the same time, but Emma woke
up next to the vella fence and unable to hear anything or speak. When
two young men found her, and she didn't respond, they became
angry. They tied her wrists and took her to Shorta. She'd been locked
up for a short while before Holly and Jack were brought to the
courthouse.

Emma was still amazed that Holly broke out of the light barrier
and stomped across the floor in her boots like she owned the place to
confront the mayor. She'd seen Holly stand up to Jack plenty of times,
of course, but never so boldly to an authority figure. The mayor and
the fat sheriff had looked genuinely bewildered. Shorta had blinked,

sputtered, and then bowed his head in reverence to Holly, which made the mayor more put out. He screamed at the guard to lock them up, but then, as if reconsidering his words, told the guard to feed them.

Holly should have known the man wasn't going to simply give up, hand over the kaleidoscope and release them. While the guard marched them across the chamber, Shorta and the mayor continued to bicker.

"This is completely unacceptable!" the mayor hissed like a spitting snake. "I will not be held responsible for your mistake!"

"My mistake? I don't understand why capturing three Farkers—"

"No, of course you don't! You inspected these girls, correct? You saw the Marks?"

"Yes, but they just looked like another bad Farker job. And they didn't act like Sisters!"

"And I doubt they are. The lightcells barely work half of the time. But if I'm wrong and they have any connection to the Coren and this gets back to Eres Daria—"

"What should we do?"

The mayor rubbed his head. "I'll send riders to Ephara to ask about any recent thefts of artifacts by Farkers."

Emma had lost their conversation when the beak-nosed guard led her into the small cell. But she'd heard enough to think the mayor was scared and would not be experimenting with the scope, at least for now. She had no idea what he meant by the Coren or Eres Daria, but she guessed they were in line for another round of harsh questions.

Leaning her head against the wall, she listened to Holly's steady breathing as she slept in the next cell. *Get your rest, little sister. You earned it.* Closing her eyes, Emma finally drifted off to sleep.

～

"EMMA? ARE YOU AWAKE?" HOLLY ASKED, HER VOICE muffled by the rough-planked wall.

"Yeah." Emma sat on the old cot next to the wall. The stitching on the hard mattress was frayed and in need of repair, much like the rest of the building. She'd slept, but badly.

"I fell asleep before telling you about the light wall." Holly's voice rose with excitement. "I dreamed about it. At first, I was pushing through the light, but then I was floating in the ocean. The water was warm, and it was super easy to stay on top. I could stretch my arms out all the way, and my hands were resting on top of the water, the small ripples moving up and down my fingers. And I started sinking in the sea, but not in a bad way. I wanted to sink, and I closed my eyes with the water wrapping all around me. When I opened them, the water was a rainbow, swirling and spinning."

Emma's hands gripped the edge of the bed. Her own experience in the kaleidoscope sounded too much like Holly's dream to be a coincidence. Floating in a red sea, deafening waves of sound had exploded and expanded into chords she'd never imagined. She had lost consciousness several times from the ear-splitting pain. However, since arriving here, her hearing seemed to be ten times stronger.

In the hallway, there was the creak of hinges, then the rustling of feet and muffled orders. The door of her cell burst open.

"Get out here," the guard croaked, his voice a mix of weariness and annoyance from having to keep watch. Emma stepped into the hall and watched Jack yawn sleepily as he emerged from his cell, his hair messed up, much like every morning at home. Emma couldn't help but smile at the familiarity.

"Move. And no talking." The guard marched them up the short hallway and through the door. Inside the chamber of the courtroom, the mayor was sitting at his bench arguing with Shorta again.

"The Eye of the Prophet?" Shorta asked, stifling a yawn. "It can't be. That's a legend."

"Believe what you like, but if it's genuine, and if no one has reported it as missing or stolen, it's mine. I mean ours." The mayor tapped a wooden box next to his elbow then leaned forward quickly. "But I'm worried about these girls. If they are under Daria's protection and I don't notify the Coren—"

"By your Marks, Mayor. If the girls were truly Sisters, do you honestly believe they would have tolerated one minute in the cells?"

They stopped talking as the guard placed Jack, Emma, and Holly into the floor circles. Shorta was sitting in a chair next to the bench. His eyes on Holly, he reached out and tapped the side of the bench. The light barriers popped into place.

Holly's eyes lit up as she moved her right hand towards the wall of light. Emma coughed loudly and when Holly glanced her way, she shook her head back and forth, mouthing the word no. Emma relaxed as Holly slowly lowered her arm. *These people were not their friends, who knew what they might do if her sister revealed more power?*

To her left, Jack stared at the floor, as usual, but he stood flat-footed, not in his usual ready-to-fight stance.

BOOM! The chamber doors slammed open, the heavy panels striking the walls with a thunderclap. Emma spun around inside her light barrier as Shorta and the mayor jumped to their feet. A beautiful woman, with a regal face set in hard angles, stood in the open doorway. Dressed in a floor-length crimson cloak and gown, she scanned the room like a hawk sizing up its prey. Buried in the echo from the crashing doors, the mayor's startled whisper caught Emma's ear.

"Daria."

The woman's head snapped in his direction. She unfastened the gold clasp of her cloak and dismissively flung it to one side. Before the fabric hit the chamber floor, a wisp of a red-haired girl, barefoot and dressed in a simple dark-red shift, dashed out from behind her and snatched it out of the air. Quickly folding the cloak, the girl took several fast backward steps like a scurrying mouse and disappeared from view behind one of the spiral columns.

Eyes still locked on the mayor, the woman crossed the room with commanding strides. As she walked, her long dark dress, cinched at the waist with a wide gold and diamond encrusted belt, swirled, and rippled out behind her, a blood-red pool of color which formed and unformed with every step. Without looking their way, she passed by Emma, Jack, and Holly and stopped.

"Ternan, stay," Daria spoke to the mayor as if talking to a dog.

"Everyone else...leave." Avoiding eye contact, their heads held low, Shorta and the guard sprinted towards the exits.

Daria stared at each of the children in turn as one hand slowly smoothed a stray hair back into place. Her brown hair, tied back tight, was streaked with gray, but her skin was smooth and unwrinkled. Not smiling, she tapped the heel of her right shoe on the chamber floor, her eyes on Jack.

"Come here."

16

FOUND AND LOST

"I CAN'T," Jack said. He tapped his knuckles on the barrier.

"Down," Daria said in a weird voice as if she were swallowing and speaking at the same time. The three lightwalls turned off as if by magic. To his right, Emma and Holly looked impressed. He walked forward and stopped in front of the woman.

Daria stared down at him. Avoiding eye contact, he looked straight ahead, directly at the low-cut front of her dress. He swallowed nervously.

She had markings very much like Emma's, but no yellow. Six bright lines of color wrapped like vines around her throat and then wove downward. Unlike Emma's pattern, two of the Marks dove straight down the center of her chest and forked across her sternum, before disappearing into her dress. He didn't know where else to look, so he dropped his head and stared at his feet.

"Your name," Daria stated flatly. Jack guessed *please* was not a word she used very often, if at all.

"Jack. My name is Jack Waite." He raised his head, carefully bypassing her cleavage this time. Her eyes were light grey with flecks of red, green, and gold buried throughout.

"And the rest?" To his surprise, she showed absolutely no reaction to his eyes. *Maybe there are other people with eyes like mine in this place after all.*

"The rest of what?"

As soon as the question left his mouth, her head jerked back, as if he'd said something rude. Her nostrils flared. He had a great view looking up her nose.

"Your line. Your lineage," she said, tapping her foot again.

Jack hesitated, not sure what answer would satisfy her ever-expanding nostrils.

"Ternan obviously failed to ask you the most basic of questions." Jack caught the tiny curl of a smile on her lips; she enjoyed tormenting the frightened mayor who, still standing behind his bench, blanched another shade of white. "In the Seven, a proper greeting includes your full name, your titles, and your line on your father's side. Of course, my greeting is unique." She placed her left hand artfully on her hip and gave a slight low wave with her right hand out to her side. Jack guessed she'd practiced this move in a mirror, perfecting the haughty pose. "I am Eres Daria-sa-gisnu, the Red Guardian of Dara and Thirty-fourth Keeper of the Light." She held the pose and Jack's gaze. She was waiting for him to bow his head down in deference like Shorta did in front of Holly. *What the heck? Maybe I can get on her good side.*

Jack assumed the resting position he used in Budo, his feet shoulder-wide, his arms behind his back with his hands clasped lightly together. He gave a quick nod of his head but maintained eye contact. "I am Jack Waite of Lebanon, son of Elishah." Their dad always went by Eli, but his dad's full name sounded closer to the formality she obviously expected.

Daria smiled at him, apparently pleased by his response. Emma and Holly stepped forward and he waited for her to acknowledge them. But instead of addressing the girls, she continued to watch him. Not sure what to do, he gestured to the girls. "And may I present Emma Cassandra Waite and Holly Teresa Waite, my sisters, also daughters of Elishah." Beside him, Holly dipped her knees in a slight curtsy.

Daria's smile vanished and Jack wondered if he'd messed up their introductions. Leaning forward, she looked the girls up and down as if inspecting them, her lips pursed.

Daria smiled thinly. "Welcome to the land of Dara. You are now my guests. Wait here with Acorn."

The red-haired girl called Acorn was standing next to him. Jack had no idea how she'd snuck up that close. She grinned, her wide-set green eyes sparkling with curiosity. She was examining every inch of his clothes, and her frenzy of red curly hair bounced with every move of her head. Before he could say hi, Daria whirled around to the mayor.

"Which one was it, Ternan? Your stupidity or your greed?" Her words grated on the walls of the chamber. "Did you even think before dispatching riders to the capital?"

The mayor's face had turned white. "Eres, I didn't want to bother you with such a mundane—"

"Mundane? What could be the Eye of the Prophet lands on your doorstep in the hands of these children and you call that mundane?" the Red Guardian said. "Did you forget my command to report all suspicious activities directly to me?"

The mayor didn't even try to make any excuses. Based on all the times Jack had been lectured by their dad, he knew the man was better off not saying anything.

"Did not the appearance of two girls with abnormal Marks strike you as suspicious?" Jack cringed at the word abnormal and glanced at Emma and Holly; they were both frowning. "Clearly, life on the Southern Edge has dulled your mind."

Beads of sweat were pouring down the mayor's face. He looked rattled, but somehow managed an answer. "On my Marks, Eres," he muttered with his head hanging down, "my poor decision was influenced by these dark times." Then the man's eyes rose slightly. "However, may I assume that since the message reached you so quickly, you came from the capital?"

"Assume nothing, Ternan." She dismissed his question with a sharp wave of her hand. "Where is the item you have found?"

The mayor hurriedly picked up the wooden case next to him and flipped open the lid. "Here, Eres. Completely secure." Looking hopeful he might do something right, he reached inside to retrieve the scope.

"STAY YOUR HAND!" Daria's voice split into multiple notes and crackled with energy. The poor mayor froze as if shocked by electricity. His body went rigid. She snapped her fingers and Acorn raced to her side. "Inside that case is a metal rod. Retrieve it."

Sprinting behind the judge's bench, Acorn popped up beside the mayor, still oddly frozen in place, his outstretched arm unmoving. She pulled a thread-worn cloth from a pocket sewn on her dress, picked up the kaleidoscope and carefully wrapped it. Walking quickly to Daria, she peeled back the edges of the cloth like the petals of a rose and held it out for inspection.

Jack hoped that Daria would have some response to seeing the scope or share some new information. Instead, she barely glanced at it.

"Ternan," Daria said his name slowly. The sound of her voice had a soothing quality, and the mayor started back into motion. He yanked back his arm, his eyes filled with fear as Daria continued. "As I suspected, this is not the Eye of the Prophet, merely a replica."

"A replica? Are you sure?" he asked dumbfounded, then threw his hands into the air, pleading. "Eres, on my Marks, I apologize for my mistake."

Ignoring him, Daria turned to Jack. "Tell the truth. Where did you get this?"

"From our father," Jack said. *She's not going to believe me.*

"Very well, son of Eli. Perhaps it is yours." She gave a reassuring smile. "And when we get to the Coren, we shall send for your father. I would like to see him."

"Yes, of course," Jack answered, trying to keep his tone matter-of-fact as if they could summon their dad so easily. He was glad she believed him, but he wasn't sure he believed her. Something she'd said bothered him. Their dad's scope could be a copy of this Eye of the Prophet, but the Mayor thought it was genuine and was obviously too scared to argue. Jack reached out to take the scope from Acorn.

Daria plucked the scope out of the girl's hands, then secreted it into the folds of her dress. Acorn ran over to the nearby column, retrieved her cloak, and ran back like she was being timed.

"And Ternan," Daria closed the clasp of her cloak with a loud snap, "we will not speak of this incident again."

Not waiting for his reply, she spun on her heels in a swirl of crimson. "Come." She strode past them. "Acorn, take our guests to Yiana's skimm." A red storm, she blew through the chamber doors and out of sight.

Stunned, Jack felt Emma's hand on his shoulder. "What the heck just happened?"

"We lost the scope. *Again.*" Emma shook her head. "And I don't trust her. What if she can use the scope?"

"I'm scared," Holly said. "What do we do now?"

"We get it back," Jack said.

Acorn spoke up, "Eres Emma, Eres Holly. Jack. Would you please follow me to the skimm?"

The small girl stood in from of them, her face bubbling with excitement as she grinned, a wide gap between her two front teeth. She bounced in place and Jack guessed she never stopped moving. Once outside the building, she skipped down the stairs and ran to a young, olive-skinned woman who was cloaked in bright red and standing by a coach. After exchanging words with Acorn, she smiled warmly and gently patted the girl on the shoulder. Turning away, she climbed into the seat mounted high on the front of a windowed coach which rested on metal runners, like a sled. In the distance, at the far end of the street, another red and gold coach was speeding away under the early morning sun,

Acorn dashed back up the stairs and skidded to a stop in front of them, a small cloud of dust kicked up at her feet. She pointed excitedly at the coach. "Eres Emma, Sister Yiana says I may ride inside the skimm with you."

"What's that word mean...Eres?" Jack asked.

"Highest one," Emma guessed. "Is that right?"

"Higher Woman, Eres Emma." Acorn smoothed the sides of her

worn dress with her palms. "I am Alla-nu. Servant to the Red
Guardian and daughter of the Coren. But please call me Acorn." She
led them down the steps.

"That's a neat name," Emma said as they walked "How did you
get it?"

"Eres, Alla-nu means 'small tree nut'. Most of the Sisters call me
Acorn." She pointed to the woman dressed in red sitting at the front
of the coach. "That's Sister Yiana. She's really nice."

"What about your parents?" Holly asked.

"Eres, on my Marks, but I no longer have parents." She hopped
off the bottom step, then pulled open the coach door and stepped
aside. The inside was spacious enough for six people, with leather-
covered benches at either end. "They gave me to the Coren when I
was five."

"Five?" Jack blurted out. "Your parents gave you away at five years
old to be a servant? Why in the world would they do that?"

She rolled her eyes at him as if his question made no sense.
Suddenly, the drastic difference—between her reverence toward
Emma and Holly and how casually she talked to him—hit Jack's head
like a brick.

Acorn had no Marks on her neck. He snagged her right wrist and
stared at it. There were no Marks on her arm.

"Because I'm a Zero, Jack," Acorn said, smiling. "Just like you."

17

THE SEVEN

EMMA STEPPED up into the skimm. It was spacious inside, with two benches, each wide enough to seat three people. The walls were covered in orange silk and the ceiling was high enough for a person to stand without bending over. Emma sat down on the forward-facing bench.

"What do you mean I'm a Zero?" Jack asked grumpily as he climbed into the skimm. He plopped onto the backward-facing bench next to Holly and crossed his arms.

Last to enter the skimm, Acorn pulled the door closed, then knelt on the floor in front of a long wicker chest that sat along the wall between the front and back benches. "We're ready, Sister Yiana."

The Sister was on the other side of the front compartment window, sitting in the glass-enclosed driver's section. She was pretty; Emma guessed not much older than her. Her braided brown hair revealed five-colored Marks that ran down the sides of her neck. The skimm pulled smoothly away from the front of the courthouse, picking up speed. She seemed to be guiding the skimm with her hands lightly resting on several glass balls mounted in a wooden panel.

"I'm sorry, Jack. I don't understand." Acorn's red curls bounced back and forth. She lifted the lid of the large wicker chest, pulled out a tray with folding legs and created a tabletop for serving. The chest was filled with fruits, bread, and cheeses which Acorn began laying out on the makeshift buffet. "Is it wrong to call an Unmarked person a Zero in your land?"

"UNMARKED?!" Jack threw his hands into the air. Acorn scooted backward and looked away.

"Jack, you're scaring her," Emma said, pointing at Acorn cowering at her feet. She rested her hand gently on Acorn's shoulder. "It's okay. Jack's not mad at you. We're just really confused right now. We've never been here before and don't know what's going on."

Acorn raised her head, then looked around at all three of them. "Yes, Eres."

"Acorn, there's no need to treat us special," she grinned. "Just call me Emma."

"And I'm just Holly," chimed in Holly, not taking her mouth off the roll of bread in her hand.

Emma watched Jack fill a small plate with food then lean back and stare out the window of the skimm. As if things weren't bad enough already for them—apparently colored marks were important in this place, and her brother had none.

Outside, the landscape raced by. The skimm was moving fast, gliding over the sand, the metal runners making soft scraping sounds when Sister Yiana changed direction. They'd left Lindur and its houses of sculptured sand behind. Now a vast expanse of desert, morning sunlight reflecting off the dunes, stretched out in all directions.

Emma picked up a red apple and took a bite, chewing slowly as she made a list of questions in her head. *What do we know?* She didn't understand how, but Jack turned on the kaleidoscope, all three of them traveled here, all with weirdly different experiences. *Where are we?* We arrived near a village—called Lindur—which is in a place called Dara and Dara is part of the Seven. They were definitely a long way from home. *What's strange? So far...Everything.* The people in Dara have colored marks—like her and Holly—but their marks don't look infected and seem to signify a social status; the mayor outranked

Shorta, whereas Daria called herself a Guardian and acted like she outranked everyone.

"Acorn, can I ask you some questions?" Emma patted the seat of the bench. Acorn hesitated, her eyes darting back and forth nervously. She climbed up and sat cross-legged on the seat. Emma smiled at her. "Acorn, what's the Seven?"

The little girl grinned. "Eres, that's an easy one. Dara, Nima, Kasa, Tera, Zala, Hema, Mora." Her smile faltered when Emma did not respond. "By your Marks, Eres, was that not right?"

"No, that was great." Emma sighed, overwhelmed by how little she knew. She wished she had a notebook. "And those are the names of..."

"The Seven Lands, Eres. Like in the song." Acorn paused for a moment, then began to sing softly.

> *On my Marks the Seven rest,*
> *and by your Marks, truly blessed,*
> *From desert Dara to the fires of Nima.*
> *The flowers fair in Kasa fall,*
> *the trees in Tera green and tall,*
> *The waters blue in Zala flowing deeper.*
> *In Hema mountains reach the sky,*
> *In Mora how the time goes by,*
> *And in the end, the darkness comes a'calling.*
> *On my Marks, the Seven rest.*
> *By your Marks, truly blessed.*

"That was beautiful." Holly's eyes narrowed. "How old are you, Acorn?"

"I'm ten, Eres...I mean...Holly." Acorn's eyes darted towards the driver's compartment as if they were being overheard.

"On my Marks... what does that mean?" Emma broke off a piece of hard orange cheese. Jack continued to sit, oddly quiet, scrunched up in the corner on the other padded bench, his eyes still fixed out a side window. He was sulking from Acorn calling him a Zero and she didn't blame him.

"On my Marks, the Seven rest. By your Marks, truly blessed." Acorn recited the words like a prayer. "It's the first thing children learn. We are all bound by our Marks. We should all live up to our Marks and we must obey those with higher Marks."

"So that's why Shorta and the mayor seemed so bothered? Because we outrank them?"

"Yes, Eres. I mean, yes, Emma," Acorn corrected herself, still looking unsettled by using their first names. "You deserve the same respect as Eres Daria and the other Guardians. There is a Guardian with six Marks for each of the lands, but I've never heard of a Seven."

Emma heard Jack huff and mutter under his breath. His plate of food sat untouched next to him; the fingers of his right hand were angrily tapping the wall of the skimm.

"They said we had fake Marks and called us Farkers," Emma said. Acorn frowned; apparently, she did not like Farkers either. "But you should have seen their faces when Holly stepped through the light wall."

"Colorcast barriers like lightcells contain four colors—red, yellow, blue, and indigo, I think. For restraining Threes and below." Acorn twisted a curl of her hair. "It wouldn't be able to hold you."

"What about walls with five or six colors?" Holly asked.

"There's no reason to colorcast cells like that, Eres. Most people only have one or two Marks."

"Well, what about the Fours, and Fives...what if they had to go to jail?"

"Arrest a Royal or a Sister?" Acorn squirmed in her seat. "Eres, please."

"Okay, wait a minute. Colorcast. What's that?" asked Emma.

"You don't know how to colorcast?" Acorn asked, then began apologizing. "Forgive me, Eres, I didn't mean to say that."

"Acorn, it's okay. Where we're from, everything is different. And remember, it's just Emma."

"And just Holly." Holly winked at Acorn and made her giggle.

"Right. Thank you, Emma and...Holly," said Acorn, still struggling with the idea of not calling them by the formal title. "Colorcasting is how people—well, the Marked of course—put color energy into things to make them do stuff, like lightsticks or hotpots or...." Acorn paused, her head turning towards Sister Yiana in the driving compartment. Acorn's lips were moving, silently mouthing words as if listening intently. She nodded, then addressed Emma, "Sister Yiana can explain it better."

Yiana's soft voice filled the coach. "Colorcasting includes the two arts of Touchcasting and Soundcasting. Colorcasters use their Marks to imbue materials, living and non-living, with enhanced properties." She took a breath. "I would be happy to show you back at the Coren."

Emma sat back on the seat, her mind spinning. Sister Yiana had listened to every word of their conversation and had spoken directly to them—from the other side of a window. Unbelievable.

"Okay, let's back up. We're in Dara. And the Guardian's name here in Dara is...Daria."

"Yes, Eres."

"Wow, this could get confusing," Emma said as she stared out the window at the sand. "And in the Seven, there are seven lands, and each one has its own Guardian with six Marks."

"So I've been told," Acorn shrugged, then added excitedly, "I met the Orange Guardian from Nima once when she visited the Coren."

"You've never left Dara?" Holly asked.

"Me? A Zero?" Acorn laughed at the idea. "Eres, I know my place. I am Unmarked. I can't have silly dreams."

"Seriously? SERIOUSLY?" Jack lurched away from the window and pounded his fist on the leather seat. Acorn scrambled into the corner of the seat as Jack continued to punch out his frustration.

"Stop it, Jack!" Emma was sure that Acorn had been struck before.

Jack stopped shouting and stood up in front of Emma. "You heard her. She's a Zero. I'm a Zero. No one cares about us!"

"We care," Holly said. "Please calm down."

"Whatever, Hol," Jack snapped at her. "Oh, wait. I forgot. I'm supposed to say 'Whatever, ERES.'"

"Knock it off," Emma said.

"Why, of course, Eres Emma. On my Marks, right?" Jack snarled as he paced back and forth like a caged tiger in the narrow space between the seats. "I'm a lowly Zero and you're a magnificent Seven. Shall I lick your boots now, your Highness? Or grovel at your feet for a breadcrumb?"

"What the heck are you talking about? You're not our slave."

"Are you sure about that?" Jack said as he raked his hands through his hair. "You heard what she said. This whole place runs on how many Marks you have. Two Marks... congratulations, you can be mayor. Four and it's come on down, you've won the rainbow lottery and you get to be royalty. But not for lucky Jack. Nope, not a Mark on me. Nothing. Nada. Zip. Lucky Jack gets to be a Zero."

"But maybe with your eyes—" Holly suggested.

Jack whirled to Acorn. "Have you ever met somebody with eyes like mine? Eyes with no color?"

She hesitated. "No."

"Awesome. I get to be a Zero and a white-eyed freak."

"Please stop," Emma said, saddened by the pain in his voice. But there was no way to downplay Acorn's description of the Seven and what its hierarchy of Marks meant for her brother. *The sooner we get home, the better.*

Jack scowled at her. "It's true. The big wheel of fate spun around and missed me completely. But not you. I bet your hearing is like a million times better here. And Holly can walk through walls of light while all I can do is thrash around like a rat in a cage. It's not fair. It's not fair."

He slumped down against the door of the skimm, crossed his arms, and stared at the floor. Emma listened to his ragged breathing and wished for something more to say. The silence filled the air, pushing them farther and farther apart.

"Lick my boots," Holly said.

"What?" Jack looked up. Emma glared at Holly.

"You heard me." She stared at him and cleared her throat. "Lick my boots."

"I'm not going to lick your boots." Jack frowned. Emma realized what Holly was doing; her little sister was really good at reading Jack's mood swings.

"You offered," Holly waggled her finger at him.

Jack was staring at Holly with his lips pursed. "I don't think so."

"I command you. Lick my boots... *Zero Boy*." Holly waved her hand regally and choked back a laugh. Jack grinned up at her; Holly's teasing was working. Emma snuck a glance at Acorn, concerned that Holly's zero joke would offend their new friend, but Acorn was giggling at their antics.

"You really want me to lick your boots?" Jack stood, his voice now tinged with a shade of his usual playfulness.

"Yes. Lick my boots, *Zero Boy*."

The smile on his face broke wide open. "As you wish." He knelt in front of Holly. Grabbing her left foot, he raised it to his mouth and stuck out his tongue.

"No, don't do it!" Emma and Acorn squealed in unison.

He pretended to drag his tongue across the top of Holly's dirty sneaker. She yanked her foot back and laughed.

Emma passed him the jug of water. "Listen, Jack. I know you're mad and this feels unfair, but right now we all need to stick together. You're not a zero to us," she said, then turned to Acorn, "No one is."

"Fine, point made." Jack climbed to his feet and sat up on the bench beside Emma. "But even if I'm not your slave while we're stuck here, other people are gonna treat me like one. And that's only one of our problems."

"You're right," Emma said. "We don't know enough."

"Like if we can get the scope back from Daria," Jack said as he made a sandwich.

"And if the kaleidoscope will send us home," added Holly.

"Can you tell me more about your home, Jack?" Acorn asked.

"Acorn," Emma interrupted. "He can tell you all about home later. Trust me, his head is full of all sorts of useless information." She put her hand up as Jack made a face. "But we need to learn what's going on first. We came here by mistake..." Emma put her other hand up to keep Jack from feeling like she was blaming him, "... and we need to get back home to our dad."

Acorn's eyes went wide. "Does he know you're here?"

"We don't know," Holly said. "We got here with the metal scope Daria took."

"So, we need you to help us," Emma added, then suddenly remembered that Sister Yiana was hearing everything. *Acorn did say she was nice.* Emma hesitated, then spoke directly at the compartment window. "Please, I'm asking for your help."

"Yes, Er...Emma. I'll try," Acorn replied. On the other side of the window into the driver's section, Yianna nodded. Feeling more hopeful, Emma turned back to the others.

"Thanks, Acorn. Now let's start with what we know."

"This won't take long," Jack mumbled, his mouth full of food.

"Chew, then talk." Emma tucked her legs under her. "I'll start. Dad hid a collection of kaleidoscopes and research in the attic. When you looked through one of the scopes—the one that flashed with a green light—we traveled from home to here. Dara."

"But nothing happened when I looked," Holly added.

Jack swallowed. "Right, and the tunnel could be a wormhole and we got sucked—"

"Slow down," Emma cut back in. "No guessing. Facts and logic."

Jack put his sandwich down. "Sorry, Em. You're right, but just because the kaleidoscope didn't work for Holly doesn't mean I'm the only one who can use it. It might work for other people."

"Right. So you have to get it back," Acorn piped up. She looked at them with a shy smile. "I'm sorry. I didn't mean to interrupt. This is very exciting."

"You're not interrupting. We need your help." Emma smiled and Acorn beamed with pride. *She'd spent her whole life as a servant. I bet no one ever asked her nicely for anything.* Emma continued to Jack, "You said you saw a light, kind of like a door, when you activated the scope. My guess is you dragged us through the door with you." She turned to Holly "He had his arm around you, right?"

"Yep," Holly said.

"And I grabbed his shoulder when I tried to stop him. So, when we go back, we should hold on to each other," Emma concluded, liking her logic. "Agreed?" She went on as they nodded. "Okay, next. We experienced different sensations while going through...traveling inside..." She searched for a better word. "What should we call it? Transporting?"

"How about worm-holing?" Jack offered up.

"Yeechhh." Holly and Acorn both wrinkled their noses.

"No, we don't know it's a wormhole," Emma said.

"Emma, how about scoped?" Acorn suggested. "You said it brought you here, right?"

"Scoped." Jack flicked his fingers in a swooshing motion, saying the word like a sound effect. He smiled at her. "That's perfect, Acorn."

Acorn pushed a mass of red curls away from her face and stared sheepishly at Jack with a huge gap-toothed grin.

Looking at her brother who was now stuffing a handful of red berries into his mouth, Emma tried not to smile. He was oblivious like all teenage boys. Acorn, her cheeks bright red, was still staring at him, an adoring look on her face.

Jack continued talking with his mouth full. "But where exactly is Dara, and why does everyone speak English."

Emma's jaw dropped. "Oops."

"Oops?" Jack said. "What do you mean 'oops'?"

"I completely forgot to tell you because it's so obvious to me."

"What's obvious? What the heck are you talking about?"

"Well, exactly." Emma took a deep breath. "The talking I mean. Acorn, Daria, the mayor... all the people here. They aren't talking in English and..." Emma paused to let the first part sink in, "...neither are we."

18

A MIXED BLESSING

"YEAH, RIGHT," Jack frowned back, thinking his sister was crazy. "Then what language are we speaking?"

"I don't know, but Dad studied languages, right? And his notebooks were filled with crazy-looking words. Acorn, do you know the name of your language?"

"Yes, Eres. We're speaking U'maan." Acorn said. "Don't you speak U'maan where you come from?"

"Nope," Jack said. "I only know English. Well, except for three bad words in Spanish."

"Twinkle, twinkle little star," Holly stressed every syllable. "Sounds like English to me."

"Let me explain," Emma said. "Me, you, Jack... we're all speaking and hearing a new language which is called...U'maan," Emma looked at Acorn for confirmation. "How or why beats me. Maybe traveling through the kaleidoscope did something to all of us. You're convinced that everyone here is speaking English because you understand them."

"Sally sells seashells by the seashore," Holly piped up again, this time moving her mouth in slow motion and holding her lips as she talked. "Nope, still English. Feels like English, too."

"Shally shells shea shells by the shea shore," Acorn repeated as Holly giggled. "Was I speaking English?"

Emma groaned. "No, that's a tongue twister."

Holly bit her lip. "Sorry. I don't get it."

"It's okay. It sounds impossible. But I can tell the differences in our speech—I think scoping affected my hearing, and made it better somehow. English is choppy, a rat-a-tat-tat rhythm. The way we sound now is much smoother, more sing-songy. It's quite beautiful."

"Okay, fine," Jack said. "I believe you, but what does it mean?"

Emma shrugged. "Not a clue. But the scope did have symbols engraved on the barrel. I'm hoping we can read the words now."

"Once we get it back you mean," Jack said. Outside the skimm's tinted windows, scattered thickets of gnarled trees dotted the hills rising in the distance. "Hey, Acorn, how much longer to the Coren?"

"Not long." Acorn finished placing the food and dishes back inside the wicker chest. Closing it with the lid, she took a seat on the top.

Jack sat up in his seat. "All right. When we arrive, I'll ask Daria to give us the kaleidoscope."

Emma shook her head. "That's your plan? And she'll hand it over to you after what she said in Lindur?"

"Probably not, but we have to get it back as soon as possible."

"I know." Emma stared at him. "But maybe you aren't, umm, exactly, the right one of us to talk to her." She traced a finger along the Marks on her neck and Jack slumped back on the bench.

"Oh. Right." He'd forgotten he was one of the Unmarked and Daria was a Six. Daria called the girls abnormal in front of the mayor, but once she understood that his sisters' seven marks were real, she'd have to do whatever they said because of their higher rank.

The outer wall of the Coren lay directly ahead. Jack leaned forward, watching their approach through the driver's window. He let out a soft whistle, struck by the sheer size, an expanse of white stone curving off in the distance in both directions, topped with giant crystal orbs mounted in metal housings. At least fifty feet high, the weathered surface of the Coren seemed ancient, maybe thousands of years old. Like the buildings in the village, the walls flowed out of the surrounding sand as if scooped and formed by giant hands.

The village buildings in Lindur, though, had windows and doors to let in the light. Those airy structures said 'Welcome, we were built for living and enjoyment'. This towering wall, its white surface polished by wind and sand, had no openings. It loomed above them, casting an ominous glow, reflecting the light. This wall was built to keep something out. This place said, 'Go away'.

"Acorn, how big is the Coren?" Jack asked as the skimm veered to the left and glided around the base of the gigantic, curved wall for minutes on end. "I mean, how many, uh, Fives live inside?" Labeling people by the number of their Marks seemed wrong especially when he didn't have any.

Acorn scrunched her face in concentration. The constellation of freckles shifted and twirled as she pulled at one cheek. "Nine."

"Nine hundred Sisters? No wonder it's so large," Emma said.

Acorn shook her head. "No, Eres. I mean Emma. Not nine hundred. Nine Sisters, plus the Eres Daria and the Coren workers."

"Nine?" Holly asked. "You mean there are only nine women who have five Marks in Dara, plus the Red Guardian who has six?"

"Yes, Holly. Eres Daria says there used to be many more Sisters long ago. But now there's only nine."

Jack was suddenly intrigued. "Why? Did something happen?"

"I'm sorry, Jack," Acorn said. "The Sisters would be much better at answering your questions. I never learned the history of the Coren since only Twos and higher go to school."

"But what about reading and writing?" Holly asked.

"Why would someone like me need to read?"

Emma sighed loudly; she was chewing on her lip, something she did whenever she felt anxious, and Jack understood why. They were playing Whack-a-Mole, like at the amusement park, and his older sister hated that game. Each time they asked a question, two more questions popped up and the answers didn't make any sense. Marked people, colorcasting objects, houses made of sand, walls made of light...he wasn't even sure they were asking the right questions. How could they when they didn't know where they were? So far, they'd already annoyed every Marked person they'd met, gotten arrested, and he'd lost the kaleidoscope to the land's most powerful person. And now, their sole friend was a Zero prone to giggles and apologies. If they were going to get the scope back and get home, they needed to do better. He needed to do better.

Beside him, Emma tapped on the window. "There's a gate."

"What's it look like?" Jack perked up. Across from him on the forward bench, Holly spun around and pressed her face against the side window of the skimm.

"Big. Really big."

HOPPING OFF THE BENCH TO GET A BETTER VIEW OF THE gate, Jack rested one knee on the wicker chest and leaned close to the side window.

Emma bit her lip in amusement. Acorn's cheeks had turned bright crimson as she scrunched against the wall of skimm, obviously trying to avoid bumping into her brother. He was unaware of the effect he was having on the girl, but there was no way she could mention it to him. With his anger at being labeled a Zero, the idea of another Zero having a crush on him would not go over well at all. Plus, she didn't want to embarrass Acorn.

The skimm glided through the open gate where two massive metal doors, towering like armored sentries at the entrance, slowly closed behind them. Cylindrical metal hinges connected them to the inner wall. Emma counted four different swirls of color embedded into the gleaming spinning metal.

Sister Yiana drove the skimm forward, gliding over a wide road of stone pavers. Rows of boarded-up buildings dotted the flat sandy landscape inside the Coren's outer wall. A network of uneven rock paths ran back and forth between the buildings; there were piles of lumber, stacks of crates, and broken wagons scattered everywhere.

Ahead of them was a gigantic domed building with clusters of smaller connected domes. More than enough room for nine women.

The skimm stopped in front of a sprawling courtyard, weed-covered and sparsely landscaped with a few striped palm trees and spiky bushes. A sand-strewn paved walkway led up to a tall arched doorway, adorned with a faded tile mosaic depicting a setting sun scattering rays of light across the desert. Emma wrinkled her nose at the red color of the sun and droplets of light. *It looks like the sun is bleeding.*

"The Coren's kind of a dump," Jack said.

"Remember, we're guests." Emma squeezed him on the shoulder. But he was right. The home of the most powerful women in Dara desperately needed a makeover.

The skimm dropped down as its weight settled to the ground.

"Jack, I have to get up," Acorn said.

"Sure. Sorry for hogging the window," Jack said as he moved out of her way.

Acorn sprung into motion. With a rag pulled from her dress pocket, she polished the chest, wiped the smudges from the windows they'd touched, slid across to the door of the skimm, and swung it open wide. Turning, she gave them a courteous smile. "Eresi Emma and Holly—and Jack. Welcome to the Red Coren, the Jewel of the Sands, and the home of Eres Daria, the Red Guardian."

Outside the skimm, two Sisters waited, one thin and tall and the other short and round, their arms folded, palms touching lightly together. With their long red dresses, bejeweled head wraps, and blank expressions, they looked like nuns waiting to confer a blessing on them. Acorn was staring obediently down at the floor of the skimm. *How strange their conversation must have been for the tiny girl.* Here in the Coren, the Fives treated her purely as a servant. She could no more look up at them than Emma could look to the sky and fly away home.

Emma waited for Jack and Holly to exit, then stepped down between them. With the lesson from the mayor's chambers still fresh in their minds, they automatically lined up in front of the two Sisters, ready for the formal greetings.

"Welcome, Eresi Emma and Holly," the razor-thin Sister spoke with an unpleasant nasal whine, "and welcome, Jack son of Elishah." Emma's ears pricked up at the woman's flat tone of voice which did not match the smile on her face. "I am First Sister Sasa. This is Second Sister Haia," she said, tilting her chin towards the plump woman next to her who said nothing. "Eres Daria has provided directions for your accommodations. Follow us."

Not waiting for a response, the sisters turned away, leading them up a path toward the intricately carved wooden door. Acorn sprinted away to the right, carrying a sack clinking with the sound of their dishes, and disappeared behind one of the smaller domes. Sister Yiana walked behind them, and Emma hung back to match pace with her. She had so many questions, and Yiana seemed much more approachable than these two new Sisters.

"Sister Yiana," Emma pointed to the towering dome ahead of them. "Coren. Does it mean palace?"

Yiana smiled down at her. She had to be close to six feet tall even without her boots. "No, Eres. It's a very old word that means birthplace. Except for the one in Zala, each Coren is thousands of years old. The First Guardian of Dara lived here."

Emma ran through the names of the Seven from Acorn's song. She was good at recalling lyrics and music. Zala was the land with blue waters. "Why not in Zala?"

"It sank. More than once," Yiana replied softly. "There's a beautifully sad song called *The Tears of Zala*."

Emma hesitated, unsure of what to say. She gestured towards the buildings behind them. "What are those buildings?"

"They are shops for displaying and selling," Yiana said, then pointed to a flat-roofed building off to the left. Several small harp-shaped instruments sat in one of the windows. "That's my workshop. I make cymbalas."

"Yiana." Sasa stopped in front of the Coren door. She was frowning at Yiana. "I'm sure our guests are exhausted after their visit to Lindur. Do not weary them with conversation."

"Yes, Sister, you are correct," Yiana said.

Emma couldn't help but notice the marked difference in how the two women addressed each other. Despite both being Fives, Sasa – *First Sister Sasa* – was treating Yiana like an underling.

Sasa placed her hand on a red circle set in the wooden door which swung open to reveal a wide stone hallway and led them inside. The hardened sand walls were filled with colored swirls of red and orange, and the light from a long line of glowing wall sconces reflected in the smooth glass-like surface.

"It's like a tunnel of starlight," Holly said, touching the wall with her hand as they walked.

The end of the hallway opened into a vast courtyard filled with gardens, pavilions, and tables, connected by winding paths. In front of her, Jack whistled as he leaned back, his neck craned up. High above them, at least thirty feet or more, the top of the domed ceiling sparkled with the light coming from hundreds of brightly glowing yellow orbs embedded into the surface.

"I'd hate to be the guy who changes the light bulbs." Jack grinned at Emma. She ignored him and studied the glowing lights but didn't see any bulbs. *They're solid glass. Based on Yianna's explanation of colorcasting in the skimm, they're probably colorcasted lights.*

In the room's center, seven graceful fountains surrounded a pool of water, its rippled surface catching the pinpoints of light from above. Sculptures, tall grasses, and fruit-laden trees lined the walkways. To the right was an amphitheater with a raised dais, and on the left was a cluster of tables, surrounded by rows of bookshelves. Unlike the untended grounds outside, the inside of the Coren appeared to be manicured and lush. The space was an oasis, exuding tranquility.

Sasa and Haia stopped at the edge of the gardens and turned to face them. "This is where we Sisters study, commune, and refresh ourselves. As is customary in the Sisterhood, we will now confer upon you the Blessing of the Light." Yiana started to speak, then stopped and stepped back from Emma when Haia cleared her throat loudly. From inside the sleeves of her robe, Sasa removed two clear faceted gems, several inches wide. She handed one of the stones to Sister Haia who moved in front of Holly.

"These crystals represent the Coren, the Jewel of the Sands," Sasa said and nodded at Haia. Emma felt a nervous twinge inside at the idea of receiving a blessing from their new hosts. *It's their tradition,* *but what if I don't want to be blessed...and Jack was being left out...*but before Emma could fully collect her thoughts, each Sister palmed their crystals and pressed them firmly against Holly and Emma's foreheads. Emma felt a small tingle of warmth where the crystal touched her skin, but nothing more. Emma relaxed; she'd been overthinking the situation as usual.

"With this blessing, we welcome you," Sasa continued. The tingling on Emma's skin grew, and curious, she crossed her eyes up as far as she could, but the Sister's cupped hand blocked her view of the crystal. "May the Light always surround and protect you."

Both Sisters quickly pulled back their hands and tucked the crystals into their sleeves.

"Eresi, we will show you to your room on the west side of the Coren," Sasa said. "Jack, your room is on the north side." She and Haia headed down a path towards the left of the complex.

Emma didn't want to be split up so soon in this new place. "Sisters, we'll gladly all share a room," she offered.

"The Coren is home to the Sisterhood," Haia stated over her shoulder. "Except for King Lugar, men are not allowed to stay here. Eres Daria has graciously made a special accommodation for Jack."

The tree-lined path snaked through the gardens. Walking beside her, Holly reached out and rubbed a triangular sculpture of dark green stone, then quickly jerked her hand away.

"That rock's alive!" Holly gasped.

"Not quite, Eres," Yiana pointed to the stone. "That was imported from the land of Tera and—"

Not stopping, Sasa spoke over her shoulder, "Sister Yiana, you must have other matters to attend to now."

Yiana slowed and glanced at them as if she wanted to say something. Instead, she gave a small nod and turned down the other path.

Emma hurried to catch up with Sasa and Haia. The Coren seemed like a wonderful place, but she had too many questions. "We need to speak with the Red Guardian right away," she said, doing her best to hide her frustration.

"Yes, of course. We will inform her of your request," Haia said.

"Yes, umm...thank you. But when can we talk to her?"

Sasa responded. "Do not worry, Eres Emma. I am sure Eres Daria will make time for you as soon as she can."

Not at all pleased by the Sister's non-answers, she hung back from the Sisters and pulled Jack and Holly in close as they walked along. Up ahead, the path ended at the entrance to another long hallway lit with more sparkling lights in the walls.

"What do we do?" Emma asked, her voice barely above a whisper, not sure if the two Sisters could hear her. Back in the skimm, Yiana listened to their conversation through the glass. But Sasa and Haia's Marks were on their arms—like Holly's; they might not have Yiana's abilities to hear. "Every minute without the scope feels like a risk. If Daria looks in it and it works for her, we'll be trapped here."

"I know," Jack said. "But we don't know where she's keeping it. And those two," he pointed at the backs of the Sisters, "aren't going to tell us anything." He gave her a forced smile. "So, for now, I vote we wait and play nice."

Emma nodded. She agreed with Jack's assessment. They really had no choice but to wait for their chance to talk with Daria. After all, they were strangers here, and based on all the commotion in Lindur, their arrival must have raised a lot of questions.

They were taking small steps, falling further behind the Sisters with their long purposeful strides. The hallway branched in three directions; the Sisters led them down the righthand corridor. They passed closed doors, several inscribed with strange writing Emma didn't recognize. *I may be speaking and hearing the U'maan language, but so much for being able to read it.*

She put her arm around Holly. "Hol? You okay?"

"Yeah," Holly said as her eyes welled up a little. Her little sister's level of talking always mirrored her level of energy. "I want to go home."

"I know, bug," Emma said, using their dad's nickname for her. "So, your vote?"

Holly rubbed her eyes. "I'm with Jack."

Emma pulled Holly to a stop and gave her a quick squeeze. She turned back to the Sisters. Waiting by one of the hallway doors, Sasa stood, tapping her foot, looking annoyed by their impromptu huddle. Beside her, Sister Haia stood with her arms crossed.

"Sisters, thank you for your patience," Emma said while dipping her head respectfully at the woman. *Like Jack said...play nice.*

Sasa pushed the door open and moved back. Not sure what to expect, Emma leaned around the doorway without stepping inside and was pleased by what she saw. Despite the Sister's words, their behavior felt pointedly unwelcoming. Emma wouldn't have been surprised if this room had turned out to be another cell, like back in Lindur, but the room was spacious and inviting. The room's smooth walls were a mix of blues and greens. Next to a stone basin with two faucets, a ledge held an assortment of cups, plates, and wooden boxes. In the center of the room, two folded piles of clothing sat on a square table. The afternoon sunlight streamed into the room through an open window.

Emma stepped through the door and walked to the window. She had an unobstructed view of the Coren's huge walls and the closed main gate. *Well, at least one thing is clear. Our only way out of here is the kaleidoscope.*

"Emma, there are clothes for us." Behind her, Holly held up a ruby-red dress with a purple sash.

"Compliments of the Coren," Sasa said as she pointed to a curtained arch on the wall. "Your bath and sleeping quarters are in there. We will give you time to refresh from your travels and then send Acorn to escort you to the dining hall for the evening meal."

Jack yanked back the curtain and stepped through the archway. Emma marveled at her little brother's lack of caution. She spent all of her time intentionally not being the center of attention.

"YOUR BATHTUB IS HUGE," JACK SAID, LOOKING SATISFIED with his inspection. He turned towards the Sister. "Though mine's probably bigger since it was used for the king, right?"

Not responding, Sister Sasa stepped into the hallway and motioned for him. "Jack, I will take you to your quarters."

"Umm, okay," Jack crossed the room but paused and looked back at them, suddenly nervous about splitting up. Emma's brow was furrowed; she was worried as well. But their room was impressive, and dinner was coming; maybe Sasa and Haia were just not used to hosting visitors. He gave a thumbs-up to Emma, then ducked out the door and joined the two Sisters.

Sister Sasa pulled the door closed, then turned to Haia. "Take both tracing crystals to Daria's quarters." From a pocket in her robe, Sasa pulled the crystal she'd used to bless Emma. No longer clear, the stone was now bright green and laced with multi-colored swirls. She handed the crystal to Haia who immediately disappeared down the hallway in the direction they had come.

Sasa turned on her heel and walked up the corridor. "Follow me, Jack," she said without looking back.

Jack followed Sasa to the end of the hallway. She turned right and then led him down a series of long winding hallways and turns. Jack tried walking next to her but snagged his foot on the edge of her long red dress. She stopped and glared down at him.

"Sorry," he said as he cracked his knuckles. "I'll walk back here."

Saying nothing, she started forward. This part of the Coren was eerily quiet as if the thick walls were swallowing the sound of their footsteps on the stone floor. They turned down yet another long empty hallway, the air stale. At this rate, he wouldn't have time for a bath before dinner.

"Wow," Jack said, still carefully avoiding the hem of her dress. "When you said my room was in the north wing, I didn't know you meant the North Pole." No reaction. "Oh, yeah, you probably don't get that since you may not have a North Pole here." Nothing. "Or snow, right?" Still no response. *Tough crowd.*

Jack resigned himself to peering in the open doorways they passed. Most of the doors were closed, but in one room, hundreds of woven baskets were filled with dried flowers and in another, wood planks were stacked neatly by color and grain.

They descended a broad ramp worn smooth by age. At the bottom, the hallway stretched on into the shadows. Thankfully, she stopped at the very first door at the base of the stairs.

"These are your quarters," Sasa said as she gestured him closer to a stone door with an intricate symbol engraved in its center. Jack reached up and touched the symbol with his finger. "This is one of the oldest parts of the Coren." She paused, smiling down at him. "This door is over two thousand years old, so watch carefully."

She reached past his shoulder and deftly traced her finger along the symbol. A shimmering cord of bright colors flowed from her fingertip, momentarily filling the engraving like molten steel in a forge, before vanishing. The stone door whooshed open and slid sideways into the wall recess.

Startled, he stepped back from the doorway but bumped directly into the Sister behind him. She grabbed his shoulders and, without a word, shoved him hard.

Jack stumbled forward into the unlit room. Instinctively, his body dropped into an over-the-shoulder roll across the gritty stone floor. He spun around on the balls of his feet, instantly recognizing the stark bleakness of a cell with bare walls, a barred window, and a cot.

Sasa loomed in the doorway. Silhouetted by the light in the hallway, her menacing shadow enveloped Jack. Her left hand reached up, poised a fingertip's width from a small matching symbol etched in the edge of the recessed stone door. Even in the dark of the cell, Jack recognized the familiar smirk of a bully. He'd spent his whole life dealing with smirks.

"Enjoy your stay, King Zero," Sasa said as she touched the symbol. The door sealed, the solid thump of stone on stone hitting Jack's ears with the finality of a coffin lid sliding into place.

19

MISSING

A FEW HOURS LATER, Acorn and an unsmiling Sister Haia came to their room and led them through the Coren gardens towards the dining hall. Walking down the hall, Emma smelled garlic and baked bread and heard the sounds of laughter and clinking silverware. But the moment Emma and Holly stepped through the doorway, the Sisters—seven of them sitting at a long table in the center of the room —stopped eating, their forks and spoons paused in mid-air.

Acorn guided them to a lone table, a good distance from where the Sisters dined together, left them at their table, and exited the hall. Bringing Jack, Emma assumed. Haia left them as well, stopped for a moment at the Sisters' table where she said something Emma did not hear, and then left the dining room.

The Sisters resumed eating but did not speak. They had been talking and laughing; now they ate in complete silence, a few of them glancing at Emma and Holly in between bites. As her annoyance grew, Emma watched the door impatiently; she'd feel better having Jack back with them. But a few minutes later, when Acorn returned carrying their dinner on a large wooden tray, she was alone. Her eyes downcast, she served the meal without speaking, not even when Holly asked about the cold green soup. She picked up the serving tray, then turned to leave them again.

Emma clasped her wrist and leaned in close. "Acorn," she said, trying to sound nonchalant, despite her suspicion, "thank you very much. Are you going to get Jack now?"

Acorn shook her head as she pulled away from Emma. "On my Marks, Eres. My only instructions are to serve you and Eres Holly." Acorn chewed her lower lip and fidgeted in place.

Emma fought down the urge to ask more questions. With the Sisters sitting twelve feet away, the small girl's reticence was obvious. Emma turned to the food in front of her, and stirred the bowl of soup with her spoon. She'd lost her appetite but forced herself to eat.

She took a few bites, not noticing the taste, but she was acutely aware of every slurp and chew from the Sisters' unsmiling mouths. She put down her spoon. If she could hear everything in the room, so could some of them. They were intentionally not sharing any information in front of her, and they were eavesdropping on her and Holly.

Holly reached out and touched her hand. "What's going on? Where's Jack?"

Emma dipped her finger into the lime green broth and drew a set of lips with an X on the tablecloth. Holly got the message, so they ate the rest of their meal in silence while Acorn stood on the far side of the dining hall. Emma ate slowly, waiting for the Sisters to leave. But after an hour, with all of her food gone cold, the Sisters continued to sit at their table, quietly sipping tea, as if they had nothing better to do than to spy on her and Holly. Fuming inside, Emma stood up. Acorn ran over, ready to take them back to their room. As they walked across the dining hall to the exit, none of the Sisters spoke or moved, but the moment they stepped through the door into the short hallway, voices erupted like a volcano, filling the hall with their loud, noisy comments.

"They're worse than I imagined!"

"It's just like Sasa said. They're freaks of nature."

Emma walked briskly down the hallway, not stopping until she reached the gardens and could no longer hear them. The Sisters were no better than a bunch of high school girls, all too eager to gossip about the girls with the strange birthmarks. Battling the urge to scream, she turned and looked back towards the dining room; one of the Sisters was standing at the edge of the gardens, her eyes fixed on her and Holly.

Shaking with anger, Emma turned her back to the Sister. "Acorn, where's my brother?"

Acorn furtively glanced at the Sister, then answered, her voice hushed. "I'm sorry, Emma. I have to do what the Sisters tell me, and if they hear me talking to you like we're friends—"

"We are friends," Holly said and raised her arms as if to hug her.

Emma grabbed Holly's shoulder and yanked her back a step. "Not now, Hol. Not while they're watching us," Emma said. "We don't want to get Acorn in trouble." She waited for Holly to nod, then let go of her. "Let's go to our room. Acorn, we'll follow you."

They walked slowly through the gardens, the Sister following them at a distance. As they passed by the central fountains, Emma stepped close behind Acorn and whispered, "Where's Jack? Why wasn't he at dinner?"

"I don't know, Eres. Sister Haia told me that she would be taking care of him," Acorn said, glancing back, her face full of worry.

Emma sucked in a sharp breath, then let it out slowly. She should have known something was wrong from the moment Daria had called them abnormal in Lindur.

As they exited the gardens and turned towards the hallway leading to their room, the Sister stopped and then walked off in another direction, apparently satisfied that they were returning to their room.

Watching the Sister disappear from view, Emma strode quickly up the hallway and stopped outside their room. Making sure there were no Sisters in sight, she knelt in front of Acorn and placed her hands gently on the small girl's shoulders. "Listen, can you find Jack for me?"

Acorn seemed to consider something, then her head bobbed eagerly. "Yes, I can follow Sister Haia."

"But what if she sees you?" Holly asked.

"She won't," Acorn assured her. "I know every inch of the Coren, better than anybody. Besides, they never pay me any attention unless they need something."

Emma rose, surprised by the small girl's confidence. "Then it's settled. Find Jack."

~

DESPITE THE COMFORTABLE BED, EMMA TOSSED AND turned all night. Every time she came close to drifting off, a new wave of worries washed in and out of her head, leaving her exhausted. Why was Jack not at dinner? Was Daria questioning him about the scope? She had seemed more interested in him than her or Holly in the courthouse. In the skimm, Acorn said she once met the Orange Guardian here in Dara. Does that mean the Guardians can travel to the other lands in the Seven? What if she leaves Dara and takes the kaleidoscope? And why does their dad's kaleidoscope resemble the artifact called the Prophet's Eye? How did their dad get it? Emma felt sick to her stomach, unable to handle the constant rush of unknowns.

The next morning, Acorn arrived bearing a breakfast platter of fruits, hot porridge, and terrible news. Jack was a prisoner, locked in one of the ancient holding cells in the north halls. Two of the Sisters were delivering his meals. So far, no one had questioned him, and Daria had not left her private quarters since returning from Lindur. She had given strict orders to not be disturbed.

"Can we get him out?" Holly asked as she poked at her porridge. "Is there a guard?"

"No, Holly, but they don't need one. The doors on those cells are made of stone and have colorcast locks made by Fives."

Holly's eyes widened. "Can you take us to see him?"

Emma took a small bite of the pear-shaped fruit in her hand. "That might be hard if the Sisters are watching us."

Acorn was shaking her head. "Last night after dinner, Sister Sasa summoned all of the Sisters and the Coren staff to a meeting. Except for this hallway and the dining hall, they closed and locked all of the passageway doors. You and Holly may sit in the gardens or walk the grounds outside, but the rest of the Coren is off-limits."

Emma frowned and dropped the fruit down on the platter; the skin was tart and bitter. *So, that's it. We're prisoners, just like Jack, except we get pretty robes and yard privileges.*

Acorn must have seen the frustration on Emma's face because she quickly spoke up. "But I can give Jack your messages if that will help. I can sneak away between my washing and mealtime chores." She then described the network of tunnels built under the Coren. They were only four feet high in most places and much too cramped for the adult workers. She lowered her voice as if divulging a secret. "I know all of them. I use them to move around the Coren and finish my chores faster. There's an out-of-use water tunnel running under the north wing. It's small, but I can fit."

After Acorn left, Emma spent the morning in deep thought, sitting underneath the window and listening to the winds swirl across the top of the Coren wall. Holly found a stash of writing supplies in a drawer and distracted herself by drawing pictures of the vella fields and sand dunes. The day dragged slowly into the afternoon mealtime as Emma anticipated an update from Acorn, but when a knock came at their door, it was one of the gossiping Sisters from yesterday. Emma didn't know the woman's name, and based on how she and Holly were being treated, she didn't want to know.

"Sister, I am Emma Waite, eldest daughter of Elishah. May I please talk to my brother?" Emma said, gritting her teeth while trying her best to sound friendly. She wanted to punch the woman in the face.

This Sister was the oldest Emma had seen so far; her skin was wrinkled, brown, and leathery. The woman stared blankly at her, unsmiling. "I will escort you to the dining hall." The woman motioned for Holly and Emma to follow, then turned and walked away.

Walking with Holly, Emma glared at the woman's back. *I should have punched her.*

Emma barely touched her food as the concern and worry for both Jack and Acorn ate at her insides. She knew they were asking a lot of

Acorn; she had no idea what would happen if Acorn got caught visiting Jack.

The rest of the day dragged. She and Holly walked the series of paths that wound through the Coren gardens and sat for a time on a stone bench by the fountains. But one of the Sisters hovered nearby the entire time and Emma felt her frustration building more and more. That evening, it was a different Sister who came to take them to the late meal. Emma felt powerless. Watching the Sisters dine at the other table, her anger grew with every bite of the food she forced down. Yet another Sister—who refused to answer any of her questions about Jack—escorted them back to their room. Emma slammed the door in her face.

Holly asked to sleep in her bed. She had seen the fear taking root in Holly's dark brown eyes, and as her little sister curled up next to her, she lied and told her everything would be all right. Emma lay there, not moving, as Holly drifted off to sleep.

20

A WALK IN THE COREN

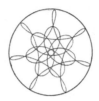

ACORN SHOWED up at their door on the morning of their third day inside the Coren, her hands full with a plate of hot breakfast rolls filling their room with the smell of orange and cinnamon. Daria had summoned her yesterday, and on top of her usual work, she'd spent the day retrieving items from the Coren archives, delivering them to the Red Guardian's quarters. Acorn said she didn't mind the extra work, except for having to beg the Ones to help carry the larger items. She rubbed her shoulders as she talked about struggling to pull down a crate of books from one of the archive's highest shelves.

So with all of the added activity, she had not been able to visit Jack yet. At night, she slept on a mat in the corner of the cook's quarters and sneaking away would be too suspicious. She promised that she would find a way to see Jack as soon as possible.

"I know you will, Acorn," Emma said, stunned by the image of Acorn sleeping on the floor. She pictured Jack in a cell and suddenly, the thought of sitting here—powerless to help him—repulsed her. She opened their door and peered down the hallway; thankfully, no Sister was waiting for them. "Let's go."

Emma stepped back into the room and grabbed two of the breakfast rolls from the plate. She handed one to Acorn who hesitated before taking the roll. "There's no Sister out there, so Acorn, I guess that means you're in charge of us. Do you have time to take a walk?"

Holly smiled and nodded eagerly as she took a bite of roll.

Glancing back and forth between the girls, Acorn slowly raised the treat to her mouth, inhaling the aroma with her eyes closed. Emma waited, afraid she was asking too much from the little girl. Acorn's eyes popped open.

"I do have a few minutes until kitchen duty." Grinning, Acorn shoved half the roll into her mouth. "Follow me."

Armed with their breakfast rolls, the girls walked to the center of the Coren without meeting anybody. According to Acorn, the Sister's personal quarters were scattered across the mostly empty compound. Sister Sasa's quarters encompassed ten rooms in the south cluster of domes. There was a ranking amongst the nine Sisters even though they were all Fives. As First Sister, Sasa oversaw the day-to-day activities of the Coren, and had named Sister Haia as Second Sister. The official ranking stopped with Third Sister Adina, and unofficially, Yiana—the one Sister who'd spoken kindly to them —was ranked last of all.

In the Coren gardens, they came across Sister Pirna, sitting at a wooden table, a box of knives next to her. Holly stared in wonder as ribbons of color flowed from the woman's fingertips directly into the blades. The edges seemed to be absorbing colors from the Sister's fingertips. This must be colorcasting, thought Holly. When Pirna looked up from her work, she scowled at them, then shut the box and walked away without speaking. As soon as Pirna was out of sight, Holly opened the box lid.

"Holly! Please don't!" Acorn pleaded as she scanned the gardens.

Holly slowly pulled her hand back. The box was divided into two compartments, with the untreated knives on the right, and the color-casted on the left. There was no visible difference between the two sets. "Sorry. Can everyone with Marks colorcast?"

Acorn quickly closed the box. "No, but everyone Marked with the first color in the item can use them." She led them away from the worktable to stroll along the path, circling the fountains. Two more Sisters sitting on a bench stopped talking as they drew near. Frowning at the girls, they stood up and strode off in the opposite direction.

Holly sat on the stone lip of the fountain. She stuck her right hand under the cascading water and looked at the four Marks: green stopped between her thumb and forefinger; then orange, indigo, and yellow, each ending at the places between her other fingers. She ran her left hand under the stream of water. She'd always liked the way her Marks looked when wet; shiny and vibrant.

The form plus the number of colors by the intensity cast at creation dictate the purpose and power of the colorcast item.' Yiana had explained on the way to the Coren, but Holly still had no idea what it meant. Emma sat down next to her while Acorn stood in front of them.

Holly dried her hands on her dress. "Since I was able to push through the light wall in the courthouse, that means I can colorcast, right?"

"I don't know, Holly. Sister Yiana would explain things much better," said Acorn.

"I'm still confused. How does a Marked person use a colorcast item?" Emma asked.

Acorn looked around then dashed over to a bench, climbing on top. Next to the bench was an eight-foot-tall light pole, topped by three glowing yellow orbs. She shimmied up the pole, removed one of the balls, dropped to the ground, and ran back to them. "This is a lightball." The glass ball was the size of a large orange. "A person with Two Marks colorcast the colors into the balls. Anything can be color-cast to light up—wands, sticks, walls—by using two colors, red and yellow. The yellow color makes it glow. The red color is what connects the object to Dara and the Marked."

"But I don't see any red color," Emma said.

"There's a little inside, enough to allow anybody with a red Mark to use the light. I'm sorry I can't explain it better, Emma." Acorn held it out. "Here, Holly, it should work for you."

Holly cupped the ball in both hands, surprised by the lack of heat. Beneath the surface of the glass, she felt a faint vibration like the internal hum of a running engine. As she rotated it in her hands, the ball glowed brighter and brighter. She wasn't sure what she was doing.

"Can I turn it off? There's no switch." Holly tapped the hard round surface with her fingers. Bursts of yellow light appeared under her fingertips.

"I don't know," Acorn said, sounding unsure. "I thought you could control it since you're Marked."

Holly concentrated on the color energy she felt; with the yellow, she detected a faint amount of red energy, but it was mixed in like wet brushstrokes in a watercolor painting. She gave up and handed it to Emma. The light immediately dimmed, back to its original brightness.

Emma spun the ball in her hands her eyes narrowing in concentration. "I can hear a humming like it's turned on, but that's all. I can't change the brightness, up or down. Is that because my Marks are in a different place?"

"I'm not sure, Emma."

"Placement of Marks matters quite a bit. I should have taught you better, Alla-nu," Sister Yiana said as she walked around the fountain. Smiling warmly, she stopped next to them and took the lightball from Emma's hands. "Eres Emma, you have the Marks of a Soundcaster, like me. Eres Holly is a Touchcaster. Colorcasting is the art of casting your color energy into other materials, using sound or touch."

"So that's why the ball glowed bright when I touched it?" Holly asked, overwhelmed by the idea of embedding color and energy into things.

Yiana looked surprised. "Not exactly. Colorcasting is a skill that requires focus and the expenditure of energy. You may be a natural, a conductor." Before Holly could ask her question, Yiana continued. "There are some Touchcasters—very few—who have a very strong affinity for colorcasting. Color energy flows effortlessly between their Marks and the world around them."

"I saw Sister Pirna putting color into knife blades over there,"

Holly pointed excitedly to the far side of the gardens. "Is that what Touchcasting looks like?"

"So I'm a Soundcaster because my Marks are on my neck?" Emma asked, cutting off Holly.

"Perhaps, Emma. You do have the Marks, but the art of Sound-casting is very—"

"Acorn!" Sister Haia emerged from the garden path to their right with Sister Pirna behind her. "You are supposed to be in the kitchen!"

Acorn's face turned pale. Nodding quickly at Holly and Emma, she ran past the two Sisters and ducked out of sight down the path.

Sister Haia scowled up at Yiana. "Where is Sister Samila? She was assigned to watch them this morning."

Yiana smiled down at Haia. "Samila and I switched turns. I've been keeping a very close eye on our guests," she said, then added as Pirna started to speak, "from a respectful distance, of course. Sister Pirna, my apologies for allowing these girls to disturb your blade work."

Sister Haia stared at Pirna, who merely shrugged seemingly appeased by Yiana's words. Haia peered up at Yiana. "Very well. Eres Daria has summoned us for a meeting of the Sisterhood. Escort our *guests* back to their room, then come to the dining hall immediately."

"Where's our brother?" Emma asked loudly. She had no interest in being escorted anywhere right now.

Haia spun around, her face livid with anger, and raised her right hand towards Emma. Holly immediately grabbed onto Emma to pull her back, but Yiana stepped quickly in front of the woman whose red face now matched her crimson robe. Glaring at the much taller sister, Haia slowly lowered her hand, then brought her stare to Emma.

"We are taking care of him."

"No, you're not! You locked him in a cell!"

"How did you...?" Sister Haia stopped mid-sentence, her jaw clenched. "Your brother is a Zero and a thief."

"That's a lie!" Holly yelled. Angry tears welled up in her eyes. She felt Emma's arms wrap around her. "The scope belongs to our dad. We already told Daria."

"ENOUGH!" Haia stepped back. "I will not be questioned by you. Yiana, take them to their room NOW!" She spun on her heels and strode down the path. As Sister Pirna brushed by Yiana, she clucked her tongue at her. Watching them walk away, Holly leaned against Emma.

"Come, Eresi," Yiana smiled down at them, then led them through the gardens towards their room.

"Sister Yiana, did we get you in trouble?" Holly asked, clutching Emma's hand tightly as they walked. Everyone was so angry and she was sure that Sister Haia would have slapped Emma if Yiana had not stopped her.

Yiana shook her head and smiled down at them. "Pay no attention to Hothead Haia. Yesterday at breakfast, she yelled at the toast." She chuckled softly as they entered the hallway, then stopped and knelt in front of them, her face close to theirs. "Acorn overstepped by telling you where Jack is. I will tell Daria that it was me, that I took pity on you because I have a little brother in Ephara."

"But why would Haia say he's a thief?" Holly asked.

Yiana rose and pushed open the door to their room. "I don't know, Eres, but perhaps I'll learn why at the Coren meeting. For now, both of you must stay put and be patient." She patted Holly on the shoulder and then gently nudged her into their room along with Emma. "And please, under no circumstances, let any of the Sisters see you wielding any Colorcasting abilities. On your next stroll around the Coren, come visit me. I can usually be found in my workshop." Turning away, she paused in the hallway. "And should Sister Haia come your direction, walk the other way."

THE FORMULA

COLORCASTING INCLUDES TWO DISCIPLINES:
TOUCHCASTING AND SOUNDCASTING.

The Primary Formula of $(F)+(C \times I) = (Pu+ Po)$ applies to both arts. The (F)orm of the cast item plus the number of (C)olors by the (I)ntensity cast into an item's creation dictate the (Pu)rpose and (Po)wer of an item.

Value is inherentely linked to an item's power and purpose. The average amount of time required to cast a lasting color effect into an item is one hour though some highly skilled casters can consistently exceed rate.

—from Chapter 1 of Luthor's Colorcasting Primer

21

SCRAMBLED EGGS

ACORN RETURNED THE NEXT MORNING, holding a plate of cranberry muffins in one hand and a basket of eggs in the other. Last night, she'd snuck away from the kitchen early, crawled through the tunnel, and spoken to Jack. "I told him that you and Holly were okay and that you've been asking about him, but there's no way for you to visit even though you *really* want to," she took a breath, continuing, "but he didn't say anything. I took him a muffin this morning, but he didn't talk."

"Not a word?" Emma asked, picking the cranberries out of her muffin. Worrying about him stuck in the cell, alone and feeling abandoned, had kept her awake again. Knowing that her brother was too depressed to talk hit her hard. The Sisters had ignored her long enough, and she couldn't keep waiting for Daria to appear. Not while Jack rotted away.

"Holly, stay here." Emma turned. "Acorn, can you stay with Holly until I come back?"

"Yes, Emma, my morning chores are done," Acorn answered immediately. She pointed at the basket of eggs. "I brought these for you to practice casting, Holly. Sister Pirna would notice if I took any of her knives, but we have plenty of eggs."

Holly picked up an egg then looked at Emma with concern in her eyes. "Where are you going?"

"I'm going to get some answers. I'm a Seven, right? It's time to act like one."

She stalked out, ready to find the Red Guardian.

"DID IT WORK THIS TIME?" ACORN ASKED.

Holly frowned at the scattered piles of broken eggs covering the floor of their room. Excited by the idea of colorcasting, Holly grabbed the basket of eggs and started practicing the moment Emma left the room. After two hours of trying and failing, all she had to show for her effort was sticky fingers and a mound of murdered eggs.

"I got it this time." Holly looked up from the table, her hands clasping the egg she'd been working on for the past twenty minutes. Pieces of exploded eggshells covered Acorn's face and stuck in her red hair. "Ready? No wait, don't say anything. Don't jinx it."

Holly slowly pulled her hands away from the egg, standing on its end. It wobbled but stayed upright. Holly slowly let out the breath she'd been holding inside. She leaned back from the table and wiped the bead of yolk dangling from her nose. She wished she knew what she was doing.

"I think it worked. I touchcasted the green color right up to the point where I felt the first hint of resistance. I was definitely forcing too much before. Good thing you brought a basket of these to practice on instead of knives."

Holly smiled and stared at the large brown egg, still upright and unwavering on the table's surface. She was amazed at how much energy she'd used to make one egg stand up on its end. Acorn told her that green was the color of life and balance in the Seven, an idea that felt right to Holly. When she held the lightball yesterday, she'd felt the yellow color, glowing with energy in her hands. Using that sensation to guide her, it took nearly an hour until she was able to find and channel the green color inside of her. But once she found it, pushing the energy out and into the egg was surprisingly easy. Controlling the amount...well that was the hard part. Her whole body hurt, and her fingers were numb. *If casting one color is this hard, making an omelet could kill me.*

Holly looked at Acorn and pointed at the egg standing motionless on the tabletop. She wanted this to work so badly. "Blow on it."

"Are you sure?"

"Yes, we're a team," said Holly. Acorn grinned back at her. Holly lowered her head to the table level and stared at her egg. She would keep this egg in honor of her first successful colorcasting. "Go for it."

Acorn puckered her lips and blew a soft puff of air at the egg. It didn't budge.

"Harder," Holly said.

Acorn took a deep breath and blew hard. The egg wavered slightly but stayed upright.

"Okay..." Holly tried to contain her excitement. "Tap it."

Acorn flicked the top of the egg with her finger. The egg toppled to one side. Holly was sure she had failed again when halfway down to the table, the egg slowed, stopped in mid-motion, and popped back up to its standing position like a boxer refusing to fall.

"It worked!" Holly couldn't stop looking at her accomplishment.

She pushed the egg onto its side. It popped right up and stood on its end. She knocked it over again. Up it popped. Grinning like a mad scientist, she laid her creation on the floor and rolled it across the room. The egg rolled to a stop by the door and popped upright.

Holly wrapped Acorn in a hug. "Acorn, you're the best teacher in all the world!" Acorn pulled back, her eyes wide, too stunned to say anything. Holly looked over at the egg still poised on its end. "I mean it, you did a great job explaining. Let's write our names on it and then celebrate with another muffin."

"Sign my name?"

"Oh, I forgot. Well then, I'll just have to teach you how to write." Holly grabbed the last two muffins, then hesitated, and put them back on the plate. "You know, I think you should take these to Jack if you can," Holly said, "and tell him about the mess we made.

Maybe it will cheer him up." She didn't like that Jack had said nothing at all to Acorn this morning. A quiet Jack was a depressed Jack.

Holly dipped one finger in the egg yolk and traced a sad face on the tabletop. She looked over at the egg standing by the door. "How many colors can something have?"

"As many colors as the caster, I guess," said Acorn. "Sister Yiana made a five-color cymbala for herself...that's a stringed instrument. Sometimes, she plays it during Market Days at the Coren." Acorn's eyes opened wide. "Holly! I think that means you could cast seven colors, well, I mean, if you had the time and energy."

"Time and energy?"

"Sister Yiana tried explaining it to me when she was making her cymbala." Acorn rocked back and forth in her chair. "She'd been working on it for what seemed like forever, and I overheard Sister Sasa yelling at her, something about missing her quota."

"Acorn," Holly stopped her. "How much time?"

"Oh, yes. She told me a five-color item takes sixteen times longer to cast than a one-color item."

"Sixteen times longer?"

"Yes. And she said six colors would be double again." Acorn fidgeted and started counting her fingers. "Which would be...umm..."

"Thirty-two times." Holly felt bad for answering so quickly.

"What about seven?" Acorn asked excitedly. "If you cast seven colors into an item, how long would it take?"

"Sixty-four times as long, I guess, assuming the time is doubled again. How many hours did Yiana work on her cymbala?"

"She said six hundred."

"Six hundred hours?" Holly had never spent more than two weeks on a painting. She couldn't imagine working that long on a single project.

"She was exhausted all the time, too, because of the energy loss from her Marks," said Acorn. "She told me colorcasting drains energy from the caster. Working with five colors is incredibly taxing, so all casters must take lots of breaks."

"Then a person could literally cast themselves to death?" Holly asked.

The room door burst open and slammed against the wall. Acorn jumped off her chair as Holly spun around. "Eres Emma, you're back." Acorn blurted out, reverting to the formal greeting she always used with her superiors. Dressed in the Coren's crimson robes, her hair tied back with a dark green and gold sash, Emma could pass for one of the Sisters.

Emma stood in the open doorway, her jaw clenched, her eyes narrowed to slits. Holly had rarely seen her this angry...and usually because of Jack.

"Did you find anything out?" Holly asked. "Will Daria let Jack go?"

"No," Emma snapped. "I mean, I don't know." She stepped into the room, slammed the door closed, and walked straight toward Holly's egg.

"Emma! Stop!" Holly yelled too late. Emma's right foot came down, smashing the egg to pieces. Holly ran forward and fell to her knees. "Oh, no. My egg."

Crossing the room, Emma frowned at the mess of splattered yolks and eggshells stuck to the walls and floors. She sank into the cushioned chair in the corner. "What happened here?"

Holly poked dejectedly at her broken egg. A few of the pieces twitched and struggled to stand like wounded soldiers valiantly trying to rise up on the field of battle. "I was touchcasting. With the eggs." She pulled the largest surviving piece from the sticky yolk and gently placed it in the palm of her hand. "Most of them exploded. Except for this one." Holly held up her hand, but Emma didn't bother looking up.

"Don't worry, Emma. I'll clean everything right away," Acorn said.

"I don't care about the mess. I'm just tired of playing hide and seek with the Sisterhood." Emma closed her eyes and rubbed her temples as if fighting a headache. "My whole morning...what a gigantic waste of time," Emma muttered as she untied the sash from her hair. "I cornered one Sister after another in the gardens and every one of them ignored me and refused to talk. I looked for Sister Yiana at her workshop—she wasn't there. Then, I found Sister Sasa in the dining hall, and when I demanded to meet with Daria, she laughed at me and told me I would have to wait."

"Emma." Acorn's face went pale, making her freckles stand out like red sprinkles on a white cupcake. "I'm sorry."

"It's okay, Acorn. It's not your fault."

Acorn fidgeted in place and nervously tugged on the hem of her shift. "Emma, Sister Sasa wasn't lying."

"What? What do you mean?" Emma said.

"I forgot to tell you this morning why all my chores were done. Eres Daria is not in the Coren. She left during the night and took the kaleidoscope with her."

22

SACRAMENT

CHAMBER...EXTEND...PIVOT...THRUST.

Jack's eyes never wavered from the waist-high black spot on the cell wall. With each repeated side kick, the sole of his foot—toes precisely curled back to form a strong striking surface— hit the mark. A satisfying thwack of flesh striking stone reverberated on the hard walls of his cell, a steady drumbeat accompanied by the sound of his controlled breathing. Jack imagined Sister Sasa standing directly in front of him. A thin smile creased his lips.

Chamber...extend...pivot...thrust.

Ten more side kicks and he switched to front snap kicks. He frowned as his foot missed the target. Since quitting the dojo, he'd neglected his practice this summer. The fight at school was sloppy; he'd relied on lazy techniques and undisciplined moves that Sensei Todd would not have tolerated. He should've trained harder but couldn't find a reason. Until now. Jack grunted from the extra effort to get a full extension of his leg. *Now I have ten reasons. Wait, Sister Yiana was nice to them, so make that nine reasons.*

Step...chamber...extend...snap.

Nine reasons who wear red dresses.

Jack grimaced as his back foot twisted and he missed the mark again. How could he save his sisters from the Red Guardian if he

141

couldn't knock out a respectable set of front kicks? Jack grinned at the imagined confrontation in his head. Him standing alone in the desert. *Step...chamber...extend...snap.* A ring of Sisters circling him like vultures in their flapping crimson robes as Jack and the Red Guardian face off in battle. *Step...chamber...extend...snap.* Feinting and moving, his steps light and his arms coiled like snakes, he moves in and then... ZAP...his world goes black as his foe flattens him with a red blast of light.

Jack stopped mid-kick and leaned against the wall. *Who am I kidding? Even if I practiced for a thousand years, I've got zero chance of fighting my way out of this mess.* Shoulders slumping, Jack slid down the wall into a sitting position on the floor as he ran the word zero over and over his tongue like a mantra. Zero chance. *I've got the chance of a Zero. It'd be funny if it weren't so true.*

A small rumble in his stomach nudged Jack out of his stupor. He looked at the door, closed his eyes, and tried to envision the space beyond. He knew he couldn't see past solid stone but he hadn't come up with a good word yet to describe yesterday's weird sensation. He'd been sitting on the floor staring at nothing when the image of two Sisters opening his cell popped into his head. One of them was Sister Yiana who had a warm smile he trusted. The other Sister—pudgy with a bad overbite—he'd never seen. A few seconds later, when the cell door opened, Yiana was there, next to a chubby Sister holding his meal tray. He could have sworn he had seen this woman—in his head—just moments before.

He blinked and couldn't be sure anymore. Deja vu was the best description, that spooky feeling of having been there before. Most likely, he'd gotten good at guessing mealtimes after being stuck in here for six days. Six long days. But training with a purpose had cleared his mind.

~

HE'D GIVEN EACH DAY ITS OWN SPECIAL NAME.

Rage. Day one after Sasa had trapped and taunted him. He

screamed at the walls. He kicked at the door over and over until his legs gave out and he stumbled and collapsed—exhausted and sweaty—onto the cot.

The whole second day, Jack barely moved from his bed, a creaky wooden cot covered with a quilt. Day two was *Bitterness*. Just like home, the people here saw him as a freak, an unworthy creature fit to be caged. He was trapped in a cell, for who knew how long. Meanwhile, Emma and Holly were not locked up and were sleeping in a beautiful room with sunshine and gardens. They were probably eating fancy meals on fancy plates. When the Sisters brought his meal, Jack scowled at the grey metal tray and barely touched his food.

Depression. Exactly what he felt on the third day after Acorn's first visit. Jack had barely recovered from the shock of hearing Acorn's voice float out of the corner hole when the reality of her news hit him. The girls had not been allowed to see Daria and the Sisters were watching their every move, she said, treating them like outcasts. But Jack stopped listening and retreated backward, weighed down by his thoughts. The possibility of being trapped in a cell for a long time scared him the most. He might survive if his captors gave him access to books, but he doubted that Daria's plans included issuing him a library card. Jack ignored Acorn's questions, waiting for her to go away and leave him alone. Then he crawled back onto the cot, laid his head on his arm, and cried.

On his fourth day in captivity, Acorn came twice, both times with muffins. When she told him that Daria had left the Coren with the kaleidoscope, Jack's heart sank even further. He told her to go away. Then he named the fourth day *Despair*.

Yesterday on day five, following his inexplicable "deja-food" moment, Acorn visited two more times, telling him about her chores and sharing bits of gossip. With Daria and the kaleidoscope gone, Emma said all they could do was wait. Sister Yiana—the nice one—was giving his sisters colorcasting lessons in her studio. The new cook —in a long line of cooks since Daria made a habit of firing them for any culinary misstep—was boastfully confident in her skills; she had catered numerous affairs in Ephara and people raved about her food, and especially her braised leg of lamb.

Jack had barely listened to Acorn as she talked since she was obviously playing the role of servant girl to Emma and Holly. Bored and waiting for something to happen, he'd started a game with himself of tracing the maze of hairline cracks in the walls, forcing himself to start back at the very beginning whenever his eyes led him to a dead end. *Waiting* was the fifth day.

~

THIS MORNING—HIS SIXTH DAY IN CAPTIVITY—HE'D grudgingly given his sisters credit for handing Acorn the tools to break through his funky mood.

"Jack, is it true where you come from the people aren't marked and are free to do what they want?" Acorn asked when she appeared in the hole again. Jack sat back on the cot, ready to start his waiting game again.

"Yeah, but I don't want to talk. Go ask my sisters." He stared at the wall.

"All right." The cell went quiet for a few moments. "You're allowed to do anything?"

Jack lost his spot on the wall. "Yes, same rights as everyone else. Live, learn, work, play, whatever."

"Like playing Budo? Emma said you like to play Budo."

"I don't *play* Budo," Jack said. He sat up and leaned forward on the cot. "Budo's not a game. It's a style of martial arts."

"So, it's art?" she asked. "How do you draw the Budo?"

Jack walked over to kneel next to the corner hole. "No, it's not like that. You don't draw Budo, you learn it and practice it and live it." Jack winced inside as the words left his lips. He wasn't living it.

Acorn cleared her throat. "I'm sorry, Jack, but I don't understand."

"Don't apologize." Jack settled his legs into the seated position he

144

practiced in the Dojo and had learned to hold unmoving for hours at a time. "I'll start at the beginning..."

After thirty minutes of explaining the tenets of Budo to Acorn, Jack felt restless. Falling silent, he stood up and stared at the wall. His train of thought raced backward and forward along the network of lines covering the cell wall. "I see a path," Jack muttered quietly.

"Jack, are you all right?"

"Yes." He squatted next to the six-inch wide hole. In the darkness of the tunnel, he made out the curly red top of Acorn's head. He put his head down close to the opening.

"Acorn." Jack stared in the darkness as Acorn raised her eyes, "I'm glad you came. Can you keep visiting me?"

"Yes, Jack. With Eres Daria gone, I mean," she stopped, and Jack knew she hadn't meant to repeat that bad bit of news, "I can probably come at least twice each day, maybe more."

"Okay, good," Jack said. "I'll tell you about where we're from, and you can tell me more about the land of Dara." Jack stuck his hand in the small hole and wiggled his fingers. "Deal?"

Jack waited for her response. In the shadows, he could see Acorn rubbing her hands frantically across her dress. He retracted his hand through the hole. *Shaking a Zero's hand might be a breach of etiquette.*

Acorn shot both of her small hands up through the opening and snagged his fingers in hers. Her palms were moist with sweat.

"Deal," Acorn said with a squeak in her voice. She released his fingers and her hands darted back into the hole. Jack heard her scrambling away.

Jack spent the rest of the morning training. Explaining Budo to Acorn had lit the spark in him to get moving. In the beginning, he stopped and started repeatedly, losing his concentration, and questioning the pointlessness. After all, what was the use of a cleanly executed spin kick against adversaries who could control color and sound? But gradually, like the laying of a brick wall, Jack's thoughts solidified and hardened around the movements, cementing the pure and repetitive motions of arm and leg, hand and foot.

Jack turned at the now familiar sound of the cell door sliding open. Yiana knelt in the doorway, carefully setting a tray of food on the floor. The buck-toothed Sister waited warily in the hall.

"Good afternoon, Sister Yiana and Sister Beaver." Jack wiped the sweat from his brow and bowed low at the Fives. "Lunch already? I've been so busy, I completely lost track of the time."

"Yes, I suppose so," said Yiana, her brown eyes looking amused by his courteous greeting. "Enjoy your lunch, Jack."

The door whooshed shut. Jack settled cross-legged on the cot with his meal tray and poked at the handful of small round fruits, purplish and splotchy and smelly. The ugly fruit had shown up before on his food tray. Jack had eaten one and come close to throwing up his entire lunch. He picked up the loaf of spiced bread and chewed on it slowly while running the name he'd chosen for day six over and over in his mind. The word grew and loomed large like a raised stone monument, a word he could rally around.

Jack surveyed the remaining food on the tray. He'd eaten everything...everything but the noxious sour fruit. He picked one and squeezed it lightly between his thumb and forefinger. The wrinkled purple skin cracked and an odor like cooked cabbage filled his nose. Lifting his eyes and staring intently at the cell door, Jack popped the fruit in his mouth and chewed slowly. The bitter liquid coated his mouth with each mechanical bite.

Revenge. Jack picked up another fruit and placed it carefully in his mouth, the act of eating the fruit a sacrament to the word.

In the year 2005, a television crew recorded Jamie Vendera as he shattered a crystal wine glass with his voice. Mr. Vendera, a rock singer and vocal coach, tried eleven different glasses before successfully breaking the twelfth.

To break glass, the singer must meet two requirements: generating an extreme volume that forcefully displaces the air molecules and sustaining a note that matches the glass's resonant frequency.

Mr. Vendera's chainsaw-like scream registered 105 decibels. The pitch of his voice exactly matched the twelfth glass's natural frequency.

The wine glass Mr. Vendera shattered measured less than one-sixteenth of an inch thick.

—Professor Waite's Journal

COLORCASTING

EMMA LEANED FORWARD and tried to focus on today's lesson. After Daria left the Coren, Yiana offered to cover 'watch duty' for several of the Sisters, who gladly accepted. Freed from the extra sets of suspicious eyes, Emma and Holly had come to Yiana's workshop every afternoon since.

However, Yiana's gracious offer to teach them about colorcasting had come with a very grave warning; Emma and Holly could not let the other Sisters see that they had colorcasting abilities. Daria had given clear instructions before leaving. "These two girls are abominations without any powers whom, for now, I am willing to tolerate. But if there are any changes, if you see an inkling of ability in either of these girls, report your suspicions to Sasa immediately." Daria could have locked them up like Jack, but instead, she'd left them out in the open to be observed like lab rats. She and Holly were being tested, and if they showed their power, they would fail.

"Closer. You've got the sustain on the back end, but you're still attacking the note. Here, listen again," said Sister Yiana with an encouraging smile. Emma still found herself taken aback each time she made eye contact with the young woman. It wasn't merely that Yiana's brown eyes sparkled with facets of ruby, her eyes radiated with a purity that disarmed her.

Sitting on an upholstered couch across from Emma, Yiana picked up the handbell, its surface polished to a mirrored sheen. Emma caught Holly's wavering reflection; her sister perched on the ledge of a counter, her hands in their usual state of constant motion since arriving here a week ago.

Seven days in the Coren. Emma wrestled with her worries constantly. During the day, she worried about Jack, still trapped in his cell. Acorn was visiting him and relaying information, but that didn't make the separation any easier. And at night, Emma couldn't stop thinking about their dad, imagining him coming home, finding the open stairwell, and grappling with the knowledge of where they had likely gone. Listening to Holly's soft breathing in the other bed, she would try futilely to control her thoughts and bring some sense of order to the chaos in her mind. She lay awake for hours, sleep firmly beyond her grasp—just like the Red Guardian.

Daria had not yet returned. Three days ago, she had used the Portal, a device located inside the Coren that connected the land of Dara to the land of Nima according to Acorn. Unsurprisingly, Acorn was not able to answer Emma's avalanche of questions about the Portal. When the small girl apologized and said that Sister Yiana could explain it much better, Emma felt horrible for making Acorn feel 'less than' again. This land was built on customs that recognized and rewarded the people with Marks, and for Acorn and the other Unmarked, those customs were stacked against them.

Trying to reassure Emma, Acorn said that Daria rarely traveled for long, but Emma's hopes grew dimmer with each passing day. The only bright spot with Daria's absence was that without the Guardian's constant demands, Acorn was spending more time with Jack, going to his cell two or three times each day. To Emma's relief, Jack had begun talking and Acorn glowed as she reported his funny comments. How would Acorn act around Jack once Daria released him? *More like if she releases him.* Emma sighed, frustrated. They were stuck here, powerless, with their fate in the hands of a woman she did not trust who, after taking their kaleidoscope, whisked off to another land.

Yiana's handbell rang out, startling Emma. "Sorry, Sister," she grinned sheepishly, "I got distracted. I was wondering...this Portal that Daria used to leave the Coren. What is it? Can anyone use it?"

"The Portals are ancient devices used to travel between the lands of the Seven. There are two Portals in Dara—one in Ephara the capital city, and one here in the Red Coren. Anyone with a travel pass can use it, but it connects directly to the portal inside the Orange Coren." Yiana grinned at her. "And it is my understanding that Eres Daria visits the Orange Coren quite often."

Emma tried to mask her disappointment. "What about the other Portal in Dara? Does it take people to a different land, someplace besides Nima?"

"Unfortunately, no. The lands of the Seven—picture them lined up in your mind. Dara, Nima, Kasa, Tera, Zala, Hema, Mora. The lands connect to the lands next to them. And please don't ask me why...I'm a musician, not a scientist, remember."

"So, the sculpture in the garden that Holly likes to rub, the Green one from Tera, went from Tera to Kasa, then to Nima before reaching Dara?" Emma asked.

"Exactly right. All imports to Dara must go through Nima, but the people of Nima can trade directly with Dara and Kasa. Which makes a sculpture from Tera or a basket of clams from Zala very expensive here."

"So, one of your cymbalas would be worth a fortune in Zala or maybe Hema?" Holly asked excitedly.

Yiana whistled softly; the sound split into three different tones. "No doubt. But with the taxes and fees levied by the Portal Guild, my share of the profits would be disheartening. Now, enough of that." She smiled and rang the bell again, and her cluttered workshop space filled with a pure B tone, two octaves above Middle C. She looked encouragingly at Emma. "The primary tone from the clapper strike is cocooned in the higher tone. For Yellow, you need to start the sound in the back of your throat to cast the overtone first."

Concentrating, Emma started to sing a low yellow note, but couldn't sustain it. She coughed and cleared her throat while shaking her head in bewilderment at the pretty olive-skinned Sister.

She'd told Yiana how much her friendship meant to them, especially since the other Sisters never spoke to them. She'd given up on expecting any answers. When she vented her frustration about Jack's confinement and asked about freeing him, Yiana listened, telling Emma to wait for Daria's return, urging caution above all. Emma chafed at the idea of doing nothing, but Yiana was right. Getting Jack out wouldn't change their situation. They didn't have the scope and even if they did, the wall surrounding the Coren was fifty feet tall making escape impossible.

As to Daria's whereabouts or when she might return, Yiana assured her that none of the Sisters would know. The Red Guardian came and went as she pleased.

"The higher tone first?" Emma scrunched her nose. "That's not logical. How am I supposed to sing the overtone of a note before I sing the actual note?"

"Logical?" Yiana laughed and used a soft rag to carefully wipe a smudge from the handbell. The clear light tones rang in the Sister's voice as she demonstrated the yellow tone structure. "Music should come from the heart, not the head. In my opinion, at least." Her large eyes flickered mischievously. "My friends in the land of Mora would disagree."

"They don't like music there?" Holly asked, her eyes still focused on the carved cup in her hands. A faint orange light flickered like a candle flame between the tips of Holly's fingers and the surface of the cup.

"It's not like that. They make music, but they don't use instruments," Yiana replied. "Last year, I was permitted to attend the annual Guardian Corenation which took place on Violet. The welcoming ceremony was purely vocal music."

"No instruments?" Emma unsuccessfully tried modulating her voice in Yellow tones. The words sounded muffled; each starting consonant smudged like a mistake.

"They believe instrumentation is unnecessary. Frankly, I couldn't survive without my cymbalas," Yiana said, as she gazed lovingly around her shop, the shelves stacked with dozens of stringed instruments, some finished but most works in progress. "That was a good attempt, by the way. Try dropping your tongue a little more."

Emma forced her tongue down, her eyes involuntarily crossing downwards as if she could see inside her mouth. Realizing how silly she probably looked, she gave up, shaking her head in frustration. With Yiana's coaching sessions, she'd learned to create the basic tones of four of the Seven already: the sustained, cool Violet tone of Mora; the crystal, metallic Indigo tone of Hema; the watery, reverberating sound of Zala; and the natural wood tones of Tera. Yesterday, she'd accidentally created her first two-note chord by singing a Violet F and C at the same time. She gasped with excitement, stunned that the layered sound had come solely out of her mouth, then suddenly felt guilty for enjoying herself while Jack was locked up.

Each color had a distinct signature tone, and since Emma had all seven Marks, Yiana assured her she should be able to generate the sounds of all the lands. With Five Marks, Yiana did not have the Marks of Indigo or Violet. She could not make those tones but was familiar with their timbre and quality from her work with other musicians in Dara. She was confident Emma's tones for those colors were very good and sounded quite natural.

Emma stood up from her chair and bumped into a set of Yiana's soundcasted wind chimes. The colored crystals, each carefully hung with a thin cord and suspended from a wooden disc, swung and bumped into one another, and an ever-changing cascade of sounds flowed through the room. Brassy Oranges sparked against the warm sweeping Red tones, invoking in her a feeling of glowing coals spontaneously flaming. In the Seven, colors were energy, a tangible force, a concept Emma was struggling to fully comprehend.

"Have you been to all of the Lands?" Emma asked, surprised by the strong urge to hear the sounds of these other worlds for herself. "I've only been here a short time, and I'm already curious."

"Yes, technically, while traveling with other Sisters on Coren business. But going portal to portal does not afford one much opportunity to see the sights," Yiana answered, not looking up as she strung a three-color cymbala. She would sell it on the next Coren

Market Day when the grounds opened for trading with townspeople and vendors from Ephara. When the Red Guardian returned from Lindur, she had canceled the upcoming market and closed the main gate, for a reason obvious to Emma; Daria was keeping their existence a secret.

Yiana plucked a string on her cymbala and smiled. "I did go one time with my family to the Flower Festival in Kasa which was breathtaking. Then again, very few people in the Seven travel extensively because of the Fade and its effects."

"The Fade? Is that when a person's energy is used up during colorcasting?" Holly asked, recalling what Acorn had explained.

"No, colorcasting fatigue is a natural process." Yiana stretched her fingers. "When I colorcast an object, I'm drained and tired. But it's a good tired from working hard. Sometimes, I colorcast for so long I can barely stand up, but when I fall exhausted into my bed at night, I'm..."

"Grounded?" Holly said, sliding off her perch and flexing her fingers for a moment before picking up the clay mug that she was touchcasting, holding it tight between both hands, squinting at it.

"... in tune with the world," Yiana smiled.

"And the Fade?" Emma prodded. "That's different?"

"I can tell you what I've seen. Twelve years ago..." Yiana paused, "...No, thirteen years ago, Eres Daria disappeared for nearly a year. I was only six, but I still remember the day she returned. Her Marks had begun to fade as if something had drained them of their vibrancy and life."

"What happened to her?" Holly asked, her eyes wide. "Where was she?"

"It wasn't my place to ask, but I assumed she was with the other Guardians and had a good reason to stay away from Dara for such a long time. You see, in the Seven, we are bound to our homelands by our Marks. The longer and farther away you go, the weaker the bond becomes."

"Like feeling homesick," Holly added. Emma nodded but said nothing. She didn't want to think about home right now.

"For Fives and Sixes?" Emma asked. "Or everyone?"

"Every one of the Marked. My red will grow stronger as I grow older," Yiana said, then pointed to the curling red lines on her throat.

Emma pictured Sister Sasa, who looked to be in her forties. Her red was more pronounced than the nineteen-year-old Yiana. And Daria was fifty-six according to Yiana; her red Mark shimmered with energy. Emma's Marks, which had seemed so livid back home, now paled by comparison.

"Shall we work on your Orange sound now?" Yiana asked. "You were doing quite well yesterday. Though you need more brassiness in your tone."

Emma chuckled at the Sister's critique. Brassy was not her nature. "Thanks, but my throat's already raw. I'm fine watching you work for now."

Yiana resumed her stringing of the cymbala body, its beautifully carved dark wood reflecting the shaft of sunlight coming through the workshop window. Judging by the stacks of carved necks, bodies, and coils of string stacked around her workshop, she loved her work. The selling of the finished instruments was very lucrative; for the price of one finished three-color-casted cymbala, she could buy three months' worth of materials. But as a Sister, she wanted for nothing and didn't care about the money. She sent a monthly stipend to her family—the rest went directly into the Coren's coffers.

Like Acorn, Yiana entered the Coren at the age of five, but in a much different manner than the young Zero. Acorn's family dropped her off unwanted at the Coren. An Unmarked child served no purpose, its presence a hardship and a burden gladly cast off. But when a family was blessed with the birth of a Five, a rare occasion, the baby's birth was announced throughout Dara. The day her parents brought her to the Coren was a truly great day for her and her entire family. Because of Yiana, her family now lived in the capital city of Ephara in a lavish house paid for by the Sisterhood.

The birth of a Guardian was an even more momentous occasion for the land. When a Guardian approached old age and felt the desire to cross into the Light, she first sent Sisters far and wide to share the news. Then, for months on end, women throughout the land came to the Coren to be blessed by the Guardian, each of them hoping to be the one chosen by the Light to become the next Guardian Mother. The arrival of a six-Marked baby was cause for a huge celebration.

The baby was then given to the Coren to raise and educate. At the age of seventeen, with her training completed, the new Guardian assumed her role as Protector of the Light. Her predecessor then crossed over, knowing the land was safe.

Daria was now fifty-six years old, the second oldest of the Guardians. The oldest, Nima-sa-gisnu had recently announced the birth of her successor. The whole concept seemed so strange to Emma; she wasn't sure if she was appalled or intrigued. How would it feel knowing the timing of her death? She analyzed and planned out every aspect of her day. Would having the date of her death inked in her mind, written down like a final deadline for a school project, push her to make different choices?

"Sister Yiana, I made this for you," Holly announced as she walked over to them and carefully placed the mug on the workbench. Yiana straightened up from her work and smiled warmly.

"Holly, thank you so very much for this gift and for your thoughtfulness," Yiana said sincerely with a well-practiced cadence in the words; the Sisters received gifts all the time from the people in Dara. Yiana touched one finger lightly to the handle. "Three colors. Red, orange, and green. Your casting skills are growing very quickly."

Holly beamed at the Sister. "The orange is for keeping your tea hot. And I cast the green to add freshness." Holly picked up the mug and filled it from the small teapot Yiana brought out to her workshop each morning. She held the mug out as if giving her favorite teacher an apple.

"I cast the orange only into the body, so the handle won't get hot," Holly explained as a ribbon of steam rose out of the mug.

"Holly?" Yiana sounded concerned. "When you cast your red for activation, did you remember to wrap the colors like we talked about? To set a stopping point?"

Her sister's eyes popped open wide.

Emma raised her hands in warning. "Hol, put down the—"

Too late. A cloud of steam from the superheated tea burst into the air. Holly squealed in surprise and dropped the mug. The mug shattered, scattering pieces across the floor. Frowning, she knelt and gingerly picked up one of the steaming fragments.

"No, Sister, I forgot to wrap the colors." Holly forced a half-hearted smile onto her lips and shrugged. "Maybe I should stick to eggs."

24

SHARDS

"Acorn, quit your dancing and get back to work!" the head cook yelled from the other side of the kitchen. The older woman turned back to the large kettle simmering on the stove. "Frazzle-headed Zero."

Acorn froze in place, not wanting to get hit again by the large ladle in the cook's hand. She risked a quiet sigh and stared at the mountain of vegetables still needing to be scrubbed and peeled.

At least the floors are done. Acorn smiled at her reflection in the spotless kitchen tiles. To make time for stealing away to talk with Jack, she'd been getting up well before dawn every morning to tackle most of her chores before lunch. Then she'd ask the Sisters if they needed anything, making sure no one would unexpectedly summon her for a task. She risked a beating every time she snuck through the tunnels to visit him. So far, no one seemed the wiser, and the Coren floors looked better than ever.

She hummed to herself as she peeled another carrot. She felt better than ever, too. Jack made her laugh out loud on every visit, and he described the most amazing things about his home on Earth: flying skimms called airplanes; sprawling cities bustling with millions of people, all Unmarked like her; a delicacy called a taco. Her favorite thing so far was the pocket-sized box that could hold thousands of songs.

Earthland sounded like a wonderful place, better than Dara for sure, and maybe better than the other lands in the Seven. Jack's description of his land—so big, fast, and strange—was surprising, but she felt most surprised by her feelings for Emma, Jack, and Holly. She never had friends. She had never even hoped to have friends. The Marked, inside and outside of the Coren, treated her like a Zero. Now her life felt upside down yet much more right. She had two girl friends —both Sevens—who talked with her and even counted on her. And she had Jack with his magical eyes.

What would happen when Daria returned? Would she keep him in the cell? When would Emma, Jack and Holly return home to Earthland? Like the mound of vegetables, her questions piled up high every morning, but she kept them hidden from Emma and Holly.

Acorn picked a grotesquely shaped Nimian root from a basket— one with sharp pointy edges and large splotches of leathery skin. She set the monster root down and pretended to be Jack, using his Budo moves to fight a shard.

When Jack asked about shards during their last visit, Acorn told him the stories, the same stories told to every child in Dara: A single pack of shards killed every man and woman in a village that failed to light its beacons; a boy ignored his parent's warning about playing outside after dark and was never seen again; shards drag noisy children who misbehave down into the dead city of Admahgon and into the waiting arms of Se'en-sii. She'd even told him the stories about the giant monster called Chaos that jumped out of the ground and destroyed villages. But Jack had laughed and, despite her protests and telling him how fast shards moved, Jack had joked confidently he could fight one off.

"When I came to the Coren, I'd never seen a shard and thought they were make-believe," said Acorn. Kneeling in the dark tunnel below Jack, she tried to keep her voice from quivering. She didn't want him to see her as a scared little girl. "Two years ago, they came."

JACK WEDGED HIS BACK FIRMLY INTO THE CORNER OF HIS
cell next to the hole, keeping his hands clasped together. Acorn had
refused to talk about shards and Se'en-sii before. The last thing he
wanted was to get her off-topic by interrupting.

"By the time we heard them coming, it was too late," Acorn
whispered.

Jack desperately wanted a clearer picture of the shards. First, the
village girl had run away terrified that he was one of these creatures.
And now, Acorn was struggling with every word of her story about
surviving an attack. So far, her description gave Jack not much more
than a puzzling set of words to piece together. Creatures, hard and
dark. Big and fast. Sharp claws.

"Go on."

"Shards whine. High-pitched and frantic like starving dogs. Their
jaws make clicking noises. It's horrible."

Jack waited in silence for her to continue. She'd described the
Corenation which took place in the capital that year, the annual gathering of Guardians and attended by the highest Marked of Dara.
Acorn worked the supply runs for the event. On the return trip to the
Coren, Sister Nami was leading the convoy but wasn't happy that
several Sisters stayed behind in the city to visit their families. Sisters
always traveled in numbers for safety.

"I was riding on top of the lead skimm that night on our way back
because I like the wind blowing through my hair." Acorn took a soft
breath and Jack pictured her gliding along the sands, the feeling of
freedom in the night air. "We'd loaded three zind-pulled carts with
fresh food and casks of wine for the Coren pantry."

"Zind? Is that what you call the Horse-Lizards?" Jack asked,
frowning at the thought of his first ride.

"What's a horse?"

"Never mind. Go on."

"There were eight of us on the dunes—me, Sister Nami, and six of
the Coren workers," Acorn said. Her voice was usually full of gasps

and giggles, but now she was speaking slowly, her tone of voice flat and lifeless. "It was Cheri who screamed first, but too late. The shards swarmed in behind us, attacked the rear cart, and it toppled over into the dark."

Jack began to rethink his chances of taking on a shard. His skin itched as he pictured the wagon going down like a capsized boat in a sea of black insects. "You couldn't outrun them?"

"The wagons were full, and shards move fast, even with their weird legs. They have different numbers of legs, three, four, six, sometimes more. Sister Haia once killed a shard that had eleven legs. It kept tripping over itself. She says it's because anything born in the Pit—anything connected to Se'en-sii—must be unnatural." Acorn was talking faster now.

"The Pit? Is that where Shen-sen...Say-un-shi..." Jack reached for the name Acorn had shared with him.

"Se'en-sii. It means the Swallower of Life," Acorn said. "The legends say Sii lives in the Pit with two terrible monsters and is surrounded by thousands of shards. In most of the stories, she's a dark queen who tricks and lures the wicked into turning towards evil."

"Sounds like a fairy tale," Jack said, muttering more to himself than Acorn. "So is Sii real?"

"I don't know," Acorn said, sounding more like herself. "Eres Daria told me the stories are for the weak-minded. She says the reports about giant creatures attacking villages are rumors and that the shards are nothing more than wild animals to be hunted down and killed."

"Acorn, what happened to the convoy?"

She didn't respond for the longest time. Jack forced himself to wait. He wanted to know what happened, but he didn't want to push her. Just when he figured she was done talking, she spoke in a hushed monotone.

"Nami stopped the skimm so hard I nearly fell off the roof. The workers from the two remaining carts cut the zinds loose and then ran to the skimm. Shards like to eat zinds, and most of the pack chased after them. I climbed inside the skimm." Jack heard a shudder in her voice. "Nami and the Ones fought the remaining shards."

"You didn't fight?"

"No, only the Marked fight shards. They're almost impossible to kill without a colorcast weapon. But I can't use colorcast items, so I'm useless in a fight. I'm supposed to run and hide."

"You hide." Jack rolled his head back, thumping it solidly against the hard wall. He stared up at the bleak grey ceiling. "That's why you kept telling me I couldn't fight a shard. Not because of their speed or my martial arts. It's because I'm a Zero."

"I'm sorry, Jack."

"No, it's okay. I don't know the rules of this place," Jack said more lightly than he felt. He imagined himself hiding inside a carriage, peeking out like a timid mouse while his friends fought for their lives.

"I watched the fighting from inside the skimm," Acorn continued. "Nami used her whips to take down the shards. They're braided leather cords with colorcast metal tips on the ends. Nami was really good with them, the fastest in the Coren. Every time she spun in a new direction, the darkness lit up with a blurred swirl of colors. The Ones fought with swords. They have to pierce the shards deep or hit them a lot. One of the survivors said he hit a shard five times to kill it."

"Five times?" Jack asked before fully picking up on her comment. He leaned over the hole in the floor and peered into the shadows. "You said survivors? How many people lived?"

The darkness wrapped around her face, her eyes haunted. "Three. Me and two of the Ones."

"What about Sister Nami? You said she was the fastest with the whips?"

"After the fighting, she came back to the skimm. She said it was all right and I could stop crying. She said all the shards had been killed." Acorn stared up into Jack's eyes. Tears were rolling down her cheeks. "There was one on the roof. It must've heard my screams and was clawing through the roof to get me. When I opened the door, the shard jumped and went straight for Nami's throat and," Acorn choked back a sob, "she died killing it. She died saving me."

There are generally four basic components of a kaleidoscope—eyepiece, external housing, mirror system, and object chamber. The object chamber is also referred to as the "cell". It is the object chamber that holds the objects you choose to view and replicate with your mirror system. When designing your own kaleidoscope, carefully consider your choice of chamber design and the objects. Rotating wheels or cells that are sealed or that can be opened to insert any variety of materials—the choices are nearly endless.

—Excerpt from The Kaleidoscope Book by Thom Boswell included in Professor Waite's Journal

25

DARIA'S RETURN

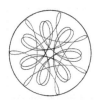

EMMA AND HOLLY followed Acorn across the Coren grounds in the opposite direction from Yiana's workshop and towards a large dome-shaped building, gleaming white in the sun. None of the Sisters had followed them outside into the searing mid-day heat, but Emma guessed that the weather had nothing to do with their lack of chaperone. The Sisters seemed to have grown bored by their presence.

With Yiana's warning ringing in their ears, she and Holly had adopted an attitude of 'do nothing and say nothing' whenever they left their quarters. Emma had reminded Acorn to treat her and Holly like strangers, but to no avail. Each day the Red Guardian was away, the tiny girl's mood improved. The change in her was obvious to Emma.

"Are you sure that you won't get into trouble?" Emma asked as she watched Acorn's red hair bob up and down as she bounced along in front of them.

"Emma, it'll be fine. The Portal room could be dirty, so I need to clean it before Eres Daria returns. Besides, Sister Yiana is on watch today, and I'm sure she won't mind your company. None of the sisters enjoy Portal Watch."

Walking backward as she talked, Acorn spun around on the stone walkway leading up to the building. She bumped into a large potted plant and playfully swatted it with the back of her hand. Acorn flashed a reckless grin. Emma had seen that same grin one too many times on her brother.

"Didn't Yiana say the Coren staff loaded and unloaded the Portal?" Holly asked.

"They do, but Eres Daria says the Ones need to be monitored by a Sister to make sure nothing valuable gets stolen," Acorn replied, spinning, then came to a stop at the base of the building. Unlike the smooth polished walls elsewhere in the Coren, these walls were unfinished, pitted and discolored from age. On their right, the dome was joined to the main complex by an enclosed passageway that, according to Acorn, connected directly to Eres Daria's quarters and used by the Red Guardian alone. To their left, the side of the structure jutted out, forming a squared-off doorway, fifteen feet tall and just as wide, now open to the inside. A sliding metal door was suspended on a metal rail on the far side of the doorway. A constant hum, punctuated by the sound of two voices, reached Emma's ears from inside the dome.

"Wait here," said Acorn in a hushed voice. She crept to the side of the open doorway, peeked inside the room, and then held up one hand. "Okay, when I say go, run to the other side."

Emma frowned. *So much for not getting into trouble.* She stepped forward to tell Acorn to stop and that they didn't need to see the Portal after all.

"GO!" Acorn whispered sharply. Holly dashed past Emma, chasing after the girl.

Darn it! Emma sprinted past the open doorway and beyond the sliding door. The wall of the building curved to her right, and she ran to catch up with them, now standing next to a closed, person-sized door.

"Acorn, why were we running?" Emma said and tried to hide her annoyance. "I thought you said Sister Yiana would be in the Portal Room?"

"She's inside, Emma. But I know you and Holly don't want to be noticed. The Ones are almost done with the Portal shipment. We can wait in the storage area until they leave." Acorn pulled open the door and walked inside.

Emma bit her lip. Acorn was trying to keep them safe.

Emma and Holly followed Acorn inside. There were high stacks of wooden crates and barrels on their left. Thirty feet ahead of them, Emma saw an open door on the inside wall of the dome. If her bearings were correct, that door led back inside the main Coren. A high stone wall on their right blocked their view of the rest of the room.

"Emma! Do you feel it?" Holly asked, her eyes wide with both hands splayed out against the stone wall.

"Probably not like you, but I can hear it." Emma closed her eyes for a moment. The level of energy on the other side of the wall seemed to have increased exponentially. The air vibrated with a low throbbing hum like the beat from a hundred bass drummers, the sound flowing into her. She felt electric.

"What does it feel like, Holly?" Acorn asked.

"Waves of heat like opening a furnace. But more. It's like..." Holly licked her lips as she searched for words. "...I can't describe it."

"Okay." Acorn sounded disappointed.

"You don't feel the colors, do you?"

"No, none of us Unmarked do," Acorn replied softly while Holly put her arm around the slightly shorter girl, like two best friends walking home after a hard day at school. It dawned on Emma that Acorn had become the first friend who instantly understood Holly's markings and talents.

Emma moved to the end of the wall to hide behind a stack of three barrels. She peered through a gap into the Portal room. Not far from Emma, Sister Yiana was sitting at a table laden with two partially strung cymbalas, a bundle of strings, and a tea service. In the middle of the floor was a twenty-foot-wide triangle-shaped platform with a stone ramp built into the side of the platform. Positioned on the other end of the platform at the triangle's point was a colorful stone cylinder, suspended at each end by metal chains attached to the ceiling. Based on the tremendous energy she was feeling, Emma had expected the Portal to be bigger, but it was maybe six feet long, maybe a few feet in diameter.

Staring at the device, waves of sound pounded inside her head. Emma swooned to one side, unsteady on her feet, and reached back to Holly for support.

Staged on the far side of the room, a dozen wheeled carts—loaded with cinched burlap bags and wooden barrels—sat in front of the tall door they had run past just minutes ago. Emma caught a glimpse of a Coren worker—a One with a single red Mark on her arms—exiting the building.

"Ferzhi, shut it down, please. That's all for today's shipment. And don't forget that you promised to play Stones with me this evening," Yiana called out to the remaining worker. Immediately, they strode to the side of the portal and touched the side of the cylinder. Emma sighed with relief as the dizzying waves of sound inside her head disappeared. She massaged her temples with her fingers as the worker walked out the tall door.

"Hello, Emma and Holly. Acorn, have you now added tour guide to your list of duties?" Yiana's voice rang out clearly in the now quiet room; she'd obviously heard their less-than-stealthy entrance.

Acorn bolted from behind the barrels, then froze like a deer. "Sister. No, I was going to..." her feet shuffled in place. "...I meant to say, I need to sweep the room. Sweeping the Portal room is one of my chores."

Yiana held Acorn with her gaze for a moment more and smiled knowingly. The Sister rotated her head, looking slowly around the room. The place was spotless. Not a single speck of dust.

"Yes. Quite the mess." Yiana took a small sip from the cup in front of her. "Eresi, would you join me for tea?"

The girls walked over and sat; Acorn didn't budge from her spot. "Your broom, Acorn," said Yiana. Acorn grabbed onto the Sister's excuse to move. Dashing to the broom propped up in the corner of the storage space, she started sweeping, her eyes now staring doggedly at the floor.

Yiana poured two cups of tea for the girls. The pungent smell of cardamom wafted across the table.

"You must not get too familiar with Acorn. I understand you have not been in Dara long and from what you've shared with me, our ways are very strange. Inside the walls of the Coren, the space between our Marks may get blurred. Outside these walls, the people of Dara will expect strict adherence to your Marks. As Sevens, I'm afraid you may find yourself destined to a life of ceremony and confronted with a new level of formality. Treating Zeros as equals will not be viewed as proper. It may even raise suspicions you do not want."

She leaned back in her chair. "On my Marks. As a Five, I should not be lecturing Sevens. Now, Holly, you're staring at the Portal behind me. You have questions, I gather?"

Holly jumped up from her seat. "Can I touch it?"

"No," Yiana shook her head. Holly sat back down a disappointed look on her face. "You could inadvertently touch the primary tile and turn it on."

Emma sipped her tea. The Portal was nothing like she'd imagined. She'd assumed a device capable of transporting wagonloads of goods would be at least wagon-sized, even bigger. But the hollow tube was barely big enough for a person to crawl through. And unlike the kaleidoscope, the cylinder was empty inside with no lenses or glass. Through the open end of the tube, the wall on the other side of the room was clearly visible.

She had been wrong about the color, too. Emma laughed at herself. After hearing Yiana's stories about the Seven and trying to master the colorspeech of each land, Emma had expected the Portal to be some sort of rainbow door. Instead, the cylinder was primarily two colors—red and orange—but in a mosaic of varying shades. The outside was inlaid with thousands of gleaming stones. A band of red circled the end of the Portal closest to them. The colors morphed into orange tones along the length of the suspended cylinder, and the far end was wrapped in a ring of fire orange. Emma closed her eyes, thinking about Jack's description of his scope sensations as the sparkling colors faded inside her eyelids.

"A Guardian made that?" Holly sounded stunned. "Every stone is colorcast, isn't it?"

"Yes, every stone. Two thousand four hundred and one, to be exact," Yiana said, yawning. "Excuse me, portal watch is very boring."

"But to colorcast all of them would take..." Holly said slowly, "....casting eight hours a day, and if I could cast one stone an hour...umm...over two hundred and fifty days. Right?"

"You're a bit under. I asked the same question the first time I saw a Portal. Sister Sasa said it would take one person twenty years to complete. Each stone is cast with a different and very precise combination of colors and requires several days of colorcasting. According to legend, these portals were made during the time of the Prophet by the First Guardians. The portal in the capitol city is the same construction —thousands of different stones—but controlled by the Portal Guild. As Guardian, Daria controls this one."

Emma pointed at the opening of the cylinder. "The portals are like the sections in the kaleidoscope."

"And the Red Portals go to Orange and nowhere else?" Holly asked.

"Yes. But the Portals in Nima have three colors – red at one end, orange in the middle, and yellow at the other. Think of them like a two-way portal."

"So, the people in Nima can travel and trade with Dara and Kasa, but Dara connects solely to Nima." Emma pursed her lips, silently reciting the names of the lands, as she tried unsuccessfully to figure out the logistics of seven lands seemingly lined up in space.

"Twenty whole years of colorcasting," Holly mused out loud, "and if it broke, no one could get into Dara?"

"No, it's the other way around. Do you see that red crystal embedded in the floor of the platform?" Yiana pointed and continued. "That crystal was colorcasted in Nima at the same time as the portal – it's connected, like a homing beacon. When the portal in the Orange Coren is turned on, it sends everyone and everything directly to that platform." Yiana shook her head. "If the Red Coren Portal stopped working, one could not use it to leave Dara. The Coren would be forced to use the portal in Ephara."

Acorn looked up from where she knelt, polishing the portal platform with her ever-handy cleaning rag. The large red crystal was inlaid on the floor, like a bullseye on a target. "Oooh, that would be bad. Eres Daria likes to come and go as she pleases."

"And I've noticed how much you like it when Eres Daria is away," Yiana teased as she picked up the pot of tea and began refilling their cups.

Acorn's cheeks appeared to flush scarlet, but not from blushing. The red glow was coming up from the large red spot underneath her. The platform erupted into an orange burst of lava light and enveloped her. Emma grabbed at her ears as a deafening rush of sizzling sound filled the room. Yiana leapt to her feet.

"ACORN! GET OFF THE PLATFORM!"

Blinded by the light, Acorn spun and stumbled to her feet. She stepped sideways off the edge of the platform and tumbled to the floor. Holly stepped forward to help her up but stopped mid-step as the orange light disappeared. Daria glared down from the center of the platform, her eyes flaring as if the colored energy from the Portal had burned away and reignited in her fiery stare. Emma braced for the coming tirade.

"Yiana. You have the watch?" Daria asked, her tone surprisingly quiet and controlled. The Red Guardian's shoulders were stooped as if she were too tired to stand up straight.

"Yes, Eres," Yiana said, her head making a small, respectful nod. She gestured towards Emma and Holly. "Our guests inquired about the Portal, and I took the liberty to give them a brief tour. I'm sure this experience of seeing your arrival first-hand has made quite the impression. Do you have any questions, Eres Emma?" Yiana paused and stared directly at them. "Eres Holly?"

"No, none at all. Thank you, Sister, for your time," Emma replied, carefully mirroring the Sister's formal tone as she turned to the Guardian. At least Daria was back. Emma fought down the urge to ask about Jack's imprisonment; this was not the moment. She would find the Red Guardian first thing in the morning. "Eres Daria, please pardon our intrusion. With your permission, we will retire to our quarters."

Daria stared back, unspeaking, peering at Emma's neck. *She's scrutinizing my Marks, searching for something.* Emma swallowed nervously. Could Daria discern differences in her Marks because of their practicing colorcasting with Yiana? The flaking skin and itching on Emma's throat had lessened these past two weeks, but her Marks hadn't changed. She prayed Daria would not ask any questions.

Daria said nothing. Her narrowed gaze moved to Holly and slid like a snake up and down Holly's arms.

Emma wasted no time. With a small nod, Emma spun on her heels, hooking Holly's arm in hers and pulling her along. She locked eyes with Holly and mouthed a silent no to keep her sister from speaking, uncomfortably aware of Daria's stare on the back of her neck as she led Holly out the doorway.

～

"GET UP." DARIA WALKED DOWN THE RAMP, PASSING Acorn without a second glance. She scrambled to her feet surprised that Daria had not given her a swift kick. "Your chores can wait."

"Have either of those girls demonstrated any skills or casting powers?" Daria addressed Yiana. She stopped next to the table and slowly picked up a cup of tea, sniffed, and took a small sip.

"No, neither has shown any powers. We have kept them under close observation as you ordered."

Daria took another slow sip of the tea. "Acorn," she said, not bothering to turn around. "Have you observed anything strange?"

Acorn hesitated. Her mind was racing from the shock of Yiana's lying to Daria, not only about Emma and Holly's powers growing every day, but about the Portal room visit, surely to protect Emma and Holly, but to protect her, too.

Acorn stared wide-eyed at Daria's back. All the time she'd spent with Jack and Holly and Emma—having so much fun—she'd forgotten what would happen once her mistress returned. Daria was the Red Guardian. She would never allow a Zero to be friends with Sevens. Emma and Holly would join the Coren and her life would go back to the way it was before: chores and cleaning and cooking and being treated like a servant by everyone. Acorn gulped. Holly, her first friend ever, would have to treat her like a Zero. Unless...

"No, Eres," Acorn lied. *Please don't turn around.* She felt like her face was melting off, her lie fully exposed. She looked at Yiana for support, but the Sister's eyes were fixed on the Guardian. "Nothing at all. Not during meal service or while cleaning their room."

Daria set down the cup of tea. "Good. Bring a platter to my quarters. Also, I want the Prophet's Cloth delivered and hung on the wall of my inner study immediately."

"The Prophet's Cloth, Eres? I don't know—"

"I don't expect you to know!" Daria snapped with a dismissive glance at Acorn. "Tell the Archivist what I want. And Yianna, bring Sasa and Haia to my quarters in two hours for a discussion about our *guests.*" Daria walked stiffly across the stone floor and out the doorway.

Acorn let out a deep breath. Standing motionless next to the table, Yiana seemed distracted, her eyes focused on the space beyond the empty doorway, her head tilted as if listening for something. Acorn started to speak, anxious to ask about the lies they had told, but Yiana raised one finger.

"Acorn. Attend to the Guardian's request so she may be well rested for the meeting." The room stood in silence as Yiana paused and looked closely at her. Acorn felt like she was examining her as if looking for an answer, and Acorn started to fidget, wondering if she had missed the question. She took a small step towards the exit, not sure if she should leave. Yiana spoke again, this time very softly. "Yes, please ensure everything is in place for Daria's meeting. I am sure the information shared there will be very important to Emma and Holly. Go on."

Grateful to be dismissed, Acorn turned and walked to the doorway, glancing back at Yiana. The Sister still stood unmoving, her eyes once again staring into space.

Acorn ran down the hallway, her mind swirling. When she reached Daria's wing, instead of running across the Coren, she turned to the wall and pushed open a decorative metal grate that covered one of the old tunnel openings. She ducked inside and raced along the low narrow passageways, taking a shortcut directly to the kitchen. Out of breath, she popped out of a wall opening located behind the grain barrels. Grabbing a silver platter, she quickly covered it with enough meat and cheese to feed three people. She tossed on a handful of dates, added Daria's favorite bread, and stepped back to inspect her work. Satisfied, she ducked back into the tunnel with the food and headed to Daria's wing, her thoughts from the Portal Room quickly catching her.

Yiana had lied about the girls' powers, and now, for the first time ever, Acorn had lied to the Red Guardian. There was something peculiar in the way Daria had asked her questions about the girls, talking quietly, casually sipping tea, asking if she'd seen anything 'strange' about Emma and Holly. They were learning new skills every day, and it would only be a matter of time before Daria and the Sisters recognized their powers. And then, her new friends would join the Sisterhood... or would they? Daria had acted as if it would be a bad thing for Emma and Holly to have colorcasting powers, but why wouldn't she want more Sisters? Acorn's head hurt and she felt nowhere closer to the answer as she approached the Guardian's quarters.

Acorn turned down the passage that led directly to Daria's study. She crouched down and peered through the metal latticework of the small, hinged door. The study was empty. She pulled open the door, ducked through, and hurried across the room, carefully weaving her way between the maze of stands and pedestals, each displaying different sculptures and artifacts collected from the Seven. Daria always paced like a bull when she was angry, and Acorn was amazed nothing had been broken. Stopping in front of the massive carved desk, Acorn set the platter down, then stepped back in surprise, her back bumping against one of the pedestals.

The kaleidoscope—Jack's scope—rested on the corner of the desk. Acorn had not seen the scope since taking it from the Mayor of Lindur, and then, for only a moment. But she knew this was Jack's by its intricate markings and seven segments. He had described the scope to her several times, telling her how badly he needed to get it back so he could take Emma and Holly home.

Acorn carefully backed out of the room and into the tunnel. Heading towards the Archives, she mulled over a question she'd asked Jack. He'd finished describing the red colors inside the kaleidoscope and before she could stop, Acorn blurted out loud if he could take her through the scope, too. "Sure," he'd replied casually, "would you want to go with us?"

Would I? His question had bothered her for days. *Would I leave the Coren?* Before Jack, Emma, and Holly showed up, she'd never thought about leaving. The Ones who staffed the kitchen, stables, and grounds were nice enough to her. A few of the Sisters like Yiana treated her with kindness. But she knew the hard truth. She was one of the Unmarked and a slave to the Coren. Nothing more.

But with Jack and the girls, she felt like so much more. They talked to her and listened to her and treated her like an equal—like a friend. *Could I leave?* Acorn stopped cold in the middle of the tunnel. The idea was crazy. She could never leave the Coren. Daria would never allow her to go.

Acorn left her thoughts behind and exited the tunnel by the edge of the dining area, already scanning the room and locating Taeni, one of the Archive workers who liked to play Stones with the others before the evening meal. Acorn ran straight through the planted garden bed, scattering dirt onto the walkway.

Haia, who won most of the games, looked up in annoyance. "Allanu, turn around and clean up that mess."

Acorn stepped over to Taeni who was setting up her stones for the next roll. "Yes, Sister Haia. Taeni, I have instructions to give you. The Archivist needs to deliver and hang the Prophet's Cloth in Eres Daria's inner study right away."

Distracted from her game, Taeni scowled over the wooden rack of colorful stones in front of her. "Not now Acorn. I'll get to it after dinner."

Acorn started to interrupt, but Haia spoke first. "By my Marks, Zero, we are busy. Frankly, Sister Sasa takes her role as First Sister much too seriously. Imagine decorating Eres Daria's study while she travels. So presumptuous." Haia glanced at Acorn and scoffed. "That means bold."

"Sister Sasa did not ask for the Cloth." Acorn paused on purpose, anticipating the next question, and already enjoying the reaction she expected. Haia never treated her nicely.

"So, who gave you the order, Alla-nu?"

"Eres Daria. She's back. And she said immediately." *That means now.*

Relishing the commotion as Haia and Taeni jumped up from the table and hurried off towards the Archives, Acorn spun lightly on her heels and skipped back to the tunnel opening.

EAVESDROPPING

BACK IN THE KITCHEN, Acorn started the slow process of making rolls for the evening meal. Punching down the batch of dough she had prepared earlier in the day, she began rolling it out into a log. With a light flick of her wrists, she stretched the bread by slapping it on the counter. White puffs of flour floated up around her like a cloud, and she peered through the dust at the light of the warm red sunset through the kitchen window.

Eres Daria would be meeting with Sister Sasa and Sister Haia any time now. She distractedly picked up the log of dough and slapped it down. *Discussing the outcome of her travels.* Acorn's fingers reached out, halfheartedly wrapping around the handle of a bench knife for forming the rolls. *Sharing any decisions made about Emma and Holly.* She raised the knife and stared at the flicker of red sunlight caught on the blade. *Talking about Jack.* Acorn's hand shook, the blade of the knife vibrating back and forth, not knowing which way to cut. *Jack's fate.*

Acorn tossed the knife aside. She had to know. She ducked past the grain barrels and ran through the tunnels. Twenty yards from her small servant entrance, she paused, letting her breath catch up to her. Voices came from Daria's study, and she moved closer, hiding in the shadows behind the small metal grate.

"Eres, forgive me, but I assumed you would present this to the entire Council," Yiana was talking. "The arrival of Sevens—"

"You assumed wrong," Daria cut her off. "Nimia and I have more experience combined than the rest of them and she agreed with me. I don't need the full Council's opinion, especially to handle a problem in my land."

"An excellent decision, Eres. You and Eres Nimia are undoubtedly the wisest of the Guardians," Sasa replied, and Acorn rolled her eyes. "Besides, you said the last Gathering was pointless."

"A complete waste of my time," Daria scoffed, her voice rising. "I made one proposal about forbidding Zeros to breed and got two weeks of never-ending questioning and prattling on about culture and rights and other nonsense only to be summarily overruled." Acorn shrunk away from the grate as the Red Guardian paced furiously about her study.

"Will we be moving the boy to a room in the west wing? To join the girls?" Yiana asked.

Daria's boots clicked on the floor as she crossed the room and took her seat.

"No, Nimia and I thoroughly considered the potential pitfalls posed by these children. With his white eyes, the boy bears too much resemblance to the legendary Prophet. The last thing we need is a religious uprising spurred on by his appearance."

"But what if he truly is—"

"Yiana, don't be ridiculous," Sasa said. "Are you actually suggesting this Zero is a reincarnation of the Prophet? He knows nothing of the Seven and has no powers."

"Tell me what is hanging on my wall, Yiana," Daria said. Acorn leaned forward but could not see farther into the room without risking detection.

"The Prophet."

"Exactly. The Messenger for the Light. And who else?"

"No one else," Haia chimed in. "According to the History, the Prophet stands alone."

"Exactly Haia. He alone came over three thousand years ago. He alone brought the wisdom and knowledge needed to build the Portals and connect the Seven. The answer is clear to me." Daria cleared her throat, then lowered her voice as if sharing a secret, "This *boy*—along with his supposed sisters—is obviously part of a Farker plot to over-throw the government. The Farker movement is growing stronger every day in Dara and across the Seven."

Acorn's breath froze in her chest in the darkness of the tunnel. Everything her mistress was saying seemed wrong. How could her new friends be involved with the Farkers or have anything to do with a prophet, whoever that was? They were from Earthland. They just wanted to go home.

"The boy, of course, must remain confined in his cell. In a few days, I will question him, but for now, Yiana, furnish his cell with a few comforts and tell the cook to feed him properly. After all, he must understand that I am not cruel."

"On my Marks. I will do what is best for the boy," Yiana replied.

Acorn wanted to burst into the room and scream. How could Yiana sit there and agree to keep Jack locked up in a cell? *Emma and Holly will be crushed.* She sat on her hands, barely able to control herself.

"And the two girls?" asked Yiana.

"They are abominations. Nimia agreed wholeheartedly with my assessment...their Marks are unnatural."

"That would explain their inability to colorcast," Haia offered up.

Acorn took in a few deep breaths to calm herself down. She didn't understand what was happening. Yiana knew Emma and Holly's Marks were real. Wouldn't telling the truth be the best way to help her friends?

"Yes, but even without powers, those two are a threat. In all of recorded history, there has never been a Seven in the Lands. If the exis-tence of these girls became known, there would be questions about their origin, questions that would lead to doubt and debate that could weaken our society, even destroy the Sisterhood. There are already too many people not happy with the Coren's influence."

"So, they will remain in seclusion?" Yiana prompted.

"No, that is not an option." Daria sighed loudly. "Freaks of nature or not, we cannot take the chance of them developing any powers. Imagine the turmoil and trouble they could cause if they harnessed the ability to colorcast with seven colors. They could impose their will on anyone. No, keeping them in the Coren—in such proximity to the Sisterhood and our natural gifts—is too great a risk to our way of life."

Acorn listened from her hiding place and waited for Sister Yiana to speak up. Daria's fears about Emma and Holly made no sense. They would never hurt anyone. Yiana must know that. Surely, she would speak up and defend them. Acorn waited and instead, Sasa spoke.

"I completely agree, Eres. I have been troubled deeply since their arrival, and the entire Coren has been disturbed as well. Their Marks are unnatural, and who knows from where they came. What is to be done with them?"

Acorn clenched her fists so hard they hurt. She wanted to shove Sasa's words back into her mouth. She heard the Red Guardian push back her chair.

"After long and careful consideration, Nimia and I came to the same conclusion. They are a threat to the Seven and as the Red Guardian and protector of Dara, I have no choice but to take action. In the morning, bring the girls to my chambers. They must be killed."

Acorn's stomach lurched violently. She slapped her hands across her lips and swallowed back the bitter taste of bile.

EMMA COULDN'T BELIEVE HER EARS. BUT SHE BELIEVED THE fear in Acorn's eyes. As Acorn struggled to share her news, Holly sat with one arm wrapped tightly around the girl's shoulders. Both girls were trembling.

Emma leaned on the edge of the table, forcing herself to absorb Acorn's story. "They must be killed," Emma repeated the words carefully as Acorn slumped against Holly. Even saying the words out loud was a struggle. "Are you sure that's what she said?"

Acorn nodded helplessly as her lower lip started to quiver again. Holly, her brown eyes wide with fear, looked questioningly up at Emma.

"I know, Hol. Let me think a minute." Trying not to fall apart herself, Emma deliberately looked away from the girls and stared up at the ceiling. In her head, Emma replayed everything Acorn told them about Daria's return and the conversation with the Sisters. "So, Yiana lied to the Guardian's face about our powers, but said nothing in the meeting about keeping Jack locked up? Or us being killed?"

Acorn sniffled. "After Eres Daria said that she was going to...umm, kill you and Holly," Acorn's voice cracked, "it was really hard to keep listening. Sister Sasa asked about the risk of Turning and the toll this could take on Daria, and then there was something about the needs of the many versus the needs of the few, I think. When Yiana asked to be excused, I snuck away."

Holly was on the verge of tears. Emma stayed at the table even though she wanted to console her, hug her, and tell her it would be all right. But none of this was all right. Emma's eyes narrowed as she raced through her thoughts, rapidly flipping every detail in her mind like the pages of a book.

Screw the hugs. We need a plan.

"Okay." Emma stood up and tried to sound stronger than she felt. Trying to ignore the shaking in her legs which was threatening to engulf her whole body, she blew out a long, slow breath and stilled her mind. The plan in her head might work, but they didn't have much time and had to act now. "Here's what we're going to do."

27

PLAN B

JACK COULDN'T SLEEP. But not sleeping was *not* his problem.

He was always oversleeping at home, forcing their dad to stomp into his room, throw on the lights, and grumble about sleeping his life away. At night, he would find reasons to stay up too late—one more chapter in a book, one more level in a video game. He was tired all the time.

Here in his cell without the alarm clock and his dad's wakeups, Jack was getting plenty of sleep. His first days in captivity, he'd slept beyond noon and awakened to find his breakfast tray and his lunch tray sitting side by side. Since day six, he woke early, eager for Acorn's first visit of the day. He ate while they talked and then spent his afternoon training, alternating between reciting the Budo codes, stretching, and practicing his kicks and movements. He then took a short nap before dinner and Acorn's evening visit.

Jack chuckled. Except for being locked up in a cell as the prisoner of a decidedly unpleasant group of red-robed witches and being thousand—if not millions—of miles away from home with no clear way to get back...he felt good. Well-rested, actually. Feeling good...*that* was his problem.

At night, he sat on his cot—counting each new star as the maroon sky turned black behind the barred window—and tried to feel bad. He knew he should, but no matter what terrible image he conjured up in his mind, he never felt truly bad. He pictured their dad and how worried he must be by their disappearance, envisioned him discovering the open door, finding the kaleidoscope gone, calling their names. Jack gazed at the ceiling, waiting for some feeling of regret to overwhelm him, but nothing happened. He felt guilty. Holly must have shed a thousand tears by now from missing their dad, and Emma was never going to let him off the hook for dragging the three of them through the scope. He stretched out on the cot with his arms crossed behind his head and smiled at the irony. *The main reason I feel bad is because I don't feel bad.*

Still not sleepy, he closed his eyes and saw Holly.

He jerked upright. Staring at the door of his cell, he grasped at the fleeting sensation of someone coming his way. In the past few days, he had felt Acorn's presence in the tunnel *before* she arrived. At first, he dismissed the sensation—likely the sound of passing footfalls or the echo from a door closing—but after sensing the arrival of his food tray the last three meals in a row, Jack considered he might be on to something special. He cleared his head and tried to picture the space past the door, into the hallway beyond.

He saw Holly coming towards his location and something else, much more subtle, like a sense of determination in her steps. Jack shook his head, confused by the vision, and tried again. Now he felt Acorn's presence, too, but not from the tunnel opening. Acorn and Holly were walking together up to his cell.

"Jack!" Emma's sharp whisper stung his ears like a dart. *Okay. So, Emma, Acorn, and Holly are at my cell door. Gotta keep working on the Spidey-sense.*

"Emma! What are you doing here?" Jack shouted as he dashed over to the cell door.

"Shhhhhhh!" Again, the stabbing whisper in his ear. "Don't talk. We're here to rescue you. I'll tell you what's happening while Holly gets the door open."

"Holly can open the—"

"SSSHHHHHH! Stop talking for once in your life and listen to me. I've learned how to focus my voice so you can—"

"No way! Emma, you're like—"

"SHUT UP, JACK!" Emma's voice ripped through Jack's head. "Yes, you were right all along. I have superpowers. Now, listen so I can fill you in. Just listen."

AS SHE TOLD JACK WHAT ACORN HAD LEARNED, EMMA nervously checked on Holly's progress out of the corner of her eye. Holly was struggling with the five-color lock on the cell door. After deciding to break Jack out while everyone in the Coren slept, Emma told Holly she would have to open the five-color lock. Holly had balked at first; she'd only cast three colors in Yiana's workshop. But after several minutes of reassuring her, Holly said she would try. Emma knew she was expecting a lot from her little sister, maybe too much. But Holly's abilities had been growing fast. Hopefully, fast enough.

Emma glanced over at Acorn, standing watch with their packs of supplies at the base of the ramp. It was well past midnight. Acorn said that no one would be around this time of night, but Emma was still worried. Holly's first three attempts to open the lock failed. Emma turned back to Holly and watched as she slowly traced her finger along the carved symbol on the cell door. This time, a faint thin ribbon of red, green, and orange light spun out of her sister's fingertip. It looked like Holly was finger painting with light on the door.

"I don't..." Holly's hand dropped. She slumped forward, resting her forehead on the door. She was muttering to herself.

Emma chewed on her lower lip and told herself to stay calm. But Holly had failed four times now, and the clock was ticking on their lives. She reached out and gently rubbed Holly's back. "You're mumbling, bug," she said, keeping her voice light. "Are you alright?"

"Yeah. No." Holly groaned as she pushed back from the door and stared at the symbol. "I can feel how it works, but the lock won't open unless I activate five colors at the same time—red, yellow, green, blue and orange. It's too hard." Using her left arm as a support, Holly positioned her right hand in front of the symbol. She pointed her index finger and took a few deep breaths as if she were readying herself to lift something heavy. A ribbon of woven colors, this time slightly brighter, darted out from the end of her finger.

Emma stared at the colors, looking hard for all five: Red, Orange, Green, and yes, a flash of Yellow this time. She leaned in for a closer look just as the colors disappeared.

Grunting in exasperation, Holly wobbled on her feet and slumped to the floor. Acorn dashed over, her face full of concern, and knelt on the floor next to her. Holly was rubbing her right hand gingerly as if she might have sprained it. "I can't do it."

"It's okay. It was a long shot anyway." Emma forced a smile and turned away to hide her disappointment. She didn't want to make Holly feel any worse or risk making her cry. "Acorn, we're going to move on to Plan B. Are you positive Daria's asleep?"

Acorn popped up, nodding, "Yes, Emma."

"Plan B? What happened to Plan A?" Jack whispered through the cell door.

Emma turned back to the cell. "Plan A was simple. First, we free you. Then, we get the kaleidoscope back, and you take us home. But Holly can't open the lock, so we go with Plan B." She waited for Jack to say something, but he didn't. She took a deep breath. "Okay, don't freak out. I suspected we might not be able to get you out. We have to leave you behind while we steal the kaleidoscope from Daria's study and escape the Coren."

"You're going to leave me? That's your Plan B?"

"Yes, because for some insane reason, Daria wants me and Holly dead," Emma paused for Jack to interrupt as usual, but there was no response. "Listen, I know it sounds bad, but if we can escape and hide the scope, she won't be able to kill us. Then, we can negotiate to get you out." Still no reply from Jack. "She obviously wants the kaleidoscope."

"Run away, hide the scope, and leave me behind. That's Plan B?"

"Yes."

"I don't like Plan B," Jack replied.

"Neither do I," said Sister Yiana as she stepped out from the shadows.

28

ACORN'S CHOICE

"Sister Yiana? What are you doing here?" Acorn asked, squeaking out the words. Next to Emma, the girl's feet shifted nervously as if not sure whether to stand or run.

Smiling warmly, Yiana walked over to them and then reached out to help Holly stand. "Eres Holly, I am very impressed. That was a tremendous effort you made trying to open the lock."

"Sister, please forgive me," Emma said while modulating her voice with a respectful formality. "I should have trusted my ears. Earlier, you protected us and Acorn, and you gave her the hint to eavesdrop. But when she said you didn't argue with Daria's plan for us, I wasn't sure I could risk asking you for help."

Yiana frowned slightly and looked over at Acorn. "Odd, I clearly remember saying that I would do what is best for the boy."

"On my Marks, Sister." Acorn looked back and forth between them, a look of relief dawning on her face. "I forgot that part."

Jack interrupted from his cell. "Hello? People outside the door. Enough with the apologies already! You're supposed to be breaking me out."

Yiana stepped over to the cell door, her hand poised by the lock. She looked playfully at Holly, still breathing hard and her face sweaty from her efforts. "May I? His manners are quite atrocious."

"I guess we have to since Daria could change her mind about him." Holly's crestfallen face had changed to a smile of relief now that Yiana was here. "And if anyone's going to kill him, it's going to be us."

The Sister effortlessly traced the symbol with her finger. The door whooshed open.

Jack stood in the doorway, tapping his wrist as if wearing a watch. Emma shook her head at him, recognizing their dad's familiar habit. "Well, it's about time!" he said with a smile so big it filled the corridor.

Emma swooped in and gave him a big hug. "More than a week in prison and the best you could do was pull a dad joke?"

Jack ignored her and gave a short respectful bow to Sister Yiana. "Thank you for helping us."

Holly looked up at Yiana. "What if Daria finds out you helped Jack escape?"

"I'm confident she will not. No one suspects that I was giving you lessons. Otherwise, one of the Sisters would have already confronted me. Of course, Daria will be furious we Sisters missed any signs of your growing powers, but she ordered us to avoid contact with you." Yiana mimed an innocent shrug and grinned. "How was I to know Eres Holly had developed the power of a Five?" Her smile disappeared. "Besides, she will have another target more deserving of her anger—Acorn."

"What?" Acorn gasped. "Me?"

Yiana knelt in front of the small girl, now starting to tremble. "Yes. You." She put her hands on Acorn's shoulders. "Now, I need you to listen carefully. You must make a choice."

"A choice?" Swaying on her feet, Acorn looked like she was drowning with only the Sister's grip keeping her afloat.

"Yes, a choice with consequence. So far, your choices—to spend time with Emma and Holly, to visit Jack, to become their friend—can be undone. Even your involvement tonight with their escape can remain hidden if you so choose."

Acorn managed a small nod, visibly unsettled by Yiana's words. Emma was even more impressed by the Sister.

"Once they take the kaleidoscope, you will have a decision to make. You can stay in the Coren. Daria will scream at you for not seeing the power in the girls. She will beat you. But she won't kill you. Good servants are hard to find, and you are a very good servant. You can choose to remain here," Yiana paused, allowing the words to fully sink in as she looked at Emma, a question in her eyes and Emma nodded yes immediately, "or you can leave Dara and go with them."

"Leave the land?" Acorn's mouth went slack. She stared wide-eyed at Emma, then at Jack. "You're going home to Earthland tonight?"

"Yes, if the kaleidoscope shows Jack the doorway back, we'll go home," replied Emma. "And you can come with us."

Sister Yiana smiled reassuringly at Acorn. "You can choose to leave. I know how scary this sounds, but be assured, staying is a risk; if Daria should learn that you helped them escape, she will kill you." Yiana reached up and gently cupped the shaking girl's chin. "Life is all about choices, Alla-nu. Usually, the choices are small, but the seemingly harmless ones add up. Tonight, you will need to make a bigger choice. Do you understand?"

"Yes, Sister," Acorn answered in a quivering voice.

"Yiana, we have to go." Emma knew they had to get moving. "The eastern tunnel exit, through the unused waterway. Acorn said it would be the fastest way out of the Coren."

"Yes, and the obvious choice for your escape which is why you have a different plan in mind, correct?" Yiana stood and smiled knowingly. "When we discover your disappearance in the morning, the search will almost certainly start to the east of the Coren."

Emma smiled, overcome with gratitude. "Yiana, I don't know what to say. I mean, we owe you our lives," Emma said. "I don't know how to thank you enough."

Yiana clasped both her and Holly on the shoulders. "Keep practicing. I expect to be very impressed the next time we sit down for tea."

"Thank you for the lessons." Holly hugged her around the waist.

She lightly stroked Holly's cheek with her fingers, then pulled back. She looked over at Jack, her face sober. "Goodbye, Jack. I expect big things from you as well." Quickly, she turned and disappeared down the corridor.

Jack shouldered the leather pack the girls had brought for him.

"Okay, Master Planner," he grinned at Emma, "how do we steal the kaleidoscope?"

29

DARIA'S STUDY

THEY MOVED QUICKLY through the servant passage, doing their best to walk quietly, cringing each time one of their packs rubbed against the tunnel walls. Jack desperately wanted to talk, and ask more about their escape plan, but the narrow passage forced them into a single file. Emma, hunched over from the low ceiling, walked ten feet ahead of him.

"Emma. Emma," Jack said her name in the smallest of whispers, like checking a walkie-talkie behind enemy lines. She had obviously developed powers with her voice and hearing. "One, two. Come in, Emma."

"Shhh!" Emma's whisper rang in his ear as if she were next to him. "I'm not a radio. Don't test me."

"Sorry," Jack whispered back. *Amazing. She can target her voice backward.*

Up ahead, Acorn slowed. The tunnel turned sharply to the right, went down a steep incline, and leveled out before forking in several directions, one path mostly blocked by a jagged hole in the floor. Acorn stepped around the dark hole and motioned them in close.

"How far?" Emma asked.

"Several hundred feet. Up ahead the tunnel will rise back up to the main level. Two left turns put us in front of my servant's door."

"Okay. And after we leave Daria's study, which tunnel would take us east?"

"That way." Acorn pointed. "Out the old waterway towards the river."

"Good," Emma said as she chewed on her lower lip. Jack realized she was mentally checking off each step in her plan. "Holly, you wait here with the packs."

Holly was shaking her head no and blinking back the rapidly forming tears.

"Fine." Emma sighed. "Everyone, drop your packs and we will *all* creep to the study. I'll listen for any sounds while Acorn goes inside and grabs the kaleidoscope off Daria's desk. Then we come back here. Got it?"

Jack gave her a thumbs-up sign as Emma turned and moved silently up the steep incline. She paused at each turn, her head slightly cocked first to one side and then the other. The only noise Jack could hear was his breathing, but he guessed she was picking up on every sound within a hundred feet. They followed her around the final corner. As Emma listened into Daria's quarters, Jack risked sliding up next to her. He took a knee next to the small grate and peered inside. No movement.

With a nod from Emma, Acorn carefully pushed the grate open. The tiny metallic click of the latch sounded incredibly loud against the dead silence of the tunnel. Jack cringed and felt Emma stiffen behind him, but Acorn squeezed smoothly through the small door and stood up. She tiptoed slowly across the room.

Jack caught glimpses of Acorn's legs as she maneuvered around what seemed to be a dozen stone pedestals. He was dying to go inside the study. He leaned forward into the doorway, but Emma grabbed his shirt collar and pulled him back. Now Acorn was nowhere to be seen. Jack scanned the room, his nervousness growing. He looked back at Emma, mouthed the words she was taking too long, and leaned towards the opening. Emma shook her head and pointed.

Acorn's thin legs were headed back but then stopped. Bending over, she waved for them to come into the study, but Emma shook her head. In one hand, Acorn held the kaleidoscope, and she waved even harder, pointing at something out of their view. Again, Emma shook her head. Acorn jabbed her hand again at the unseen thing.

Jack couldn't resist. He yanked out of Emma's grip and scrambled on all fours into the study. He stood up next to Acorn, looked past her outstretched arm, and blinked in disbelief. His face was on the wall.

As if caught in the inescapable pull of a black hole, Jack walked forward and stared at the image of himself in the large woven tapestry hung on the wall. He frowned. *It can't be me.* The fabric appeared ancient, its threads worn smooth and waxy as if handled and passed from generation to generation. Rips and tears dotted the edges, and a huge crescent-shaped scorch mark marred the right corner. *The picture is way too old to be me. There just happens to be a picture of another white-eyed guy hanging by Daria's desk.*

Jack studied the scene depicted on the tapestry. The white-eyed man was not having a good day. His face grimaced in pain, and above his head he held a rainbow in his hands, the seven colors shooting outwards like the rays of the sun. A row of jagged black towers surrounding a dark pit loomed below him. In the upper corner, a giant red turtle was sitting on a domed mountain. Under the mountain was a huge mandala filled with a maze-like pattern. All around the man, in a chaotic swirl of shadows, thousands of black figures swarmed over the fields and villages.

He had read way too many dystopian books to not recognize the scene's meaning. *It's the Apocalypse, the end of the world, and my ancient twin is right in the center of the action.* But he couldn't tell whether the white-eyed man was fighting against the enemy horde or spreading the desolation. *No wonder Daria doesn't like me.*

Jack sensed the tapestry's importance. Burning the image as much as possible into his head, he turned around. Acorn was back in the passageway, but Emma was leaning out of the hole and staring at the tapestry, her eyes filled with concern.

"Maybe Holly and I aren't the only ones with powers." Emma's whisper filled his ear.

"Rainbow Man...to the rescue." Mouthing his reply, Jack bowed with a flourish, bumping his hands against the pedestal behind him. CLINK! He spun around as a blue crystal rod rolled off the edge. He dove forward and caught it inches from the hard floor. Jack sighed in relief.

"RUN! NOW!" Emma's voice ripped through Jack's head. "She's awake!"

Daria's robed silhouette appeared behind the curtained doorway on the other side of the room. Jack dropped to the floor and scrambled on his hands and knees, hoping to stay out of sight. Behind him, the metal curtain rings jangled, and he spun around and hid behind a pedestal, keeping the base between himself and Daria. He sat, expecting to be caught, but nothing happened. *What was she waiting for?* The seconds passed by. Unable to take the suspense any longer, he slowly inched backwards towards the hole, certain that Daria would catch him. When his foot tapped the open metal grate, he froze. She was standing motionless in the doorway on the other side of the room.

His eyes fixed in horror on the Guardian's face. Her whole head was encased in a thick layer of shiny pink slime. Her eyes and mouth were closed, covered by goo; two straws stuck out of her nose, and two more stuck out of her ears.

She can't see me! Jack relaxed and inched backward, trying to not make any noise.

Daria's head whipped in his direction. She strode quickly into the room, stopped at the edge of her desk, and placed her hands on top of the empty velvet pillow where the scope had been moments ago. She turned away from Jack's position as her hands frantically patted the top of the desk, feeling for the kaleidoscope. Jack crawled backward and stuck his feet in the opening. Still searching, Daria bent down, checking the floor next to her desk. He moved farther into the hole. His shoulder bumped into the grate.

"OOUUHM!" Daria yelled, her words unintelligible with her mouth sealed shut. Bolting upright, she clawed at her face, and tore a thick piece of the gelatinous jelly from one eye, then stared directly at Jack as he backed fully into the passageway and grabbed the grate with his right hand.

He stared back, feeling the time stretching outwards. He was convinced time had stopped. If he stayed motionless, the world would stop along with him.

"YOUOUHHMM!" Daria's muffled shout bounced off the walls. She ripped the slime off her mouth. Jack slammed the grate shut.

"NO!" Daria screamed, her voice guttural and iron-hard. The metal grate crumpled like paper crushed by an invisible hand. It ripped off its hinges and flew into the study. Jack stumbled to his feet and raced down the tunnel, around the corners and down the incline. Emma was holding the scope with her pack shouldered, but she wasn't moving. Acorn and Holly were already gone.

"What are you waiting for?" Jack asked, taking the kaleidoscope from Emma. He grabbed his pack by the straps, shoved the kaleidoscope inside, then pointed down the tunnel to the river. "We're taking this one, right?"

Emma grabbed him and clamped her hand over his mouth. "Yes, Sister Sasa said to go that way, down the TUNNEL to the old WATERWAY on the map!" Emma was shouting, her voice loud and clear as if she was making an announcement. Motioning for him to stay silent, she pointed her free hand at the hole in the floor. Jack shook his head in confusion. *Why was she shouting? What map?* Emma pointed again at the hole and this time pushed Jack towards it. Jack got it. He threw his legs over the edge and dropped to the floor of the dark space. An underground cavern lay ahead. A few hundred feet away, Holly waved a faint light, and Acorn was next to her. Emma kept shouting from above. "Holly and Jack, when we GET TO THE RIVER, I'll SIGNAL to SISTER SASA and her FRIENDS. Let's go." She dropped down next to him, her hand raised to quiet him still. Looking satisfied with his silence, she took off toward the girls, moving stealthily across the cavern floor.

Jack followed her through the silent cave and marveled at his sister's composure. He guessed the choice to jump down here instead of taking the waterway tunnel was another part of her plan. *Maybe they were on her Plan C or even Plan D by now? And the shouting out of their plans to throw Daria off their trail—did she already have that comment about Sasa worked out in her head?* Emma's ponytail bounced back and forth as she jogged ahead of him. *Yes, ladies and gentlemen, inside that blonde head lurks the mind of an evil genius.*

Acorn led them downhill through the winding passages, putting distance between them and the Sisters. The glow from Holly's lightstick blinked in and out of view like a firefly as they threaded around the stalagmites and sharp outcroppings of rock. More than once, Acorn disappeared into barely perceptible fissures in the passage walls. As Jack squeezed through the narrow gaps in the path, he became more and more confident that no one could be following them. As he yanked himself free from another dark crack, Acorn stopped.

"We're here," she said, her voice sounding smaller than usual in the darkness. They had reached an apparent dead-end and were standing in a small cavern, less than eight feet across. "I wish you weren't leaving."

"Where are we?" Jack asked as he knocked the rock dust off his backpack. "And did you see Daria's face?"

Emma pointed at Jack. "Forget about Daria. Take us home."

While Jack pulled out the kaleidoscope, Emma hugged Acorn. "We're going to miss you too, Acorn. Please be careful."

Emma stepped back. Sniffling, Acorn wiped her nose, then hugged Holly. Jack wasn't surprised that Acorn was choosing to stay in the Coren. He'd spent most of his life wishing his life could be different, but now, after three weeks in Dara, all he wanted was to go home. If Acorn went with them, she'd be leaving her home forever.

"Thanks, Acorn. I won't forget you," Jack said as he fidgeted with the scope in his hands. She ran over to him, threw her arms around his waist, and buried her head in his chest. He squeezed her back, then gently pushed her away before waving the scope at the girls. "Ready?"

Stepping to either side of him, Emma and Holly linked their arms with his. He winked at Acorn, then raised the scope to his right eye, aiming the end of the scope at the bright glow of the lightstick.

There was no doorway, no light showing inside the scope. Nothing. No wavy image of the study or their house, or anywhere. And the red doorway he'd seen and stepped into, the portal that had delivered them into Dara was still gone. Suddenly, the cavern seemed very cold.

Jack shifted the scope to his left eye, but it made no difference. The inside of the scope was dark red. Putting his fingers at the end of the barrel, he waved them back and forth.

"We're ready," prodded Emma.

"Umm..." Jack frantically switched eyes again. On his left, he felt Holly loosening her grip on his arm.

"It's not working, is it?" Holly said.

Shaking his head, Jack slowly lowered the scope. "There's nothing. No portal home and no red portal, either." He tried twisting both ends of the scope, hoping to find other moving parts besides the small knobs that opened and closed the tiny compartments, and he heard a faint click. Jack excitedly pressed the end of the scope to his eye and... nothing had changed. The kaleidoscope was still dark. With the girls watching him, he fumbled with the scope, his frustration building. He stepped away from the girls, raised the scope above his head, and shook it back and forth.

"Jack, stop! You might break it." Grabbing his arm, Emma took the kaleidoscope from him. "It's okay."

"But I'm supposed to take you home," Jack argued. Staring at the ground, he shook his head in disbelief. He felt like a failure.

Emma held the kaleidoscope out to him, waiting for him to take it back. "You will take us home. Right after we figure out how to make it work."

"Does this mean you're staying?" asked Acorn eagerly. Jack glanced up and saw the hope in her eyes. *Well, at least I made one person happy.*

Emma walked to the far end of the small cave. "Yes, Acorn. Since we can't use the kaleidoscope yet, we're going to run, just like we talked."

"Emma, are you sure?"

"Run where? We're in a cave," Jack said, desperately wanting to be part of the plan. He walked over to where Emma was standing.

"Tiraseh, the South Forest," Acorn replied. "We're underneath it." She raised her hand and pointed her finger at the tunnel ceiling.

Except there was no ceiling where they were standing. They were directly below an opening, four feet above their heads. A large, gnarled tree root gripped one side of the hole like a giant hand.

"We had three ways to escape if the kaleidoscope didn't work," Emma said, dropping her pack. She pulled out a long length of cord, tied one end to her pack and threaded the rope through each of theirs, knotting the end off with Jack's. "The Coren main gate has a five-color lock but was not worth trying if Holly failed to open your cell door. The waterway tunnel to the east was another option, but as Yiana said, the obvious choice. I made up the stuff about Sasa and giving signals. Hopefully, it will distract Daria."

"It'll distract Sasa for sure." Jack relished the idea of the nasty Sister Sasa being in trouble. "So, this is your Plan C?"

"Yup. Acorn's sure nobody knows about this opening."

"When my mother brought me to the Coren, I missed home so bad. While looking for a way to escape, I found these caves. I was so lonely, but I was never brave enough to leave," Acorn said, her voice quivering.

"Well, we're with you now. We'll be brave together," added Holly.

Emma placed her hand on Acorn's shoulder. "Yeah, we want you to come with us. But remember, like Yiana said, it's your choice. You'll be our friend no matter what."

"Thank you, Emma," Acorn said. She bowed her head for a moment as if thinking, then stood up straight. "I will never serve Eres Daria again. I want to stay with you."

"Acorn, that's wonderful!" Holly smiled and hugged her.

"But you don't understand why I never tried to escape this way from the Coren. I wasn't afraid because I was alone."

"Then why?" Jack asked. He stared up at the dark hole, already guessing the answer.

"It's after midnight and there's no moon now. No one ever goes out at night, especially not at moondark."

"Because of the shards," said Jack.

Emma shouldered her pack. "But I don't know what else we can do. We're dead if we stay here."

Emma looked around the group, but no one spoke as the darkness swallowed their thoughts. Wordlessly, she climbed up the hole and led them into the dark forest above.

The predominant tree type in Dara is the Pamuli, an amazingly resilient and long-lived species despite the searing heat and harsh conditions. The roots of the Pamuli–which means 'desert spring'–dive hundreds of feet down into the soil pulling water and nutrients to the surface. When properly maintained and judiciously tapped by a skilled Segan, a single healthy tree can provide a steady source of water for hundreds of years.

—from the "Plants of Dara" by Tag of Kurun, Master Segan.

30

THE BLIGHT

HOLLY SHIVERED.

The dense forest air tugged uncomfortably on her skin, its weight like a heavy invisible coat. Sweat ran down the back of her neck as she struggled to step over another mass of exposed roots. Stumbling a bit, she thrust her right hand out against a tree to catch her fall.

She shivered again. A cold sensation licked at her hand, and nausea filled her insides as she yanked her hand back. Fear welled up inside her as she took a long breath and stopped the group with a jerk on the cord binding them together.

"Are you okay?" Jack asked, coming up from behind, gathering up the slack in the cord Emma had used to connect them. "What is it? You're as white as my eyes."

"The trees. There's something wrong with them." Holly shook her hands to fend off the unwanted sensation, foul and lingering. "They feel sick to me."

"Sick?" Jack placed a hand on the bark of the tree.

"What's wrong?" Emma had doubled back with Acorn.

"The trees are sick. Every time I touch one with my hands, it hits me."

"It's the Blight," Acorn said quietly.

Holly looked unhappily at the dark twisted shapes. They had been walking for close to an hour, and it seemed like they were going nowhere. She desperately wanted to get away from these trees.

"The villagers say it's a disease. Trees, fields, crops...they say it's getting worse every year."

"All I know is I don't like it," Holly said. "Are we close to getting out of here?"

"I'm not sure," said Acorn, her troubled face highlighted in the glow of the lightstick Holly carried. Since climbing out onto the forest floor, Acorn had been directing Emma to the north, away from the Coren to a small town located in the foothills beyond the forest.

"It's all right," Emma said as she turned her head from side to side. "Besides, I haven't heard anyone following us yet, so we must be putting distance between us and the Coren. You ready, Hol?"

Holly stepped carefully around the tree as Emma began leading them forward again. More like one step forward, two steps right, and three steps left in some crazy dance as she stumbled behind Acorn. Emma was doing her best to keep them on a straight line through the woods, but the tightly spaced tree trunks and piles of fallen branches formed a dark maze that constantly blocked their efforts, obscuring the bright bundle of stars Acorn had said to follow, guiding them northwards. Another protruding branch snagged at Holly's pants leg, and she stomped it down in frustration. At least I have pants. She and Emma had stuffed their Coren robes in their packs, choosing to change back into their own clothes and shoes. Holly took her eyes off the dark forest floor for an instant, wondering if Acorn had any idea how much tougher she was than the three of them.

Acorn was wearing her short faded red dress, the only clothing Holly had ever seen her wear and was barefoot, her sandals stuffed in her pack. She skipped and hopped effortlessly over the branches, moving with the natural grace of a squirrel, instinctively knowing the right place to land. Holly tried to imagine herself barefoot, climbing and gliding across the rocks and branches, and laughed to herself. Of course, Acorn belongs here. She was born in this world and they were intruders.

Holly slipped, the sole of her sneaker sliding off the top of a slick root. Her free hand grabbed onto a broken branch, and new slivers of revulsion shot up her arm as she fell on one knee. She groaned, sickened at the awful sensation. Jack put his hand on her shoulder.

"You want me to take the light? So you can balance better?" He helped her up.

"That'd be great, but the lightstick won't work for you." She started walking again after Acorn.

"Maybe you can change it to an always-on setting?"

Holly considered the idea. Jack had a gift for asking interesting questions that were always better than her own. She could draw circles around him when it came to art, but he seemed to see the world differently, effortlessly connecting the dots, putting ideas together like pieces in a jigsaw puzzle.

"Maybe," Holly replied, thinking about the lightballs surrounding the Coren fountain. "But I'd probably have to colorcast it again with a lot more red. Or yellow. I'm not sure."

"Huh? Remember, you're talking to a guy who spent the last two weeks shoved in a hole."

"Sorry," She said, recalling Yiana's teaching. "The person who made this lightstick cast a little bit of red color into the handle. There's enough to activate the light source, which comes from the yellow color, but not enough red color to stay on without my power."

"Wow. If you were trying for confusing, you nailed it."

Holly smiled. She liked the feeling of having to explain this to Jack. "Try it this way. There's enough red color cast into the handle to connect the user to the yellow light. It's kind of like an invisible wire. When my hand touches the handle, there's a faint vibration. Like a humming in my fingertips."

"And you're the battery? You're powering the light?"

"Not the light, just the tiny amount of red to activate the item. Since everyone in Dara...well, except for Acorn and you and other Zeros...has a Red Mark, items are always cast with a small amount of red color. But not everyone here would have Yellow Marks, so the light has to power itself. The maker cast a lot of yellow energy into this stick. I'd guess enough to keep it glowing for weeks." Holly paused. "Get it?"

Jack didn't answer, and Holly walked along thinking about Sister Yiana. She became vaguely aware of a tapping, vibrating through the ground and into the soles of her feet.

A new shiver, this time like unseen hands raking clammy fingers up her skin, hit both of Holly's legs. She stopped as the sensation grew, perplexed. She hadn't touched anything.

Jack stepped up behind her. "You okay?"

"No. I got hit with another blast of..." Holly struggled to define the feeling. It wasn't cold and it wasn't wet, but it was worse than the sick feeling from the trees. She knew there had to be a right word, but couldn't find the right word, and now the scraping, like dead branches dragged across the dirt, seemed to be growing stronger. A panicky knot pulled tight in her stomach, and another tremor clawed into Holly's shoulders. She looked up, her eyes darting about in the darkness, still searching for the right word and then, Emma was directly in front of her and the right word, the word that captured all her terrible feelings, grabbed her and the word was...

"...wrong. There's something terribly wrong out there."

"I know," Emma said, her voice tight. "Shards."

Holly couldn't move as her skin began to itch.

Jack grabbed Holly and shook her. "Can you tell where they are?"

She blinked, and his white eyes came into focus, driving the awfulness a step back. "That way, about the same distance as across the lake back home." Holly closed her eyes and concentrated on the vibrations pulsing through her legs. "They're coming closer."

Emma, Jack, and Acorn all turned their heads, staring into the darkness. "That's less than two hundred yards."

"Yards?" Acorn asked.

"Like two hundred really big steps," Emma explained. "Can we outrun them?"

Acorn shook her head. "No, they're too fast."

"Can we hide?"

"I don't know. I'm sorry, Emma." Acorn bobbed up and down as fear overtook her.

Emma looked at them in silence and chewed on her lower lip, not sure of what to do. "Um, I guess we—"

"Can shards climb?" Jack asked excitedly. "Acorn, you told me some have extra legs and they thrash around, right?"

"I've never heard about them climbing. But they can jump."

"Okay, we gotta get off the ground, and somewhere high," Jack said. "And I know where to go. Okay, Hol?" His jaw was clenched, and he was leaning forward, his weight up on the balls of his feet ready to pounce, a stance Holly was all too familiar with. He stood the same way in the schoolyard, and the alley, and every other place he had fought for her.

He spun around and backtracked the way they had come. The cord tied off between Jack and Holly's pack snapped taut, and before Holly could take more than a few steps, he tugged hard on the cord. She glued her eyes onto his feet, following his route through the trees.

Not more than twenty yards back, Jack veered hard to his right and led them into a new patch of darkness, the underbrush now a dense and tangled mass. Pushing through branches, he ducked under a fallen tree and stopped, waiting for them to regroup.

"There." He pointed at a hulking hill. Its nearest side was strewn with broken boulders and pockmarked with holes like the ground had a skin disease. On the hilltop stood a lone tree with a massive ebony trunk supporting an expanse of dead branches. Holly guessed it was at least sixty feet tall.

"How in the heck did you see that?" Emma sounded impressed. "A black tree in a black forest on a pitch-black night."

"Lucky, I guess," he said modestly, and Holly suspected he wasn't saying something.

They ran up the slope, covering the distance to the tree in under a minute. At the top, Emma paused with head cocked slightly in the direction of the coming shards. Steeling herself, Holly knelt on the mossy ground and closed her eyes. She could feel the vibrations of something scraping and scratching its way across the soil. Like insects.

She opened her eyes. "They're closer."

"Yeah," said Emma, dropping her pack. "The sound is getting worse, but clearer like individual notes instead of one big noise."

"How many notes?" Holly didn't want to ask.

"Twelve. At least twelve."

"What's it matter? Two, twelve, or twenty. Time to climb, people." Jack grabbed all their packs and piled them at the base of the tree. The first branch loomed eight feet above them, impossibly out of reach.

"Emma, I'll form a base. You'll have to step on my knees, and then my shoulders to reach the branch. Once you're up, Acorn and Holly can climb on me, and you can pull them up."

Holly started to say something about Jack's plan, but she stopped herself. She figured Emma recognized the determination in his eyes as well.

He stomped on the pile of packs to stand on. Feet spread and knees bent, he planted his back into the trunk and waved Emma over. Grabbing Jack's head for leverage, Emma stepped onto his thighs. He grunted but stayed steady. Holly and Acorn stepped in behind and pushed her as she stepped up onto Jack's shoulders. Emma reached up and over the branch with her arms. Shifting to stay upright, her left foot rammed into Jack's forehead, scraped down his ear, and dug deep into his neck.

"Emma!" He winced but held his position. "Climb the tree, not my face!"

"I'm sorry! I need a boost."

"Fine," Jack grunted in response. Groaning with exertion, he straightened his knees. His back inched up the tree, raising her higher. His body began to shake. "Hurry up."

Emma placed her left foot on top of his head and kicked herself onto the branch. Collapsing onto the pile of backpacks, he looked at Emma up in the tree.

"Smooth." Jack stood, twisting his neck back and forth. He retook his stance against the tree. "Okay, Acorn. Same plan and Emma will pull you." Jack looked at her expectantly, but she was hesitating. "Come on, it'll be easy."

Her cheeks now flushed, Acorn stepped onto his bent legs. She raised her right foot to his shoulder but wobbled to one side. Jack grabbed her knees and guided her feet onto his shoulders before straightening up. Emma grabbed her outstretched arms to pull her onto the branch. She was smiling at Acorn and said something encouraging, but Acorn didn't notice. Her eyes were glued to Jack.

"Your turn, Hol," Jack said. "How much time we got?"

Her voice quivered. "Not much." She reached past his head and grabbed the rough bark.

Holly swooned as an icy shock gripped her hands. Her hands clenching involuntarily, her arms slid forward. She faceplanted on the tree. The sickness, the horrible wrongness, oozed like slime across her cheeks and mouth. Gagging as a sour taste filled her throat, she threw herself off Jack's legs and fell to the ground.

"Holly!" Emma called down. "Are you all right?"

Gasping for breath, she raised herself on all fours. "The tree...it's got the Blight."

"Get up, Hol. You have to try again," Jack urged.

Still woozy, she stumbled to her feet and looked up at the tree. Like the body of a giant dead spider, its branches hung motionless above her head in the night air. She took a deep breath and stepped onto Jack's legs, this time avoiding any contact with the tree. She grabbed his hair with both fists, stood up on his thighs, and then raised one arm. She wasn't close enough for Emma to reach her.

"You gotta get on my shoulders." Jack sounded tense. They were running out of time.

Holly readied herself. Grab the tree, step, and go. Grab, step, go. She grabbed the tree. The Blight surged through her sweat-covered hands. A musty smell of rotting vegetables seemed to fill her nose. Holly threw her right foot onto Jack's shoulder. Her stomach started to tighten. She slid one hand higher, ready to bring up the other leg, as her stomach heaved uncontrollably.

She retched and the vomit came, filling her mouth and nose. Both knees buckled and she collapsed, taking Jack to the ground with her. They landed in one of the holes.

"Holly!" Acorn screamed. She felt Jack slide out from under her. Her eyes were closed. Curled in a ball, she sensed the shards coming their way. They were moving faster now and were close to the hill. She tilted up her chin and looked up at him. I'm sorry. I'm so sorry, she wanted to say.

"Stay down and don't move. No matter what, all right?" Jack held eye contact with her until she managed a weak nod. He grabbed their packs and piled them on top of her, hiding her in the hole. Holly nudged one of the packs a few inches to one side and peered through the gap.

Jack stared down at her, his white eyes narrowed like two crescent moons. "Stay in the hole. No matter what."

31

THE RESCUE

"JACK, HELP ME GET DOWN!" Emma yelled.

"NO! Stay in the tree!" Jack ordered, staring up at Emma and Acorn. He cut Emma off before she could argue. "You'll both be safer up there. Yell at me if one of them gets too close." Running over to a pile of broken branches, Jack picked up a five-foot-long branch. He took a few practice swings.

"You can't fight them," Emma said, pleading with him, but he ignored her as the noise from the shards filled the forest, a high-pitched whining mixed with inhuman clicking and chittering. "I can't see anything, but it sounds like they're circling us."

Jack could see them. He'd watched the black creatures break into two groups. He'd lost sight of the first group as it crawled around to the other side of the hill. The shards were surrounding them like a pack of dogs cornering their prey. Below at the base of the hill, six shards had formed a ragged line, a line that refused to stand still or stay in one place.

He shuddered. Acorn's stories had been dead on. Most of the shards were down on all fours or five or even more legs—he couldn't get an accurate count—but one of them was standing upright. They were the size of large dogs, the size you don't want to mess with, their bodies covered in a patchwork of shiny black plating and clumps of wiry hair. Each one had a different number of legs, some sticking out at horribly wrong angles. Three quivering appendages jutted out of the back of the largest shard, its thick body resting on four more spiky legs.

Jack studied the one shard standing on its two hind legs. In the inky black space he assumed was the monster's face, he could pick out two glassy spots, its eyes most likely. If it had a nose, he couldn't tell, but the thing's mouth was obvious. A ragged gash, grotesquely large and filled with long curving teeth, opened and closed spasmodically as if it never stopped chewing.

Its torso was short and round, covered with more wiry fur. The thing's back flared and curved across its body, then sloped up behind its neck and head. Jack tightened his grip on the sharp stick in his hands. *Their hard spiky backs protect them like a shield.* On all fours, these things would be impervious to damage. And impossible to kill.

A wave of clicking noises surged up from behind Jack on the other side of the hill. The group of shards to his front echoed back in response, their whining and clicking tripling in volume. The standing shard, the nasty one he had been watching, dropped onto all fours like it was a sprinter readying in the starting block.

"Jack?" Holly whispered from underneath the packs. "What do you see?"

"Nothing yet. It's too dark," Jack lied. Describing them would make it worse for her. "Stay there."

He held his breath, waiting for the attack. Tucked in his belt were the kitchen knives that Acorn had swiped and stored in the packs. The branch in his hand was pointy on one end, but not blade-sharp. He tried to picture the fight in his head. Keeping them at bay by swinging the staff in wide circles, spearing them when they exposed their bellies, and switching to the knives when they closed in. Deep down he knew he was going to die.

Running would be useless. They would chase him down. His brain recoiled at the idea of being clawed from behind with his back turned. He'd take the fight head-on. He hoped the shards wouldn't find Holly's hiding place. He hoped they couldn't climb trees.

A scream ripped the air and the pack launched itself up the hillside, scurrying like a swarm of cockroaches in and out of the holes and around the rocks. Jack took four steps forward, distancing himself from Holly's hiding place. He dropped into a fighting stance, right leg back, the staff ready to strike.

"TANNOR, TAKE FRONT. I'VE GOT THE CENTER!" A gravelly roar of a man's voice hit Jack's ears from behind. Before he could react, a young man wielding a long, curved sword and dressed in scarlet and black burst past his left shoulder and ran straight toward the oncoming shards. Jack froze in place, stunned.

The same deep voice as before, now right behind him. "Get down, boy!" the man commanded as an iron-hard grip clamped the back of Jack's neck. The hand shoved him down hard and pinned him face-first on the damp ground. The voice growled, close now to his ear. "Do not move from this spot. Grunt if you can understand me."

His face crammed in the dirt, Jack eked out a muffled yes. The heavy hand stayed on Jack's neck but backed off its pressure. "Good. Turn your face to the left." The hand slid away.

Jack had no idea what to expect. Spitting the dirt out of his mouth, he lifted his head towards the owner of the voice.

It belonged to a ghost. *More like a grey ghost of a man.* The stranger was dressed all in grey—leggings, flat-soled boots, and a long-sleeved tunic cinched at the waist with a belt of woven leather cords. On his faded cloak, a few dark spots of green were visible around the edges.

Frighteningly, the man's skin matched the grey of his cloak. Jack had never seen a corpse in real life, but he'd read a million books about the kind of creatures with skin this color: vampires; ghouls; zombies. He had a feeling this man was none of those things, not with the sharp gaze of his light green eyes nor by the stern way he was looking at Jack, sizing him up. Jack took him for a soldier. A soldier with skin the color of death.

"Your name?" The man stared at Jack's eyes without blinking, as if he typically spent his time discovering white-eyed boys in the middle of a black forest.

"Jack." All around him, the hillside echoed with the shrieking of the dying beasts. Faint unexplained flashes of light briefly illuminated the tree line. This man—and the man dressed in scarlet—were saving their lives right now for some reason. No time for hesitation.

"Why are you not up in the tree with your companions?" The man's question sounded more like an accusation.

"Two are in the tree. My little sister couldn't climb up."

With his right hand, the man reached up and stroked the stubble on his cheeks. With his left, he continued to lean on a long straight sword, its blade gleaming despite the darkness of the hilltop. The man's wide-set eyes reminded Jack of a jungle cat—watchful eyes that see everything. The man tilted his head at the pile of packs. "So, you chose to fight shards alone armed with a pointy stick?"

"CAPTAIN!" A shout rang out from the hillside below.

The grey man sprung to his feet. Sword leading, he spun away from Jack and took a quick step to his right. A shard leapt out of the shadows at the hilltop's edge. It landed on two legs, its body and head raised, waving three more clawed legs, all mismatched in size. Already in position to strike, the man thrust his blade deep into the creature's belly. As it shrieked in pain, he pulled the sword back, twisting it with a subtle turn of his wrist.

The shard lurched sideways to the ground, flailing as thick black liquid oozed from the wound in its midsection. A green light ignited inside the chest cavity like someone had lit a candle from within its body. Its legs curled inwards and clawed frantically at its wound while the light grew brighter, doubling in size and then bursting with a bright flash that illuminated the exoskeleton from the inside. Its body shriveled like burnt paper, disintegrating into a puff of black ash and dust that floated down and covered the grass in front of Jack's face. His head reeled, the image of the shard seared in his mind.

The gruff man's big hand grabbed the back of his shirt, and with a yank, Jack was back on his feet. From over the rise, the scarlet warrior appeared, his sword now hanging at his side. Brushing what Jack guessed was the dust of dead shards from his clothes, the young man strode past him without any acknowledgment. He had short-cropped hair, a thin scar slashed across his right cheek, and the same fierceness about him as the man called the Captain. Two other men appeared, dressed in sleeveless tunics over loose-fitting red pants, from opposite sides of the hill. They too were covered in black dust and armed with curved swords. The four men came together, talking quickly in hushed words Jack couldn't make out.

The grey man was their leader, and as the three men pointed over the hill and talked in turn, he acknowledged each report with a nod. He clapped the two men in tunics on their backs who then turned and walked past the base of the tree and out of sight. The man in scarlet knelt next to the pile of packs hiding Holly. Jack headed towards the tree, but the man in charge blocked his path.

"I need to—"

"Be quiet and listen." The man's voice, rough like gravel, cut him off. Without thinking, Jack clenched a fist and looked up defiantly at the grey man.

"Check that temper, boy. You've made enough bad decisions for one night."

"Bad decisions? What do you mean?"

The large man scowled down at Jack. "You're deep inside Tiraseh at moondark. You were making enough noise to attract Se'en-sii herself, let alone a pack of shards. You left the Red Coren with no effective weapons and meager supplies."

Jack didn't know what to say. The man was putting all the responsibility *and* all the blame on him. He looked away to the young man—the one called Tannor—lowering Acorn and Emma out of the tree. Holly stood next to the packs, her ashen face streaked with dried tears. His face feeling warm, Jack forced his gaze back to the man and remained quiet.

"Better. This is not the place nor time for questions." The man's eyes scanned the darkness. "Grab your packs and tell your companions to stay close. I'll lead while Tannor takes the rear. We'll reach camp in a few hours." The man waited for Jack to nod.

"You haven't told me your name," Jack said.

The man paused and seemed to consider something. "No, I have not. You can call me Captain. Now, no more questions."

"Thank you for saving us....Captain," said Jack awkwardly, trying to sound like a soldier. The big man nodded, with a small hint of a smile on his face. He began to turn away.

"Wait, how did you find us? How did you know we came from the Coren?"

The man stopped, all traces of the smile instantly gone. He seemed to go somewhere else, somewhere well out of reach from the dark hillside. Jack didn't expect to get an answer.

"I've been waiting for a man with white eyes."

32

THE SHAKING OF HANDS

JACK SMELLED MEAT. A smoky sweet aroma wafted past the cloth stretched across the opening of the small shallow cave. He propped himself up on one elbow and sucked the air into his nose, holding on to the smell.

He closed his eyes. For a moment, he pretended he was back home in his bed as their dad filled the house with the sounds and smells of lazy Saturday morning breakfast. He'd fry bacon and make the big pancake: an oven-baked golden concoction of eggs, milk, and flour that puffed up like a balloon. The four of them would sit around the well-worn kitchen table and rip the pancake apart with their fingers, messily dipping the pieces in syrup or dusting them with powdered sugar. They always argued over the last piece of bacon. Jack took another long slow breath, wishing he could go on dreaming.

"Get up already," Emma said, pushing aside the edge of the stretchy vella. She held a cup in her hands, a small plume of steam floating up. "Tannor and Acorn made breakfast."

Jack pushed the sleep out of his eyes and his hair off his forehead. "Tannor?"

"One of our new..." Emma stopped. Biting her lower lip, she shrugged at Jack. "Whoever they are. They saved us."

Last night, the man called the Captain had kept his word about answering no more questions. They had hiked with the men in silence for nearly an hour, then emerged from the forest. A chain of mountains loomed in the night shadows beyond. After leading them to a rock wall, the Captain placed his hand in a crack, revealing the shallow cave as if by magic.

"It's like camouflage," Jack said; the rock wall was a piece of cloth. As the cloth wrinkled back, the pattern shifted to stay perfectly matched with the rocks on either side.

Holly stroked the fabric with her fingertips. "It's vella fabric, like the fence from the farm fields, but it's been colorcasted." Her voice was hushed as if she were in a museum appreciating a work of art. "Where did it come from?"

"Not now. No more questions," The Captain said. Emma tried to speak, but he cut them off, his hand held up to silence them. He looked at each of them in turn, as if daring them to speak. "Good. Now sleep."

Too tired to argue, they ducked into the low-ceilinged cave as the vella closed behind them. In minutes, they had fallen asleep, too tired to talk.

But now, with the morning sunlight streaming into the cave, Jack had questions. He hadn't heard the girls get up and leave the cave. "Why were they looking for us?"

"Tannor doesn't know the reason." Emma sat down on the ground, her face silhouetted by the morning sun behind her. "He said they follow the Captain. The Captain said they had to find you, so that's what they did." Emma took a slow sip.

"You meant *find us*," Jack corrected her.

"Nope. They were looking for you alone. They were tracking down rumors of a white-eyed stranger seen in Lindur and discovered there were three of us. He said the Captain looked surprised. And according to Tannor, the man is never surprised." Emma shook her head and frowned. "When I told him we came from Earth and not from the Seven, he didn't even blink or ask me anything."

"He's angry if you ask me. I don't think I'm who he expected."

"Why?"

"He said he'd been waiting for a *man* with white eyes. Not a boy," Jack said as he played with the knots in his sneaker laces. "They're soldiers?"

"More like mercenaries, hunting shards. They move around, getting paid to protect villages. Tannor's been riding with the Captain for three years." Emma handed Jack the cup. "He said the Captain never talks about his past back in Tera."

"He's from the Green land?" Jack stood up, picturing the remnants of green color on the man's faded cloak. "Then he's a long way from home. He must have come through the Portals to get here, right?" Jack tried to slide past Emma, but she blocked him.

"Hey, before I forget." Emma held up a hand, her face serious. "Two things. First, keep the kaleidoscope hidden for now, our secret. I only told the Captain that we traveled from Earth and that we were arrested in Lindur. Their voices have a ring of truth to me, but we have to protect the scope. After all, it's our only way home. I already told Holly and Acorn to say nothing."

"Sure. It stays in my pack. You said two things?"

"About last night and your choice to stay down on the ground to fight."

"Yeah, I know." The grey man's harsh comments still stung. "I wasn't thinking."

Emma suddenly wrapped her arms around him, hugging him. "Thank you. It was the bravest thing I've ever seen."

Jack pulled away, embarrassed. "Thanks, Em. But I didn't feel brave. Just scared."

"Me too," Emma said. "But it was still brave." She pulled him out of the cavern and into the bright sunlight. "Come on. I saved you some meat."

They walked down the short slope, across sparse patches of grass working hard to survive. Four zinds grazed contentedly at the forest's edge, less than twenty yards from their campsite. Less menacing now in the light of the day, the trees gathered gracefully, their branches spread wide, most covered with thick leaves. One tree stood out, its bark marred with ugly black spots, its branches bare. Even in daylight, the Blight looked bad. *No wonder Holly can't stand touching them.*

Camp consisted of no more than a cooking pot and a small pan. The girls were sitting close by the young man called Tannor who was laughing, an easy-going smile on his face. With his dark cropped short hair and his square jaw, he reminded Jack of an athlete, like the quarterback on a football team, though Jack had never been friends with anybody popular. The Captain and two other men were nowhere to be seen.

Sitting cross-legged on a low flat rock, Tannor looked completely relaxed, quite a different image than the grim-faced hunter from last night. He was young; Jack guessed he was no more than twenty. His leather belt and boots sat in a small, neat pile, a compact crossbow and his curved sword lying next to him, the hilt within easy reach.

"So, the sleeping warrior arises," Tannor announced. Effortlessly and much faster than Jack expected, he popped up to meet him, quickly taking a few strides forward. He'd stepped into his boots and held the sword in his left hand with a casual confidence. He may have appeared relaxed, but the man's guard had been up the entire time. He sized Jack up and down, and seemingly satisfied, he thrust out his open right hand towards Jack.

"Emma told me in your Earthland, a shaking of hands is the proper greeting. Will you shake with me, Jack?" Tannor said as he stuck his hand out further, poking him in the chest. Jack forced himself not to laugh at the odd choice of words. Daria had made a big deal about greetings. Deep down, he knew this was an important moment. Stepping back, he firmly grasped the man's hand.

"I am Jack Waite of Lebanon, son of Eli." Jack shook his hand but did not let go.

Tannor smiled broadly and Jack instantly liked him.

"And I am Tannor of Ephus, second son of Tanok. Welcome to breakfast."

Holly squeezed between them, breaking up the handshake. She hugged Jack and stepped back. "That was for last night."

Jack shrugged his shoulders. "Thanks, Hol. I didn't know what else to do."

Acorn darted past Holly and wrapped her arms around him, her head buried in his chest. Jack froze, his arms stuck at his sides, and waited for Acorn to step back. She didn't move. At all. Jack looked up, feeling helpless. Emma made a patting sign with her hands, but Jack hesitated. Hugging his sisters was already bad enough. She made the sign again. "Hug her back, stupid." Emma's whisper filled his ear.

Jack put his arms around Acorn's shoulders, trying to make as little actual contact as possible. He patted her shoulder blade with his right hand. Acorn relaxed as if she had come unstuck. She stepped back quickly, her cheeks a bright red as she stared at the ground. "Thank you, Jack. I think you were very brave last night."

"Thanks, Acorn." Jack looked awkwardly around the group. "But we were all brave. Especially you. We'd still be trapped in the Coren, or worse, if you guys hadn't pulled off the escape. Besides, the Captain didn't seem very impressed with me last night." He walked over and sat down next to the fire. Before he could ask, Acorn handed him a wooden bowl filled with an oatmeal-like mixture that smelled like warm bread. A thick flat strip of meat, brown and tough like jerky, was shoved in the mix. Jack looked up at Emma.

"Like a spoon. And take off little bites as you go. Trust me, you'll love it."

Jack was starved. Taste was the least of his concerns. He shoveled in several mouthfuls of the porridge and bit off the end of his jerky spoon. The combination tasted like a roast beef sandwich. Jack closed his eyes and sighed. The food they gave him in the Coren was decent and filling, but he'd never enjoyed the meals. Feeling like every meal could be your last tended to sour your appetite. He took another bite, savoring the sweet taste of beefy freedom.

"Don't mind the Captain," Tannor said. "In my three years with him, I've gotten four kind words. He's not one for compliments."

"Where is he? And the other men?"

Tannor settled himself on the flat rock, his sword still in reach.

"Durk's on watch at the neck of the valley where he can observe anyone approaching. The Captain sent Byrn to a village not far from here. He'll grab supplies and listen for any news. The four of you are fugitives from the Red Coren. People are bound to be talking."

Jack took another big bite, talking with his mouth full. "And the Captain?"

"Over there." He pointed up the slope past a large boulder. "Sleeping."

Amused, Jack grinned triumphantly at Emma and Holly. "Guess I'm not the only one who oversleeps."

"The Captain needs to rest," Acorn said.

"He's not sleeping late," Emma frowned at Jack like he'd said something wrong. "Tannor told us he never sleeps at night, just during the daylight hours and no more than a few hours each day."

"Wow, no wonder he looked so tired and pale," Jack said. Emma frowned at him again. "What? What'd I say wrong this time?"

"He's got the Fade," Emma said as Jack shook his head. "Oh, yeah. You weren't around when Yiana talked about Daria showing signs of the Fade."

"Prison cell. Ring a bell?"

Emma ignored him. "People with Marks are bound to their home-land. The longer and farther away you go, the weaker that bond becomes." His sister looked at Tannor as if for confirmation, and seemed pleased when he nodded in agreement. "It's like an illness. Your colors fade and you have no energy."

Jack pictured the Captain's pale grey skin. In the chaos of the fight and hiking through the dark woods, Jack had not seen any Marks on him. "It sounds like being homesick, but worse," Jack said, thinking out loud. "And he looks like a ghost from three years of Fading?"

"I've known him for three years," Tannor cleared his throat as the Captain strode into view, fastening his sword belt. "I've already said more than I should. Stories have power and should not be shared lightly. Bear that in mind with him." He stood up to go but paused. "He's never confirmed the rumors. But there are folks in the outer villages who say he's been haunting the land of Dara for much longer. They call him the Grey Ghost."

"How long?" Jack asked.

"Ten years. The Captain has been Fading for ten years."

While precise measurements are impossible due to the nature of the beasts, we can estimate the tunneling rate of shards based on the multiple reports from hunting parties who have cleared established nests in Dara and then observed the egress points of the remaining animals. The average time—from the initial disturbance of the nest to the emergence of surviving shards up to one hundred strides distant—is four minutes. Factoring a fifty percent decrease for a sustained and less agitated pace of digging, I contend they can tunnel a distance of one daan in sixteen hours' time.

—from the Study of Shards by Sarak, First Ummi of Tandur

33

THE TRACER

BYRN—A short man with one Mark who never smiled and rarely spoke—returned along with Durk to their camp later that day with fresh supplies, cloaks for the four of them, and horrible news. Two Sisters were walking the village and asking about strangers. According to a merchant, the Sisters were hunting for a pack of rebellious Farkers —their bodies tattooed and modified with false Marks—wanted for crimes committed in Ephara. As they shared their news, neither man made eye contact with her, Holly nor Jack.

Byrn's voice was rife with fear. According to Tannor, most people in Dara lived their whole lives without ever setting eyes on one of the Sisterhood. The Sisters kept to themselves, rarely venturing far from either the Coren or Ephara, the capital city. Seeing two Sisters together was akin to getting caught between two sandstorms on the open dunes. You knew it could happen, but you never wanted it to happen to you.

Hearing the news, the Captain frowned in Emma's direction and then pulled Byrn and Durk aside for a private conversation. Visibly not happy, the men gestured toward the village. Byrn was talking loud and fast as he told the Captain going against the Sisterhood was more than he could handle. If Daria discovered he was helping these children, her punishment would be swift and merciless. She'd confiscate his land and farm in Goral. Durk said they both had families and children of their own to think of.

Emma's stomach tightened in a knot of outrage. She knew she shouldn't be surprised that Daria would take these men's land, maybe do even worse things to their families. Daria had been ready to kill her and Holly—commit murder—all to protect the status quo and her position as the highest-marked person in the land. She wouldn't think twice about punishing two men who were Ones.

Emma knew she shouldn't be eavesdropping on their conversation. She forced herself to focus on the sounds of the forest behind her, and the words of the Captain and the other men faded into the background. They each knelt in front of the Captain. He lightly touched the top of Bryn's head with his hand and repeated the gesture with Durk. Looking relieved, both men rose and strode away, not looking back.

"Byrn and Durk are leaving," Tannor said. "He released them from his service."

Emma turned to face him. He was right behind her. Her eyes traced the thin scar zigzagged across his cheek.

"They joined us to protect people. They've risked their lives a hundred times over. But protecting two girls with Seven Marks and a white-eyed boy—fugitives wanted by the Sisterhood—is too dangerous for them. Shards are terrible, but all of Dara knows the wrath of the Red Guardian is far worse. You wouldn't believe some of the stories of what she's done," he paused, then raised his hand. "By your Marks, Eres, I guess you would."

"But you're not worried?" Emma asked, thrown off guard by his addressing her formally.

Tannor smiled down at her, and Emma swallowed nervously. He glanced at Jack who was sitting nearby with Holly and Acorn, cross-legged on the ground by the cooking pot. "What kind of gentleman would I be if I abandoned you?"

"Emma, was I unclear this morning?" Walking up next to them, the Captain stopped and crossed his arms. The frown on his face was set deep and hard, a crack in weathered stone.

"Excuse me? Unclear about what?" Emma asked.

"This morning. I asked you to tell me everything. You didn't."

"Yes, I did," she said, frowning at him. Earlier, she'd shared everything that had happened to them since arriving in Dara. Well, everything but the kaleidoscope.

She said they came from Earthland, and when he didn't ask her how they traveled to the Seven, Emma was relieved; after the Mayor's and Daria's reactions, she wasn't ready to reveal any information about the kaleidoscope. She then took him and Tannor through the timeline—their capture in Lindur, the first meeting with the Red Guardian, the time spent training in the Coren with Jack stuck in his cell, and the escape—while carefully omitting any mention of the scope. Except for asking Acorn to confirm the Guardian intended to kill them, the Captain never reacted. Tannor was right about him; the man never looked surprised. Now, though, he looked angry. She started to wonder what else Byrn might have said. *Were the sisters telling the villagers that Emma, Jack and Holly had stolen something valuable? Were they telling people about the kaleidoscope?*

The Captain stared down at her. "There are two Sisters in that village, dangerously close to our position here, and they have a Tracer." He stood there unmoving as if his last statement was carved in stone and should be monumentally obvious to her.

"What's a Tracer?" Holly asked. The Captain's expression softened as Holly approached.

"A metal box, the size of a small chest. It tracks people," Tannor replied. "They're very expensive. When my brother was in the Guard, he used one to hunt down deserters."

"But how does it work?" Jack asked.

"It locates a person by their Marks. First, you need the crystal containing the patterns of the Marks from the person you want to find, called a Tracing. You put the Tracing inside the box, and it vibrates and changes colors, then you read the colors on the outside of the box like a map to pinpoint the location of the person."

Emma searched her mind while looking at Holly and Jack for

help. "But the Sisters would need a Tracing of us, right? We spent time with Yiana, but the other Sisters never touched—"

"Yes, they did," Jack interrupted as he stood up, waving a half-eaten stick of meat in his hand. "With the Blessing ceremony. Remember when Sasa and Haia held crystals on your forehead? Those crystals changed colors and Sasa gave them to Daria." Stopping next to Emma, he shrugged matter-of-factly. "You got Traced."

"Why didn't you say something before?" Emma said, remembering the tingling sensation of the crystal on her skin.

"Well, as I recall," Jack made a face at her, "right after you and Holly got blessed and welcomed like royalty, I got tossed in a prison cell. I was a little busy."

Emma's arm whipped out and smacked him lightly on the side of the head. Like always, he grabbed his head, pretending to be hurt, and for a moment, Emma forgot where she was. She smiled as Jack grinned back. Tannor chuckled, amused by their antics.

The Captain cleared his throat with a grumbly growl. Emma did not like the look of vindication on his face, but she relaxed knowing the kaleidoscope was still a secret.

"Fine. I left out one detail," Emma lied. "So, what are we going to do?"

"We get out of range."

∼

THEY PACKED QUICKLY. WITHIN MINUTES, THEY WERE mounted on the zinds and heading north through the forest of Tiraseh. As they rode through the night, Emma wished she could get more than two words at a time from the Captain. She tried asking him questions each time they stopped riding, but every time, he either gave no answer or, even worse, gave one of his non-answers.

Up ahead, the Captain dismounted, scouting forward on foot again. She rolled her eyes in annoyance. She'd offered to help and proved her hearing was better than his by having Acorn whisper at them both from thirty feet away. But instead of being impressed, he rejected her idea, instead spouting off another one of his cryptic responses. "Listening takes more than big ears." Big ears or not, she'd heard more than enough half-answers out of the man. Emma vowed to get some clarity from him when they stopped for breakfast.

She turned her head to the left and the right, checking for noises. Nothing different; the creaking of the woods to her right, the stony whisper of boulders on her left, and the nagging voice in her head. The Captain reappeared, mounted, and dropped his hand with a forward wave telling the group to continue.

He'd given them instructions on following his hand signals—gather up, retreat, maintain silence—while they traveled. Emma started to kick her heels into the speckled yellow zind—the name for the lizard-skinned horses—she shared with Acorn, but she needn't have bothered. The zinds were amazingly well trained, and hers started on its own, taking its signals from the pale zind Jack and Holly shared ahead.

The trail wove lazily in and out of the forest edge. Beyond the blackness of trees, the land of Dara appeared to be more of the same desert landscape they'd first encountered upon their arrival by the village of Lindur. Starlight illuminated the dunes which stretched to the horizon. The few times that they came within sight of a home or dwelling, the Captain steered them back under the trees, clearly intent on keeping them hidden as they fled north.

She shifted uncomfortably in the saddle, stretching her leg muscles. The Captain knew quite a lot about the Tracer and had called it range-limited. The vibrations from the crystals put in the metal box passed through the ground in all directions. When the vibrations came in contact with the person with those original Marks, the vibrations would stop, and the box changed color. Setting up the Tracer and getting a reading took time. As long as they kept plenty of distance between them and the device, they could avoid detection, and since the Tracer signal passed through the ground to locate its target, he had ordered her and Holly to stay off the ground as much as possible. The whole night, he'd let them dismount only once after Holly said she had to go. She flexed her legs again.

Morning light began filtering through the trees. She'd questioned the wisdom of riding at night with the threat of shards, but each morning, the heat in Dara rose fast. By noon, the temperature was unbearable, the air stiflingly hot. She'd spent nearly all her time indoors in the Coren, not realizing how harsh and unforgiving the Red Land could be.

Finally, the Captain motioned for them to stop to eat breakfast. Jack and Acorn climbed down from the zinds, but she and Holly stayed in their saddles. While Acorn helped Tannor prepare food and cups of hot tea, Emma eyed the Captain, wondering what the best way was to get him to talk. She needn't have bothered. Jack was already talking.

She leaned back in her saddle. The Captain had been hard on Jack so far. He'd criticized her brother's choice to defend them against the shards, and since then, at camp, he scowled at Jack as if something was wrong. Jack hadn't said anything to her, but he didn't need to; he'd kept his head down and his eyes averted from the Captain, the same way he always did back home. The Captain had responded only slightly better to her, ignoring most of her questions, but his demeanor with Holly was completely different. When he had lifted Holly onto the saddle before leaving camp, Emma could have sworn she saw a trace of a smile on his lips.

Jack was asking questions about shards. Emma hoped the Captain would respond to Jack's eagerness to learn, like one warrior to another warrior...well, at least a wanna-be warrior. After all, Jack had shown his willingness to stand against a dozen shards and surely, the man would give him some credit for being brave.

"Do you have to use a color weapon to kill them?" Jack asked. He looked very small standing between the Captain and Tannor.

"No, but non-cast weapons take a lot longer. And it gets messy," Tannor said.

"Why do they have different numbers of legs and arms?"

"No one knows," Tannor said.

"Where do they come from?"

"The Pit," Tannor answered again as the Captain slowly sipped his tea.

Emma rolled her eyes. *Geez, Tannor. No wonder the Captain never talks.*

"Where Se'en-sii dwells in the darkness?" Next to Jack, Acorn nodded vigorously.

"That's a legend. No one has ever seen Sii." *Tannor again.* Emma hefted the hunk of dense bread in her hand and considered throwing it at him.

"So shards are out-of-control monsters? Like giant insects running around Dara and attacking people because they're hungry?" Jack asked.

"Shards don't eat the people they kill," Tannor said. "But they can be controlled."

"Like hunting dogs? By whom?"

This time, Tannor didn't answer. Emma leaned forward in the saddle. Tannor's eyes were haunted. Clearly distracted, he mumbled about checking for any sign of pursuit and walked away.

The silence grew uncomfortably, but then Jack spoke. His voice was hushed with a sensitive tone that surprised Emma.

"I'm sorry, Captain. I didn't mean to offend him."

The Captain sighed as he pulled a small knife and a partially carved wooden female figure from a pouch on his belt. "You did not offend him. You merely opened a memory he carries with him."

"What memory?" Holly asked from atop her zind.

"Tannor's story is not mine to tell." He flicked his knife, shaving off a small slice of wood. The group dropped into silence again. The Captain looked at each of them in turn, then hesitantly clasped Jack's shoulder, before turning away. "Finish up."

Still whittling the wooden figure, the Captain slowly walked up the trail. When he stepped out of sight into the trees, Emma nudged her zind closer to Holly, then motioned for Jack to join them.

"Acorn, we need you, too," Emma said. Acorn looked up from where she was stowing the food into a pack and dashed over. Emma leaned down in her saddle. "I think we have to make a choice about showing the kaleidoscope to Tannor and the Captain," she paused, as the others nodded at her, "so far they've helped us, but the Captain... it feels like he's not saying something."

"Maybe he's quiet like that all the time. Tannor did say he's sick, right?" Holly suggested.

"Could be," said Emma, unconvinced.

"Maybe he hates kids," said Jack.

"Not based on the way he's treating Holly," Emma said as Holly grinned sheepishly. The Captain's treatment of her was markedly different. "Forget all that. The question is...do we trust them enough to show them the scope? Remember, Daria wasted no time taking it from us and we can't lose it again." The voices of Tannor and the Captain came from the woods, heading back to their location.

Jack combed his fingers through his hair as he looked around the group. "Do we all trust Tannor?" Emma nodded along with Holly and Acorn. "Okay, well if we trust Tannor, and Tannor trusts the Captain, then we can trust the Captain. Right?"

The two men stepped onto the trail up ahead. Jack's logic was shaky at best. The transitive formula of when A=B, and B=C, then C=A, worked great in math class. This was not math class. This was life. But she didn't have any other choice. The kaleidoscope brought them here, and until they figured out how to make it work, they were going nowhere.

"All right, I agree. We'll show them the scope. Maybe they'll know what we have to do to get back home."

"There's no sign of the Sisterhood," Tannor said as he strode over to his zind and pulled a cloth sack from the saddle bag. He rubbed the back of his neck with one hand. "We'll set up camp here."

Emma sighed with relief, more than ready to get off the zind and give her sore legs and back a respite from the rigors of riding. She started to dismount, but Tannor raised his hand and stopped her.

"No, you and Holly stay mounted," he said. Then he handed the sack to Acorn and pointed at a grouping of trees to their rear. "Vella hammocks. One for each of you. We'll string them up over there."

Emma spun around on the back of her zind and rolled her eyes as she watched Acorn, Jack, and Tannor stretch and secure the hammocks to the tree trunks. Hadn't Tannor just said there was no sign of pursuit? Surely, she and Holly could walk around and stretch their legs for a few minutes? Fed up with sitting, she threw one leg over her saddle.

"Stay there," ordered the Captain.

Emma stopped with her left foot in the stirrup and right leg hanging above the ground and looked back toward Holly. The Captain had her sister tossed over one shoulder like a sack of potatoes and was walking towards Emma. She could only see Holly's backside but could hear plenty of angry complaining coming from Holly's frontside.

There's no way I'm letting him carry me.

He strode past Emma as Holly tried to wriggle free, a scowl on her face. He spoke without looking back. "Tannor will carry you to a hammock."

"He'll what?" Emma sputtered. Tannor was walking towards her. *Alright. This up-in-the-air routine is going way too far. I mean, do the math.* "The probability of the Tracer being in range, set up, and active at the exact time of me stretching my legs for a minute is, well...um..." Emma skipped the math. "It's low, darn it." Not waiting, she jumped off the zind and landed right into Tannor's waiting arms.

He straightened up, holding Emma easily with one arm under her knees and the other supporting her back.

"Got you," Tannor said sounding amused. "And I thought he was the stubborn one, Eres."

Suddenly uncomfortable, Emma's stomach tightened, but not from any concern of falling as he carried her effortlessly towards the hammocks. Her arms sat like wooden sticks in her lap. She knew the natural, normal response would be to wrap the closest arm around his shoulder. Why was she acting so weird? He had to be feeling the stiffness of her body. *He's going to think I'm mad at him instead of the Captain and his dumb order.* She decided she should move, but her arm wasn't cooperating. She stared at the useless limb and begged it to move. *Come on, arm, lift yourself. Up and over his shoulder like it's the most natural thing in the world and means absolutely nothing.*

Without warning, Tannor dropped her onto a hammock. "Stay there, your Stubborness." He turned and walked away to unload the zinds.

Her left arm decided to shift into a comfortable position on the hammock. "Great. Now you decide to move." Exasperated and not entirely sure why, she flopped back onto the hammock, her body still exhausted from riding, but now, very awake.

34

A SHOW OF TRUST

SINCE BREAKING CAMP THAT MORNING, Emma's arms had several chances to act more naturally around Tannor. Each time he had lifted her, she lightly wrapped her left arm around his neck. Not too tight because she didn't want him to think she was holding on to him, but again, not too loose which might say she didn't appreciate his help. All in all, Emma was quite pleased with her arm's behavior.

But her eyes were not cooperating. When he picked her up, her eyes decided to drop down, fixating first on his strong arms, then his shoulders which seemed a great deal bigger than Emma had first thought. Early this evening, they had stared nervously at his two Marks—dark scarlet and orange lines—that began at his throat, ran squarely down the center of his muscled chest, and disappeared under his shirt. Yup, she and her eyes were definitely going to have words.

They stopped for a few hours in the heat of the day before heading again to the north. When the Captain awoke from a brief nap —his eyes bleary and his face grim—he said they should keep moving into the wilds of Tiraneh, the North Forest. Emma decided to wait on telling him about the kaleidoscope. His reaction about the Tracer had been harsh, and she didn't relish the thought of revealing another piece of information to him, this time something she had intentionally hidden.

Up ahead on the narrow trail, the Captain raised his left hand, the signal to stop. In the waning light of dusk, she watched as he paused on the trail and listened again for any sounds of Sisters. His head moved slowly from side to side. In camp, he walked stiffly as if warding off a deep and constant pain. She wondered how much of that was from the Fade and how much was from age. She couldn't pinpoint how old the man was, but everything about him—the gruff demeanor, the deep creases around his wide-set eyes, and the quiet growling under his breath whenever one of them asked a question— said the Captain was old, an aging tiger past his prime.

Night closed around them. They rode in silence for another hour along the top of a ridge that provided a clear sightline of the trail they'd been following through the forest of Tiraseh. There was still no sign of them being followed, and the Red Coren now lay far behind them to the south, out of sight. The Captain, still atop his black zind, peered at the trail, and after several long minutes, dismounted and, to Emma's surprise, motioned that she and Holly could get down as well. Tannor pulled two glowcubes from his pack and they sat as a group in a circle eating dried meat and dates. Tannor shared a funny story of a terrible banquet he and the Captain had suffered through where the hostess passed out from too much drink and the host tried to give the Captain one of his daughters as a token of gratitude for saving their village. Watching the Captain chuckle softly as Tannor talked, Emma sipped her tea and tried to come up with a good way to change the subject. She needed to tell the Captain about the kaleido-scope without destroying the mood.

"Were you a Captain before you came to Dara?" Jack asked. "And how did you get here?" Emma couldn't help but smile with relief. She desperately wanted to know more about his background and his reason for helping them. She tipped the cup in her hand back and forth, studying the rising tendrils of steam, and hoped he would answer.

The Captain sat motionless, his hands now still, no longer carving the small figurine he'd pulled from a pouch on his belt. His eyes studied each of them in turn and then dropped down to stare at the carving. Jack was getting ready to say something else; worried he might accidentally redirect the conversation, she quickly raised her hands to her lips, giving him the quiet sign. As if speaking from a faraway hill, the Captain began:

"Yes, in Tera, I carried the rank of captain. On my twelfth birthday, the age of decision for all young men, I pledged my service to the army, although that went against my father's wishes. He expected me to join in our family business. But I had dreamed of nothing but war and glory my whole life, and I saw no honor in the making and selling of furniture. I'm sure if the Light ever blessed me with a family, my sons would surely reject my path as well. Betrayal is the nature of men and women." He looked right at Emma. She swallowed nervously.

"You became a soldier at twelve?" Jack asked.

"Hardly." A glimmer of a smile crossed his pale and drawn face, the first one they had seen. "A new recruit is not worth a soldier's belt buckle. Not even a Three. I mucked stalls and slopped livestock. I lugged rations, fetched water, and scraped the dung from the officer's boots. But I learned, and I listened. I learned first how to follow orders, and then how to give them. At nineteen, I became Captain of the Coren Guard."

"The Coren on Green is guarded by men? What about the Sisters there?" Holly asked as she reached out her hand and Acorn handed her another dried date.

"Wait, did you say you're a Three?" Jack asked. They had not seen any Marks on the Captain's neck or hands, but Emma wasn't surprised. Tannor had two Marks—Byrn and Durk were Ones. It made sense he would be higher Marked.

"Yes, Eres Holly, in Tera, the Coren was open to all. At least it was during my time there." He held up the back of his right hand. "And yes, I'm a Three." Jack edged in closer to inspect the Captain's hand.

Acorn leaned forward a few inches, obviously hesitant to act too familiar with a higher Marked. Since being rescued, Acorn had reverted to her servant mode with the men. Emma wondered if she would ever think of herself as more than a Zero.

"He's got three Marks. They're so faint, I'm not sure what colors,"

Jack announced as he looked to the Captain, who changed the subject.

"You asked how I came to Dara. I came through the Portal in the capitol. I was sent here as a sentry," he looked thoughtfully at Jack, "my mission to wait for a white-eyed man whom I must now assume is you. I stayed in the shadows at first, keeping to myself, naively believing my mission would be short and my return to Tera swift. But I could not sit idly by as Daria tightened her grip on this land. She rules Dara like a tyrant, choking the life from these people. So, I recruited men, trained them, and have been patrolling Dara ever since," he paused and stroked the thick grey stubble on his chin, then smiled wryly. "It's been ten long years since I made that journey. My protection of these people—both from shards and from the Red Coren's injustice—did not sit well with Daria. I've been called a rebel. I am forbidden from entering the capital city of Ephara or accessing the Portal located within. I have no way home." He chuckled softly then inclined his head towards Tannor. "Tannor likes being a rebel. He's been with me three years now. Since the age of sixteen." Emma glanced at Tannor who was sitting next to the Captain, and their eyes met. Suddenly flustered, she quickly looked back at the Captain.

"And after this white-eyed man arrived? What then?" Emma asked, clearing the lump in her throat.

"My mission was to protect him and bring him back to Tera and the Forest Council. As to why...well, do you know anything about the Prophet?"

"We know a little," Emma said. The tapestry image—with the man and his crazed eyes alight with fury—popped into her mind. "Daria fears that people will treat Jack as a new Prophet, because of his white eyes, I guess." Emma hesitated as she gathered her nerve to tell him about the kaleidoscope.

The Captain nodded. "The legends speak of a white-eyed man who came here three-thousand years ago. A man with the eyes of a prophet, supposedly. He revealed the existence of the other Lands to the people, chose the First Guardians, and then with his knowledge, constructed the very first Portals, uniting the Lands. If you believe the stories. Many people still do, calling him all sorts of names... the Father of the Seven, the Prophet, the Bringer of Light." Eyeing Jack, he stopped speaking for a moment. "There's no room in Daria's world for a religious uprising, nor would there be any room for two girls with Seven Marks, which makes her behavior puzzling," he said as his eyes settled on Emma. "All three of you are clear threats. Why did she not kill all of you immediately?"

Emma sucked in a deep breath and blew it out. ""Show him," she said, then nudged Jack with her elbow. She stood up as Jack opened his pack and pulled out the kaleidoscope. Tannor whistled in awe. She held out her hand and after Jack laid the barrel of the metal scope into her palm, she held it up. "We have this. Daria called it the Prophet's Eye, but we've been calling it the scope, short for kaleidoscope." She stepped around the cooking pot and placed the scope into the Captain's hands. "We found it in our dad's room on Earth and when Jack looked inside, he saw a red light."

"More like an open red door into Dara," Jack added.

"Right, a door like the Portal we saw in the Red Coren," Emma continued as she sat down. "It works for Jack and no one else as far as we know. He stepped through the door and pulled us along with him."

Turning the scope over in his hands, he ran his index finger over the engraved symbols on the barrel, then tapped the green rune on the fourth section. "So, it's this *kaleidoscope* that has the power of a portal and brought you here. And Daria called this the Eye of the Prophet?" he mused out loud, then frowned at Emma. "You should have shown this to me sooner. You have to trust me."

Emma gulped. She'd been surprised by the Captain's calm; she'd been expecting a much angrier reaction, not a conversation about trust and sharing, especially coming from a man with the conversational skills of an oak tree. She squinted at him for a long time. Then again, he had just shared quite a lot, and he and Tannor had given them every reason to trust them.

The Captain hefted the scope in his hands, as if checking the balance of a forged weapon, then twisted one of the small metal knobs on the scope. The tiny slot opened on the side of the barrel, revealing the empty chamber beneath. "I think this may be why Daria wants Jack alive. As Guardian, she would have a deep knowledge of the prophet and the power of this device." He turned to Jack, then spoke, his voice quiet. "And what about your father? He can use this scope as well?"

"Our dad?" Jack scoffed. "No, it wouldn't work for him. He has normal eyes. Blue. He had a huge collection of kaleidoscopes; this was one of them."

"He's an ancient history professor," added Holly.

"And now that we're in Dara, the kaleidoscope doesn't show anything, no red light and no door back to our home," Emma said as the Captain handed the kaleidoscope to Tannor.

"I don't know how to make it work," Jack sighed.

"None of us do." Emma patted Jack on his shoulder. "Captain, we want to go home. You saved us and you're keeping us away from Daria and the Sisters, and we're thankful. But we need to go home, back to our dad." Holly leaned into her, and she wrapped her arm around her shoulders, hugging her tight, before turning back to face the Captain. "We need your help; we don't know how to make— Tannor!" Emma gasped as Tannor placed the end of the scope to his right eye. Too stunned to move, Emma held her breath.

Tilting his head back and forth, Tannor then aimed the end of the scope at Emma. "Nothing, no light's getting through at all." As he pulled the scope away from his eye, Emma recovered enough to step forward. She snatched it from his hand. Tannor recoiled from her, then lowered his eyes to the ground and cleared his throat. "On my Marks, Eres. I didn't mean to do anything wrong or to offend you."

Emma handed the scope to Jack. "No, I'm sorry Tannor. I overreacted. Like I said, we're pretty sure the kaleidoscope only works for Jack, but until we know more, we need to be careful." Emma paused and when he looked up at her, she smiled at him and tried to sound reassuring. "We need your help, too."

Grinning, Jack slid the scope into his pack "Yeah, and if you accidentally scoped, who'd carry her back and forth to her hammock?"

Emma laughed along with the others, but she felt her cheeks getting warm. She grabbed her cup of tea and raised it with both hands to her lips, hiding her face and avoiding eye contact as the laughter died off. For a long moment, the camp was quiet.

"Very well. Then our course of action is clear," announced the Captain.

"It is?" Holly asked.

"Yes, Eres," said the Captain as he smiled at Holly. "This kaleidoscope has the power to return you to your home in Earthland, and I suspect, may also have the power to take you to the other lands in the Seven," he said pointing at the scope in Emma's hand. "That green sign on the barrel, the one in the shape of a tree. That symbol is on the flag of Tera, my homeland," he said, then stood up. "We must learn how to use the Eye of the Prophet and there is only one option." Then the Captain reached down and rested his hand on Tannor's shoulder. "I'm sorry, Tannor."

Tannor nodded as if in acknowledgement, but then, Emma watched his eyes go wide. He jumped up and wheeled to face the Captain. "No, you can't be serious?" He waved his arms in the air. "Please, no."

The Captain grabbed Tannor by the arm and led him over to the zinds at the edge of camp. The two men huddled close together, speaking in hushed tones with Tannor shaking his head as he argued. Emma dumped her tea on the ground and busied herself with packing up the food and cooking pot, all the while, focusing her hearing in their direction.

"Let it go, Tannor."

"You know I can't. Besides, I'm not the only one with ghosts the last time I checked."

Emma was dying to know more about the pasts of these two men. Instead, all she got was a long, tired sigh from the Captain. They went quiet for a moment, unsaid words hanging in the air between them. Finally, Tannor spoke, with a small cough.

"So, that's the move? There's no one else?"

"No. We need more information fast."

"What about the archives in Ephara? I still have friends in the Guard."

The Captain glanced their way. "Too risky. The Sisters would have already spread the news and put up a bounty. Every person within twenty daan of the cities will be looking out for these three."

"Fine, but I don't like this. He talks too much. And the last time we met, the idiot tried to take my sword. My brother's sword!" Tannor sounded furious. "Are you sure you can trust him?"

"No, but he owes me," the Captain declared, with a small chuckle in his voice, "and right now, he's all we've got. We find Roi."

35

THE COMPELLING

THEY SLEPT that night under a dark sky bereft of clouds. At first light, they headed out, this time leaving the forest trail and riding to the east. Going mostly downhill now, the trees thinned out, eventually giving way to open fields and a shallow river, barely waist deep. When they came within sight of a small village, Tannor rode ahead to scout out any news of Roi's location as the rest of them made camp and waited.

The morning dragged slowly for Jack. He didn't love riding—he kept waiting for the zind to leap into a wild gallop—but at least traveling had provided a distraction from the worry of being hunted by the Sisterhood. Sitting in camp, waiting for something to happen, was intolerable. Emma tried asking the Captain about Roi (she had been eavesdropping last night and overheard Tannor's concerns about this man), but the Captain only responded that she needed to trust him then promptly went to sleep under the shade of a large tree.

Jack tried practicing Budo, but after a few minutes, he gave up. What good would a front kick be against a jaw-snapping wolf-beetle anyway? He waded in the river and tried skipping stones with no luck. Besides the water was hot like the air.

Jack wandered over and sat on the ground by Holly, Acorn, and Emma. The Captain had relaxed his rule on keeping his sisters suspended in the air. He'd concluded that they were a safe distance from any of the Sisters. They'd been riding consistently to the north before heading east; they'd crossed the shallows of the river Enabsa that flowed down from the western foothills and across Dara to the Sea of A'abak on the Eastern Edge.

The four of them tried to make sense out of the markings engraved on the kaleidoscope's barrel, but quickly grew tired of guessing – the green symbol was tree shaped and the orange symbol looked like fire, but that meant nothing to them. When Tannor came riding into camp later in the day, Jack almost cheered.

"We're in luck. Roi is in Silig, a few hours ride down river. He's working in a tavern called the Cracked Rib," Tannor said as he dismounted. He was grinning more than usual as if he'd heard a good joke.

"I told you to bring him here." The Captain set down his still full plate of food; he'd taken only a few bites from the roasted game bird and hard roll. Acorn dashed in, taking his plate, as if she were serving in the Coren. Jack frowned as she backed away respectfully. She shouldn't be treated like a servant. Not after how much they owed her.

The Captain returned her gesture with a slight nod of his own. "Your cooking is excellent."

"Thank you, Captain. But you need to eat more," she chided while waggling one finger at him. Jack relaxed. Acorn was serving the Captain not because she had to, but merely because she wanted to.

Tannor sat on the ground with them, took off his boots and stretched his legs. "Getting him may not be simple. He's in a tricky spot."

"Roi is always in a spot." The Captain said.

"That's putting it mildly." Tannor shrugged, then leaned forward. "Let me tell you about Roi."

According to Tannor, Roi's thievery was aimed at a very specific kind of target. Instead of stealing money, jewelry, or practical goods to barter, he stole knowledge. Roi was obsessed with the history of the

Seven. He was convinced that the Sisterhood had secrets and somewhere behind the Coren walls was the answer.

"The answer to what?" Jack asked, intrigued. Next to him, Emma was frowning and wrinkling her nose as if Tannor's story about Roi smelled rotten.

"The answer to everything. Why we're here and meaning of life nonsense," Tannor said. "Frankly, he's crazy—or a lunatic who has spent too much time sniffing the ink off scrolls. He'll steal anything—papers, artifacts, carvings, weapons—anything he thinks is linked to the legend of Sii or the Sisterhood or the Red Guardian. Especially her. He tracks that woman's every move."

Jack wanted to forget about their up-close experiences with Daria. Anyone who wanted to spend time with the Red Guardian had to be nuts. But with his obsession for ancient treasures and legends, Roi sounded like the right person to help them unlock the secret of the kaleidoscope.

This fascination was the reason for Roi's current predicament. The town of Silig was Daria's birthplace, and as the custom, her home and all its belongings had been turned into a shrine, a physical remembrance of where the Light had blessed a child to become the next Guardian. Roi—probably on one of his crazy searches, Tannor explained—had broken into the shrine and gotten caught. Half of the townsfolk came forward and called him out for not paying his debts. Then, the other half came forward and called him a nuisance.

"He's under arrest?" Emma asked, sounding angry. Jack sat up straight; he was sure her voice had split into more than one note. Across from him, the Captain was watching his sister, a wary look in his eyes.

Smiling at the group, Tannor finished. "The town Shorta, who also happens to own the tavern, is punishing him by making him pay off his debts in a very public way. He's working at the Rib."

"That doesn't sound too bad," Holly said, lying on the ground and clearly enjoying not being stuck in a hammock.

"Hard work is a good thing for any man," The Captain replied.

"But the town is shaming him. Roi is a Two. Mopping floors and fetching drinks is beneath his Marks."

"Let me get this straight," Emma said. She was scowling at him, and her voice was hard, a chiseled edge like flint. "Your *master plan* to protect us from the Coren and help us get home is to seek advice from a half-crazy convicted thief who is stalking the Red Guardian? The woman who wants us dead?"

Jack braced himself, sensing his sister's frustration. His sister was the most organized person in the world and of all the things that wound her up back home, not knowing the plan was the worst, which was why they'd gotten into the habit of making decisions together and voting as a family. But the Captain was a soldier; he probably had no idea how much his giving orders and not explaining everything was winding her the wrong way.

"Yes," the Captain said, letting the word drop like a stone and then staring at her. Jack wondered if he should say something to save the poor man.

"YES? That's *all* you've got to say? The best you can do is a one-word answer?" Emma stood and stepped in front of the Captain. Jack watched his sister's anger rising up...literally. Her Marks were glowing brighter from deep in her chest and into her neck. "What if he turns us in? What if Roi tries to steal the scope like he did Tannor's sword?"

"Trust me," the Captain said.

"No, that's not good enough! ANSWER ME!" Emma's voice split into four different tones at the same time and ripped through the air like a windstorm. Vibrations of sound hit Jack's head like a closed fist. A few feet away, Acorn grabbed her ears and fell to her knees. Tannor looked stunned and stared open-mouthed at Emma.

Surprisingly, the Captain's face looked calm, as if he had been waiting, expecting her hard-as-a-hammer scream. He stepped in close to Emma, her head shaking and a confused look in her eyes. "That's called Compelling, what you did with your voice."

"You knew that was going to happen?" Emma said. Her voice was quiet as if she was afraid to let her voice get loud again.

"I suspected. Over the past days, your questions have gotten more and more direct. This morning, when I ignored your questions about Roi, I heard hints of three colors in your voice. Indigo, Green, and..."

"Violet," Emma answered. "You made me mad on purpose?"

"No, he's been testing you," Tannor said, still rubbing his temples. "Trust me, he does it all the time."

"I chose to push your limits," said the Captain.

Smirking, Tannor crossed his arms. "Sounds like a test to me."

Ignoring him, the Captain continued. "Sisters and Guardians are capable of compelling others with their voice."

"But it didn't affect you." Emma paused; her brow was furrowed in concentration. "I didn't do it correctly."

"No, but you were very close. For a Compelling to work, you have to include all of your target's colors—in my case, Red, Green, and Violet—plus Blue and Indigo. Five colors."

"I can't do Red yet. Orange either. Sister Yiana, who helped our escape, was coaching us but we never finished the lessons."

"Yes, but your soundcasting powers are growing incredibly fast. You told me that Marks stand for nothing in Earthland and that you had no colorcasting abilities, yet in less than three weeks on Daran soil, you have developed significant power," the Captain rose to one knee in front of Emma. "You need have no worries about Roi. You are a true Seven and for Roi to betray you would be to betray his own nature." The Captain clasped Emma's hands in his. "By your Marks, Eres, will you forgive my soldier ways?"

Emma's face looked overwhelmed, and Jack guessed it would take her a while to fully process the past few minutes, and not just her sudden outbreak of power. Jack saw the significance. The Captain was kneeling in front of his sister and had called her a true Seven, and then addressed her as Eres, like a knight pledging an oath to a queen.

Emma nodded, then smiled softly. "Yes, Captain."

The Captain rose slowly, then looked around the group. "Now, let us rescue Roi. Based on his plight, he should be pleased to see us."

Tannor grinned. "Captain, I think he'll be very pleased."

ROI'S PERFORMANCE

WALKING into Silig with a zind for Roi, Jack followed the Captain—riding his zind—and kept his eyes glued on the beast's oversized hooves, perfect for traversing the sand dunes. Acorn, her pack loaded with several of their colorcast cooking pots in need of recasting, was walking somewhere to his right. She made clunking sounds with each step.

The zind's hooves kicked up another cloud of dust into Jack's face, but he kept his head lowered. He reached up, scratched his nose, and tugged the hood on his cloak farther over his eyes. The Captain had not minced words earlier. "Keep your head down and your eyes on the ground at all times. You are a Zero."

And now I look like a Zero. Jack stared down at his dirty bare feet. He'd relented and changed into the plain cloak and clothes—a sleeveless brown tunic and loose pants cinched with a plain leather belt. Days ago, Emma and Holly had both changed into their new clothes —full-length dresses with loose, long sleeves and hooded cloaks to deflect the hot sun—but Jack had stayed in his jeans, t-shirt, and sneakers. His clothes felt like home to him. When he stuffed his sneakers into his pack, he felt like he was giving up on going home, like he was accepting his new place here as a Zero. Worse, now he was barefoot.

Acorn had eagerly offered her own coaching. "Remember, Jack. Nobody pays any attention to the Unmarked, especially when they are in service. Stay close behind the Captain at all times, like you're waiting for him to give you an order. You'll be fine."

Emma and Holly stayed behind with Tannor, and Jack had given the kaleidoscope to Emma for safekeeping. The Captain originally had planned to leave them all with Tannor, but if shards or the Sisters found them, protecting all four children from an attack would be difficult. Even for Tannor.

More hot dust flew up Jack's nose, and he willed himself not to sneeze. Around him, the streets were noisy, blanketed with a jumble of conversations, shouts from vendors, and the clattering of rolling wagons—more than loud enough to cover the sound of one little sneeze. The problem was that his sneezes were never little. He didn't sneeze; he squealed. The girls yelled at him every time, and their dad once likened Jack's sneeze to the sound of an angry pig being shot out of a cannon. He raised his right arm, vigorously rubbed his nose, and tried to focus on his surroundings—at least the eight feet of dirt in front of him.

He'd caught quick glimpses of Silig as he, Acorn, and the Captain rode two of the zinds down from the hills on the western side. A sandwall, twenty feet high with several guarded gates, surrounded a collection of several hundred houses and buildings. Most were carved from sand like the village of Lindur, though with fewer openings and less adornment. Larger buildings made of wood lined the open square in the center of town. Unlike Lindur, all of the buildings had either wooden shutters or metal grates on their windows. Protection from shards, Jack guessed. Groups of armed men stood at the ready at the main gate. With its fortifications, the town felt ominous, like a clenched mouth full of sharp teeth.

Surprised at his own skittishness, Jack edged closer to the Captain's mount as they navigated up a narrow, crowded street. The chance of being caught chewed on his nerves. A group of men were arguing loudly to his right, talking about an attack. A pair of heavy, dusty boots supporting a pair of equally heavy legs came into Jack's limited field of vision, and he veered to the left to avoid a collision. An unseen voice, male and respectful, hailed the Captain. Jack imagined the Captain nodding back, not wasting any words as usual. Another group of sandaled feet pressed in all around him, filling Jack's nose with the earthy scent of tea and spices. A woman's voice—close behind—reached his ears, asking him a question, something about the Captain and would he be interested in trying her Sunset blend. Jack hunched his shoulders and said nothing and hoped the voice would go away.

The Captain's zind stopped and the woman's voice moved mercifully on. With a clunk of her pots, Acorn stopped beside him. "Jack, we're here. Give me the reins and follow the Captain inside." Relieved, Jack slid the rope into Acorn's outstretched hand. He risked taking a small glance at her from under the edge of his cloak. She had a reassuring twinkle in her eyes. "Keep your head down."

Next to him, the Captain cleared his throat. Jack fixed his gaze on the Captain's boots. The design of a tree was stitched into the leather. A symbol of his Green land, Jack guessed, as they started up the steps and entered the Rib.

Dim. That was the word that came to Jack as he followed the Captain inside. Each table had a small glowing cube that cast a yellow light on the patrons. As they passed by, an old man on their left reached out and tapped the cube, its yellow glow immediately turned off. The man's table slid into the dimness, his face covered in shadows.

They stopped at the edge of the long stone bar. The Captain asked for Roi, and a woman's voice replied that he'd be back soon from an errand. Apparently satisfied with the answer, the Captain turned and led them to the far corner of the room. He stopped in front of an occupied table, the one closest to the wall but with clear line of sight to both the front entrance and the breadth of the room.

"Toran. Deel," The Captain said, obviously familiar with the men seated at the table. "Would you mind?" His voice sounded polite, but Jack knew right away the question was an order in disguise.

"Not at all, Captain," answered the men quickly in unison. The men picked up their plates and mugs and walked off towards a different table. Sitting down with his back to the wall, he extinguished the table cube. "Sit. The chair in the corner."

Jack sat and lowered his head, still thinking about the men giving up their table so willingly.

"Welcome back, Captain." The woman sounded pleased. Two shapely hands with thin Red Marks came to rest on the table as the woman leaned in. She smelled like cinnamon. Jack kept his eyes fixed on the dead yellow cube. "Will you be staying a few days?"

"Not this time, Meera. Passing through." His voice was surprisingly friendly. "My usual. And stew for him."

"I don't like stew," Jack said as Meera sauntered off to another table. A question popped into his mind. "Do you have a family? Like kids or a wife?" Jack raised his head.

"Head down." *So much for the friendly voice.* "You need to sit quietly. Zeros work in taverns; they don't eat in taverns. But leaving you outside in the open with Acorn would have been too risky. Mind though, bringing you inside here could cause trouble." The Captain's voice softened slightly as if anticipating Jack's next question. "I rescued Meera once. She will not cause a problem."

Jack nodded and contented himself with listening to the conversation of two men at a nearby table. Meera returned and set a large clay cup with a straw and a platter piled high with food in front of the Captain. The roasted meat smelled delicious. Jack was hungry.

"Meera, the town's on alert. Why?" asked the Captain.

The woman made a clicking sound with her tongue. "You don't know? Lindur was attacked. A bad one, too, by all reports—a horde of shards and that beast Chaos. They're saying the whole center of town was destroyed."

"No, I hadn't heard. I've been patrolling out by Tiraneh."

A bowl of stew and a clay cup slid noisily across the table to Jack. A glop of lumpy brown sauce dangled from the edge of the bowl and stubbornly refused to let go.

"Thank you very much, Eres," Jack said, not sure how anyone could be thankful for a bowl of mystery goo, keeping his head down, not sure how to address her.

"Eres," Meera laughed but sounded pleased. "Still training this one, Captain?" She laughed as she moved to another table.

The Captain dug into his food while Jack tried to digest Meera's news about Lindur. They'd just been there a few weeks ago. Acorn had told him about Chaos, but stories of a giant-clawed monster big enough to crush buildings seemed unbelievable. Meera said the center of town was attacked. Jack wondered what that meant for the fate of the Mayor.

With a sigh, Jack picked up his spoon and eyed the bowl of goo in front of him. He understood the reason for ordering something fit for a Zero, but why did it have to be stew? Jack liked soup and with soup, you at least knew what was in the bowl. Stew was a dark mystery, filled with unknown ingredients and suspicious-looking chunks of who-knew-whats. Even the word— *ssteewww*—sounded bad, like muck or swamp. He stirred the brown surface and pictured a hand reaching up from the muck, yanking the spoon and pulling him down, body and all, down into the depths.

Jack nudged the bowl aside. Opting for the cup instead, he took a tentative sip from the straw made from a cut piece of reed. The distinct bite of alcohol, mixed with a sweetness of thick honey and lemons, filled his mouth. Jack's eyes popped wide. He took another sip, not sure whether he liked or disliked the taste.

The Captain tapped the bowl with his knife. Taking the hint, Jack grudgingly tried the stew. No chunks and a taste like scorched metal. He spooned a few more bites into his mouth—still no chunks. He stirred back and forth through the bowl: nothing but gravy and not a single piece of carrot or potato. Jack understood. Meera may not cause a problem for the Captain, but she wasn't wasting any good food on a Zero. Now annoyed by the missing chunks he didn't want, he finished off the bowl.

Adjusting his hood, Jack lifted his eyes and peered at his surroundings. The Cracked Rib was long and rectangular; the place was about half full, with more than twenty men sitting in groups of two or three around the sturdy wooden tables. All of the men were armed with curved knives or swords, like the one Tannor carried, and by the looks of their scars and hardened expressions, these men were not simple farmers. Besides Meera, three other women—all Ones—served the tables. The massive bar was a grey block of stone as big as the moon; they'd probably built the tavern around it. At the far end of the room, a small stage sat empty.

He immediately understood why they called it the Cracked Rib. The long walls on either side were framed by massive wooden supports, dull white like the bleached bones of a dead animal. They started at the floor and curved inwards, coming together in sharp points at the roof's peak like bones forming a rib cage. Most of the supports showed deep cracks and breaks. Very much like the men inside.

The Captain leaned forward, and made a small motion with his hand to catch Meera's attention. She hurried over from another table.

"Nother, Captain?" She said as she grabbed their empty dishes.

"Yes. Is Roi back yet? I'm looking for him."

She laughed as if he'd said something funny. "Oh, you won't have to look very hard." Still chuckling, she turned back towards the bar. "No, not hard at all."

The Captain growled impatiently under his breath. Leaning forward, he propped his elbows up and rested his chin on his hands. With his thumbs, he slowly stroked his stubbled beard, peppered with grey, as his eyes settled into a blank faraway stare, something he'd done several times over the past few days, usually at the back end of their camp conversations. Jack sat back and looked around the Cracked Rib for anything more interesting than this man's grim silence.

A woman appeared in the doorway at the back of the stage. Clothed in a shabby dress and head wrap—both faded blue like a rain-weary sky—she edged to the center of the stage while keeping her back to the audience. With each step, her feet dragged across the wooden planks. Jack leaned forward at the prospect of any entertainment, though this woman did not seem very excited to be there.

The woman, her back still toward the men in the crowd, stood still, her large hands balled up into fists. Jack frowned. There were some rather tall girls at school who had quickly outgrown him, but none of them had hands that big. Neither did they have arms so long they stuck out of their dress sleeves like two overgrown sticks.

Some of the men in the crowd began yelling for her to turn around. Some of the calls seemed rude to Jack, and as the woman's shoulders slumped, he felt sorry for her. Wow, what a bad crowd. *No wonder she doesn't want to do her act.*

A table over, the men started chanting "Sing, sing" and the chorus quickly spread throughout the room, bouncing loudly off the ribs. Jack hoped the woman would leave the stage and refuse to perform, but she slowly turned around. Jack tilted so far forward he nearly fell off his seat.

Pasty white like a subterranean cave dweller, she had a long bony nose and big eyes that seemed stuck in a state of perpetual gawking. Beneath her large ears, two lines of color, red and yellow, threaded down her throat. The singer was the homeliest girl he'd ever seen. Or else...

Jack reached out and tapped the shoulder of the Captain, his eyes now closed, ignoring the crowd. "You said Roi was a Two?"

"Yes." The Captain opened his eyes at Jack.

"And he's skinny?"

The Captain scanned the bar. "Yes, like a stick with feet. Is he here?" Taking a drink, he turned his head back towards the stage. That's when the Captain—who was never surprised—spit out his beer in disbelief.

"He's supposed to sing," Jack said, feeling terrible for the skinny man in the faded blue dress.

Up on stage, Roi looked miserable. In a different setting, without the dress and the pained expression, he could pass for a scientist, like someone who spent too much time in the lab, forgetting to eat. But now, he looked whipped, like a dog grown used to repeated beatings, his head and shoulders hunched down as if ready for the next blow. Like the Captain's thousand-yard stare, Roi's eyes fixed on a spot twenty feet above the head of the taunting crowd. But his gaze was more than blank and unfocused. His eyes held no hope.

A deep harsh voice boomed from somewhere near the bar. "Get on with it, you louse! And make it a good one."

Roi's focus came down from the rafters as his head jerked towards the voice. He sighed, took a deep breath, and fumbled to adjust his head wrap. The crowd snorted with laughter.

"Very well. A good one," Roi repeated. Jack grinned at the sarcasm in the response. Maybe he's still got some spirit left. Roi stepped forward and spread his hands as if welcoming the crowd to a party. "The Brothers and the Bucket." With a slight curtsy, he launched into a song, a song about three brothers who lived on a farm and all of them chasing after the same pretty farm girl. Every time one of the brothers got close to catching her, he slipped and fell into a bucket of...

Jack cringed at the words. It was the dirtiest and funniest song he'd ever heard. During the first verse, he tried holding his laughter in, not wanting to draw any attention. By the end of the second verse, he didn't try to hold back; the men in the Rib were all singing along and laughing loudly. Next to him, the Captain sat unmoving, not smiling.

Roi hit the third verse—"And 'fore he reached the bedroom door, he slipped in a pile of..." He stopped singing, while the crowd kept going into the chorus. He was staring in the direction of their table, probably aware of the Captain, but as Roi continued to stare, Jack felt more and more like he was the one being watched. Not sure what else to do, he shrank down in his chair and yanked his hood lower.

The crowd faltered without Roi's singing. Several men yelled angrily at him to get on with it. Jack peered out from underneath his hood. Roi was looking right at him. The hopelessness in his eyes was gone, replaced with curiosity and determination.

Roi strode to the front edge of the stage and gazed at the crowd. The laughter and heckling in the room quieted, seemingly in response to his sudden shift in manner. The men fell silent. Reaching up, with an air of dignity this time, he untied and removed the wrap from his head, then undid the top two buttons on the dress, exposing his two Marks, red and yellow. After raking the fingers of both hands through his hair, he clasped his hands together in front of his chest. Jack recognized the stance, the same welcoming gesture used by the Sisters at the Coren.

"The Beginning Song." And with a small nod of his head this time, directed right at Jack, Roi began to sing. Unlike the casual rough tone used for the bucket song, his voice now rang out clear and pure, a warm tenor that reverberated off the walls and rafters:

> *Before first morning, Ashala lay sleeping with Kiru*
> *   bound to her side,*
> *and Kiru cried,*
> *"Ashala, my darling, give me your love to keep me*
> *   warm."*
> *"What will you do with my love?" Ashala sat on her*
> *   throne,*

None of the men spoke or moved. The women slid quietly into empty chairs.

> *and Kiru cried,*
> *"Oh, my queen, with your love I will create a burning*
> *   fire."*
> *"What will you do with my fire" Ashala raised her*
> *   head,*
> *and he cried,*
> *"Ashala, my guide, with your fire I will create a golden*
> *   sun."*

As one, the men at each table reached out and tapped on the light cubes. The yellow glow filled the room. One of the burly men wiped his eyes.

> *"What will you do with my sun?" Ashala lowered her*
> *   veil,*
> *and Kiru cried,*

> *"Ashala, my bride, with your sun I will create a green*
>   *field."*
> *"What will you do with my field?" Ashala unbraided*
>   *her hair,*
> *and he cried out,*
> *"Oh, my lover, by your field I will create a sparkling*
>   *river."*

The men picked up their mugs and took a drink as if making a silent toast. With Roi's voice in his ears and the men's movements, Jack felt like he was in a church ceremony.

> *"What will you do with my river?" Ashala drank*
>   *deeply,*
> *and Kiru cried,*
> *"Oh, my enchanted, in your river I will hide a royal*
>   *treasure."*

Rising to their feet, every man in the room pulled out his sword or knife and held it forward. Jack turned to his right. The Captain was standing, his sword held in both hands.

> *"What will you do with my treasure" Ashala fingered*
>   *the blade,*
> *and he cried out,*
> *"Ashala, my heart, with your treasure I will create*
>   *eternity."*
> *"What will you do with eternity?" asked Ashala*
>   *holding her breath,*
> *and Kiru cried,*
> *"Ashala, my darling, in eternity I will love you forever."*

As if on command, each man plunged his blade downwards towards the floor.

"Then I will give you all my love," Ashala gasped as she
*   fell on the throne.*
Before first morning, Ashala lay sleeping with Kiru at
*   her side,*
and Kiru cried... and Kiru cried.

No one spoke or moved as the last sounds of Roi's voice faded into silence. Like mourners at the close of a funeral, the men sheathed their weapons, sat down, and tapped off the table lights. The room sat in shadow, the remaining light coming through the small windows high up on the walls. His shoulders no longer slumped and his feet no longer dragging, Roi stepped off the stage.

He was headed straight at Jack with an eager, no, desperate look on his face, and Jack had a terrible feeling Roi would make a scene and draw attention. Exactly the kind of unwanted attention he'd been trying to avoid.

"Don't move." The Captain commanded. Rising quickly, he strode forward and met Roi head-on. He grabbed onto his shoulder and stopped him, turning him away from the table, and whispering a short set of commands at the man. Letting go, the Captain walked across the room toward a big man sitting close to the stage.

Jack fidgeted in his chair and tried to stay calm. Roi had stayed put, which Jack guessed was on the Captain's order. But the skinny man's big eyes kept peering in his direction. On the other side of the tavern, the big man, who had stood at the Captain's approach, was exchanging words with the Captain, but his eyes kept drifting to the side, lingering on Jack.

Spooked by the man's scrutiny, Jack carefully folded his hands together on the table and lowered his chin. Nothing special here, just another bored Zero obediently waiting for his master. Doing his best to act natural, he slowly rotated in the chair, away from both men and faced the entrance. The door of the Cracked Rib swung open.

Sister Sasa walked in.

S-KNEES-ING

JACK FROZE as the room erupted into waves of motion flowing away from where Sasa stood anchored in the doorway. Chairs rocked and tables capsized, knocking over mugs and spilling ale across the floor, as the men in the Rib surged to their feet. The burly man gasped for air as if hit in the face with a cold bucket of water. Floundering away from the Captain and spreading his hands wide in welcome, he hurried across the floor towards Sasa.

Jack didn't know what to do. The Captain edged closer to the bar, his eyes never leaving the Sister. He wished the Captain would give him a sign, a signal to stay put or move. Jack stayed put, slumped in his chair. At least, with all the men now standing in the bar, Sasa had no clear line of sight over to his corner.

"Get under my dress."

Jack jerked up. Roi had slid next to his table. "What?" Jack whispered.

"Master. Get under my dress," Roi whispered at him out of the corner of his mouth. "You can't sit in a Sister's presence, but you can't stay in the open either. Crawl under my dress. Now, for the sake of the Seven."

Feeling stupid, Jack dropped to the floor, crawled under the table, and knelt behind Roi. He lifted the bottom of the blue dress and hesitated. The fabric reeked of stale beer and dried sweat. Jack wrinkled his nose in disgust. "What if I hid behind—"

"No. She will catch you. Get under my dress, Master." Roi shifted his feet apart.

I can't believe I'm doing this. Holding his breath, Jack slid under the fabric and wedged himself between Roi's spindly legs. Sitting on the floor, he pulled his knees into his chest and wrapped his arms tightly around his shins. As best as he could tell, none of him was sticking out.

"What's happening?" Jack whispered, hoping Roi would be able to hear him since he had Soundcasting Marks on his neck like Emma. Vague shapes and blurs of light rippled across the thin, blue cloth, accompanied by the grating of chairs across the wooden floor and the shuffling of feet.

"Sasa is talking to the Shorta. A few men are waiting to greet her, but most of them are leaving," Roi said. "Are you the Prophet?"

"No. I'm Jack." He tried to not breathe through his nose. Roi's legs, even paler than the rest of him, were sweaty and smelled as bad as the dress.

"But you did come from the land beyond the Seven?"

"Yeah, I did. With my sisters."

"And you have the white eyes?"

Roi had already seen his eyes from the stage. "Yes, I do."

"And you carry the Eye?"

"Carry my eye?" *What the heck is he talking about...* "Oh, you mean the scope." Jack stopped himself, worried he'd already said too much. He wasn't sure if Emma would want him to talk to Roi about the kaleidoscope, especially with the man's history of stealing. "No, I mean...I don't know anything about an Eye."

Roi shifted his feet to the right. The dress fabric rippled back, and Jack tried to pull himself into a tighter ball. The inside of Roi's knee, warm and sticky, pressed against his cheek and Roi's sweat ran down onto Jack's face. Tilting his head up and away from Roi's leg, Jack groaned in disgust.

"Shhh!" Roi whispered sharply. Visible through the fabric, a swath of bright red stopped dangerously close to them.

"Sister Sasa, by your Marks." Roi squeaked, his voice quivering. The Sister was probably used to people being nervous around her. "I am—"

"I know who you are." She cut him off, the same condescending voice she had used with Jack in the Red Coren. "You are that horrible pest and museum thief. A Two not worthy of his Marks. Why are you not in jail?"

"The townspeople were gracious to me, Eres. They gave me this opportunity to show my repentance." Roi's knees bent slightly, and Jack cringed as he pictured Roi nodding and bowing his shoulders in deference towards Sasa despite her nasty comments. Jack wanted to kick her in the shins.

"More grace than you deserve. Nevertheless..." She paused and stepped in closer to Roi. Her voice shifted down in volume. "I would also like to give you an opportunity. A chance to redeem yourself in the eyes of the Coren."

"Thank you, Sister Sasa. I am always for the good of Dara," Roi replied drily with another half-bow, shifting his stance again. His right leg bumped into Jack's nose.

"Yes, of course you are," Sasa replied cooly. "Now, with your particular area of interest, I assume you know about the three thieves from Ephara?"

Roi cleared his throat. "Of course, Eres. Though I didn't get all the details. What exactly did they steal?" Roi asked, his voice shaky. His legs were trembling against Jack's face.

Beads of sweat rolled onto Jack's forehead and down onto his nose. He had no idea if the sweat was his or Roi's, but that was the least of Jack's concern right now. Halfway up his nose, he felt the beginning of an itch.

"What they stole is not your concern. They're despicable Farkers. Have you heard anything about their whereabouts?"

Roi's voice cracked into pieces. "No, Sister. Nothing."

"Nothing at all?" Sasa scoffed. "With the company you keep and your interest in the Coren? Certainly, you have picked up some information: two girls with abhorrent, fake Marks, traveling with a young boy, a Zero with abnormal eyes. You're telling me you've neither heard nor seen anything?"

Jack scrunched his nose, desperate to shake off the bead of sweat. His hands were locked around his knees, and he couldn't risk moving them with Sasa right in front of him. He tried turning his head to the side, tried to dig his nose into Roi's knee, but the urge to sneeze burned like a fiery pinprick.

"On my Marks, Sister. I wish I could be more helpful." Roi's twitchy legs shifted another gear into a knee-knocking quiver. More sweat dripped onto Jack's nose. Jack bit down on his tongue, hoping the pain would override the sneeze. "But my time has been spent making my amends to the town. I have nothing to hide."

"Ahhh-cheessh-HAH!" Loud as a rifle shot, Jack sneezed. His head jerked forward causing Roi's dress to billow out. Sasa's feet stepped in towards Roi, her body a red blur of motion, and Roi flew up and backward into the air and crashed onto the table behind them. Jack stared up at the Sister from the floor. She sneered at him, her face a hardened mixture of surprise and fury.

"Jack." She said his name like a reprimand as if he were a child to be scolded for bad behavior. "First Acorn and now this pitiful excuse for a thief. I see that your choice of friends has not improved."

From the corner of his eye, he saw the Captain stepping up from behind, holding the hilt of his knife like a club.

Jack smiled at Sasa and faked a loud chuckle to hold her attention. The Captain's blow struck her solidly on the back of the head, knocking her unconscious. She slumped to the floor in front of Jack. Unable to resist, he leaned in close to one ear and whispered. "On the contrary, you nasty red witch. I've chosen my friends very well."

38

TEACHER'S BOND

Emma paced back and forth as she waited at the edge of the woods outside Silig. Holly was colorcasting a stick, coating the leaves with a layer of frost. At the sound of riders, both girls ducked behind a tree.

"It's Jack and the Captain. They got him," Tannor called.

Filled with relief, Emma stepped out. Acorn was riding with the Captain, but on the other zind, Jack was riding in front of a skinny woman in a blue dress.

Holly stood beside her, the frozen branch in her hand. "Is that Roi?"

Emma didn't answer as she watched them approach. Jack looked worried, but Roi was grinning wildly.

"Mount up," said the Captain as they pulled to stop. "Roi has a place east of here where he says we'll be safe."

"Safe? What happened?" Emma asked.

But before Jack could answer, Roi leapt to the ground. He took three steps toward Emma and Holly, then fell on his knees in front of them. "You're real! You're really real!" I knew there had to be Sevens, somewhere, somehow," he paused, gasping for breath as he stared at them. He had big eyes, the kind of eyes that stuck out and seemed to be looking everywhere at the same time. Still kneeling, he bowed his head. "By your Marks, Eresi, forgive my lack of manners, but meeting you is such an honor. When Master Jack told me that he came to Dara with two sisters and—" Roi raised his head, and at the sight of Tannor bringing their zinds over, his grin disappeared. "Oh, hello Tannor. You're not still mad, are you?"

"Roi, not the time." The Captain grabbed Roi by the shoulders, yanked him to his feet, and shoved him toward one of the mounts. "I'll take Acorn. Jack, you can ride with Tannor. Roi, lead the way."

Emma watched Roi as he hiked up his dress and climbed onto the zind. As she held the reins and steadied the zind for Holly, Tannor and Jack drew up beside her.

"So that's the man with all the answers?" Emma looked up at Tannor.

Tannor shook his head. 'Don't say I didn't warn you."

AFTER FLEEING THE TAVERN AND MEETING UP WITH THE others, Roi led them at a gallop east along the river Enabsa. Once out of sight from the town, they took the zinds into the shallow river and continued to the east, exiting the water to the north onto the loading dock at the deserted remains of an old grain mill. Satisfied that their tracks were not visible on the wooden dock, they rode north at a gallop. An hour later, they angled into a mass of rolling hills and valleys and arrived at Roi's home.

Roi quickly dismounted, ran onto the small porch attached to the front of his house, and disappeared through the door. No one spoke, but Emma watched as Tannor dismounted, drew his sword, and positioned himself between them and Roi's porch. No, Emma thought, porch is too generous of a word for the broken boards attached to the front of the man's house—also too generous of a word for the sad little shack where Roi had brought them in less than a half day's ride to the north of Silig.

A few minutes later, Roi came running out holding two necklaces. "Eresi, please put these on. Master Jack has told me you were traced by the Sisterhood. These crystals will shield you from the Tracer."

"Can I have the green one?" Not waiting for the answer, Holly took the necklace with the heavy emerald crystal from Roi. She held it up in the sunlight; the dance of color spun a leafy pattern across the back of her hand.

"And you're sure this will keep us from being found by the Tracer?" Emma asked as she slipped the orange crystal around her neck.

"Yes, Eres." Smiling awkwardly, he reached into his dress and pulled out his amulet, also orange. "These were given to me by one of the Capitol guards—"

"Stolen more likely," Tannor interrupted as he stepped off the porch and sheathed his sword.

"—And though I too have been traced—"

"While in jail, no doubt."

"—This amulet has always shielded me from detection," Roi finished, ignoring Tannor.

"Can we get down?" Holly asked from astride her zind. The Captain nodded yes; his attention was focused in the direction they'd come. He pointed to the line of rocky hilltops they had passed by earlier. Without saying a word, Tannor remounted and rode away towards the hills to take a lookout position.

"How does it work?" Holly put on her necklace then dismounted.

"I'm not sure, Eres, but I do have an interesting theory." Roi talked fast, and his words came in broken spurts. "To find me, the Tracer sends out vibrations using the crystals made with my Marks. So when those vibrations reach me, they must cause my Marks to vibrate and send a signal back to the Tracer." He paced back and forth excitedly. "Or perhaps, and this is the exciting idea, it's not the signal that makes my Marks vibrate. What if my Marks are the source of the vibration and it's me that is making the amulet vibrate?"

On the ground, Emma stretched her legs and smiled over at Jack and Acorn. "You know what I'm thinking, don't you?"

Jack rolled his eyes and shook his head. "Go ahead."

"We finally found someone who talks more than you," she teased. Acorn giggled.

Roi was still speaking, his right hand smacking his left as he hit each point. "I believe when these amulets vibrate, they must send out a pure tone which overrides—"

"Stop talking." The Captain placed a hand on Roi's shoulder. Immediately, as if the Captain had hit the off button, he stopped. "We can talk once we're inside." He glanced past the shack and into the edge of the barren foothills. A shadow of concern passed his eyes. "Acorn, we'll have to tie the zinds out of sight beyond that rise."

"Captain. I have a paddock." Roi pointed to the front door hanging askew from one hinge, the other hinge dangling broken on the frame. "Inside."

"Inside there?" Emma couldn't hide her skepticism. His shack looked smaller than her bedroom back home. Tannor was right. The man in the dress was delusional.

"Yes, Eres." Roi bowed towards Emma. From the moment he met her and Holly outside the village, Roi had addressed them both as Eres, much like Sister Yiana had done in the Coren, acknowledging them right away as Sevens. "If I may, please follow me inside along with your mounts. Though, one at a time would be best." He shoved open the weathered door, gave a wave of his arm like a waiter's welcome into a fancy restaurant, and walked inside.

You've got to be kidding me. Exasperated, Emma shook her head at the Captain, then grabbed the reins of her zind and followed him. Stepping inside, her eyes took in the whole of Roi's home in one glance, and she pushed back on the urge to cough from the deep layers of dirt and dust: A small bed, the mattress sagging; a battered table with a few rolls of water-stained parchment; a rumpled pile of clothes in one corner. Emma sighed and hitched the reins to one of the cracked table legs.

Her host stood by the back wall, a patchwork of broken boards. In his frayed dress and surrounded by filth, Roi looked like a five-year-old orphan girl eager to give his new mother a present.

"Would you do me the honor, Eres? For you, of course, a trivial display, but I've never had the chance to watch someone else open the lock. I'm quite proud of the design of my colorcast."

"Open the lock. Your design?" Emma's stomach reeled. *Maybe he's not crazy after all.* She scanned the wall behind him as a wave of performance anxiety filled her. *He's asking me to demonstrate my powers and use them to open a door. But what lock?* All she saw were dirty, broken boards. Emma squinted, acting like she was thoughtfully considering his request. He was staring at her. *He thinks I'm a real Guardian, and I can't say I have no idea how to do anything.* Emma took a deep swallow and looked right at him.

"Thank you, Roi, but I can't."

His face, all puppy dog eagerness a moment before, drooped. "Oh, yes, of course. On my Marks! Forgive me for my impertinence."

"No, that's not what I meant," Emma cut in. She felt stupid and wasn't entirely sure why. "I don't know how to open the lock. To be completely honest, I don't know what lock you are talking about. Maybe the Captain hasn't fully explained our situation, I mean Holly and – well, not Holly since she seems to be a natural, but my situation. Yes, I'm a Seven but I don't know how to use my powers. In our world, these Marks have no meaning, no purpose, which is why the Captain sought you out. So you could teach me." Emma took a deep breath. "I need your help."

"You...need...my...help." Roi repeated the words slowly as if trying to make sense of their meaning. "A Seven asking for my help." He ran his hands through his hair and tilted his head upward, staring towards the ceiling, and Emma felt he was looking somewhere far beyond the confines of the squalid little shack. "A teacher. For a Seven." His eyes were closed, and she started to wonder where he had gone in his mind.

His eyes snapped open. With an excited smile on his face, and to her surprise, he stepped in closer. "Eres, on my Marks, I humbly accept your request. May I initiate the bond?"

Emma's insides squirmed. She wasn't sure what Roi meant by bond, but she had just asked him to teach her how to use her powers, and he seemed really excited by the idea. It was probably some sort of teacher pledge that she was expected to repeat. "Yes, Roi," Emma said, "go ahead."

"To create our bond as teacher and student, I must synchronize my Marks to yours." Slowly, Roi raised his arms and placed both of his hands on top of her shoulders. Caught off guard, Emma forced herself to not flinch. She felt the tips of his fingers on her neck and resisted the urge to step away. *He's touching my Marks.* His thumbs came together at the base of Emma's throat and rested on top of the Green Mark in the center of her throat.

His fingers were hot, but his hands didn't move. After a moment, the skin on her neck began tingling. Roi smiled down at her. "Eres Emma, I, Ber-ha-roi, am your teacher. Your success is my success. I will not fail you." His eyes were wide as he continued to stare at her.

Emma fidgeted nervously. He was waiting for her to say something in response. Was she supposed to say thank you? The whole situation was laced with formality and felt like one of Jack's Budo ceremonies. Emma chewed on her lower lip. *If he says he's my teacher, then I would say...I should use his full name...*

"Ber-ha-roi, I, Emma Cassandra Waite, am your student," she replied in a solemn tone. Like a spark, the heat on Emma's throat surged and flashed out. Roi pulled back his hands and dropped his arms. His smile grew bigger than before. Part of Emma knew she had said the right words; the other part of her was worried. What if the right words might turn out to be wrong?

"Roi!" The Captain shouted from outside, his irritated voice ricocheting off the walls. "Is there a problem?"

"No, Captain, no." Like a startled bird, the smile flew off Roi's face. He stepped away from Emma, spun towards the boarded-up wall, and pointed at two squiggly lines, carved into the highest board covered in dust. "Notice, Emma, how I placed the lock well above one's normal line of sight. People never look up." He raised a finger as if to make another point, glanced out the doorway, and stopped. "Never mind. We'll have to keep this lesson short." He twirled his upraised finger.

Still trying to make sense of Roi's pledge to be her teacher, Emma gasped as his voice rang out and split into two notes. She'd completely forgotten about the two Marks on his throat. He had the ability to soundcast. As he sustained the two-note chord, the small marks engraved in the wall began to glow. and then two red lines raced along the seams of the boards, tracing a saw-toothed path down to the floor. The boards split open in the middle, and each side folded backward, coming to rest against the walls of a surprisingly long and well-lit tunnel carved into the hill behind the cabin. Roi pointed down the sloped passageway.

"After you, Emma. Halfway down and to the right, you'll come to my paddock. My quarters are at the far end." He smiled. "I'll help Acorn tend to the zinds once everyone is safely inside."

Impressed by the lock but still skeptical that there was room for all the zinds inside, Emma untied the reins and led her zind through the door. Something about Roi's manner felt different, but she couldn't pin it down. Halfway down the corridor was an eight-foot-wide doorway framed with timbers. She prodded her zind into the smoothly carved-out space—a large and low-ceilinged room paved with stone blocks, big enough for all of their zinds and then some. Lightcubes embedded in the walls illuminated the room with a blue glow. Along one wall was a water trough and feed sacks. *Son of a gun. He does have a paddock.*

"Wow, I bet this took forever to dig!" Jack said, nudging his zind past Emma's shoulder and into the paddock. She didn't respond. "Hey, are you okay?"

"Jack, get out of the way," Holly said. She led her zind inside. She spun around slowly, then ran her hand along the walls, feeling the cubes of blue light. "Look at this, Emma."

"She's not listening." Jack elbowed Emma gently in the side. "Emma. Hello?"

"Um, yeah. Fine." But she wasn't fine. She was still stuck in her head, stuck back in the shack, thinking about earlier. She rubbed the Marks on her neck; they felt no different than usual, but she was sure something had happened back there with Roi.

"Hey, do me a favor," Emma grabbed Jack and Holly by their

arms. "Don't show Roi the kaleidoscope just yet. Not until we're sure about him." Then she followed Jack and Holly down the hallway and to a closed, wooden door. Jack pushed it open and walked in.

"Holy packrat," Jack swore with an impressed chuckle.

Emma stopped next to Jack. Roi's home under the hill sprawled in front of them, a cubelit space as big as a small-town library. Immediately to their left was a living space; a rumpled bed, a cooking area, and a massive oak table surrounded by mismatched chairs. The rest of the cavern overflowed with a sets of shelves, towering racks, and long tables, every flat surface covered with piles of scrolls and knickknacks.

"The Captain wasn't kidding. He's a thief. And a good one," said Jack. Next to Emma, a huge grin crossed Holly's face as she gazed in wonder at Roi's collection.

Looking at the chaos in front of her, Emma tried to stay calm. Tannor had warned her that he didn't trust Roi, and now, the idea of showing the kaleidoscope to a man with an obsession for artifacts seemed like a risky move. But the Captain had vouched for him, and despite her nagging concern about the teacher ceremony, nothing about Roi's behavior or words had sounded off to her. He had a kind voice, a high tenor. *Just because he lives in a hole in the ground filled with a stash of stolen goods doesn't mean he's crazy, right?*

Emma turned away from the jumble of shelves and walked over to the heavy wooden table in the middle of Roi's living space. Next to the wall, a life-size stone bust was perched on a round pedestal. Emma gasped in disbelief.

She was looking at the Red Guardian. The likeness to Daria's unforgiving face was eerily spot on.

Wrong. My new teacher is a nut.

THE BEGINNING SONG

Before first morning, Ashala lay sleeping with Kiru bound to her side.
And Kiru cried, "Ashala, my darling, give me your love to keep me warm."

"What will you do with my love?" Ashala sat on her throne.
And Kiru cried, "Oh, my queen, with your love I will create a burning fire."
"What will you do with my fire?" Ashala raised her head.
And he cried, "Ashala, my guide, with your fire I will create a golden sun."

"What will you do with my sun?" Ashala lowered her veil.
And Kiru cried, "Ashala, my bride, with your sun I will create a green field."
"What will you do with my field?" Ashala unbraided her hair.
And he cried out, "Oh, my lover, by your field I will create a sparkling river."

"What will you do with my river?" Ashala drank deeply.
And Kiru cried, "Oh, my enchanted, in your river I will hide a royal treasure."
"What will you do with my treasure?" Ashala fingered the blade.
And he cried out, "Ashala, my heart, with your treasure I will create eternity."

"What will you do with eternity?" asked Ashala holding her breath.
And Kiru cried, "Ashala, my darling, in eternity I will love you forever."
"Then I will give you all my love." Ashala gasped as she fell on the throne.

Before first morning, Ashala lay sleeping with Kiru at her side.
And Kiru cried... And Kiru cried.

39

SEEING THROUGH THE EYE

ONCE THEY WERE ALL SAFELY inside Roi's house in the hill, they filled Roi in on their adventures with Daria and the Coren. He asked a thousand questions, interrupting them about the inner workings of the Coren, asking Emma and Jack about life on Earth, clarifying who the three of them had met in Dara. When Roi learned that they had been arrested in Lindur, he told them about the attack on the town.

"It was the beast Chaos and a swarm of shards," Roi said shaking his head. "The Mayor and his men are presumed dead, buried under the courthouse rubble."

"Chaos?" Emma asked.

"It's a monster, like a giant shard," Jack offered. From her perch on the pedestal, Acorn bobbed her head in confirmation.

Roi swallowed hard. "I met a survivor who saw Chaos and threw herself down a well to hide. Pure fury, she said—a lumbering beast, black and wet as the darkest pit. It takes no prisoners."

Roi paused and for a moment, the room fell into respectful silence. No one seemed able to move past his words as they wrestled with the image of the giant monster.

The more they talked, the worse Holly felt. She didn't want to imagine the mayor or his men getting crushed by a giant beast. She didn't want to talk about Earth or home or their dad. So, after another flurry of questions and talking, she wandered away from the table and started exploring the items in Roi's collection.

Listening from across the room, Holly knelt on the floor by one of Roi's many shelves. She wiped away the thick layer of dust on a glass jar that had caught her eye, its contents a snail the size of her fist with protruding eyes, unblinking, floating in a bluish liquid. By the amount of dust and cobwebs coating the hundreds of other items stacked on the wooden racks, this jar—and everything else in Roi's collection—had not been touched or moved for years. There were also no labels on any of the items or any sense of order as to where the items were sitting; strands of jewelry were hung on wooden carvings that leaned on glass bowls sitting on top of open books lying on stacks of closed books. Holly wrinkled her nose. Her room at home looked like it could barely contain her art supplies and projects, but every-thing was organized by color, by media. Roi's accumulation of stuff was one pull away from turning into an avalanche.

"Before the first morn, Ashala lay sleeping with Kiru at her side....and Kiru cried...and Kiru cried." Roi finished singing. Jack clapped for him as the last notes of the song echoed and faded into the room.

"It's so sad," said Acorn. She sat cross-legged on the stone pedestal where the bust of Dara had been before Emma asked Roi to move it somewhere out of their sight. "Sister Yiana always sang and played it for the villagers on Market days, but the song sounds so much worse with your voice." Holly looked up at Acorn's flushed cheeks. "No, I meant the story is much sadder sung by a man instead of a woman. Master Roi, please forgive me for speaking so rudely."

"No need to apologize, Acorn." Roi propped a bony elbow on the messy, wooden shelf behind him. A pile of scrolls cascaded to the floor. "There is also no need for formality. I'm overjoyed to meet someone with such personal knowledge of the Coren's inner work-ings. Call me Roi."

"The song is about the Seven, right?" Holly asked, as she stood, still holding the jar. Jack had asked Roi to sing the song for them; he said it might be important, and now Holly understood why. She stepped out from between the rows. "Seven verses. Seven colors. Seven lands."

"Yes, Eres, my interpretation exactly," Roi replied, smiling with appreciation at her latest find. "You have found a Zalan sea snail. A gift from a trader friend of mine." Holly set the jar on a small table, amongst the dozen or so things she'd already scavenged for closer inspection from the shelves. The snail blinked, and Holly jumped back, as Roi continued talking. "I believe you'll find my collection of orange items from Nima quite intriguing. Two shelves to your right."

"How old is that song?" Emma asked.

"Very old. My grandmother sang it to me as a child. Same words. Same tune," the Captain remarked from his chair near the room's entrance. Despite Roi's assurances that they were his first visitors and that no one in Dara knew about this place, the Captain had not let down his guard.

Jack spoke up. "That's why I think it's related to the—"

"To our situation," Emma cut in, stopping Jack before he inadvertently mentioned the kaleidoscope.

"Right," Jack added, "our situation is like that song. Complicated...and colorful." Looking pleased with himself, Jack grinned at Holly. She frowned back.

The Captain stood up and stretched, his knees popping loudly. With his graying hair and wrinkled skin, the color of faded parchment, Holly wondered how old he truly was. "Which brings us back to why I sought you out. Roi, I've been waiting ten years to complete my mission, ten long years for the arrival of a white-eyed man, and now he's here. Tell me how to get these three to Tera."

Standing up straight, Roi clasped his hands and walked to stand beside Jack. "Captain, I believe I can help. But first, I must examine the item in Master Jack's bag."

Jack's eyes went down to where his backpack was lying on the floor, before quickly looking back at Roi and shrugged. "What's in my bag?"

"The Eye of the Prophet, Master Jack." Roi's smile was politely deferential like a butler; to Holly's amusement, he insisted on addressing Jack as Master. Unlike the Captain and Tannor, Roi fervently believed the legends of the Prophet. "I believe you called it the 'scope' when you were under my dress."

"You already told him?" Emma shook her head. "Why didn't you tell me?"

The Captain took a seat by the table. "Show it to him. He knows."

"You were under Roi's dress?" Holly asked, her eyes wide as Acorn giggled.

"No, I didn't tell him anything!" Jack argued back. "And it was Roi's idea, trying to hide me when Sasa showed up!" Holly laughed out loud as Jack tried to explain. "It's not funny, Hol!"

"By your Marks, Emma, do not blame Master Jack," Roi said, the excitement growing in his voice. "Legend says the Prophet had white eyes, came to the Seven with the Eye, and then helped to create the portals in the Corens. Since you arrived in Lindur and not through the Coren Portal, you must have it in your possession."

Across the table from her, Emma was watching Roi intensely. Then she sighed and leaned forward. "The Captain's right. We have to trust him."

Jack pulled the scope from his backpack, then extended his arms with the scope resting in his open palms. The burnished colors in the metal gleamed, reflecting the glow from the set of light cubes strung from the roughhewn ceiling.

"Master Jack, may I?" Roi's hands twitched, the nervousness showing down to his fingertips. He carefully took the scope and rotated it in his hands. Working gently like a jeweler, he peered closely at the first of the barrel slots, turning the knurled wheel with his thumb and watching the slot open and close. "These chambers. All empty?" Roi asked, glancing at Jack for confirmation. "And when you looked into the scope from your land of Earth, what happened?"

"I saw red light, a door, and what seemed to be blurry sand dunes. The scope took us to Lindur."

Roi pointed to the first engraving on the barrel of the kaleidoscope—a wavy red line. Jack sat up. "Oh yeah. That marking glowed with a red color when I held it back home. Nothing happens now."

Emma poked Jack in the shoulder. "You didn't tell me that the first symbol glowed! What about the other sections?"

"No, Emma, only this symbol for Dara would have glowed, not the others," answered Roi as his fingers lightly traced the engravings on the barrel of the scope. "It makes perfect sense."

"It does?" Jack and Emma asked at the same time.

Roi nodded vigorously. "Yes, these seven large engravings..." Roi placed the kaleidoscope in the center of the table. Everyone stood up from their chairs, leaning in closer; Acorn hopped down from the pedestal and squeezed between Emma and the Captain. "...each one references one of the Seven Lands. That mark on the second section means fireflower in Landspeek."

With her finger, Holly touched the engraving, which looked like a letter U with a line in the middle. She smiled; the symbol was a stick-figure flower.

"What's Landspeek? Isn't the language in the lands called U'maan?" Emma asked. "Doesn't everyone speak the same language?"

"Yes, the people in the Seven speak U'maan, but in my searches, I've found bits and pieces of another, ancient language, closer to symbols than writing. I can't read it—I would need a lot more material to work with and to study—but I can recognize a few symbols. That's why seeing the Eye and holding it in my hands is amazing. Each of these symbols must be a reference to each of the lands. If I can figure out the meaning of the symbols, I can use the knowledge to decipher more."

"Like a code key," Jack said.

"Exactly, Master Jack," Roi said as he rubbed his hands in anticipation. "I've long suspected many of the Coren's deepest secrets could be revealed in the old writings."

A frown on her face, Emma picked up the kaleidoscope. "That's great, but I'm not sure how learning another language helps us. What we need is to know how to make this thing work so we can go back home."

"Exactly, Emma! As I said, once all seven chambers are filled, the kaleidoscope will show the doorway to your homeland, the last symbol," said Roi, his face beaming, seemingly oblivious to their confused faces.

"Huh?" Jack asked. "What are you talking about?"

Holly reached up and grabbed Roi's hand, getting his attention. He looked down at her, his smile fading. "You didn't say we had to fill all the chambers or anything about a symbol for Earth."

"I didn't? I thought I explained how the Eye works."

"No, but that's okay. Explain it now," Emma said. She sat down in her chair and propped her elbows on the table in front of her, the scope resting in her hands. "Slowly."

As the rest of them took their seats, Roi scrunched his eyes closed as if concentrating deeply. "I once saw a drawing of the Prophet's Eye —it was in an ancient tome on display at the Archives—and now that I've had the great honor of holding the Eye itself, I understand how it works." His eyes popped open. "The Eye, the kaleidoscope as you call it, is the original portal, likely created by the Prophet, though of course, I can't be sure of its true origins, nor why the kaleidoscope must be wielded by a person with white eyes." Roi pointed to Jack as if they needed to be reminded. Jack stood up from his chair and bowed.

Holly suppressed her giggle. "Roi, how does it work?"

"Yes, of course. There are nine symbols on the scope. The seven large ones engraved on the sections—those symbols reference the color energy for each land. The fire flower on the second section refers to the legendary orange fireflowers of Nima. To activate this orange section," Roi reached across the table and tapped the second section on the scope. "...one must insert a piece of fireflower into the second compartment."

"And for the other sections? We need to put a colored piece into every compartment?" Holly asked.

"Yes, adding the color to the Red compartment will activate the connection between Dara, the Red Land, and Nima, the Orange Land." Roi leaned back in his chair. "Master Jack could then travel between Red and Orange. Based on the cylindrical design and its dimensions, I'm convinced the kaleidoscope inspired the design and construction of the Portals throughout the Lands."

"Roi, you said nine symbols?" Emma asked skeptically.

"Look closely at the side opposite the compartment openings. On the eyepiece, the maker of the kaleidoscope inscribed a small symbol, the same shape engraved on the Dara section. I believe that symbol creates a red doorway viewable solely in the light of your Earth." He continued, now tapping the table with his long fingers. "On the other end of the scope is another small symbol with a circle consisting of seven segments."

"And a white eye in the middle!" Jack lunged across the table and snatched up the scope. Still standing, he examined the scope, then pointed excitedly at Roi. "Our dad's study—where we found this and all his scope stuff. There was a window exactly like this!"

Roi sat down. "There's a mosaic in the Royal Hall with this same design."

For a moment, everyone was quiet. Across the table from her, Emma was deep in thought. As Jack showed Acorn the small inscriptions on the underside of the scope, Holly struggled to share his enthusiasm. His explanation had been clear, but knowing how to make the Kaleidoscope work was a very small start. If Roi was right, they needed to get hold of seven different colored materials, and he knew only one of the seven items—a piece from a legendary flower the color of fire. The other six materials might be impossible to find, and they didn't know what they were. Holly tried to push down the sadness, but it was hard. A sense of hopelessness began to overwhelm her. She blinked back a tear and wiped at her eyes. Across from her, the Captain was staring into space, his face grim and resolute. He'd reached the same conclusion as her; they could be stuck in the Seven for a very long time.

"Roi, do you know what is needed for the Red section of the kaleidoscope?" The Captain asked his question slowly.

Roi hesitated and Holly saw him swallow before answering. "No, Captain, I do not."

The Captain leaned forward in his seat. "Roi, you've heard their story. I can't hide them from the Red Sisterhood forever. They're the most wanted fugitives in Dara."

"After the way you knocked out Sister Sasa, you might be the biggest fugitive in the room." Jack joked and the Captain glared at him. "Um, I mean, sorry," Jack stammered. "Captain."

The Captain waved his right hand at the long rows of shelves. "Roi, you must know a secret way into the Red Coren. Surely, there's a map of the Coren somewhere in all this mess."

"You can't seriously be thinking about going back to the Coren? They'll kill us," Emma said as she glanced at Acorn. "Besides, by now the Sisters must know how we escaped. They'll be watching every tunnel, including the passage we used to get out."

"And we can't climb the walls," added Holly. She walked over to them, and sat down at the table next to Jack, bringing the jar with the sea snail with her. She felt sorry that it was trapped in a jar, alone and far away from its home. She would ask Roi to set it free.

"Captain, by your Marks," Acorn said as she fidgeted nervously with the strands of her hair. "Emma's right. Even if the tunnels looked unguarded, it would be because they've set a trap." Holly nodded along with Jack and Emma; returning to the Coren was a sure death sentence for her friend.

"Very well. We can't go in the way you got out." The Captain raised his hand to silence Emma as she started to speak. He stood up and paced slowly with measured steps. "Nor am I suggesting we scale the walls. But I need options." He stopped next to Roi who merely shrugged.

"Then we have no choice," the Captain stated, more command than comment. "We'll have to try for the Portal in Ephara. That won't be an easy task since I'm a wanted man in the capital. But Tannor's brother had friends in the King's Guard. If we can enlist their aid to sneak into the city undetected, we can then bribe a Guild worker for Portal tickets." He paused for only a moment. "In Nima, we'll have to act fast, but once we reach Kasa, you'll be safe; I've met the Yellow Guardian and the Kasans are a kind people." He placed one hand on

Emma's shoulder. "We'll need to move you three in secret, of course. Roi, we'll need a skimm. How soon can you get one?"

Emma didn't move or acknowledge that the Captain was speaking. She sat very still.

"Excuse me?" Emma said. She was staring straight ahead, somewhere in space between Jack and Holly on the other side of the table.

The Captain pulled his hand away from Emma's shoulder. "You heard him. The kaleidoscope can't take us to Nima unless we have some piece of red color, and he doesn't know what it is. The scope is useless to us as a means of escape."

Emma sprung out of her chair and wheeled to face the Captain. Her jaw was clenched. "Then we find it."

"We find it?"

"Yup," Emma said as she crossed her arms. Holly smiled, surprised, but pleased by how firmly her sister was holding her ground against him.

"Don't be ridiculous. You're being hunted by the Coren. Every minute you remain in Dara you're putting yourselves in danger." His voice hardened. "The mission is to keep you safe and deliver all three of you to the Green Coren. As fast as possible."

"No, that was your mission." Emma pushed back, her voice getting louder. Behind the Captain, the glassware on Roi's kitchen counter rattled.

"But it's an oath I've been carrying for ten years!"

"I don't care!" Emma shouted at him. "We don't want to be here!"

A glass bowl shattered, scattering broken glass across the floor. Stunned, Emma dropped into a chair.

"I'm sorry."

Roi walked over to Emma and placed a steadying hand on her shoulder. She flinched but took a slow breath. She looked down at the broken pieces on the floor, her forehead creased. "Getting us to your home may be the end for you, but not for us. We'll still be stuck here, lost and no closer to getting back to our home." She slowly raised her head and stared at the Captain. "You can't even be sure your Council remembers you or your oath. I'm sorry, but we need to figure this thing out." She paused for a moment. "Please. Let us try."

He didn't respond, his face impassive, holding Emma's gaze.

Emma started to say something else, but Roi responded first. "If I may, Captain, I'm confident that I can decipher the red symbol on the kaleidoscope. Fleeing Dara now would be premature."

"Premature! Taking them to safety is premature? I'm talking about saving their lives. The Green Council can deal with getting them home." Shaking his head with frustration, the Captain turned away from them and began slowly pacing back and forth, between the table and the entrance door. He stared up at the ceiling, muttering under his breath. After several long minutes, he stopped and faced the group.

Emma stood and mouthed the word please again. Holly held her breath.

"Til morning." His eyes settled on Emma. "I'll give you until dawn to give me a plan—a reasonable plan—to justify staying here for a minute longer. If there's no plan, we're going to the Portal in Ephara, even if Tannor and I have to tie you down and drag you there." Grabbing his sword, he opened the tunnel door. "Roi, make sure to let Tannor in." He spun and strode down the tunnel, his cloak quickly disappearing in the shadows. Exhausted, Emma sat down hard on the floor and dropped her head in her hands, her bangs falling over her face.

"Well, that went well." Jack whistled softly. "I think the bowl shattering was what changed his mind."

Holly walked around the table and sat on the floor next to Emma who leaned into her. "Plus, Roi saying he could figure things out," Holly added.

"Eres, about that," said Roi as he swept the broken glass into a bucket. "I may have overstated my level of understanding to the Captain."

Holly rolled her eyes at him. "You have no idea what we need, do you?"

"On the contrary, Eres, I already know what we must do," Roi said, "but I feared the Captain would reject the idea out of hand. I thought it best to tell you first. We have to locate Balgagaar."

"Who's Balgagaar?" Jack asked.

Roi grinned sheepishly at all of them. "That's the problem. Balgagaar is not really a who. He's more of a what."

Emma climbed to her feet. "Roi. What kind of *what* are we talking about?

Roi set the bucket of broken glass on the table and winced slightly. Holly saw a spot of red on one of his fingers where he had cut himself picking up the pieces.

"Balgagaar is a dragon," Roi answered, "the legendary Red Dragon of Dara who is said to dwell somewhere under the mountains of Kursagar." He sucked on the tip of his finger, then shrugged. "And we need his blood."

The colorcasting of items with more than three colors is superfluous. Single or dual colorcast objects are more than adequate for most jobs. There is no purpose in creating items that exceed the Marks of the majority. If a sword of a single color is needed to dispatch a shard, the subsequent time and effort used to cast a two-color weapon is time and effort wasted.

In the history of the Seven Lands, only the fabled Twins of Mora have successfully created a seven-color item—a ceremonial sword—by simultaneously casting their colors into the blade. And since in the history of the Seven, no person with Seven Marks has ever lived, the sword remains unused and untested in battle all these years.

—an excerpt from "Ruminations on Colorcasting and Society" issued by the Guardian of Zala, circa 1800 Y.O.P

40

HEALING TOUCH

Leaning back in her chair, Emma counted to three in her head, trying to stay calm. *This is absurd!* Here they were—three kids, a servant girl, and a singing thief—sitting together around a table while sipping sweet beer called sika, concocting a plan that would put their lives at risk, starting them on a journey that would consume their every waking moment until they could get back home. If ever. The idea was too big, more than she could handle right now, and she tried shoving it into the back of her mind.

After Roi's declaration that they would have to find the dragon named Balgagaar, Jack described the tapestry they'd seen in Daria's quarters. Looking elated and muttering to himself, Roi dashed away and disappeared amongst the rows of racks and shelves.

While they waited, the four of them passed the kaleidoscope around the table studying the various symbols inscribed on the kaleidoscope's barrel. When Holly pointed out that the wavy line looked more like a sand dune than the blood of a dragon, it had been easy to rule sand out as the answer; Holly ran outside, brought back a handful of the cinnamon-colored sand, and gave it to Jack. They held their breath, too nervous to talk, as he carefully placed a few grains of sand in the first compartment and closed the slot with a turn of the tiny knob. But when the red symbol did not glow, they all groaned in disappointment, even before Jack held it up to his eye and shook his head.

Jack set the scope on the table, then walked back and forth behind his chair. "Okay, maybe it *is* dragon's blood. But even if Roi's right, the Captain said he wanted a plan that's *'reasonable'*—he made air quotes with his fingers and stretched out the word.

"Would you sit down? Bouncing around the room is not helping." More amused than annoyed, Emma shook her head at her brother as he paced. Jack's aversion to sitting still at a table was legendary in their household. Whenever they played a game, he spent most of the time standing, throwing down his cards like knives. "And don't say 'reasonable' like that."

With a roll of his eyes, Jack pulled back his chair but didn't sit down all the way. Like a bird perched on a wire, he squatted on the seat. He was energized by their conversation. "All I'm saying is when we tell him our *reason*..." Jack stressed the word again, "…. to stay is because we need to find a mythical Red Dragon who might have the magic red stuff we need to put in the scope, he's not going to like it. Even saying it out loud sounds ridiculous." He spread his arms wide and wiggled his fingers. "Now playing at the Lebanon Regency! The Search for Dragon Blood!" Sitting beside Holly, Acorn giggled.

Roi emerged from the far end of his storage shelves. Smiling broadly and waving a rolled-up scroll, he crossed the room and plopped into his seat. "This is it!" He leaned forward and took a drink from his cup, his elbows resting on the table. "And Master Jack, may I suggest we propose our plan to the Captain in a slightly less dramatic manner?"

Emma smiled, glad for Roi's suggestion. Between Jack's joking, Acorn's giggling, and Holly's fascination with Roi's collection, she'd started to think she was the only responsible person in the room. Now that Roi had changed clothes—out of the dress and into a faded mustard-colored tunic and dark brown pants, similar in style to Tannor's clothes—she could take him more seriously.

"Roi's right. We need to go at this like a school project. Organize our thoughts into an outline to convince the Captain."

'What? That we're *reasonable*?" Jack chimed in, looking for another laugh.

"Wow. So not funny." Emma glared at him; Acorn kept quiet. Jack slumped deflated into his chair while taking another sip of sika. "Listen, I know it's crazy. And it's horrible. But Holly has stopped crying from being homesick every night..." She glanced at Holly and mouthed the word sorry, "...and I've stopped blaming you for dragging us into this mess. The least you can do is take it seriously." Emma backed down as Jack slumped down further. "Sorry. Just take it down a notch. And do not drink all of that sika." She pointed at Roi. "Tell us more about this map and the dragon before Jack starts talking again."

Roi touched a red, blue, and indigo circle embossed on the outside of the scroll; it unrolled itself, revealing a map of a circular maze drawn on the two-foot-wide piece of thin vella. "It looks like a kaleidoscope picture," Holly said as she ran her fingers across the design filled with an intricate pattern of intersecting lines.

"A mandala," Emma said. "I saw the word in Dad's notebooks."

"It's the same design on the tapestry in Dara's quarters," Acorn said.

"I thought so, and that's why this mandala..." Roi seemed to enjoy saying the word. "...is our key to finding Balgagaar, the Red Dragon of Dara. This is a copy of the maze from the Prophet's Cloth. And before you ask, I did not steal it." He grinned. "I paid an acquaintance—one who used to work in the Coren Archives—to make it for me."

Emma guessed he was lying, but that wasn't important. Jack pointed to the poorly done, rough drawing in the center of the maze. "And what's with the three-legged dog?"

"The dog?" Roi looked momentarily confused. "Oh, no, Master Jack. That's not a dog. It's my drawing of the dragon." The animal had terribly sad eyes and appeared to be missing a foot.

"It's not my best work," Roi admitted. "However, I'm convinced the inclusion of Balgagaar on the Prophet's Cloth signifies that the first chamber of the kaleidoscope must be filled with material from the dragon. Countless legends describe Balgagaar as a creature of immense power, filled with red energy."

"But how do we get blood from a dragon?" Jack asked. "Just walk in and ask?"

"Exactly! Balgagaar the Wise is a talking dragon," Roi hesitated, then grinned sheepishly, "according to stories, that is."

Emma picked up the scope. The slots for inserting materials inside were narrow and less than an inch long. "How can you be sure it's the dragon's blood?" Emma asked. They would need air-tight logic to convince the Captain. She was afraid Jack's jokes about the insanity of chasing down a dragon were all too true. "Are you sure this symbol means dragon's blood? You said earlier you only recognized the second symbol."

"True," Roi said as he stirred his sika with the straw. "But the word engraved on the second section means fireflower and in the second verse of the Beginning Song, the goddess offers Kiru a fire. So, if I'm right, this first mark must refer to the warmth in the first verse. And what could be warmer than the blood of a dragon?" He grinned and looked at them all. "Right?"

Emma grabbed her cup of sika and raised her straw from the bottom of the cup before taking a small sip; if you didn't, you got a mouthful of grainy sediment. Roi's reasoning seemed to make sense: The Prophet's Eye was designed for the insertion of seven powerful colored materials; the items' identities were engraved on the barrel of the scope; the words of the Beginning Song described the same materials; and the Prophet's Cloth, the ancient tapestry depicting the Prophet wielding the kaleidoscope, included a picture of the Red Dragon Balgagaar and a map. Now, all they had to do was convince the Captain to let them try.

"Yeah, I guess so. The symbol is wavy like flowing blood," Jack said, sounding unconvinced. "And you're sure we can find this dragon with your map?"

A light cube hung above the door to the tunnel blinked a bright red.

"Is it supposed to do that?" Holly asked.

Roi pushed himself back from the table. "Yes, Eres. I cast the cube to be in harmony with my door lock. If someone touches the door, the cube alerts me. Tannor must be knocking."

As soon as the door closed behind Roi, Emma rapped her knuckles on the table. "Okay, let's make sure we all agree before he comes back with Tannor."

"Agree on what?" Holly asked.

"On the three—wait, make it four—things that have to happen before we scope to Nima." Emma raised two fingers. "One, we will try the Portal in the capital city only after we try to find the Red Dragon and two, we don't give up unless all of us agree."

"Got it." Jack leaned in. "But if the dragon eats me, we should probably give up."

"Good point. So don't get eaten," Emma said eliciting a giggle from Acorn.

"I'll protect you, Jack," Holly smirked. "Acorn will too." Acorn giggled more.

"Three," Emma held up a third finger, "when we leave Dara, we ask Roi to come with us. If we're going to have any chance of finding what we need for the scope, we need someone who knows the history and the stories."

"But he's from Dara. He might not be much help in Nima or the rest of the Seven," Jack argued. "Besides, what about the Fade? He'll get weaker the farther we travel."

"The Captain's been Fading for ten years. We won't be here that long.

"There's another reason to take him," Holly said to Jack. "Roi can protect you. You can hide under his dress."

Jack blushed. "It's not funny. Hiding from Sasa was a serious situation."

"Yeah, seriously funny."

Trying not to laugh, Emma rapped the table again to get their attention. "Funny or not, it's another reason to take him. We'll need quick thinking." She raised a fourth finger and smiled at Acorn. "Are you still okay with your choice to leave Dara?" Acorn started nodding immediately. "Good, we need you, too, Acorn," Emma replied, adding a solemn and respectful note to her voice.

"Emma, you forgot a point." Jack rested his chin on one thumb, while his index finger rested along the side of his nose.

A wave of homesickness surged through Emma. Their dad did the same thing with his hand when he concentrated while reading papers in his office or considering how many tricks to bid while playing cards. Jack looked too much like him right now.

Jack grinned impishly. "Tannor. Don't you need him to protect you?"

Emma blushed and she felt the heat rush unbidden into her face. Holly quickly looked down avoiding any eye contact with her. Her feelings for him must be way too obvious if they both already had her pegged.

"Get off me! I don't need your help!" Tannor's shouting filled the room as the door from the tunnel burst open, followed by Tannor stumbling into the room, his pants shredded, exposing jagged claw marks on his left leg. Grunting in pain, he limped forward with Roi at his side, dragging his left leg and leaving a trail of blood on the floor.

"Acorn, the second cabinet to the right! Bottom shelf. I have a healing kit," Roi called out, pointing at the kitchen as he grabbed onto Tannor and led him to a sturdy wooden table covered in books and scrolls. Holly and Jack ran over to the table and shoved everything onto the floor, clearing it for Tannor.

Acorn dashed to the cabinet and ran back to Tannor's side carrying a round box. Setting the box down carefully, she latched onto his hands with hers as he leaned unsteadily on the table. Long dark streaks of dried sweat mixed with shard dust covered his pale face. "Lie down on the table, Master Tannor. I've had a lot of practice." She opened the shiny metal box while sparing a glance towards Holly. "Treating the Sisters after attacks." Pulling out a thin-bladed knife, she quickly sliced around the top of his left pants leg and pulled off the blood-soaked fabric. Torn flesh hung like ribbons above his knee.

"It's not bad at all. I'll have you smooth as sand in no time." Acorn pulled a jar, filled with an orange and blue striped gel, from the box and set it on the table. "Holly, would you take off his boots for me, please?"

Still across the room, Emma felt sick to her stomach. She couldn't move from her chair. She stared blankly at Tannor's leg as a rushing sound crashed like waves inside her head. Acorn was saying something to him, but she couldn't focus.

Holly quickly undid the straps and buckles on Tannor's boots, glancing up. "Emma!" she whispered sharply.

Emma blinked and made eye contact. Holly gave her a reassuring smile. "Acorn's got it under control. Why don't you get a drink? Maybe bring some water for Tannor?"

Emma pushed herself up and out of the chair. "Water would be good. Thanks, Hol." She walked to the kitchen and leaned on the stone countertop, keeping an eye on Tannor the whole time as she took a drink of water. On his back, his eyes closed, Tannor was gripping the edge of the table. Sweat beaded his forehead.

"Would you like an ice crystal? There are two in Roi's kit." Wiping her fingertips clean on a rag, Acorn held up a small lump of shiny purple that looked like rock candy. Emma assumed it was a painkiller.

Tannor grimaced but shook his head no. "Save it." Acorn frowned but said nothing as she put the crystal back inside a glass vial. From the treatment box, she pulled a pair of pointy tweezers along with a short and very sharp-looking knife.

He rolled his head to the side, waving one hand at Holly and Jack. "Ice crystals come from Indigo and are worth a small fortune. You steal those, Roi? Or something else you borrowed?" He chuckled, causing him to grimace again from the pain.

"Jack, Roi. Could you hold his legs? I have to clean his wounds now," Acorn said. She leaned her face close to Tannor's as they grabbed his ankles. "Tannor, try not to move."

He leaned his head back onto the table, then closed his eyes as Acorn began to clean the gashes on his left thigh, using the knife and tweezers to dislodge and remove bits of dirt, dipping the tweezers into the small bowl of water each time she pulled something out, trimming away a small section of skin from the edges of the wounds. She pushed the tip of the knife under the edge of the deep gash along the outside of his thigh, wiggling the blade. As Tannor grimaced and swore under his breath, Emma felt faint. Tannor's leg flinched and twitched, but Jack and Roi held him in place as Acorn pulled out a sharp curved fragment, a black piece of claw two inches long. Tannor leaned his head back with a loud sigh of relief.

Emma took several deep breaths, inhaling and exhaling slowly, steeling herself. *Snap out of it, for heaven's sake! Everyone is helping him and I'm hiding by the kitchen sink.* Forcing herself away from the counter, she refilled the cup with cold water and slowly crossed the room.

"There now! All neat and clean." Acorn dropped the tweezers and knife into the bowl. She twisted open the lid of the orange and blue jar; a pungent citrus odor filled the room as she dipped a flat blade into the jar, stirred the contents, then carefully scooped out a large dollop of the mixture. Emma stopped beside Tannor's left shoulder as his eyes opened. Propping himself on his elbows, he grinned at her, then swore as Acorn began spreading a thin layer of the swirled gel on the wounds.

"I bet you stole the healing gel, too. Didn't you, Roi?"

Roi shrugged innocently. "Tannor and I had a minor misunder-standing a while back. Ever since he's been content to wrongly label me as a common thief."

"Minor misunderstanding??" Tannor yelled up at the ceiling as Acorn stitched up the wound with a needle and blue thread. "You drugged me and stole my sword!"

"Not true, Emma." Roi apparently felt more comfortable arguing with Tannor through her. "I observed him having a rather rough night. When he passed out at his table, I took his sword and money as a precaution, for safekeeping. He cannot handle his drink."

"Can't handle my sika!" Tannor shouted. Holly moved around the table and held him down as he tried to rise. "You lying sack of zind dung. You knew full well what day it was for me. You brought the sika to the table!"

"Master Tannor, please hold still!" Acorn raised her voice. "I still need to apply the vella wrap. Quit moving!"

Emma pulled a chair closer and sat down next to Tannor, placing her hand on his shoulder. "Calm down and listen to Acorn. She's trying to take care of you."

Tannor lay back and looked at her. Carefully, he placed his hand on top of hers and squeezed her fingers. He smiled. "Yes, Eres." He shifted his gaze back up to the ceiling and said loudly, "Backstabber."

"Ruffian." Roi muttered back.

"Dirty thief."

"Lying drunk."

"Pretentious pile of—"

"Stop it!" Acorn shouted at Roi, her head whipping around, a tornado of red hair and fiery eyes. "Be quiet!"

"Yes, Acorn." Roi looked at her stunned as Tannor chuckled under his breath.

She whirled on Tannor. "You, too! Not one more word!" She slapped his good leg. "And do not move. Do you understand?"

"On my Marks, Acorn." Tannor grinned up at Emma. His eyes crinkled up at the corners when he smiled.

Emma turned her head away, not sure where to look. She picked up the glass of water with her free hand and took a slow drink. His hand was resting on hers. His fingers were calloused, rough.

"Done." Acorn finished binding the wound and repacked the kit. Picking it up, she hesitated. "I apologize for striking you, Master Tannor."

He sat up and gingerly swung his legs over the table edge. "It's okay, Acorn. I was being rude."

Acorn smiled at him and then carried the kit to the kitchen.

Tannor tried to stand. Emma grabbed his elbow to steady him. Upright but wobbly, he tested his leg by putting his weight on it. A muscle in his jaw tightened, and he sucked small breaths through his clenched teeth.

"Good tight dressing." Rubbing his bandaged leg, he wobbled again as she helped him walk across the floor.

"You need to sit down," Emma said. She turned him slightly and lowered him into a chair at the dining table.

"And you need new pants," Jack added as he and Holly sat down at the table.

Roi stayed standing in the room, his arms crossed and not looking happy. "What happened?"

"I turned left instead of right." Tannor joked. "This one's my fault. After the Captain relieved me, I was distracted, thinking about what he'd said. A runt—a three-legger at that—caught me blind on my way back. Pretty dumb, considering how many I've already put down today."

Apparently over his anger at Tannor, Roi brought a pitcher of sika and a large mug to the table which he filled and placed in front of Tannor.

"There are a lot of them out?" Acorn asked as she shrank into her chair next to Holly. "How many?"

"More than usual. I killed eight after sunset. No, nine including the last runt." He drained the entire mug of sika. Jack was amazed at how nonchalant he seemed about fighting and killing nearly a dozen of the nasty creatures. The image of the shard close up from the attack on the hill assaulted his mind. "Definitely lots of activity."

Holly's eyes widened with concern. "But won't the Captain need help tonight? On watch in the dark?"

"He'll be fine," Tannor said, draining his mug. He reached for the pitcher but paused at their worried faces. "The man is never surprised by the shards. Honestly, he seems to have an unnatural instinct for where they are and how to anticipate their moves. I've seen one pass right by him within arm's reach because he's so stealthy." Refilling his mug, he grinned at Emma. "What did you say to him? Because whatever you said made him mad. Very mad."

"I told him no."

Tannor let out a long whistle.

"We disagreed with his plan to leave Dara without first trying to get what we need for the scope," Jack spoke up. "She argued with him, and she shattered a bowl. He told us to come up with a better plan or else he'd drag us out of here."

Tannor laughed. "He'll do it, too. So, do you have a better plan yet?"

Roi, still leaning against the wall, spoke. "Yes, we do." He stepped towards the group and grabbed the back of a chair. "According to my—"

Tannor raised his hand. "No way. Not from you." Roi stiffened as the left-over tension from their argument filled the room.

"Tannor, calm down. And Roi, sit down please." Emma put her hand on Tannor's forearm. "We're all part of this. Can you two at least pretend to get along?"

Roi looked away and flicked his head dismissively. "I can pretend."

"Fine," Tannor grumbled. "But you, Jack or Holly have to do it. The Captain's keen on rank and structure. If you expect him to follow your plan, one of you needs to share it. He has to know you fully understand all the details and all the risks." He paused and looked at Jack.

"Me? Why me?"

"Because it's your scope."

"Huh? No, it's not. We found it together. If anything, the scope is my dad's."

"Yes, and you took it, you used it, and now you're here. Taking ownership of the plan...and your scope...will go a long way with him."

"He's right, Master Jack." Roi said, though not looking pleased to agree with Tannor. "The Captain will expect you...as a man...to shoulder the burden."

"Yeah, okay, but I'm not a man," Jack said. "I mean, not legally. I'm thirteen years old."

"He'll be fourteen soon," said Holly.

Tannor sat back in his chair. "In Dara, the age of passage is twelve. You're old enough to choose your trade or start your colorcasting apprenticeship. Old enough to pledge a bride."

"Pledge a bride?" Emma said, astonished at the idea of her little brother getting engaged. "Are you saying he's old enough to choose a wife? He doesn't have a girlfriend...." Emma snapped her mouth shut as Acorn begin to blush wildly beside her.

"That's not true," Holly said. "He's been under Roi's dress."

"That's not funny!" Jack jumped up, waving his arms. "I had to hide. I had no choice!" Emma feared his head might spin off his neck as he wheeled around at all of them.

"You're right," Holly said, grinning. "So, does Roi have nice legs?"

Everyone but Jack burst out laughing. He hung his head down, a man caught, condemned, and mocked to death.

Tannor laughed the loudest. "Well, if that doesn't count as a rite of passage, I don't know what does. Welcome to manhood, Jack!" Tannor leaned back and crossed his arms behind his head. "Now, pretend I'm the Captain and tell me your plan."

41

MISSION STATEMENT

PRACTICING with Tannor and the others last night had definitely helped Jack. "You're presenting a mission statement," Tannor had coached him. "State the objective up front. You have to be clear, concise, and commanding. Also, no jokes. He needs to know you are serious."

The next morning, despite Emma's protests, Tannor left to take the watch, reminding her that the shards avoided the daylight and swearing he would stay mounted on his zind the entire time. Jack sat on the steps of Roi's shack, watching their heated exchange. When Tannor rode away, Jack smirked at his sister, but she stormed past Jack without looking at him, sang the two-note chord to open the secret door, and disappeared up the tunnel.

Emma had never had a boyfriend, only her small circle of girl-friends in Hartford before moving to the old house in Lebanon, and she'd never talked about liking any particular boy, but she liked Tannor. Jack did, too. He chuckled to himself. He royally screwed up when he used the kaleidoscope and pulled the three of them to Dara, and they might be stuck here forever, but on the bright side, Emma had met a boy.

Awaiting the Captain's return, Jack leaned back, propping his elbows behind him on the steps of the dilapidated porch. Waiting there had been one of Tannor's suggestions as well. "When he approaches, stand up to show respect. Choosing to meet him alone and outside the safety of the house...he'll acknowledge that even though he'll likely curse at you for being outside. Don't wait for him to start. Jump right in."

"Why are you outside?" Jack jumped to his feet and whirled to his left at the sound of the Captain's voice. Leaning against the wooden railing, the Captain stood a few feet away, frowning down at him. He must have approached from the wooded hillside behind the house. Tannor wasn't kidding. *He moves like a ghost.*

"Captain, I..." Jack paused as his mind went blank. He'd rehearsed his speech in front of Tannor and the others last night and rattled it off easily for Holly while eating breakfast. The Captain said nothing as Jack struggled to remember the words he'd practiced.

"Go inside. It's not safe for you out here," said the Captain flatly, yawning, visibly weary from patrolling the night. He stepped away from the railing to head inside.

"Captain, before we go with you to use the Portal in Ephara, we must find Balgagaar, the Red Dragon of Dara, and retrieve a sample of true red color. Putting this material in the first of the kaleidoscope's seven chambers will activate the chamber and open the scope's doorway into Nima. Once in Nima, we will pick a fireflower to activate the scope's second chamber and the door into Kasa. If we succeed, we'll be safe in the Yellow Land and we'll have the first two materials we need to get us home."

Jack stopped to catch his breath. He had stated the mission as planned, though a lot faster than he'd practiced. The Captain's intense stare and hard expression made him nervous. Plus, the man was exhausted and probably hungry. He could let him go inside and get breakfast, then share the plan, wait for him to be in a good mood. Jack felt the urge to apologize for bothering him but caught himself and stayed quiet. *Who am I kidding? He's never in a good mood.* He met the Captain's gaze and willed himself not to blink.

"Convince me." Stepping past Jack, the Captain unbuckled his belt, then sat down on the top porch step, laying his sword next to him before resting his hands on his knees. Jack gulped at the splattered drops of dried black liquid on the back of the man's hands.

He let out a slow measured breath, counted to three in his head and recalled Tannor's words. "He'll listen to your idea. If he hates it, he'll shut you down fast with a hard no. But if he sees any merit in your plan, he'll ask you for more. No reason to be nervous. If he asks for details, your chances are good."

Yeah, right. I'm going to vomit. Jack squeezed his fists together. As rehearsed, he knelt down by his backpack, slid out the kaleidoscope, and held it up.

"Based on the writings and the other kaleidoscopes in our father's study, he was researching ways to make a scope like this one. My father only has one good eye—a blue one—so he couldn't use the kaleidoscope. But he collected hundreds of different materials and colors. We think he was trying to open a portal into the Seven." Jack took a breath.

"Go on."

"The scope works for only me and my white eyes. We don't know why or how. But we know combining all the colors creates white light. So, to create the portal for Earth—there's a sign for it on the end of the scope, right here—we need to combine the colors from the different lands. You know...in the scope," Jack added, handing the scope to the Captain who peered at the symbol. He paused, trying unsuccessfully to read the Captain's silence and unchanging expression.

Last night, Roi had pulled out a large chunk of crystal to demonstrate light splitting into colors, like sunlight making a rainbow on a misty day, and suggested that Jack tell the Captain all of their theories about the kaleidoscope's inner workings. Tannor was adamant that he should keep it simple. "Never mistake his silence for a lack of understanding. He needs one solid example to decide if you've put the right level of preparation into your plan. Give it to him straight and wait."

"What makes you think this dragon exists or has this red material?"

Jack relaxed a little. He had worked on answering this question with Roi for quite a long time. "Three reasons. First, hanging on the wall in Daria's room is an ancient tapestry called the Prophet's Cloth. We saw it when we broke in to get the scope back. It shows the Prophet holding the scope—this scope—and a picture of the red dragon breathing fire. Second, Roi knows the stories about this creature and where it lives. Third, he found a map that will lead us into the dragon's cave."

"He *found* a map?" asked the Captain, the hint of a smile in his eyes.

"Stole," Jack admitted. "He's confident the dragon existed."

"Existed?" The Captain said. "Is he sure the beast is still alive?"

"No, he's not," Jack said, counting on his practice to pay off. "But a search is worth the risk. The stories say Balgagaar's home is at Kursagar, and Roi said that would be a short detour on the way to Ephara." The Captain was nodding as if in agreement, and Jack fought to contain his excitement. "If we come up empty-handed, we'll move on to the Portal in Ephara. Your plan."

The Captain crossed his arms. "Very well, but what material will we get from a dragon?"

"Dragon's blood," Jack said, trying to sound fully convinced himself. He remembered their doubts when Roi brought up the idea last night. "The meaning of the Prophet's Cloth is clear. The Red Dragon was in Dara at the same time as the kaleidoscope thousands of years ago." Jack hesitated, knowing full well that he was stretching the facts, but he couldn't stop now. "We need him, or her, to do it again. Um, we don't know if the dragon is a girl or a boy. Not that it matters." Jack stopped, furious at himself. He was babbling now, exactly what Tannor had warned him not to do.

"Are you finished?" The Captain's meaning was clear. Time to stop talking.

"Yes, I mean, no." Nervous sweat ran down the back of Jack's neck. He was afraid he'd messed it up and the Captain was going to refuse their plan. The possibility of never finding a way home hit Jack in a very real and hard way. "We know it's a long shot, sir. And the chances of success are probably zero. But, we have to try, and we need your help."

"Very well."

"Does that mean you're done listening to me, or that you agree with me?" Jack asked, not clear from the short answer.

"I agree, but now you need to understand my terms. I don't like this. We need to get out of Dara, and I consider every minute spent on this plan risky and foolish. If we run into any significant danger, I expect all of you to hold up your end of the bargain and give up on this plan. And the moment we find no dragon—which is how I think this will play out—we head straight to Ephara, take the Portal to Nima, and then find a way to Kasa."

"But we'll need to find a fireflower in Nima."

"No. Think about it. If there is no dragon, you will not have the red color you're seeking which then makes searching for that flower in Nima less important. Once we reach the Green Coren, they can give you their guidance and may provide exactly what you need."

"Yes, Captain." Jack hated the idea. Leaving Dara and passing through Nima without getting the red and orange items for the scope put them no closer to getting home, and possibly even further away. Daria wanted the kaleidoscope and was trying to kill his sisters. Once they made it all the way to Green, the chances of coming back were slim.

The Captain interrupted his thoughts. "Also, you will not fight or try to defend your sisters. Your actions on the hilltop were brave but foolhardy. From now on, if we encounter anything more dangerous than a sandwasp, I want you to hide behind me, Tannor, and the others."

Jack's cheeks turned red as if the Captain's words had slapped him across the face. "But, but, what..." Jack's words sputtered as his thoughts swirled, "...what if they need my help?"

"Your purpose is to use this scope. You said it—you're the only one who can, so getting yourself killed helps nobody." The Captain stood up, handed Jack the scope, then put one of his huge hands on Jack's shoulders. "Face it. You are Unmarked and can't wield a color-cast blade. Your sisters' powers are growing every day. They won't need your help." He looked down at Jack whose teeth were clenched in anger. "Be mad if you must. Tell me you agree."

Jack kicked at the ground with the toe of his sneaker. All of the bitterness he felt while trapped in the Coren rose like bile up into the back of his throat. The Captain was a soldier, and he was Marked, like Roi and Tannor and Emma and Holly and everyone else in this stupid place. It didn't matter what words the man used or how many times he patted his shoulder as if he cared; the Captain didn't understand him and would never truly value him. He would always think of him as a helpless Zero and expect him to be like Acorn, cowering inside the skimm while others bravely fought and died. Jack felt tears pushing into the corners of his eyes and did not want the Captain to see him cry. He exhaled slowly. "Yes. I agree."

Not waiting, Jack ducked inside the shelter and pounded on the door. As soon as Roi opened it, Jack pushed by, walking quickly to the paddock where he slid into the shadows next to one of the wooden stable walls. He waited, motionless in the dark, until the Captain and Roi passed by in the tunnel. Blinking back tears of anger and frustration, he punched the rough-sawn board of the paddock wall, again and again until he felt the wood splinter against his scraped and bloody knuckles.

"She comes in colors."

—A quote by a man named Jagger written in the margins of Professor Waite's Journal

ROAD TO KURSAGAR

RISE AT DAWN. Cook. Eat breakfast. Pack the camp. Load the zinds. All while the Captain sleeps for two hours after his night watch. Mount up, with Tannor in the rear and the Captain in the lead, scouting for danger well in front of the group. Stop each time Emma hears the Captain's brusque command to hold up. An hour's break at midday to rest the zinds and eat lunch while the Captain naps. Mount up and ride. Two hours before dusk, stop. Make camp for the night—vella hammocks suspended high in a tree for Roi and the kids because of the heavier shard activity in northern Dara. The Captain eats and Tannor takes the early watch. The next morning...do it all over. Wash. Rinse. Repeat.

Last night, while lying in her hammock, Emma had fallen asleep to the rhythm of the whispered conversation between the two men camped at the base of the tree. As usual, the Captain's voice was barely more than a few staccato words and grunts. Tannor's voice, a warm baritone, rose and fell like a cello sonata.

From Roi's house, they had set off to the east, staying well out of sight from any traffic on the river which flowed from Silig to Ephara before spilling into Carithabsa, the Eastern Sea. This morning, after circling the town of Nasir, their trail had turned hard and rocky, a slow series of switchbacks and zigzags as they made their way into the foothills that dressed the mountain range base in a rolling skirt.

Eighty yards ahead, the Captain disappeared from view as the trail veered left. A moment later, the sound of his voice reached her ears, telling her to halt. Emma raised her right hand in a fist, the agreed upon signal to stop. She pulled gently on the reins and then patted the head of the spotted zind that she and Jack were sharing. She'd started calling it Pepper, despite Tannor's insistence that the mounts in Dara were dumb beasts. Behind her on the sun-dappled trail, Roi softly muttered a command as he stopped his zind. A moment later, the sound of Acorn and Holly, pulling up on the zind they were now sharing, reached her ears. Emma leaned back in the saddle nudging Jack with her shoulders, aware of the mild stiffness in her body from the past three hours of riding. But she was pleased overall; she was getting used to the constant traveling.

They'd ridden steadily on towards the mountains bordering the eastern side of Dara. Legends said the dragon's lair was the peak of Kursagar, a rocky dome set on the edge of the mountains lying to the north of Ephara. That's where they would find Balgagaar, the Red Dragon. *If he even exists.*

Twenty feet up the trail, Roi was engrossed with the contents of a scroll. Each time they stopped or made camp, he opened the faded set of documents he kept rolled up and tied with a leather cord. The first night on the trail, he had brimmed with confidence when sharing his plan to locate the dragon. Balgagaar was revered as the wise and ancient caretaker of Dara; Roi fully expected Balgagaar's lair would be graced with a grand entrance, easy to find.

"Balgagaar means turtle by the way," Roi announced at camp. Holly and Acorn giggled. He wasn't joking.

"Did you say turtle? 'Has a shell, moves slow and eats bugs' kind of turtle?"

Roi rubbed his chin, seriously considering her question. "Emma, I can't speak to the dragon's diet or speed, but based on the stories, a shell is quite possible."

"Great. As if convincing the Captain to follow this plan wasn't hard enough already." She rolled her eyes at Jack, hoping he'd respond, but he stayed silent.

But by the second day of riding, Roi's confidence had faltered. Each time they stopped, he spent all of his time thumbing through the books he'd packed for the journey or poring over his maze-like map, copied from the Prophet's Cloth. Reaching the rumored dwelling place of Balgagaar would not pose a problem he assured them. Every person in Dara was familiar with the story of the ancient dragon who could turn into stone, and besides, Kursagar was shaped like a big sleeping turtle. But he admitted that he did not know when they would need the map nor how long it might take them to find their way through it. When Emma pressed him, Roi muttered and sounded less sure in his answers. She had opted not to tell the Captain or Tannor—at least not yet.

"Jack, you okay? You need to hop down to stretch your legs?" she asked, but he didn't respond. He'd been oddly quiet since leaving Roi's house. "Use the bathroom?"

Not answering her, Jack slid off Pepper's back and dropped to the ground before walking away. He ducked behind a tree ten feet off the rocky trail.

They hadn't seen a real bathroom since leaving the Coren. Roi had a sheltered latrine at the back of his house with a hole in the floor and a rail to hold for balance. She'd never imagined herself as the kind of girl who would be comfortable squatting behind trees, but now, everything had changed. Like it or not, she needed to accept their daily life, and their very survival would depend on this entirely new, disciplined routine, which apparently did not include bathing either. Except for the brief stop in sight of a small village yesterday which Tannor and Acorn entered to restock their rations, they'd stuck doggedly to the trail and out of sight. When she'd suggested to the Captain that they stop at an inn—for a chance to eat a decent meal and bathe—he'd instantly balked at her idea, despite the fact they'd seen no sign of the Sisterhood behind them.

Jack reappeared from behind the tree and walked slowly over. As he patted Pepper's flank, Emma caught a whiff of Jack; she wasn't sure whether it was her brother's t-shirt, the same one he'd now been wearing for weeks, or if it was him, but he smelled rank. She really wanted a bath, but Jack was a teenage boy and he *needed* one. Most days, she would have teased him, knowing how much he enjoyed teasing—and what's not funny about body odor and stinky armpits—but since leaving Roi's, he'd been downright sullen.

"One more day to the mountain from what Tannor said," Emma said to him, not expecting a response from her brother. He'd been subdued since getting the Captain's agreement to their plan. He should've been excited, but when she'd asked him for details of the conversation, he'd given her a short three-word summary, saying the discussion went fine. When she'd pressed, he'd gone rigid, his voice like a tight cord, and refused to say anything more.

At first, she wondered if having to ride behind her was making him mad. The Captain had decided since Emma and Acorn were more confident riders than Jack and Holly, sharing mounts was the safest choice. If they had to ride quickly to avoid the packs roaming the forest, a smaller group would be easier to direct and defend. Usually, she was thankful for any silence on Jack's part, but these past three days of sharing a zind with him had been uncomfortably quiet.

"Clear," the Captain's gruff voice filled her ears. She peered up the trail; he was out of sight. With her hearing growing more acute every day, he needed only to whisper the word. Though shards rarely attacked during daylight hours, he'd told her and the others to stay well behind, giving him plenty of leeway to clear their path.

"Climb on, Jack," Emma said, as she waved her arm forward, the signal for moving ahead.

"Wait." Holly's voice reached her ears. "Acorn isn't back yet."

Emma spun around in the saddle.

"She walked back up the trail, towards Tannor," Holly added with a worry.

"Okay. Jack, climb on with Holly." Emma tugged on Pepper's reins. "Roi, We don't have Acorn. We're going to backtrack." Doing her best to aim her voice at the Captain's location, she modulated her voice with tones of orange. "Captain. Acorn is missing. I repeat... Acorn is missing."

Riding past Holly and Jack, she rode slowly up the trail as she scanned the woods, cataloguing the sounds surrounding her: the rustle of the wind in the leaves; the rhythmic rumbling of Pepper's breathing; and a faint clicking somewhere off to her left, somewhere lower.

"Hol, do you feel any shards moving close by?" She pulled Pepper to a stop and looked over her shoulder.

Holly shook her head. "No. But with all the trees covered in Blight, I constantly have that icky feeling."

Click. The terrible familiar sound again but muffled like the it was under something. She scanned the forest with her ears waiting for another click to pinpoint a direction.

"Should we call for her?" Holly asked as Jack slid to the ground.

"No, the Captain's orders are to keep quiet on the trail," Roi said while quickly dismounting.

"Emma." *Click.* "Emma." Intermingled with the clicking of the shards was Acorn's voice, coming from somewhere below where they stood and back along the trail.

"This way!" Emma ran farther along the trail as the others followed.

A short distance ahead, the path swerved sharply at the edge of a steep drop into a ravine. Tannor was there, breathing heavily as if from running, his sword drawn. His eyes were narrow slits, his gaze fixed on a point at the bottom of the slope. He raised his hand in caution as they approached.

"Stay quiet," Tannor said. "Acorn slipped and fell into the ravine. She's on a nest."

43

SHARDSPEEK

THIRTY FEET BELOW THEM, at the bottom of the ravine, Acorn lay face up on a large mound of churned dirt, her arms and legs motionless, splayed wide as if she'd landed that way and had not yet moved. The hard shiny backs of at least six sleeping shards broke though the dirt's surface. Like a jagged pincushion, their hideous extra legs poked out of the ground.

"Help," Acorn whispered as her eyes locked onto Emma's. The shells rose and fell with their breathing. Dangerously close to Acorn's chest, a pair of misshapen legs swayed slowly back and forth in the dry still air.

"Acorn, don't move. We're gonna get you out of there," Emma said as she reached out and squeezed Tannor's hand. She felt his fingers tightly gripping the carved pommel of his sword. "What do we do?"

"Oh, no," Roi gulped. "They sleep during the day and burrow into the dirt to avoid the light. There could be dozens under there."

Tannor was gritting his teeth as he studied the nest. "Roi's right. At least a dozen, likely more. If I slide down and disturb one of them, that whole mound will explode with activity." He paused and then looked Emma in the eyes. "Even if I made it out—and they do move slower in the heat of day—I couldn't keep her safe."

Emma squeezed his hand again. Acorn's breathing was getting faster and faster; any moment, the girl's fearful crying would awaken one. Roi had his arms wrapped protectively around Holly, and next to them, Jack had picked up a pointy branch, his thoughts all too obvious.

Where is the Captain? She looked up the trail, searching for any sign of him. *He should be here by now.*

Her eyes wide with panic, Acorn moved her legs to the left, then shifted her body, trying to get to her feet. Emma held her breath. Acorn's right arm pushed against the creature's leg closest to her. The back of the monster shuddered, sending clods of loosened dirt down the pile and onto the exposed back of another shard.

"Tell Acorn to stay still!" the Captain's urgent whisper hit Emma's ears. "I've got her." He leapt into view on the other side of the ravine.

Next to her, the others gasped as the Captain, his sword drawn, sprinted along the far side. She aimed her voice downwards, passing his order to Acorn. Like a soldier called to attention, Acorn froze in place as the serrated leg lowered, hovering inches above her chest.

Now directly across the gap from the group, the Captain stopped, raised his left hand, and made a closed fist. In unison, the group nodded in understanding at his clear message for them to stay in place. Next to her, Tannor sighed as he raised his own fist in response. She guessed he was not thrilled by the order, and neither was she. He'd already said entering the ravine would trigger an attack. If the Captain was going into the nest, surely he would need Tannor's help.

Seeing Tannor's signal, the Captain lowered his fist and raised his sword, his right arm cocked back. Anticipating the worst, Emma gripped Tannor's hand tighter. But instead of charging down into the ravine, the Captain's arm whipped forward. His sword looped through the air in a high arc. It spun end over end and landed with a quiet thud, point first in the dirt trail three paces from where Tannor stood.

The Captain slid carefully down the ravine slope, his boots making the smallest of scraping sounds on the hard dry dirt. Safely at the bottom, he paused for a moment then stepped lightly onto the chewed-up dirt at the edge of the nest, a silent stag entering a desolate garden filled with black thorns and jagged stems.

Emma glanced at Acorn. The leg had dropped fully on to her chest and was now twitching excitedly. Close by, the legs of another shard began scrabbling at the dirt as its segmented back shifted.

With his hands now stretched away from his sides, the Captain climbed slowly up the slope of the nest. He was taking small, measured steps as he wove in and around the black limbs towards Acorn's position on the top of the mound. A foot's length from the edge of the still partially buried shard—its back now arching up out of dirt—he knelt down and lightly ran the fingers of his right hand across the shell. As if lulled back to sleep, the back of the beast stopped moving and settled into the soil. Emma blinked; not sure she could trust her eyes. But watching in disbelief as the Captain rose to his feet and then stroked the leg of the shard pinning Acorn to the ground, Emma fully trusted her ears.

She'd missed it at first. She'd been too overwhelmed by the sight of him moving up the mound. But she heard him now—talking while he climbed across the nest, his lips barely moving and his voice much too soft for anyone else to hear.

Emma's insides churned when he lifted the leg away from Acorn. The leg drooped sleepily off in the other direction and stopped, motionless. The sick feeling grew in the pit of her stomach as he lifted Acorn into his arms, moved steadily over the nest, and climbed up their side of the ravine. Behind him, the nest of vicious monsters remained quiet and peaceful.

As the Captain reached the top of the ravine and placed Acorn into Roi's waiting arms, Emma turned away from him. She needed time to process her thoughts and make sense of what she'd heard.

He'd been speaking the entire time. And as best as Emma could tell, he'd been speaking to the nest.

Speaking shard.

44

AN UNDERSTANDING

STILL DISTRACTED by the ugliest tree yet, Holly tried to not burn their lunch again with her attempts at casting heat into one of Acorn's non-colorcast cooking pots. The first batch of stew steamed like a blackened lump of lava on the ground. Gracious as always, Acorn had laughed off Holly's mistake, rinsed the pot and quickly made a second helping of chopped roots and red spices with water drawn from a nearby stream. Acorn had come out of the shard's nest with nothing more than small scratches, and she'd been extra bubbly and quicker than usual to help with any camp chores trying to make up for falling into the ravine.

Her grip light on the handle, Holly colorcasted the outside of the cooking pan. As small tendrils of orange light cascaded from her fingertips onto its surface, she sensed the inner surface heating up quickly. She forced herself to focus, staring doggedly at the stew while the limbs of the ugly tree threw a net of disturbing shadows over their camp.

Yesterday, she started counting the trees with Blight along the trail, as if anyone could call them trees anymore with their diseased bark and black limbs covered in swollen knots. She asked Acorn to keep their distance as they rode past the sick trees. But the further north they rode towards Balgagaar's lair in Kursagar, more and more of the forest had succumbed to the Blight. In the last hour of riding before this stop, she had counted well beyond two hundred black trees before giving up. Here in the small grove the Captain had chosen for the midday rest, she felt surrounded and nauseous. She wouldn't be eating any stew.

"Holly." Acorn's hand clasped her wrist. "The stew's done."

Holly snapped out of her thoughts and dropped the handle. She'd come close to burning the second batch. "Oops. I'm sorry." She glanced at the twisted shapes. "I can't stop looking."

"That's okay, I understand," Acorn said. "I mean, I understand they bother you, of course." Acorn pulled the stack of nested wooden bowls from her pack along with a loaf of hard bread. "Do you feel something, without touching them?"

Holly stretched her fingers outward as if feeling the air around her. "A little bit. It's like I'm holding my hands close to a block of ice and the vapors are licking my palms." Holly shivered in the mid-afternoon heat. "Do you know why we keep seeing so many more of them?"

"The Pit," the Captain said quietly as he sat up from his brief midday nap, the shadows from the trees darkening the already deep circles under his eyes. Holly and Acorn had urged him yesterday to sleep longer after Acorn's misadventure, but he had dismissed their concern, grunting that he was fine. An obvious lie. The way that he looked, he would need years of sleep to fully recover from the Fade. "Roi's map shows your dragon lying on the lower dome of Kursagar, which is less than four daan from the Pit. Still a two-day ride, but closer than any sane person should be." He looked over at Jack who avoided eye contact as Acorn handed him a bowl.

"It's not our dragon," Jack said, stirring his stew.

Holly turned towards the creek where Emma was practicing her color speech again with Roi, and whispered, "Lunchtime." Emma looked up immediately and Holly smiled, amazed at how strong her sister's hearing had grown.

She took a filled bowl and set it down next to the Captain. "The Pit causes the Blight?"

The Captain tore off a piece of bread and dipped it slowly in and out of his bowl. "Some people say."

"Is that what you say?" Holly asked, not confident she'd get an answer.

He looked up. His eyes, more grey than green, came back from somewhere far away and focused on her. "If there's a light in the world, the Pit is the farthest from it." For a brief moment, Holly felt he was about to say something else entirely. "The Pit is three-daan wide and filled with an impenetrable darkness. There's no life and nothing good in that place. The poisoning of the trees; perhaps there's a connection," he stood on his words for a moment, "I can tell you what I've seen these past ten years: the people oppressed by the Coren; the woods blackened by the Blight; the towns terrorized by shards. These are dark times in Dara."

"You didn't sound frightened yesterday," Emma said sharply as she walked up. "In fact, you seemed pretty darn comfortable."

"Spit it out, Eres. You've been wanting to ask me all night."

"Ask him what?" said Jack.

Emma crossed her arms. "How he speaks to shards." She pointed a finger at the Captain's head. "You talked to them in the nest."

The Captain stood up. "I've been here a long time." Fastening his sword belt on his waist, he stepped close to Emma and put a hand on her shoulder. "Which means I've spent too many hours in the forests at night, alone and surrounded by their infernal chittering. I can't speak their language, but I have learned to imitate some of their sounds."

He closed his eyes and began making a rhythmic series of clicks and scratching sounds deep in his throat. Holly cringed. Even the sound of a sleeping shard was horrible.

"And on my Marks, I've spent too few hours in the company of others. Looks like I need to relearn how to speak U'maan." The Captain smiled at Emma who visibly relaxed.

"Thank you." Emma clasped and squeezed his arm. She sat down by Acorn and grinned up at him. "So, since you're explaining things, can you tell us more about this thing Tannor mentioned to you the other night? The thing he called Order."

The Captain scowled at her, but his eyes held a grudging respect. "Eavesdropping on private conversations is not polite."

"I guess we're all learning new skills," Emma teased back.

"Tannor's story is his to tell, so you'll have to ask him yourself." Then he pointed at Roi whose mouth was full of stew. "They need to learn the legends and know what's out there." Striding to his zind, he turned and waved his finger at Roi. "But nothing about Tannor." Riding away, he called over his shoulder, "and Roi, keep it short."

THE SIGNS

Roi took an enormous bite of bread and scratched his head.

"Short. Sum up everything I know about the history of Dara and the Seven and keep it short." He looked baffled by the Captain's direction. "Hmmm...I could start with the appearance of Order...or maybe I should work my way backward."

"Start at the beginning," Emma interrupted him, her voice firm. "We'll ask questions if we need to."

"Excellent suggestion, Emma. Very well," Roi said, then leaned forward, "according to legend, over three thousand years ago, the Prophet came to Dara. I believe he must have used the kaleidoscope, Master Jack's scope. When he departed, a terrible war—one hundred years long—raged across Dara. Sadly, I've been able to find scant information. The historical evidence about this war is gone. The library in Ephara was ravaged by a shard attack years ago."

"Who was fighting?" Holly asked.

"Oh, forgive me, Eres." Roi put his fingers to his forehead. "The Hundred Year War was between the people of Dara and Se'en-sii."

Jack sat up, beating the others to the question. "Sii? The evil queen that dwells in the Pit? But Acorn, you said Sii was a legend, a story to scare children."

Acorn blinked, looking nervously at Roi. "She's real?"

"Honestly, I don't know. I've spent years looking for proof of her existence, but besides the old stories, I've come up empty handed," Roi said. "However, in recent times, there have been signs."

"Signs?"

"Yes, there are bad things happening in Dara, more in these past few years than I can ever remember: the prevalence of the Blight for one. Shards were first sighted in Dara ten years ago, and their numbers have increased more and more each year. Then, there are the senseless attacks upon our villages—like the recent one in Lindur I told you about—reportedly spearheaded by the monster called Order."

"And these are signs?" Acorn asked.

"Yes, all signs point to something unseen. All ends must have a beginning."

"Roi, tell us more about Order," Emma reminded him, hoping he might shed light on Tannor's experience with this creature.

"Oh, yes. First there was Chaos—that beast came to Dara not long after the appearance of shards in the land," Roi paused before continuing, "Nearly six years ago, a new creature began plaguing the villages. The women told stories of how it rode in the night like a general of darkness, packs of shards marching behind like trained dogs of war, herding their men like sheep and taking them captive. I've never seen this thing—called Order ironically by the people— but Tannor," and Roi paused briefly as he glanced in the direction the Captain had left, then spoke, his voice low, "he has personal experience with Order. The creature killed his brother and I fear Master Tannor has sworn revenge."

Emma bit her lip as a sense of dread crept over her. Tannor had a temper – she'd seen repeated flashes already – and everything about his bold manner only supported Roi's conclusion. If given the chance to avenge the death of his brother, Tannor wouldn't hesitate. He'd leap into battle even if this Order creature was surrounded by a horde of shards.

"Roi, you believe Sii is real, don't you?" Jack asked. They could all see the underlying dread in the thin man's eyes. "First the shards appeared, followed by this giant shard called Chaos, and then Order showed up. If all these signs are ripples in a pond, and the Pit is at the center," Jack said as he sat up straighter and clenched one fist, "then someone or something started it all."

"Yes, Master Jack."

"THAT'S IT!" Emma shouted as she jumped to her feet and closed the gap between her and Roi in seconds. "I knew something was different since you agreed to teach me."

"Different? I'm not sure what you mean, Emma," Roi said, backing away.

"You did it, again! You call me Emma now, but you're still saying 'Yes, Master Jack' and 'Of course, Eres Holly'. Why?"

Roi grinned at her. "Because you're my student. As your teacher, my position is higher than yours even though you are a Seven. My apologies. I should have told you when we made the bond, but I was so excited. I forgot."

"Higher? You forgot?" Emma cringed at the bothered tone in her own voice. She had no right to be annoyed by this. "Sorry. I don't like talking about one person being higher than another."

"It's our way," he said. "Each according to their Marks. Thus, I must address Holly as Eres."

"But I don't have any Marks, and you keep calling me Master," Jack said. "Not that I'm complaining."

"Yes, Master Jack, but you wield the kaleidoscope, and you have the eyes of the Prophet. This may sound blasphemous, and I have no proof yet, but in my opinion..." Roi hesitated a bit, "...I believe you may be the highest of us all."

The girls rolled their eyes, knowing what would come next.

The big grin on Jack's face was impossible to ignore. He raised one hand—two fingers up with the others curled under his thumb—and began making blessing motions at them like a priest presiding over a ceremony. "I, Jack the Wise, grant peace and good tidings to you, my lowly sisters."

"Seriously?" Emma laughed. She was thrilled by the spark of life in her brother; he'd been so depressed since leaving Roi's house.

"Excuse me, oh Person of the Lower Status. You must speak

loudly since I am so high and far above you." Jack cast his arms wide as if searching for the source of the sound.

"This is all your fault, Roi." Emma shook her head in mock exasperation.

"It's okay." Jack aimed his wave of blessing at Roi now. "Like any wise teacher, you have restored balance to the universe. And Roi, please don't call me Master Jack. I'm not in charge of anything." He dropped his arms, laughing, as he turned to Emma. "Speaking of teaching, did the Professor teach you anything new today?"

Roi looked shocked. "Oh, no, Master...I mean Jack, I do not deserve such a title."

"Ignore him," Emma said. "And yes, he did. If you're done, I'll show you." She stepped closer to the trees as Jack sat on the ground with the others. "He's been helping me with my colorspeak. I'm close to a five-note chord. And I can speak all of the colors now, including red. Listen."

Her eyes closed, Emma focused on a healthy tree to their left, its leaves a dark umber. Back home, she could identify the note made by the wind moving through the branches. Now, she listened to the tree itself. Roi had explained since all things were made out of colors, and colors had their own distinct sounds, she should be able to hear the sounds inherent in each and every thing. This tree's sound, a D note, hummed softly in her ears. The tone was warm and sustained like the playing of a viola, the same tonality that permeated Dara.

Emma sang, matching the note of the tree, her voice vibrating like the strings on a violin, and when she opened her eyes, Holly and Jack were gaping at her in amazement. Still holding the D, she modulated her voice into the color blue. The tone softened into a piano-like ahh, the sound of rippling water. Holly's eyes opened wider. Enjoying herself, Emma changed the tone once again, this time to the fiery tone of the color orange. Her voice, still wrapped around the original note, grew louder and louder, a brassy horn blaring into the tree leaves.

"SILENCE!" The Captain's harsh whisper sliced into her ears, his voice coming from south of the trail, down towards the edge of a cliff they had ridden past earlier in the day. Emma clamped a hand over her mouth. She raised her hand, signaling the others not to speak.

The Captain's words, tight and tense, rang in her ears again. "Emma. Tell everyone to keep quiet. Have Roi, Acorn and Holly pack up camp and start leading...not riding...the zinds up the trail to the northeast." Emma started to ask why but his urgent tone stopped her. "Tannor will meet them on the trail. Come find me. Bring Jack with you."

Waving everyone in close, she relayed his orders. Quickly breaking camp, the others headed along the rock-strewn trail as she and Jack made their way towards the cliff.

Behind them, on the lowest branch of the dark umber tree, one of its leaves continued to vibrate from the sound of Emma's singing. In its edges, thin orange threads of color formed like droplets of rain. They pooled together, weaving through the inside of the leaf, following the veins down to the base. Now shaking violently on its stem, the leaf curled as tendrils of smoke formed at its edges. Suddenly, the latticework of burning orange inside flared bright and the leaf burst into flames.

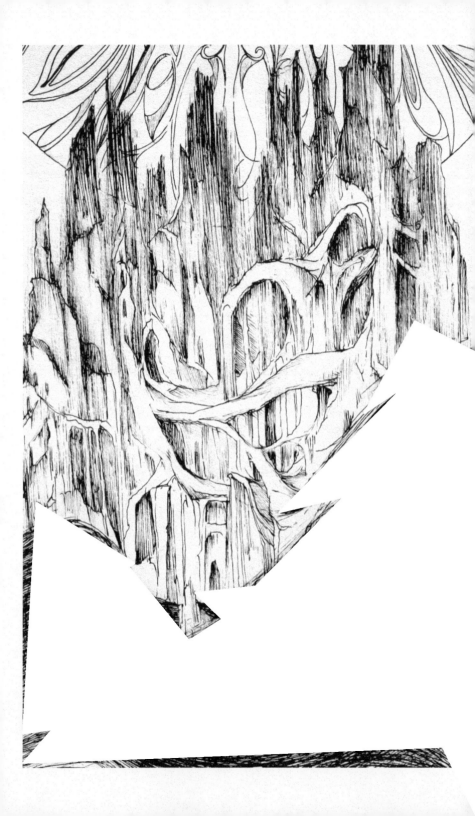

46

THE PIT

JACK FOLLOWED behind Emma as she led the way through the dense forest. Each time his foot crunched on a fallen branch, her hand shot up in the air, warning him to be quiet. By the third time, his nerves were frazzled. He wanted to ask what was going on, but she said nothing at all.

Roi's explanation for why he was using the title of Master had improved his mood, but Jack was still frustrated. He wanted to talk with Roi, find out more about these dark creatures, know more of Tannor's story and how his brother died. Had Tannor only seen Order or had he fought against the monster? Jack bet Roi would have kept sharing despite the Captain's warning.

How would you fight against something that controls an army of shards? Jack's mind jumped back and forth, keeping beat with his feet as they stepped over the branches. *And what's with all these things starting ten years ago?* The Captain's arrival in Dara, the start of the Blight, the attacks on the Land...it all seemed connected somehow.

He bumped into Emma, who was stopped and crouching by the trunk of a tree. Ahead of them, the ground gave way to a clearing. A few man-sized boulders rested heavy at the cliff's edge. Like a rock himself, on the ground and slightly back from the edge, lay the

Captain, his faded green cloak blending seamlessly with the ground. He motioned for them to get down and crawl to his position.

Jack crawled on his belly behind Emma and slid next to the Captain who leaned in close; the man's stubbled beard rubbed against Jack's ear.

"Do not talk. When I move forward, move with me, but keep your head low. Watch and observe. When I tap your leg, crawl backwards until we reach the wood line. Nod that you understand." Even as a whisper, his voice sounded commanding. Jack nodded along with Emma. Crawling forward with their heads down, they edged to the sharp drop off. From this height in the mountains, hundreds of feet above the valley floor, a wide expanse of the northern desert filled their view; a reddish-brown swath of unbroken sand stretched towards the horizon. Waves of light and heat shimmered on the dunes.

Jack peered over the edge. At the base of the cliff sat a single skimm, decorated in red and gold just like the one that had taken them to the Coren. The door of the driver's compartment swung open.

Jack gasped at the sight: a flash of dark hair laced with silver and a crimson cloak. The driver stepped onto the sands, her dress rippling like blood and shadow.

Daria.

～

"THIS CHANGES THE PLAN," THE CAPTAIN SAID FLATLY AS they rode higher up the trail, narrow enough now to force them into single file. His surprise at seeing the Red Guardian this far from the Coren had been obvious. "We should turn back now."

"Why? She doesn't know we're here. Sister Sasa saw us in Silig, but that was days ago and nobody has followed us. Roi's amulets made us safe from the Tracer." Visibly flustered, Emma kept turning around in the saddle to argue with the Captain who was riding behind them. Jack wished she would keep her eyes on the trail but he couldn't help smiling at the combination of annoyance and determination on his sister's face. She'd always hated confrontation, and he found it funny how often she'd been forced to argue since scoping into Dara. He doubted she would see the humor.

"True, or else, she'd be on our heels," the Captain conceded gruffly "But what other reason would she have to be this far from the Coren?"

"She goes to Ephara at times, right? Which is south of here."

"Yes, and if she has put the city on alert for you three, getting access to the Portal will be close to impossible." The Captain looked over his shoulder as if expecting to see Daria rise out of the dunes, then pointed at Emma. "This had better work."

Emma spun around again, almost elbowing Jack in the face. "It will. We're too close to Kursagar to give up now, and Roi has a map. We'll find Balgagaar."

"If there's a dragon to find," the Captain said. Jack felt the weight of the Captain's words on his shoulders.

Emma frowned at him then whipped her head back around to the front. Ahead of them, Holly and Acorn rode together. Roi and Tannor were farther up the path, coming in and out of view as their zinds wound around the mountain side.

Jack felt a surge of nervous energy. They were less than an hour's ride to their destination, the domed top of Kursagar.

Jack risked a glance over his shoulder. The Captain's eyes, scanning side to side constantly like a hawk on the lookout for its prey, alighted on him for a moment.

"You said we're close to the Pit?" Jack asked.

"Yes. When the tree line opens at the next rise, it will be visible. We're within a two-days ride, but even this distance is closer than anyone should be. The hills this far north are infested with shards."

Jack swallowed, involuntarily looking at the mass of dark trees to the side. "So, even as the Red Guardian, Daria is taking a huge risk coming this far out into the dunes?"

"As are we." He sounded grim. "Come nighttime, we'll be overrun. Daria may be a Six, but she's not indestructible and a hundred shards won't care how many Marks she's got. Nor how fast I can swing a blade." His watchful eyes went back to the tree line.

Apprehension clutching at him, Jack scanned the forest. Daria's presence here made no sense. He and the others had left Roi's house unseen and moved steadily through the forest, out of sight for days. Tannor had picked up supplies from a small village they passed, but if he was recognized, no one knew they were traveling together. And like the Captain said, if they'd been seen, she would have already swooped down on them.

The trees thinned out ahead. The late afternoon light, still uncomfortably hot, pulsed in Jack's eyes, light to dark, dark to light, as he passed in and out of the shadows from the trees. He frowned, still uneasy that the woman who planned to kill his sisters was this close to them. So, if Daria wasn't following them, what reason could she have for traveling all alone towards the Pit? Acorn said the Sisters always travelled in groups across the dunes. Daria was taking a huge risk; she must have a reason. Their dad didn't believe in coincidence, always lecturing them about choices, how their actions connected. No, Jack thought, there must be a reason for her showing up now, this close to them and the mountain.

Like a blister, black and infected, the Pit swelled into view far below and to the northeast. The Captain had described the Pit as stretching three daan in length; a daan equaled seven miles which meant it was close to twenty-one miles across, but Jack struggled to comprehend its true size. Around the edges, the smooth sands of the Galasag desert fractured into a chaotic pattern of broken boulders and jagged chasms with no sign of water or life on the cracked dirt. He strained with his eyes to pick out any detail, but from this high vantage point, nothing showed but darkness, like the Pit was filled to its rim with a black tar that the sunlight could not pierce.

On the far eastern rim stood the hollowed and cracked ruins of Admahgon, the dead city. Sandcast towers riddled with a honeycomb of holes loomed hundreds of feet in the air. Circular buildings and domes, their roofs caved in and aching with age, spiraled out from tower bases. Jack imagined how beautiful the city might have been once, standing unbroken with its streets not covered in rubble and years of drifting sand.

"Are you seeing this?" Emma whispered to him.

"Yes, it's—" Jack searched for the right word. The black hole was bigger than anything he had ever imagined. Epic or legendary or…

"It's wrong. Very, very wrong." Emma said. "Holly's feeling something."

Jack's eyes shot ahead to where Holly and Acorn were riding. Like them, Holly stared at the Pit, her eyes unblinking, her hands clasped together, writhing as if unable to stop. She rubbed and pulled at the skin on her palms as if she'd stuck her hands in a sticky goo which stubbornly refused to come off.

"Can you hear anything coming from the Pit?" Jack asked, still watching Holly's reaction, and feeling sorry for her.

Emma smiled just a little. "My hearing's not that good and we're miles away. I'm kind of surprised that Holly is sensing something."

The trail mercifully turned left, taking them away from the tree line and out of view of the Pit. Emma turned their zind to the left, following the switchback path which rose steeply for fifty feet and led up to the top of the rocky dome. Roi had dismounted to lead his zind around the last narrow turn after Tannor, who was already out of sight on top of the mountain. Jack relaxed a little, ready to stretch his legs and shake off the dark image of the Pit.

Emma's body tensed in front of him. "Oh, no. Holly wasn't feeling the Pit," she muttered as she jerked on the reins and looked over her shoulder. "It's shards. I can hear them."

"Where?"

She closed her eyes. "They're close, but definitely below us on the mountainside." Her head tilted to one side as she bit her lip in concentration. "Except," her eyes flashed open, "there's some up there. On top with Tannor!"

"CAPTAIN!" Roi's yell ricocheted down the rocky trail.

"Hjahh!" The Captain spurred his zind forward. Pushing his way past theirs and Acorn's mount, he kicked his heels into the flanks and drove the animal up the trailhead. One hand on the reins, he drew his sword, its blade glowing with a steely green aura. Taking the last turn, he leapt from his zind, over the rocky outcropping and out of view.

Emma kicked her heels into the side of their mount and their zind leapt forward. Rocked backwards, Jack grabbed onto the saddle as the zind jumped up the trail. Emma leaned into the neck, urging it forward. Halfway up the steep slope, Jack could finally hear for himself the sounds echoing down from the clearing above, a terrible mix of cursing from Tannor and high-pitched whining.

47

ORDER

"COME ON, PEPPER!" Emma cajoled their spotted zind forward one more step, but the spooked animal was shaking its head, yanking them to the right, backing down the trail. Emma had to get up there, but the zind was desperate to get away. In front of her, Acorn and Holly struggled to keep their mount steady.

"Here!" Emma barked. She dropped off the side of Pepper while tossing the reins at Jack. She ran up the hill. The squealing raked across her skin, like sharp fingernails scraping a blackboard. Ten more feet. Another grunt, a sharp intake of breath from Tannor, still out of sight. She pictured him wounded, a claw slicing into him. Five more feet to go. Scrambling upwards, her shin banged into a jagged stone, cutting her, and she fell hard to the path, landing on her hands and knees. Almost there. Ignoring the pain in her leg, she pushed her sweaty hair back from her eyes. In front of her, hiding behind a cracked boulder, crouched Roi.

Emma pushed herself up and ran towards Roi. His face contorted in shock, he frantically waved his arm, urging her to stop and get down, but she ignored him and rushed by as he tried to grab her. She stumbled past the boulder and stepped onto an expanse of flat rock. Ten feet to her left, the Captain was battling two shards, keeping them away from the trail, but Emma's eyes locked onto Tannor.

His back to her, he stood at the far edge of the rock dome. All of his energy and focus were on the three in front of him. He slashed at the one to his left, lopping off three of its five legs at once. Black liquid squirted out like fountains, splashing the already dark sticky ground. With his leg, he kicked the large shard at his right, forcing it down on to four legs and propelling it backward across the slick rock. At the same time, he brought his sword upwards, the return stroke from the slash. The blade slid between the writhing legs of the five-legged beast standing directly in front of him with its misshapen face, squashed brow and dark eyes. Tannor's blade sliced into its sectioned underbelly and with a small grunt of satisfaction, he pushed the point deeper. The shard made a gagging sound and a red spark ignited inside its torso. Tannor wrenched out his sword, and the shard burst into a cloud of black dust and ashes.

Not hesitating, he stepped in toward the wolf-sized shard to his right. The creature had spun around and was starting to scurry away. Emma didn't know shards could choose to retreat or possessed any intelligence; this was pure instinct, an animal fleeing from a predator.

Tannor's eyes were charged with the energy of battle. He jumped forward and plunged his sword into the beast's back, the tip expertly finding the gap between its armored back and head. The animal squealed in agony as a red spark burst inside of its body. Spinning around to dispatch the injured one, still writhing on the ground with its severed legs, Tannor saw her standing there across the clearing. As the dying shard behind him burst into a black cloud of dust, he grinned at her, a cold gleam still in his eyes. Emma shivered.

"Welcome to Roi's folly. I'll be right with you," he said, then casually turned back to the writhing creature as it tried to drag itself away with its two remaining legs. Emma was speechless, stunned by his ability to joke right now.

"Coming here was unwise, Eres." The Captain stepped in front of her, and Emma forced her eyes away from Tannor to stare at the Captain. His left sleeve was torn at the elbow, as if shredded by claws, and the black shard dust coated his shoulders. "I didn't know you were behind me and could not have protected you. And neither could he." The Captain pointed at Tannor, who was now standing next to a carcass and wiping his blade, the metal still glowing a faint red. As the others gathered around, Jack stopped next to her, whistling in awe at the large pools of black blood blanketing the ground.

Emma stood in silence, embarrassed by her actions. She'd panicked and she'd run up the hill without thinking. She took a deep breath to calm down. Past the Captain, beyond the treeline, the main peak of Kursagar towered over them, steep and imposing. The small dome of rock they stood upon dropped off sharply at the edges. The only way down was the rocky trail they'd traveled.

"Emma. There's more of them." Holly nudged her and pointed to the drop off. The sounds of shards resurfaced in her ears like sharks had been circling under the water. She closed her eyes for a moment. "Hundreds."

Tannor stepped close, completing the circle with Roi and the others around Emma. "What? Did you say hundreds?"

A deafening chorus rushed up from far below and drowned out his words. Whimpering like starving dogs, the shards shrieked as if being goaded to attack while still leashed. As Tannor ran toward the edge of the cliff, Acorn grabbed onto Roi's arm, and Jack threw his arm protectively around Holly. Emma winced; the clicking of their mandibles drilled into her ears.

"Captain, down there!" Tannor called from the edge. "At the trailhead."

"Everyone to the middle of the clearing!" The Captain ordered. "Tie the zinds next to Tannor's. Roi, pull my second sword from my mount and pretend you know how to use it," he yelled over his shoulder as he strode to the edge and joined Tannor.

The mountain went silent as a booming voice called out from below.

"Tannor of...Ephus, son...of Tanok. A...supreme pleasure." Each word was spoken slowly with chiseled precision, but with abnormally long pauses between each word, as if the speaker needed to search for what to say. The voice, slick like oil, paused again, then issued a loud, grating sound, more cough than laugh. "You are...afraid. Your...brother....was also afraid."

Tannor recoiled, took a step backward and just as quickly stepped forward again. Emma gasped. He was leaning forward as if ready to throw himself at the unseen voice. The Captain stepped in, wrapped his arms around the younger man's waist in a bear hug and heaved him off his feet. Spinning around, he set him down several feet back.

"It's Order," Tannor spoke the word like a curse. His voice cracked, as he choked back his emotions. He gripped the Captain's shoulders. "I have to try. Don't take that from me."

"Any other place, but not here. And not now," as Tannor started to protest, he continued, "we have to get them to safety, out of Dara."

"But it killed him. On my Marks, Captain! It left him in pieces on the ground. I may not get another chance."

Tenderly, like a father calming his child, the Captain placed both his hands on each side of Tannor's head and drew him in close. He spoke softly into his ear; Emma focused on the words. "Your chance will come." Tannor's whole body heaved as he fought to control the rage. "I swear. It will die. By your hand...or by mine." He held his gaze, waiting for him to calm. "Agreed?"

Tannor's shoulders eased a fraction. The Captain released him and stepped to the sharp drop of the cliff. Emma couldn't stand still any longer and ran towards Tannor with the others behind her.

"You, I do...not...know." The alien voice reverberated up the cliff, the overlapping tones a dark minor key which Emma could not identify. "Will you...greet me?" Another long pause, followed by a raucous gravelly laugh that lasted too long and felt strangely out of place as Emma and the others crept close to the precipice.

Dark general. The description Roi had shared earlier had been accurate but completely inadequate. Like a gigantic obsidian statue, the thing called Order stood eight or nine feet tall, maybe more. This creature was not created by nature, but by the work of hands unholy. The body had too many muscles, too many bones—as if carved by an amateur sculptor with no training on human anatomy. Its head was warped: the chin too big and the planes and angles of the face askew and asymmetrical. Save for its glossy skin, which reflected the evening light like cut gemstones, the creature was horrible to behold.

This thing called Order stood like a man and gestured like a man, but apart from a long red cape secured around its neck by a large gold ring, the creature wore no clothes. Hung from his waist by a banded metal belt was an iron broadsword. Order loomed in front of the black mass of creatures, lined up in columns and rows. The shards swayed slightly back and forth in a spooky unison as if they were soldiers standing in formation.

Tannor moved next to her, fumbling with his belt.

The Captain sheathed his sword. "Crawl back to the Pit and I won't kill you today."

"Ahhh...a Greenling. How...captivating. You are...lost...far from home," Order said.

"Save your lies, foul beast," The Captain shot back.

A bolt, fired from Tannor's compact crossbow, flew down, aimed squarely at Order's head. Its right hand flicked up, surprisingly fast, deflecting the bolt harmlessly to its misshapen feet.

"Tsk, tsk...last...son of Tanok." Order picked the bolt from the ground and snapped the steel bolt between his fingers like a pencil. "By your Marks—"

Tannor launched two more bolts. Order slid effortlessly to the side. The bolts flew past him and blasted into the beast directly behind him. The creature screamed in pain. Within seconds, two red sparks flamed in its abdomen, and it exploded into a ball of ashes. At once, the others screamed in rage, pawing frantically at the air with their legs.

Order picked a piece of ash from its shoulder, then fastidiously smoothed out a wrinkle on his cape.

"It is time...for my greeting," said Order, the pitch of his voice modulated down an octave into a thundering bass that shook rocks loose from the wall of the canyon, the words fragmenting into dozens of notes, a dark orchestra. The lines of shards behind him fell silent. He raised the huge black sword and aimed the point at them. "I am

Sutesuru, Master of the Pit, Lord of Admahgon. You may call me...
Order."

Order said no more, standing motionless while the horde rocked
back and forth, the mountainside eerily quiet. Tannor shook with
rage, his fists clenched, staring down at the monster who had killed his
brother. The seconds passed; yet the creature held his position.

"What's he waiting for?" Emma mused out loud.

Jack stepped to the edge and clapped his hands.

As if on cue, Order's crooked mouth stretched open, his chin
dropping sharply and to the right, off kilter. He began to laugh, loud
and raspy, while slowly lowering the sword to his side.

Jack turned back to the group, shaking his head in wonder. "An
audience. I think he wants to be liked."

"It's waiting for nightfall to attack," the Captain said with a quick
glance at the sun setting bloodred on the horizon. Then he reached
out and grabbed Roi by his arm. "You need to find an entrance to the
dragon's cave. Now." Roi gulped.

Down below, at the base of the hilltop, Order continued to laugh.

48

THE GATE

"YOU'RE TELLING me you brought us all the way to this mountain...this close to the Pit, and you don't know where the entrance is?" Tannor was yelling now.

"Um, it should be here. Somewhere." Roi scanned the top of the dome, his eyes bewildered. "I was sure there would be a gate. A big gate. You know, dragon-sized."

"I'm going to kill him," Tannor said as he raised his sword and took an eager step forwards. Roi flinched and backed up two steps.

Jack and Holly laughed nervously, but Emma was deeply bothered. She knew he wasn't serious, but his underlying tone, a vindictive note without remorse, struck her as much too dark. Given the justification, Tannor might actually kill him.

"Enough," the Captain said as he strode up and pushed one massive finger into Roi's quivering chest. He turned his head to Jack, Emma, and Holly. "This is what I warned you about. Sunset is less than an hour away. Our best chance is to retreat through the woods and climb higher, using Kursagar to stay ahead of them."

Emma pulled Holly and Jack to one side, then leaned in close. They'd discussed this possibility back at Roi's. All of them needed to agree on when to give up on their searching.

"Gate first."

Jack didn't hesitate. "Yup. We may not get another chance."

"Okay, but he's right," Holly said softly. "That's a lot of shards."

Jack faced the Captain. "We'll all search for Balgagaar's gate. If we don't find it, then we'll run."

"Make it fast," the Captain said, frowning as he pointed his finger at Jack. The fabric of his left sleeve was stained with blood.

"The tapestry in Dara's room showed the Red Dragon sitting on top of Kursagar," Roi jumped in, eager to make things right. "The entrance to his lair must be here."

Holly studied the hard ground, kneeling down to rub her hand across the slick surface. "Yes, but that was thousands of years ago. Maybe the weather wore everything away, so now there's nothing left."

"Maybe not," Tannor said, standing north of the dome's midpoint. He pointed to a spot by his feet. "Something's carved here on the rock."

Barely visible in the remaining light, a palm-sized symbol, similar to the mark above Roi's door, was etched in the stone. A second symbol—six inches to the right—appeared to be incomplete, obliterated by the passage of time. The symbol looked crooked to Emma.

"How in Dara did you find these? That was very...um, I mean..." Roi hesitated and coughed.

"He meant to say good job," the Captain scowled, his displeasure with their bickering clear. He tapped the first symbol with the toe of his boot. "Roi, what next?"

"Those are musical notes in U'maan, Emma; the lower part of the symbols. All musical notation is written—"

"Roi!" Jack, Emma, and Holly yelled at him in unison.

Emma patted Roi on the shoulder. "Not a good time for a music lesson. Can you unlock the gate with these?"

He scratched his head as he stared at the symbols. "I'll try. To be safe, everyone move." As they stepped back, Roi quietly sang a single note, a G-note, that Emma immediately recognized. The first symbol glowed red like a hot coal, and Roi's face lit up with excitement. He paused and sang one whole step higher, an A-note, and this time the other symbol glowed, including the erased part. Looking positively delighted by his progress, he took a breath and sang both notes at once, a dissonant combination. The timbre of his voice was rich and steady, like the long pull of a bow across the strings of a cello. He was singing the notes in the color red, the natural key of Dara.

Under the ground, something clicked, like the tumbler in a combination lock. Grinning with anticipation, Roi held the two-note chord.

Nothing happened. he increased his volume, his chin now pointed down, aiming his voice at the symbols. They burned a fiery red color, but there was no new sound, no movement as his body trembled from the effort of sustaining the notes.

Like a broken whistle, his voice wheezed and sputtered. Roi gasped for breath, hands on his hips. He gave an embarrassed shrug. "It didn't work."

"What gave it away? The fact there's no open gate or that we're still standing here?" Tannor snapped at him.

"Tannor! Keep watch on Order!" The Captain commanded. "And do not, I repeat, do not shoot again." Tannor stomped away, scowling back at Roi. Beyond the mountains, the sun had settled into a glowing ball on the horizon, painting the rocky hill in shades of crimson and gold. "Roi, unless you have another idea, we need to flee."

Emma stared at the placement of the symbols on the ground. *The second symbol's not crooked. It's rotated.* "Hold on. Watch," Emma interjected. Starting with a G-note, she sang up the scale. Like fireflies tracing a circle on the ground, the first two symbols and then four more, completely invisible until hit with the right note, blinked on and off as Emma hit each note. "Roi, how many notes in the circle?"

"Six. G, A, B, D, E and F#."

Emma frowned. "But no clicks. Singing each note individually didn't trigger the lock."

"Try a chord of three notes," Roi said eagerly.

Emma's stomach flipped as she digested his words. Deep down inside, she realized that singing three notes would further open the unseen lock—but not all the way. The information on the Prophet's

Cloth had proved to be true, had led them to Kursagar, and now they'd found this entrance to Balgagaar's lair. But the gate was protected by six-colors, a lock that only a Guardian could have color-cast which meant only one thing. She would have to do something she'd never done.

"Six. It's gonna take a six-note chord to open. I can combine five."

"What if Roi sings two and you sing the other four?" Holly asked. "Together as a team?"

Emma liked the idea. "Sing high. Same octave." He sang out the G and the A at the top of his tenor range. The first click of the lock as before. She layered on the other four notes, the chord like a quartet ringing from her mouth. Nothing new happened. There were no other clicks.

"Darn it," Emma cursed. The difference in the tonality of their voices was clear. "The lock. It needs all six notes from the same voice."

Jack's sigh echoed her frustration. "Which means a Guardian made the lock."

Tannor hailed the Captain. "They're moving. Half to the south to take the trail we used. The others are going north to trap us. Order hasn't budged from his spot. He's content to wait and watch us get pushed off the edge."

The Captain clasped Emma on the shoulders. "Eres, you have one shot to get this open. Everyone else—packs on and ready to move."

Horrible nausea gripped Emma's insides. Everyone was staring at her, waiting for her to sing. She felt like she might throw up, like when she had to be on stage for piano recitals. Acorn looked worried and small; the oversized pack balanced on her shoulders. Roi was motioning with his hands, miming the act of singing as if he was her vocal coach. Holly kept glancing at the opening to the clearing, her hands fidgeting, as she sensed the scrabbling of shards climbing the trail.

But the Captain wasn't watching her; his eyes were on the woods framing the back northern edge of the dome., his sword in his hands, ready to lead them away. *He's expecting me to fail.*

Jack stepped next to her, his face unexpectedly calm. He smiled and then spoke softly. "You've got this. Seriously."

Emma was not feeling confident at all. She'd try to hit a five-note chord first and then—

"Six. Don't mess with five," Jack said, guessing what she was thinking. "Remember. You're a superhero."

Emma chuckled; she felt calmer. Picturing the chord on the piano keys, she took a deep breath, stared at the ground and she sang all six notes at once.

All six symbols on the ground burst with red light, forming a glowing circle. The first click reverberated sharply under their feet. She held the chord. A second click, a third, a fourth and...the fifth symbol for the E-note glowed weakly, dimmer than the others. She pushed her voice, driving the note slightly higher in pitch. The fifth...a click...and then the sixth...a clunk, loud and solid like a stone falling into place. Too afraid to stop, she kept singing.

The ground shook beneath their feet. Red lines raced outward from the symbols like spokes on a wheel and formed a completed circle. Each section began to lower in succession. Emma jumped backward. The successive parts of the stone circle dropped, each one lower than the one before, as the scraping of heavy stone echoed across the clearing. The last section slid down and out of sight.

"You can stop singing now." Jack was grinning at her.

"How did you know I could do it?" She studied his face. He had seemed oddly confident.

He started to answer, but Roi grabbed them both. "Time to go. We're not alone anymore." He pulled them towards the hole, filled with the set of stone steps Emma's voice had exposed. Tannor, Acorn, and Holly with a glowing light stick in her hand, were already halfway down.

Shrieking surrounded the hilltop, coming from every direction now. Behind her, the zinds whinnied in terror, their hooves pawing desperately in the dirt. They were no longer tied to the tree; the Captain must've freed them while she sang. Pepper bolted past her disappearing into the tree line. The Captain's strong hand clamped onto her shoulder and pushed her down the steps behind Jack and Roi.

"Keep moving! Will this close up after us?"

She hit the fourth step. "How should I know?" Claws scrabbled on the rock dome above them, and she pictured a pack of skittering cockroaches converging towards a shower drain.

The steps ended in front of a carved stone doorway with columns flanking each side. In the large room beyond, the others huddled behind Tannor, his sword drawn.

"Emma, sing!" Jack yelled at her.

She whirled around without thinking and sang the six-note chord. The chamber reverberated with the sounds of the stone pieces sliding back into position. The bottom step, the fifth and then fourth in succession began slowly spiraling back up to the surface. The Captain stood next to her, his sword a barrier between her and the closing hole. The final steps rose back and began locking into place, exposing a system of metal weights and counterweights that must have been created long ago. With an ominous last thud, the six stone wedges connected and sealed them underground.

WRONG WAY

"Ewww," Acorn squealed.

Holly groaned and wrinkled her nose at the overpowering stench. Fragments of legs, trapped and crushed between the stones, dangled from the ceiling. Drops of thick, black liquid hung and stretched down like hot tar. Apparently, when shards were killed without colorcasting, they stank.

"Emma, I'm so proud of you," Roi said with a sheepish grin on his face as he stepped out from behind Tannor. He waved his arms. "Your control! Your awareness to bring each note into tune...so impressive!"

Standing next to Holly, Emma was shaking. "I didn't realize how much that would take out of me," she muttered with a weak voice.

Holly wrapped her arms around Emma and helped her take a seat on the ground. Then she noticed something strange about Roi's neck. "Roi, you're glowing." The faint glow of his Teacher's Marks was impossible to miss in the dimly lit chamber.

Dropping his sword to the chamber floor, he craned his neck back and forth. "They are? I wish I could see for myself." Still contorting, he spun himself around in a circle.

"For Dara's sake, man, you're like a dog chasing its tail!" Tannor barked at him. "Don't we have a dragon to find?"

"Tannor's right." The Captain gestured to the back wall of the circular chamber. "Roi, stop twirling and tell me that those doors are on your map."

Tannor activated a second lightstick as they surveyed the circular room, its walls hewn in the grey stone. On the opposite side of the chamber from the stairwell door, three doorways were spaced evenly on the wall. Stone columns framed the sides of each opening. Except for a different symbol carved into the rock above each doorway, they looked identical.

The space beyond each doorway loomed black as night.

Roi fished the rolled parchment map out of his pack and frowned as he rolled it open. "No, not all three doors. The map of the maze shows one main entrance," he jabbed the air with his finger, "but I think we should enter the door with that symbol."

"Because?" Jack asked.

"That is the symbol on the red section of your kaleidoscope. The symbol for the dragon's blood."

Holly stepped closer to the middle door. Darkness hung like a black curtain, covering the space, keeping any light from entering or exiting. She reached out with the lightstick, its glowing tip inches away from the door.

"Eres, I don't think that's a good idea."

Ignoring Roi, she stuck the lightstick into the darkness. The light disappeared as if swallowed whole.

"What the heck?" Jack swore.

Holly pulled the stick backward. Inch by inch, the light reappeared as it slid out of the black. She pushed it back in, a different spot this time. Again, the black covered the yellow light completely.

"I'm not feeling anything from the darkness," Holly said. "Nothing hot, nothing cold. And nothing sick like the blighted trees or the shards," she paused to gather her nerves. "I'm going to stick my hand in."

As Roi started to protest, she shoved her hand wrist deep into the darkness. The blackness appeared to cut her arm off like a knife, but she felt fine. She pulled her arm back, and like the lightstick, her arm reappeared.

Holly smiled, fascinated by the effect. She jabbed her hand in and out of the doorway, watching her hand vanish into the inky dark. "I don't think the lightsticks will be much help."

"Or the map," The Captain said. "Unless you have it memorized."

"Memorized?" Roi gulped. He rolled out the map between his hands, splaying it out for them.

"There's no way," said Jack and Holly agreed. At Roi's house, they'd looked briefly at the drawing of the maze, then once again while making camp, but never with the goal of memorizing the pattern.

If the map was correct, the maze formed a circle. The entrance into the outer ring—drawn in crisp lines—was the door they were standing in front of now. In the maze's center was an open circle, the endpoint with Roi's drawing of a dragon in it. In between those two points, hundreds of passages twisted and turned, a seemingly endless series of curving corridors and junctions.

But worse were the several very conspicuous blank spots on the map. Roi had pointed out the gaps in his drawing when they first developed their plan. They'd agreed with him that night; guessing which way to go in the maze a few times was a risk they'd be willing to take. But that was when they thought they would be able to see inside the maze.

Jack stepped away from Roi and let out a long whistle. "Even if the map were complete, it'd be impossible in the dark."

"Wait, this map's not finished!" Tannor exclaimed, examining Roi's drawing for the first time. He jabbed at one of the undrawn spots. Based on the scale, there could be dozens of unknown turns in that area alone. His finger moved to the center of the maze and jabbed at Roi's sketch of Balgagaar. "What in the Seven is this supposed to be? It looks like a fat dog with wings!"

"Did you know about this?" The Captain stared angrily at them.

Holly, Jack, Tannor, and Roi all started answering at once, their voices bouncing off the stone walls.

"EVERYONE!" Emma's voice blasted them into silence. Stumbling to her feet, she pointed back across the chamber, her eyes fixed on the sealed entrance. "Quiet. Something's different up there. The shards aren't moving outside."

"Which means Order has arrived," The Captain said, his hand moving to the hilt of his sword.

"Can he open the gate?" Acorn asked and everyone turned to Roi.

"I don't know," Roi said meekly.

"Then we enter the maze," The Captain announced, his demeanor grim.

Looking almost relieved, Roi stepped back from Tannor who was still glaring at him. Roi gripped the map tightly with both hands and stepped towards the maze entrance. "Follow me."

"Not so fast," the Captain grabbed him by his shirt and yanked him away from the door. "First, study that map."

Tannor pulled a length of yellow cord from his pack. Looping it loosely around Roi's waist, he cinched it with a knot and the cord started to glow. "Quick. Line up behind him." His hands moving fast, Tannor tied them all to the rope in the same way, explaining as he worked down the line. "Not sure the glowcord will work in there, but this will keep us together. We don't want anyone falling down a chasm."

Acorn tugged at the knot around her waist. "There are holes in there?"

"I don't know, but trust me, little one. These knots are secure." He flashed a wicked grin. "Except for Roi's."

"Conceited oaf," Roi muttered under his breath, his eyes fixed on the map.

"Good for nothing bookworm."

"QUIET!" The Captain growled as he tied himself. "Roi. Take us in."

Roi folded and tucked the map into his belt, then as he snuck a glance over his shoulder, gave the knot at his waist a hard tug. Holly pretended not to notice.

Roi inched up to the doorway, his shoulders hunched together, the lightstick shaking in his hands. He reached into the black opening, his hand moving tentatively like he might get burned. His hand, then his arm slid out of sight. Sighing with relief, he stepped through the door and disappeared.

The rope around Jack's waist stayed taut, pulling him towards the opening. He glanced back at Holly; he was frowning with a look of deep concentration written on his face. Then with a deep breath, he walked quickly through the door. The length of cord between them snapped tight and pulled Holly through the door.

Blackness surrounded her with no light from the glowcord. Blinking a few times, she shoved her hand to her face, against her nose, but saw nothing. She felt Emma brush up behind her. Stepping forward, she ran into Jack.

"Jack, keep going forward. The others are trying to push their way in."

"Sorry, Hol. This is the second time I've been blind in Dara," Jack said.

"You're not—never mind. Roi, are you moving?"

"Yes, Eres, but I'm taking small steps given the circumstances," he answered with a shaky voice.

"We're tied together. We won't let you fall," Holly said.

Holly let the tug on the rope guide her steps. The murmurings of the others filled the black passageway as they repeatedly bumped into each other. Tied together, like a seven-person spring constantly stretching and constricting, they moved slowly along the tunnel.

Roi called out each time he made a new turn in the maze. Both Jack and Emma were counting out loud, tallying their progress. Holly dragged her hands along the walls. They were smooth as glass. Whoever had designed and built this maze had been careful to leave no variations in the surface. Even with light, there would be no clues, no identifying marks to use for guidance.

"Left again," Roi called out another turn. They had made nineteen turns so far. Sounding confident, he rattled off another change in direction. Holly doubted Roi could go much farther before his memory of the map gave out.

"Right...I mean, um..." Roi's voice trailed off. Hands still spread wide, she collided with Jack. Like a train wreck with each railcar running into the one ahead, Emma ran into her as the others crashed into one another.

"What's wrong?" the Captain's bass voice filled the darkness.

"Nothing, Captain," Roi answered, a nervous hitch in his voice. "I'm picturing the next turn."

Holly grimaced. They had reached the end of Roi's memory. She felt Jack reaching out with his arms as well, first to the left and then to the right. The rounded corners on both sides of the tunnel meant they were at a T-junction or a cross passage. Roi had to choose.

"Left. Turning left everyone," Roi announced.

She felt Jack lurch forward. Suddenly, the rope around her waist cinched tight and yanked her off her feet. Holly tumbled onto the stone floor next to Jack and Roi as Emma, Acorn, and the others were ejected through the far left door in the rock chamber. They were back where they started.

Jack rolled towards her, shaking his head and blinking. "Well, I didn't see that coming."

Two wrongs don't make a right, but three lefts do.
—Anonymous

50

A-MAZE-ING

"SHARDS!" Tannor yelled. Across the room, the stone sections of the stairs had lowered down into place. Behind the columned archway, two shards crept onto the bottom step. Behind them, more scrambled and pushed against each other, a wriggling black mass filling the hole.

Tannor untied himself and pushed past the others. His crossbow already out, he stepped over Jack and fired bolts into the two shards. They fell back in pain, writhing and momentarily blocking the doorway into the chamber. He continued to launch bolts into the stairwell, wounding the creatures and bringing them down.

"The maze kicked us out. We have to try again," Jack said as they clambered to their feet.

The Captain said nothing as he rapidly untied the glowcord. A pile of black bodies blocked the stairwell. Tannor had chosen normal crossbolts, without any colorcasting. He was wounding them to stop up the stairwell like a clogged drain. The smell of rotten meat filled the chamber. "We'll hold them back for as long as possible. Memorize the maze for another try." The Captain spun away and crossed the room to the stairwell.

"But how did they get in?" Acorn asked. Holly had her arm around the smaller girl. "Was it Order?"

Emma shook her head. "It should take the singing of a six-note

344

chord to open the gate. Maybe Order has that power." She grabbed one end of the map from Roi and spread it out between them. "Everyone, memorize as many turns as you can."

They scanned the map. A chorus of directions—muttered lefts, rights, and more lefts—rose between them. Wedged between Roi and Holly, Jack kept losing his place and his concentration. Looking at the size of the maze, he couldn't imagine this working.

"Silently...memorize silently!" Emma yelled at them. "And take different sections in order. Holly, you follow Roi. I'll start here." They fell silent, their lips moving as they each studied the tunnels and turns in the maze.

From across the room, the smack of the Captain's sword on a hard shell rang out. Jack gave up on learning the map.

Broken and dead bodies littered the space outside of the stairwell. Jack cringed at the squealing body of a badly wounded shard wriggling itself out of the tangled mass. As soon as it tumbled to the ground, another pushed through the newly formed gap and leaped at Tannor. He ducked and thrust his sword up into its exposed belly. While the monster sparked and exploded into ash, two more squeezed through the hole.

"They're eating through each other to get in," Tannor yelled. Lines of shard dust, mixed with sweat, ran down his face.

The Captain finished off another with a sweeping arc of his blade that cleaved the jaw from the thing's head. Its body lit up with a sharp green spark and burst into a swirl of black dust. Swinging his sword while backing up, he yelled toward the group.

"Time's up." He strode over and picked up the trailing end of the cord. His face bleeding from a ragged cut on his forehead, he gestured at Roi. "This better work. Tannor, fall back!"

Roi stepped into the black doorway, dragging Jack and the others behind him. Walking faster this time, he led them through the maze. He called out every turn...ten turns, now fifteen, then twenty...left again, this way, another ten paces before the next turn to the right...

Roi was doing his best, describing every move so he and the others could better visualize the maze. But as he rattled them off one by one,

Jack felt his mind drifting away from the twists and turns. *This isn't going to work.* They could only go so far with the information they had. At some point, they would have to make a choice in the dark, a choice between right or left. *A choice between life or death.*

Jack shook his head, not sure where that thought came from. He listened again to Roi, still sounding confident with the directions; but now, Jack knew for sure that much like the sensation back in the Coren, when he had known dinner was coming or known Acorn was approaching, Roi would forget what came after turn thirty-four.

"Right at the next turn," Roi called out the thirty-third change in direction and led them another ten paces. "Right again," he said as they made the thirty-fourth turn, the rope still taut around their waists. Jack followed him down the corridor. "And...now it's...I'm not sure."

Jack pulled up immediately. Roi couldn't picture where they were in the maze. *But that won't matter because Holly is going to take over.* The image of Holly leading had come unbidden into his head. The group talked excitedly behind him, and Tannor was imagining feeding Roi to the shards. Jack frowned. *Had Tannor said that out loud or not?*

"I've got it," Holly spoke up behind him. Pulling herself free of her loop, she slid past Jack in the tunnel. "Roi, switch with me." Roi sighed loudly with relief as he pushed past Jack and took Holly's place in line.

Holly moved ahead, calling out each turn. In the dark, Jack half-listened to her directions. Moments before he had been sure Holly would be so confident, but how had he known? Intuition perhaps: Holly was an artist, and studying the details of the maze would be second nature.

I'm overthinking and too stressed out. Jack tried to calm his mind. He felt a hitch in Holly's step. The rope between them went slack. *She's finished. She wants to tell us to go to the right, but she's not sure.* He couldn't see her or the intersection, but something told him she was right to hesitate. The next turn needed to be left.

Holly stopped in the darkness. Jack placed his hand on her shoulder, not sure if he wanted to ask the question. "What's wrong?" He tried to convince himself the maze, the total darkness, was messing with his mind.

"I'm stuck. We could go right, but I'm not sure," she whispered.

Jack's head spun with her answer. He felt light-headed.

"Don't move. Switch with me," Emma said as she worked her way up to the front.

"Why have we stopped again?" the Captain asked.

"I'm taking the lead from Holly." Emma's tone was reassuring, but Jack guessed she was anything but calm at this point.

"Emma." Jack replayed his last thoughts through his mind. "You know which way to go, right?"

"Yeah," she whispered in his ear. "But it won't matter. We're nowhere near the end, and I only memorized a few more turns from here."

Jack needed to test his hunch. "Before you move again, the next turn is to the left, correct?"

"Yup. I wasn't sure you memorized this far into the maze."

"Just a lucky guess." He looked to the left and tried to picture the layout of the maze in his head. Nothing. "What about the next set of turns...right, right and left?"

"Nope. Left, right, and straight at an intersection," Emma replied. "I'm moving now, okay?" Without waiting for his response, she announced the left turn to the group and turned the corner.

Jack focused on his sister, as she quietly counted her steps to keep track of their location. She called the next left turn. In his mind, he saw them heading left and moving down the tunnel. Emma called out again, and the same eerie feeling came over Jack—she was making the right choice. The feeling continued as they crossed the intersection.

"You're doing great, Emma," Roi spoke up from back in the line.

"So far," Emma muttered, still counting barely loud enough for Jack to hear. When she reached eighteen, her words dragged, slowing the count. "Okay, a few more steps, we'll take a—"

A vivid image of Emma choosing left and continuing in the maze saturated Jack's mind.

"Left," Emma said. She took three more steps and led them around the unseen corner.

He tried to picture the next turn, but his mind stayed blank. He didn't know the next direction. He focused again on Emma and waited.

"All right, there should be another intersection ahead and we have to go—"

To the right. Like before, Jack knew she was choosing to turn right. But this time, they wouldn't stay in the maze.

"To the right." Emma turned before Jack could stop her. The rope snapped and like cattle dragged to slaughter, they were ejected from the right door of the maze. The group stumbled into the starting chamber.

Acorn's screams pierced the air.

Shards were lined up in jagged rows and filled the far side of the chamber. The one closest to Acorn shrieked, but did not charge, its body rocking wildly on three, misshapen legs. Tannor jumped to the front of the group, then kicked it hard and sent it crashing into the formation. The room exploded into a nightmare of clicking and whining, but the pack stayed in place, not breaking ranks.

"The stairwell," Roi gasped. It was completely clear of bodies.

"What are they waiting for?" Holly asked.

"Order," the Captain said. He pulled his knife from his belt and handed it to Acorn who took it without question. "Roi, pick up the sword you dropped and get ready to fight."

Jack grabbed Emma by the shoulders. "Go back in the maze."

"What?" Emma pulled her eyes from the small army of monsters. "Jack, it's hopeless."

"No, it's not." The others turned to him. "Trust me."

The cavern plunged into an icy silence as the shards stopped their keening. A blast of cold air, coming from the stairs, hit their faces. Still tied together by the glowcord, they backed toward the entrance of the maze.

"Oh, no," Acorn said meekly as Order came into view on the

stairs, moving regally like a king descending from his throne. With each step, its feet scraped on the stone.

Much taller than the opening, Order spread his arms wide, touching the columns with three, blocky fingers on each hand. Slowly lowering his head beneath the doorway, Order peered into the room. Upon seeing them huddled together, his face contorted into a toothless smile.

"Roi, Acorn, form a line with me and take down as many shards as you can," the Captain said as Tannor reloaded his crossbow with colorcast bolts. "Tannor, now's your chance."

"No! Our best chance is the maze!" Jack poked the Captain in the chest.

The Captain shook his head. "We can't defend ourselves in there if they follow us. We'll make our stand here and now."

"Sorry, Captain. I'm with Jack," declared Emma. Like an arrow, she shot through the middle doorway and into the maze. Jack latched onto Roi's elbow and dragged him forward, not stopping until he ran into Emma standing at the first junction.

"Em, is everyone inside?" he asked softly.

"Yeah, I can hear the Captain cursing under his breath back there," Emma said as she began to squeeze behind him in the tunnel.

"No, stay in front of me."

"What?" Emma sounded surprised. "Aren't you taking the lead?"

"No," Jack said. "I want you to go steady and keep calling each turn and change in direction. But—and this is important—when we get to the unknown part, wait for me to say yes or no before you choose."

Emma pulled them down the first tunnel. Not bothering with directions, she led them past the first dozen turns, familiar to the entire group. Behind them, the maze was quiet with no sounds of pursuit.

"I don't get it," Holly said from back in the line. "If you're going to tell Emma if she's right or wrong each time, why don't you go first?"

"I'm not sure I can explain it," said Jack.

Walking quickly, Emma began counting each of her steps out loud. At each junction, she paused to call out the direction she planned to take. Jack listened intently to her every word. She was making all the correct choices, and he kept repeating the word yes over and over again, confirming each move.

Within minutes, they reached the spot where Emma had taken over from Holly the time before. "Okay, Em, keep it up and be ready to stop. And I mean it. Do not move an inch if I say no."

"Okay." She sounded unsure but moved forward. Jack focused on her voice. This was the most attention he'd ever given her; his mind was usually distracted. "Fourteen, fifteen...we have an intersection ahead and I'm going to go right when we get there."

"No." A brief vision—Emma turning to the right and falling out of the maze—struck Jack's head. "Not right. Go left."

Emma stopped walking. "And you're sure?"

"I'm sure. Going to the right would be the wrong choice."

"Okay, we're going to the left up here." Moving forward, she took the turn. They were still in the maze. "You still want me in front? We're farther than I memorized."

"Yep, just keep your hands on the sides of the tunnel. When you feel a corner and you're at an intersection, stop, then choose a direction. Call it out, but don't move unless I say yes. Same rules."

They kept going, with Emma stopping at each junction, calling out her choice. Jack answered back immediately with a firm yes or a sharp no. Each time, he saw the result before she moved. To his rear, the others followed without talking and so far, there was no sound of shards behind them in the corridors of the maze. Jack's mind flashed with an image, a steady stream of shards scrambling into the maze, taking wrong turns and getting tossed back out.

"How's he doing it?" Acorn whispered to Holly.

"Be quiet," Emma hissed. "Eight, nine...don't break his concentration...twelve, thirteen..."

Jack smiled. "It's okay. You can talk. I'm not concentrating on the maze."

Emma stopped in front of him. "Jack, we're at another T-intersection. I am going to go left."

Another ejection from the maze filled his mind. Jack clasped her right arm and squeezed. "No, go right." Emma turned that way, heading along the tunnel.

Roi's voice pierced the darkness. "Master Jack, this is fascinating. Are you seeing through the walls because you have the white eyes of the Prophet?"

"Do you have x-ray vision?" Holly asked.

Jack chuckled to himself. He'd always wished for superpowers. "No, that's not it at all. I'm not seeing the walls or which way to turn. It's more like I'm seeing Emma and which way she *should* turn." Emma stopped again, announcing a right turn. "Yes, to the right," Jack said as if he were her conscience.

"So, you're seeing Emma inside of the maze?" Tannor called out, sounding doubtful. "Like a bird's eye view?"

"No, that's not it either. Em, hold up." As she stopped before the next junction, Jack turned sideways in the tunnel and waited as the others closed the gap. He cleared his throat with a cough. "The first two times in the maze when we chose the wrong direction, we returned to the chamber. Each time we chose correctly, we stayed in the maze." He hesitated, trying to find the best words. "I don't know what changed, but right before Emma chose wrong the last time, I saw us get kicked out...before it happened." *They think I'm crazy.* "So, I'm paying attention to Emma and when she makes a choice, I can see the result. It's like I'm one small step ahead."

"That's super weird. Even for you," Holly said.

The Captain interjected. "You are claiming you can tell the future?"

"No, I'm not sure what I'm saying," Jack said. His whole body felt heavy and tired. "This feeling...seeing things a little ahead of time...I've had it two or three times since scoping into Dara. I don't understand it." Even in the dark of the tunnel, he felt like everyone was watching him. "Ready Emma? Choose a direction."

"We're at another T-intersection. I'm choosing to go left."

Jack took a deep breath. "Listen, everybody. I can't explain it but I'm positive if Emma turns left, we'll be tossed back onto the chamber floor at Order's feet. But if she leads us to the right, we'll be out..." he paused and tried to picture where they were going, but nothing came. "Out of this maze and into somewhere else."

He pointed into the blackness and the unseen end of the maze. "Turn right."

51

BALGAGAAR

HOLLY HELD her hands up to her face, making a tent to shield her eyes from the blinding light. Red flashes of color pulsed with energy beyond her closed eyes, scrunched tight. She cracked open her eyes a tiny sliver and peeped through her eyelashes still intermingled, making everything blurry.

No one in the group moved as they also struggled to make the transition from the sightless black of the maze to this new space. Holly opened her eyes a bit more. They stood on the edge of a huge, bowl-shaped cavern that seemed to stretch endlessly in every direction. But as her eyes adjusted to the light, the walls, dizzyingly tall, came into focus. They curved upward to the cavern's domed ceiling that shimmered hundreds of feet above them. Every surface in the cave gleamed in glossy sheets of red, thousands of shades blended and mixed together.

Holly knelt and stroked her hand across the colorful swath of apple red underneath her feet; her hand reflected in the glassy depths as if the floor had been coated with a million layers of shellac. Mountainous stacks of papers and scrolls crowded the cavern floor like papier-mâché stalagmites; and in the middle of it all, rested a forty-foot-long grey dragon.

"I don't believe it," Tannor whistled softly.

The dragon's wings—folded into the shape of a turtle shell—stretched forty feet long, curved on the sides and met at the top in a smooth flat dome. A tight seam ran down the middle where the two wings came together. At the bottom edge of the wing closest to them, sticking out from the underside, were three pointed claws, slightly curved, but no sign of a head or tail, hidden from view underneath the impressive shell-like expanse of grey, a stark contrast to the red floor.

The floor sloped down to the center from all sides of the cavern. The precariously stacked paper towers made concentric rings around the creature. Holly imagined the mess if the dragon ever sneezed.

A few steps away, she watched Jack lean tiredly against Emma as she untied the glowcord from around his waist. Leading them through the maze must have exhausted him like colorcasting affected her. Emma was talking to him softly.

"So, now what?" Holly asked Roi, whose face was a mixture of shock and elation.

"Eres, are you expecting me to take the lead?" Roi asked nervously.

"Yes, but I'll be right beside you," the Captain said before she could answer as he strode over to them, his sword drawn. He gestured towards the dragon with its point. "There is your dragon. Four words I did not ever expect to say." The Captain stepped down from the ledge and walked towards the middle of the cavern.

Roi's eyes darted back and forth between the group and the shell of the dragon. The Captain stopped and turned back to face Roi. He pointed at the black doorway behind them, identical to the one in the chamber. "Let's go. We may not have much time."

Resigned to his fate, with his face three shades whiter than usual, Roi stepped off the ledge and joined the Captain. Even from this distance of several hundred feet, the rocklike body of the dragon loomed large. Holly and the others followed a short distance behind them. Next to the Captain, Roi crept forward, holding his arms out in front of him, hands open wide as if warding off the danger. Halfway down the slope, he stopped and looked to the Captain as if for a reprieve, but the Captain prodded him forward with the flat of his sword.

The huge stacks of papers towered above their heads. Edges of the individual sheets fanned out from the sides of the stacks, and Holly marveled at the care and patience it must have required to organize them. She gently rubbed a corner of one sheet between her fingers. Unlike paper, it was thick and leathery. As best as she could tell, every sheet and rolled-up scroll was covered with symbols, written in the same style as the markings on the kaleidoscope. In Roi's tales Balgagaar the Wise was a talking dragon and from the look of these scrolls, he was a writing dragon, too.

Twenty feet away from the dragon, the Captain and Roi stopped. The grey wings of the dragon had not moved. Holly walked up behind them and stopped next to Roi. The Captain frowned at her but let her stay.

"Now what, Roi?" asked the Captain.

Roi's eyes were fixed on the exposed tips of the dragon's claws. "How long are those, do you think?"

Holly took hold of Roi's left hand and squeezed it. His hand was sweaty.

Roi exhaled. "Right. I must ask for his assistance, explain that we have come with the Prophet and need the red material for the Eye."

Holly rolled her eyes at the reverential way Roi referred to Jack. By her brother guiding them successfully through the maze, Roi seemed fully convinced he was the new Prophet. Holly didn't want to go there yet. Her brother was already obnoxious enough. There was no way she was going to call him Master; he'd be impossible to live with.

"Oh, that's all?" Tannor scoffed from behind them. The dragon hadn't moved yet, but its monstrous wings and claws were a mere twenty feet from where they stood. "Besides, your dragon looks dead to me."

"Maybe he's asleep," said Holly.

"Balgagaar is reputed to be fierce but also full of knowledge," Roi said as he pointed at the scrolls. "I'll appeal to its *wise* side."

"And if Balgagaar greets us with its *fierce* side? What then?" Holly asked.

"We run, Eres. We shall run," Roi said as he gallantly held up his shaking hand, nudged her backwards, then crept forward.

A loud burble, followed by a snort, came from inside the closed wings. The taut leathery surface of the wing rippled. Roi flinched and stopped immediately. "I believe this is close enough."

The claws curled, the sharp tips raking the floor with a loud screech. Roi jumped backward four feet, landing right where he had left Holly standing before his brief moment of bravery. The Captain stepped to his left, putting himself in front of her and Roi.

A cracking sound filled the chamber as the gigantic wings retracted from the top, and the solid surface of the wings wrinkled. The underlying structure, a fan-like pattern of tendons and bones, collapsed and came together, folding the thick elephant-like skin of the wings backward.

Holly stood mesmerized and felt strangely calm. Balgagaar's claws, four on each foot, were almost as long as Holly's arms. The tail, its tip covered in spikes, slowly unrolled like a giant cable and came to rest on the cavern floor only a few feet from them. Its neck still curved away, hiding its head and face from view.

To Holly's surprise, Roi stepped in front of the Captain and then dropped to his knees. "Red Dragon of Dara!" Roi yelled as he threw his hands up in the air like he was worshipping. "Balgagaar, the mighty. Hear me, Balgagaar, the wise!"

Holly glanced over her shoulder at the others standing behind them. Tannor, his sword drawn and ready, was smiling, trying hard not to laugh.

Roi kept shouting, his voice breaking with nerves. "We have journeyed far to seek your counsel, Ancient Master of Dara. We know your legends. The Prophet requests an audience. We ask for your mercy—"

Balgagaar's head swung in a slow arc and stopped, its flat snout poised an arm's length from Roi's head, each deep and raspy breath blowing Roi's hair straight up. Roi froze, mid-speech, his mouth open. Behind him, the Captain's sword was at the ready, its tip aimed directly at the dragon's snout.

No one moved or spoke as the dragon's head slowly retracted a few feet. Its round eyes were set high above its mouth, and it scanned the group, looking at each of them in turn, before focusing its gaze on Holly. The deep folds of skin surrounding the eyes gave the dragon a kind expression, Holly thought, like a grandfather peering down at his grandchildren.

"I was not sleeping, little Guardian," Balgagaar addressed her, his words coming slowly. His voice wheezed from his chest like a creaky train engine. Holly had never heard something so old, so tired. "I was waiting." Another rumbly wheeze. "With my eyes closed."

And then Balgagaar the Wise, the Red Dragon of Dara, winked at her.

Examples of the written Landspeek are extremely rare; archeological digs have uncovered a handful of inscribed items. As documented in these Kaleidoscope Chronicles, the rune-like Landspeek appears on two very significant discoveries by the Three: the Scrolls of Balgagaar and the Kaleidoscope itself.

—Loremaster Roi

THE SACRIFICE

HOLLY WASN'T sure if she should reply, though Balgagaar's voice sounded friendly and good-humored. If Jack had said something like that, she would have joked right back, but she had no idea how to read the massive face which was an odd mix of box turtle on the top, dragon on the bottom.

His eyes, a pale red, sat high and forward on his round wrinkled snout. His mouth curved sharply down to a point in the middle and arced back in a sinuous curve to a spiked jawbone. Like the faded eyes, the scales lining his neck and body were rust colored, mottled with patches of grey and brown like a weathered brick building, sun-washed and worn. Based on the deep creases covering his body, she guessed the stories of the dragon's age weren't exaggerated. He looked as old as the mountains.

But she felt his power, old or not. Holly looked down at her hands; her red marks glowed brightly, as if powered by currents of energy. The power—a rhythmic surging that tingled her skin—was coming from the dragon himself.

"Balgagaar!" Roi had recovered from the shock of a dragon's mouth hanging so close to his own head. "I am Ber-ha-Roi, son of Hurato. Can you help us?"

The dragon winked again. Holly looked back at the others. They had seen it, too. Everyone except for Roi.

"Who is the sacrifice? Ber-ha-Roi?" Balgagaar's tail curled away from Holly and came to rest next to Roi's kneeling body.

He leaned backwards on his knees. "The sacrifice?"

"Surely, if you know the ways of old, you know that a sacrifice is always required."

Roi fell forward, his arms stretched out on the cavern floor as his body began to shake. Balgagaar turned his head to Holly. The dragon definitely had a smile on his face.

Holly smiled back. She tapped Roi on his back, but he wouldn't move. "Roi, you can get up. He's not going to eat you."

He slowly lifted his head, tears on his face. "I'm not the sacrifice? Then who's the sacrifice?"

The Captain stepped forward. He lifted Roi to his feet. Backing away slowly, Roi's eyes did not leave the dragon's mouth. He bumped into Tannor and turned to the group. "I was ready."

Acorn hugged him around his waist. "We saw. You were very brave."

Jack grinned. "Yeah, especially for a guy named Ha."

Emma's arm whipped out and slapped the back of Jack's head. "Seriously. Can we focus on the dragon?"

"My gravest apology, Ber-ha-Roi," Balgagaar spoke slowly as if each word needed time to travel to his mouth from somewhere deep inside. He shuffled to the left and extended his neck another three feet, adding to his length and making him more dragon-like. "You are the first visitors I have had in a very long time. Yes, a long time." His head swung and swayed slightly back and forth. "But first things must be first. The greetings."

Balgagaar rose to all four feet, forcing them to step back as his bulk expanded. His chest arched as he extended his tail into the air behind him. "I am Balgagaar the Wise, the Red Dragon of Dara, Well-spring of the World, Protector of the Land, the Mighty...oh, never mind with the rest." He bent his massive striped head toward the men.

The Captain stepped forward. "Permit me, for the sake of speed since we did not come unfollowed. The monster called Order waits at the entrance to the maze." He pointed at the others. "This is Tannor son of Tanok, a warrior of Dara, who serves as my First. This is Allanu, known as Acorn, former servant to Red Guardian, and now loyal to us." The Captain pointed to Roi. "You have met our Loremaster. And I am—"

"You need no introduction, Captain. Thank you for protecting Dara. Your time here has not been in vain." Balgagaar gazed at the door. "As for Order and the pestilence he commands, we have time. Nasty creatures, shards." The dragon's head swung closer to Holly and Emma. "Now, who might you be? I have never been visited by two Guardians at the same time, nor by ones so young."

Emma brought her hands together in the formal greeting position. "My name is Emma Cassandra Waite, daughter of Elishah and this is my sister, Holly Teresa Waite. We came from our own land, a land very far away from the Seven." She dropped her hands. "We're not Guardians. In fact, we had to escape from the current Guardian, Daria, because she wants to kill us." Jack nudged her in the side. "Oh, and this is Jack, first and only son of Elishah. Our brother."

Balgagaar's round eyes blinked once. "Your brother...ah, siblings." His eyes closed. "How very interesting...and so the time has finally come..." Balgagaar coughed violently, his chest heaving up and down, his neck convulsing, as he gasped and wheezed for several minutes. After a long wait punctuated by one last cough, Balgagaar opened his eyes. "Forgive me. My age is showing."

"How old are you?" Acorn asked, her tiny voice filled with concern.

"As old as the beginning, little tree nut. Four thousand years, give or take a few." Balgagaar's neck retracted as he settled back onto his belly, his front legs crossed and folded up under his chest. He chuckled, his voice a light rumble. "I do confess to sleeping through a few centuries, but the land was quite calm in the first millennia. The arrival of the first Prophet changed everything, of course. Then Se'en-sii waged the Seven Wars, and those were dark times. I must have written...oh, I'm rambling, and you came for a reason."

With a heavy groan, Balgagaar shifted his weight and his head tilted to one side. "That's odd. Order is making faster progress through the maze than I anticipated. Never seems to be enough time. Four thousand years comes down to one moment." He addressed Jack. "Son of Eli, you are carrying the Eye of the Prophet?"

Jack pulled the scope from his bag and held it up.

"Good. I will make my third sacrifice for you. For the three of you," Balgagaar said. "You must take one of my scales."

"Ahh, a red scale from the Red Dragon." Roi shrugged at the others. "That makes sense."

"I'm taking a scale?" Jack asked.

"No, not you son of Eli." Balgagaar pointed to Holly with one claw. "Daughter of Eli, come." Without hesitating, Holly stepped up next to Balgagaar's thick, front left leg. Unbidden, she reached out and placed her hand on his skin. "You can feel my red power, yes?"

The dragon's skin was warm. The energy pulsed like blood under her fingertips. "Yes, it's all over you and in you."

Balgagaar smiled at her. "But to take what you need, you must bring all of the power down into one of my scales."

"How?" Holly asked uneasily, remembering her failure with the cell door in the Coren.

"You have colorcast into items before. This is the opposite. Place your hands on a single scale and pull the color towards you. I will help you by pushing my color towards that point," Balgagaar reassured her. "When you feel the power concentrated, push up on my scale and nod. Your Captain will shear it off at the base."

Holly's eyes widened. She hated the idea of causing him pain. "But won't that hurt you? What about your power?"

"My energy will return, little one, like the times before. Perhaps, a long nap will be warranted." Balgagaar winked at her.

Holly rubbed her hands together and placed them on Balgagaar's front left leg, down towards his foot where the scales were smaller. As Roi stepped in next to her for a closer view, she chose one the size of her palm and gripped the edge with both hands. The scale was rough on top, but smooth on the underside where her thumbs rested. Red energy like a steady current of warm water flowed across her fingertips. She focused on drawing the color towards her fingers, oblivious to everything but the deep pool of red inside of the dragon.

"Now, before we are interrupted, I must give you two more things," Balgagaar spoke, his voice ragged. Holly continued to pull at the color; the red mark on her right arm vibrated with energy, and the scale began to glow from within like molten steel in a forge. "Loremaster, I have a gift for you."

Roi didn't respond, transfixed as he was by Holly's channeling of the color. Jack poked him in the ribs. "Loremaster, pay attention."

"The scroll at the bottom of that stack." Balgagaar pointed to the base of one of the large paper towers where a rolled scroll bound with strips of red leather lay on the cavern floor. Roi grunted as he picked it up; the scroll consisted of seven tightly rolled sheets. "While I cannot tell you what will come, I can give you the gift of knowing what has come before. This is the history of the Seven Wars. Sadly, it is far from complete and many of the details were relayed to me secondhand by my daimons. But it is likely the sole record left in existence, for Se'ensii thrives in darkness. She has done a very thorough job of destroying this information." Cradling the scroll carefully in his arms, Roi carried the scroll back to the group.

Balgagaar groaned uncomfortably. His skin had turned the color of ash, the pale red color in his eyes had faded to grey. "It is time, little butterfly."

Holly pushed up on the brightly glowing scale with all her strength. Reaching in with his knife, the Captain sliced across its base. The scale came loose from the dragon's foot, leaving a red mark in the soft flesh underneath. Holly stumbled backwards, clutching the still glowing scale in her hands. Balgagaar let out a windstorm sigh, scattering papers across the cavern floor.

"It is done," Balgagaar pronounced. His body sagged heavily to the floor, and the muscles in his long neck trembled as he struggled to hold his head aloft. "I have given my power freely. My red scale will open the Prophet's Eye, but though I am large and mighty," he laughed weakly, "my gift is small. For the Eye to see the Light, a much bigger gift is required." Turning to Jack, he spoke in an endearing tone, "Son of Eli, come close," as he tapped the cavern floor in front of him.

Jack walked past Holly and stopped in front of the old dragon's face. Blood oozing from the wound, Balgagaar curled his left leg around Jack, then wrapped his claws tightly behind his waist. "I must say, you look very much like your father, son of Eli. You have his eyes."

Acorn screamed and all of them whirled around.

Shards were scrabbling through the black doorway. A wave of nausea washed over Holly as Order stepped into the cavern.

I didn't find the Kaleidoscope. It found me.
—a quote from Professor Waite

ESCAPE TO NIMA

BALGAGAAR RELEASED Jack and stretched his head towards the group. "Sadly, it appears we have reached the end of our visit. Shards make horrible houseguests."

Looking down on them, Order stepped forward with both hands outstretched and palms down, as if holding back a rising flood while the shards stayed at his side, mewing and whining like feral cats, their legs sliding on the glassy stone surface. Their shrieks ricocheted sharply off the cavern walls. Behind Order, more shards squeezed through the doorway.

Jack stumbled away from the dragon. "What did you say?" His head was reeling. "You've met my dad?" Jack muttered, his voice drowned out by the noise in the cavern.

The Captain pointed his sword towards Order. "Balgagaar, is there another way out?"

"To your left, in the wall."

Thirty feet up the sheer wall was a small ledge with an opening. There was no way to reach it.

The dragon shifted, turned to his right and lumbered towards the wall. "Come now. The tunnel will take you to safety while I entertain my new visitors."

Looking over their shoulders, they ran across the cavern floor behind him. Order stood like a statue carved from dark ebonite, not blinking, watching and waiting. His hands stretched out like a conductor as the shards filled the ledge.

Stopping at the base of the wall, Balgagaar unfurled his wings to each side and flattened the one closest to the cavern floor. The other, he stretched out and up into a curve that reached the ledge.

Unspooling the rope from his pack, Tannor leapt onto the wing and tossed the end of the rope to them. "Grab a loop and follow me." He turned and stepped higher, keeping his feet on the underlying structure of bones and tendons. Acorn, Holly, and Roi slid the loops of rope around their waists.

The Captain didn't budge.

"No, Captain, you will not stay and fight," Balgagaar spoke. "You have wandered too long, Green Ghost." He smiled. "Besides, what good is one sword against a thousand claws?"

A terrible whirring sound rose from the dark doorway behind Order. Emma and Jack, now crossing Balgagaar's back, spun around. Order raised both hands as if lifting an invisible curtain.

The sides of the maze door cracked and crumbled as the horde burst through and poured in the cavern, like a torrent of black water, rushing and spilling off the ledge and down the slope. Their claws scrabbled on the stone. They flopped and rolled and fell, scattering wildly in all directions as the sheer numbers of them pushing through the collapsed doorway propelled the others forward.

The Captain ran up the wing and shoved Emma and Jack towards the ledge. Tannor pulled hard on the rope from above. Within seconds, they reached the top. Jack fell to his knees, then wheeled around as Balgagaar retracted his wings and backed away from the wall. He gazed up at them, seemingly unconcerned about the approaching black wave.

"Our time was cut short, Jack, son of Eli. Never forget that above all, Sii desires the kaleidoscope. You must keep it from her and..." Balgagaar paused, and for a moment, his head drifted lazily to one side as his eyes slowly blinked. Then with a start, his eyes snapped alert and fell on Emma, Jack, and Holly. "The one became the two, and the two became the three. Now the three have become seven. Farewell, my friends."

With a wink, Balgagaar flexed his shoulders. His wings flew up and outwards and then crashed down to the floor, forming a shell completely around his body.

"Jack, we have to go," Emma said, tugging at his arm.

His mind was spinning. He couldn't make sense of what Balgagaar had said. He needed time, somewhere safe to figure things out. Letting Emma pull him to his feet, he backed away from the ledge and stood with the others.

The cavern floor was black, covered with shards. They swarmed up and over the shell of Balgagaar's wings, smothering him like a pile of attacking ants. Where his wings touched the floor, they clawed and pulled frantically, searching for a way inside. Acorn was crying next to him, and Jack put his arm around her. He felt sick. One of the Captain's big hands clamped onto his arm and pulled him into the mouth of the opening. Balgagaar disappeared under the darkness, covered in a writhing black blanket. Forcing himself to turn away from the horror, Jack walked quickly behind the others into a winding tunnel.

They moved fast, Tannor and Emma holding lightsticks to illuminate the passage, its walls blanketed by thick moss and lichen, the floor sloping up, leading them higher with every step. Each time the tunnel straightened, Jack caught a glimpse of the group as they made their escape. Roi carried the history scrolls, rolled up tightly, and Holly clutched the dragon scale in her left hand, the glints of red sparkling between her fingers.

His head hurt. He had a million questions for the dragon, but there had been no time. If true, Balgagaar's information was overwhelming. Se'en-sii was supposed to be a legend, not a real thing. How could he stop something like that from taking the scope?

Then again, was it possible that Balgagaar had been warning him about Daria? Maybe the old dragon said 'she', not Sii; they sounded the same and the noise in the cavern had been deafening. Jack ran behind the others and tried to replay Balgagaar's words, but his mind was reeling. Besides, Daria had taken possession of the kaleidoscope, and nothing had happened.

And when he was sure nothing could surprise him any further in this strange land, the dragon knew their father. But their dad didn't have white eyes; he couldn't have used the scope. Balgagaar had to be mistaken—he did seem addled by his age. The idea brought him to a sudden stop. Balgagaar might have been thinking about the Prophet from three thousand years ago, but had he said something about a third time? That would mean...Jack gave up. His head hurt.

Ahead, the tunnel narrowed, then ended at a skinny gap in the rock no more than two feet wide. Jack squeezed through the crevice. The morning sun had risen, glowing red with an orange rim. Tannor and the others, already outside and standing in the tufted grass, said nothing as he approached. They had their packs on, everything stowed and secured, but their shoulders slumped with fatigue.

"You need to look at something," Holly said, her eyes wide as she pointed at a weathered stone, stuck in the ground next to the tunnel's exit. Jack turned and couldn't locate the crack hidden in the hillside he had come through; he guessed colorcasting masked the entrance. Without the stone marker, no one would ever find it. He started to walk away, but Holly stopped him. "Look closer."

Jack knelt next to the marker and jerked back in shocked recognition. Scrawled on the stone, like someone had scratched the surface with a sharp knife, were three letters. E-J-W. Jack stared at the initials, stunned by the significance: Elishah John Waite. Balgagaar wasn't confused, after all.

"Dad was here," Holly said.

"But..." Jack sat on the ground, "he never told us. Why wouldn't he tell us?"

"We'll ask him when we get home," Emma said. She was smiling down at him. "This is good news."

Jack had no clue what she meant. Nothing was making any sense to him.

Emma held out her hand to pull him off the ground. "If Dad was here, it means we made the right choice to find Balgagaar and get the scale. And, if Dad made it back with the scope, so can we."

"Then we have to go back inside and ask more questions."

"We can't," Emma said, the pain in her voice wound tight like a string about to break. "Shards are coming up the tunnel."

"And Balgagaar? Can you hear him?"

"No, but that doesn't mean anything. If he's wrapped in his shell—"

"Yeah, but what if—"

"No more what-ifs." Holly held up the scale, not glowing anymore, but now the color of blood. A shiver coursed through Jack; Balgagaar's words about the gift and the sacrifice echoed in his mind. "We found what we needed and now we have to go."

Emma and Holly were right. There were so many questions, so many things they needed to understand, but now was not the time. No matter what happened next, they had made it this far, together.

He slid the scope from his pack, and the metal barrel glinted in the rising sunlight. Jack turned the wheel next to the first chamber, then held the scope in front of Holly with the open slot on top. Roi and the others crowded close to them as Holly raised the scale. Tentatively, she stuck the sheared tip of Balgagaar's scale into the slot. Jack held his breath with the others.

"I hope this works." Emma said what they were all thinking.

The red color drained from the scale. Jack felt a surge of power and the scope vibrated in his hand. Glints of orange and red, like sparks in a fire, lit up the symbol engraved on the first section of the scope. Jack shut the slot and then rotated the eyepiece counterclockwise as far as it would go, feeling the embossed ring click one time. He put the scope to his right eye. An orange doorway revealed a cluster of vine-covered trees on the other side.

"It works! There's an orange door," Jack announced. Breathing a sigh of relief, he smiled at the others. Acorn nearly knocked him over as she hugged him tight, then started to pull back from him. Jack stopped her and wrapped his arms around her, holding the hug for a few more moments before letting go. Acorn was crying but grinning up at him and Jack realized he'd been so wrapped up in his own problems since starting their quest for the dragon that he'd lost sight of the others. Acorn had as much to lose as any of them.

"I'm really leaving Dara," Acorn said as she wiped her eyes. "I'm free."

Jack grinned at her. A few feet away, Tannor was congratulating Roi and slapping him on the back, which left Roi speechless for once. Emma was silent, her eyes focused on the tunnel exit, listening for the approaching shards.

Holly knelt on the ground and carefully tucked Balgagaar's scale —now drained of color—into her pack. She had a faraway look in her eyes as she stood.

"Do not worry for Balgagaar," said the Captain, stepping close to Holly, "I have a feeling that this is not the end of the Red Dragon of Dara."

Holly nodded and gave the Captain a half-hearted smile. "I think so, too." Then she looked over at the stone with their dad's initials. Suddenly her breath hitched, and her eyes brimmed with tears.

Jack watched as the Captain followed Holly's gaze. He knelt in front of his sister and gently clasped her hands in his. "On my Marks, Eres Holly Teresa Waite, I will get you home." The Captain reached up and tenderly stroked her cheek with one finger, wiping away the tear. "On my Marks."

Jack turned away and gazed one more time at the stone with their dad's initials. *Now I know why you didn't tell me about the Seven, why you could never show me the kaleidoscope. You were protecting me, preventing me from making the same mistake.*

Emma strode up to him. "Time to go. The shards are getting close."

Jack turned back to the others. They were watching him, waiting for him, his sisters, and his friends, six people who had fought for him, six people he would willingly die for. Together, seven strong. The Sisters couldn't catch them. Daria couldn't hold them. Shards couldn't stop them, and Order couldn't beat them. And now, they were one step closer to getting home.

"Okay, form a circle and link arms," Jack said, remembering how they had been touching when they scoped into Dara. He hooked Holly's arm with his left, and gripped the scope in his right hand as the Captain clamped a huge hand onto his arm. Across from him, Tannor had not yet linked his arms with Emma and Roi, his eyes fixed on the tunnel opening that led back into the mountain.

Jack cleared his throat loudly. "Tannor, you're coming with us, right?"

Emma let go of the Captain's arm and spun to face Tannor. "You're not seriously thinking of staying? Please, don't."

Still hesitating, Tannor glanced at the Captain, then scanned the group, his eyes conflicted.

"We want you to come with us," Emma said. She reached out quickly and took hold of his hand.

Suddenly, Tannor's face broke into a wide smile, his deep brown eyes crinkling. Jack saw Tannor's cheeks flush as he returned Emma's gaze. Holding on to her hand, he stepped forward and linked arms with Roi, completing the circle. Seven strong.

"Captain?" Jack asked, thinking the Captain would give a final order, but he simply nodded.

Roi spoke instead. "Into Nima, the Land of Fire." He raised his voice as if making a toast.

Tannor chimed in. "Great. Out of the burning sand and into the—"

"One more thing," said Jack as he raised the kaleidoscope to his eye. The orange portal glowed and shimmered directly in front of him. "This might hurt."

Jack stepped through the door.

APPENDIX A

Important Figures, Groups, Creatures and Places

Jack: (a Zero) The second eldest of the Three. Brother to Emma and Holly. Born with white-colored eyes and Master of the Kaleidoscope.

Emma: (a Seven) The oldest of the Three. Sister to Jack and Holly. A Soundcaster and student of Loremaster Ber-ha-roi.

Eres Holly: (a Seven) The youngest of the Three. Sister to Jack and Emma. A Touch-caster and creator of Inkadu, the Staff of Color.

Professor Waite: The father of the Three.

Alla-nu, known as Acorn: (A Zero) A young girl and a faithful companion to the Three. A native of Dara, Acorn was the personal servant to Daria-sa-gisnu, the Red Guardian.

The Captain: (a Three) The Former Captain of the Green Guard. Due to the Fade, his Marks have lost their color. A close personal friend of mine.

Tannor: (a Two) A good-hearted fellow but rash. A close personal friend of mine.

Ber-ha-roi: (a Two) The Loremaster of the Three. A lifelong scholar and amateur collector of historical artifacts. The Historian of the Kaleidoscope Chronicles: A Firsthand Historical Record of the Three (note: this is my working title and will likely change.)

Balgagaar, the Red Dragon: Dwells under Kursagar. A noble, intelligent creature.

Daimons: Wondrous creatures that nurture the lands. A protected species by law. Each land has its own species especially suited to care for the environment.

The Blight: Widespread and growing, this disease is killing trees and crops. The cause of the Blight is undetermined, but the disappearance of Daimons is believed to be connected.

The Prophet: Came to the Seven thousands of years ago. Wielder of the Kaleidoscope. May have battled Se'en-sii. Viewed as the Father of the First Guardians and his influence led to the creation of the Portals.

The Kaleidoscope: (The Eye of the Prophet) A powerful artifact of unknown origin associated with the Prophet (The Bringer of Light) The Kaleidoscope can be used to travel between the lands while in the Seven. If fully activated by the insertion of rare color materials, the Kaleidoscope opens a portal to Earthland.

The Unmarked: called Zeros (not derogatory) or Unchosen (derogatory since it implies the Zero was snubbed by the Creator of Light). Treatment of Zeros in the Seven varies by societal attitudes. In Dara, Zeros are relegated to servant class only, given away by their parents at a young age (five years old) to work for the Coren, the Royals, or wealthy Threes. The Master/Mistress provides food, clothing, and shelter for the Zero, relieving the Zero's family of the burden.

Se'en-sii: known as Abaddon, the Angel of the Abyss, Swallower of Life, Eater of Light. Resides in the Pit (legend). "The deceiver of the Lands; The darkness deepens, the fear spreads over the hearts of men." —Otera the Minstrel of Hamasa. Commonly referred to as Sii (pronounced shee). Sii is the subject of countless stories and legends and portrayed with female attributes.

The Pit: A vast black hole and the legendary home of Se'en-sii and the Shards.

Admahgon: The City of the Dead which borders the Pit.

Order: (Sutesuru) An evil sentient creature. In my opinion, Order's appearance coincides with the increased Shard sighting over the past ten years. Order is man-shaped, stands more than 9 feet tall with shiny, crystalline skin. Origin unknown. "I am Order" —a quote attributed to Order

Chaos: A giant monstrosity. A horrible clawed creature with jointed insect legs able to bound great distances in the air. Often accompanied by Shards. Origin unknown, but widely believed to dwell in the Pit (see Admahgon, also called the Dead City).

Daria-sa-gisnu: (a Six) The 43rd Guardian of Dara. I have nothing good to say about this person.

Sister Sasa: (a Five) (name meaning – Sting) The First Sister of the Red Coren. I also have nothing good to say about this person.

Red Sisters (an incomplete list): Sarra (Azalea); Haia (Peacock); Dusia (Quartz); Yiana (Harmony).

Shards: Wolf-sized with ravenous jaws and beetle-like features. Shards have a random number of legs - from 1 to 12 based on documented sightings. They sleep in Nests (burrowed under the ground) and are nocturnal beasts that avoid bright lights and sunshine. Their undersides are furry and matted with a coarse bristly hair is hard to damage. Their eyes are round, black and wide set above nasal slits and a wide jagged and hinged mouth. Best killed by colorcast weapons. When a color cast weapon penetrates a Shard, a spark of color flashes inside the Shard, consuming it from the inside. Shards killed in this manner burst into a cloud of black smoke and ash. Shards struck with non-cast weapons do not explode. When pierced, a thick liquid oozes from the wound. This liquid is not harmful to humans but—as I can personally attest—Shard blood reeks and smells horribly and requires a great deal of scrubbing to wash off.

Dust: When a Shard is struck by a colorcast weapon, an internal reaction causes the Shard to combust and burst into a cloud of black powder. This fine powder can be collected in mid-air using glass vials (clear glass is the only material that does not react with Dust).

Duster: A person who is addicted to snorting Dust. The inhaling of Dust gives a short-lasting burst of physical energy and a drug-like feeling of euphoria and invincibility. Habitual use of Dust contaminates the person's Marks and eventually leads to either death or conversion into Tarjeda.

Tarjeda (plural – no singular form): also called "Turned" or "Shades". A person is Tarjeda when their Marks change to black. If a person makes evil choices consistently, his/her Marks will turn grey, and if the evil behavior continues unchecked, the Marks will eventually turn black. The ingestion of Dust (see Dust) will also change a person's Marks. The treatment of Tarjeda varies in the Seven. In some Lands, execution is condoned, while in others, the treatment may be banishment.

Farker: A person with fake Marks tattooed on their body. The reasons for Farking are myriad: to fake a higher number of Marks to gain social status or access; to protest and subvert the societal system of Marks; to cover grey Marks (reference Tarjeda).

The Children of Eternity: A small enclave of people who dwell in Zala and who refuse to die. They pay people to continually colorcast energy into their bodies to stay alive. The oldest resident of the Children is a man named Oosh who is four hundred and fifty-nine years old.

The Games: a physical competition held every five years in the Seven. Teams and individuals compete in tests of strength, speed, and agility. The athletes on each team work as a collective, enhancing their abilities and skills by colorcasting. Recent games have been marred by the absence of participation by teams from Dara and Nima.

Colorcasting Academies: Though apprenticeship is the most common method of training Touchcasters and Soundcasters, there are several well-known schools dedicated to the art of Colorcasting. The most notable are Luthor's Colorcasting College located on the Isle of Elutasa, and the Arcadium of Sound in Mora.

APPENDIX B

The Sound of Colors (Emma's notes from her lessons with Sister Yiana)

Red - passionate, warm tones (strings like violins)

Orange - fiery, hot tones (brass and horns)

Yellow - light, chiming tones (bells)

Green - natural wood tones, resonating (like woodwinds)

Blue - watery, reverberations (piano-like)

Indigo - crystalline and metallic (striking tones with percussion)

Violet - sustained, cool tones (vocal)

APPENDIX C

Emma's Lesson Notes: I have included an excerpt from the notes Emma wrote during one of our first lessons while in Dara. —Loremaster Roi

The Land, Color and Capitals / What's each land like /
Color energy / Color Item we need to activate the
Kaleidoscope?

Dara, Red, Ephara / Mostly desert, dry and windy /
Love and Heart/
Balgagaar's breath...nope, it was a scale

Nima, Orange, Turas / Jungles and Volcanoes / Fire
and Heat /
Roi says we need a fireflower petal

Kasa, Yellow, Skyrras / Pastures, Flower Fields /
Light and Air / ???

Tera, Green, Paladur / Deep Forests / Life and
Nature / Could be another plant?

Zala, Blue, Lasulhi / Mostly Ocean with Islands /
Water and Motion / blue water? Probably not
that easy

Hema, Indigo, Sedu / Mountainous, the coldest place
/ Stone and Structure/ ???

Mora, Violet, Perkana / Snow covered Mountains and
Plains / Logic and Head/ ???

About the author

Rob likes to hike in the woods, play guitar and make stories, among other things. When he was young, he played with Star Wars action figures. When he was less young, he played in a folk band and married a wonderful girl. Several years ago, he had an idea for a story that refused to be ignored. He began to write it down.

Nowadays, Rob spends most of his days writing. He lives with that same wonderful girl in the woods in a green wooden house filled with two needy dogs, four guitars, six or seven cats, and an abundance of love and grace. He still has his original action figures. From their vantage point on his study shelf, they watch him, twelve tiny merciless overlords.

Milton Keynes UK
Ingram Content Group UK Ltd.
UKHW010641080724
444940UK00001B/1